SNOW ANGEL

ALSO BY MARGARET LUCKE

SNOW ANGEL

A JESS RANDOLPH MYSTERY

Margaret Lucke

OAKLEDGE PRESS

ISBN 978-1-939030-03-0

Cover design: Sharri Wolfgang
Author photo: Charles Lucke

Oakledge Press
Hercules, California
www.oakledge-press.com

For my sisters

PATRICIA HARRIS and SHARRI WOLFGANG

with love

CHAPTER 1

O N A BLUSTERY JANUARY AFTERNOON, Amy Gardino, age
seven, walked away from her schoolyard and vanished.

She was supposed to arrive at three-fifteen at the home of
Evelyn Talbot, a grandmotherly woman who watched Amy and
her friend Hannah after school. Evelyn was absorbed in attaching a
waistband to a pleated skirt, so at first she didn't notice that Amy
was overdue. But when three-thirty chimed on her antique clock
and Amy wasn't there, Evelyn phoned the little girl's house.
Hannah was home with the flu. Maybe Amy was sick in bed, too.

No answer.

Worried now, Evelyn called Amy's mother, Terri, at her office.

"Oh God! Keep looking. Don't panic!" Terri sounded panicked
herself. "I'll be there quick as I can. I'm leaving this instant."

As she waited, Evelyn searched her house. Amy was a playful
kid, not above pulling a prank. Around her neck she wore a leather
cord with a key to her own house and one to Evelyn's front door.
Perhaps she'd let herself in and hidden somewhere. Evelyn had
read about that sort of thing—kids tucking themselves into some
nook or cranny and falling asleep, hours going by before they were
discovered by frantic parents.

"Amy!" she called.

She looked under her dust-ruffled bed, peered into cluttered
closets, poked behind cobwebby boxes and broken furniture in her
garage. She climbed on a chair to lift the hatch to the attic and
knelt to check the cabinet below the kitchen sink.

No Amy.

1

Evelyn tugged on a jacket and went into the yard.

"Ay-mee!"

Dark clouds roiled overhead, making the day as gloomy as dusk. Wind clattered the metal walls of the garden shed as she looked inside.

Amy wasn't there.

Nor was she crouched in back of the woodpile or under the rhododendrons or behind the photinia hedge.

Evelyn heard a car jerk to a stop out front. She hurried around the house to find Terri pounding on her door.

"Terri!"

"Where is she?" Terri pleaded. "Have you found her?"

"No. I've searched everywhere."

They got in Terri's car and drove two blocks to Creekhaven School, following the route Amy would have walked.

The street was empty. No sign of anything amiss.

They caught Amy's second-grade teacher as she was opening her car door to leave. Spatters of rain gusted across the parking lot as they asked about Amy.

"Oh no!" the teacher cried. "I hope she's all right."

"Did anything happen at school today?" Terri asked. "Did something upset her? Did she talk about going anywhere?"

"No, it was an ordinary day. Amy was her usual cheerful self."

"And when school was over?" Terri demanded. "Did you see her leave?"

"I wish I'd noticed," the teacher said. "The end of the day is always such chaos, getting the kids into their jackets and making sure they have the right lunchboxes. And this afternoon they were all stirred up with this storm blowing in." The teacher glanced at the turbulent sky.

Evelyn gazed at her watch. "Amy was due at my house more than an hour ago."

"Come on. I'll help you look for her."

Together they scoured the school corridors, the classrooms, the playground. Then they sped to Terri's bungalow, where they searched as thoroughly as Evelyn had done at her home.

"Amy! *Ay-mee!*"

No answer.

Terri phoned Hannah's mom and the parents of as many of her daughter's friends as she could think of.

No one had seen Amy.

Finally, desperately, the women went through the gate that separated Terri's backyard from the Blackberry Creek ravine. As the last light bled from the sky, they followed the narrow, mud-slick path that rimmed the canyon. In the summer the creek far below was a trickle, but now water surged and leaped along its rock-strewn bed. Wind rattled the eucalyptus trees. Drizzle soaked the searchers; twigs slapped their faces.

"Amy! *Ay-mee!*"

They poked sticks and beamed flashlights into dead leaves, tangled berry canes and clumps of poison oak—hoping, dreading, that they would glimpse a sock, a sneaker, a blue jacket sleeve, a strand of straight brown hair. Every time a wild creature skittered or a bird screeched, they stopped to listen, praying the sound would turn into a child's footsteps, a call of "Hey, Mom!"

Nothing.

No sign of Amy.

Frozen and fearful, they returned to Terri's house, slamming the door just before the storm's full fury hit.

Terri called the Creekhaven police to report her daughter missing.

Then she phoned the homicide squad in San Francisco. She asked for Inspector Nick Gardino.

"All right, you son of a bitch," she said. "What have you done with her?"

CHAPTER 2

THAT WAS THE STORY Nick Gardino told me the next morning when he arrived at Parks & O'Meara Investigations to ask for my help. He'd pieced together the details from Terri's frantic call and the questions he'd been asked by the Creekhaven cops.

"She's gone, Jess. Completely disappeared."

He was slumped in the chair beside my desk. His eyes were red, his skin grayish; his thick dark hair stuck out in jagged peaks. He looked much older than he had the last time I'd seen him, not two weeks ago.

That day, his daughter Amy had been with him.

He lifted his hands, dropped them into his lap. "I'm supposed to be the big, tough cop … I feel so helpless. What am I going to do?"

Amy had been missing for nineteen hours. The news gripped my heart like an icy hand.

"This is dreadful, Nick. I'm so sorry." Such inadequate words.

Nick groaned. "How could Terri imagine for one minute that I'd do anything to Amy? Terri and I've had our troubles, God knows, but I'd never—Christ, why would she accuse me of this?"

Outside, rain slashed at the windows. The damp and chill seeped through the brick walls of the nineteenth-century whiskey warehouse where P&O had its office.

"It's hope as much as blame, Nick," I said. "If you stole Amy, at least Terri could know she's not in physical danger."

"Yeah. I want to know that myself. Christ, I'm scared—Amy's

so small. So ... vulnerable. And, believe me, I know better than Terri does what kinds of monsters are out there preying on kids."

He shut his eyes for a moment, then turned to watch the rain. O'Meara, one of the partners in the firm, padded over to offer solace. He licked Nick's hand and placed his head on the homicide detective's knee. O'Meara was an Irish setter. More than one person had pointed out a family resemblance between the dog and me. Our hair was the same auburn color, and we both had long, lean frames.

Tyler Parks, my employer, colleague and mentor, was happy to share top billing in the private investigation firm he founded a dozen years ago. "It's easier being in business if you have a partner," he would explain. "It lets you be diplomatic. Suppose I want to turn down a case that makes me uneasy, or turn off a pesky salesperson—I just say I have to check with my partner. Then I can report back, with regret, that O'Meara's answer is no."

I'd been hired as P&O's first employee when I graduated from the San Francisco Art Institute nearly ten years ago. I began as the receptionist, but under Tyler's tutelage I'd put in the hours to earn my own private investigator's license. It was hard at times to balance two careers, artist and detective, but I couldn't imagine living my life any other way.

Though Nick was stroking O'Meara's silky fur, he seemed almost unaware that the dog was there.

"Maybe there's a simple explanation," I said to him. "Amy spent the night at a friend's house and forgot to call home. Or she went for a walk and got lost—" The idea stopped me short. *Lost* was not a consoling thought, especially in this brutal weather.

He shook his head. "We're trying to cover those bases. But Amy knows she's supposed to go straight to the babysitter's. And I can't believe she suddenly ran away. She's been snatched, Jess. Someone grabbed her, and it wasn't me."

Nick took five photos from his pocket and fanned them out on my desk like a winning poker hand. Amy riding a pony ... playing in front of a Christmas tree ... standing on ballerina tiptoes in a tutu and gauzy wings. The one that showed her features best was a headshot, probably a school portrait. She had favored the photographer with a wide grin. She was clearly Gardino's child: they shared brunette hair, bronze-colored eyes and a habit of tilting their head to one side when they smiled.

God forbid, I thought, that anything has happened to extinguish Amy's smile.

The fifth photo surprised me. I picked it up: Amy and me, working together at the easel in my studio at home. She was painting mountains and trees—bold strokes of brown and green and purple.

My stomach clenched at the thought of losing her.

"I didn't know you took this."

"That first time she was at your place. New Year's Day. You two were so engrossed in what you were doing, you forgot I was there."

Nick patted O'Meara's head. O'Meara thumped his tail on the floor—sympathy, canine style.

"That's why I'm here, Jess. Did Amy say anything to you during her painting lessons? Any little comment that might clue us to where she is?"

I tried to think, tried to capture an elusive thought niggling at my brain. "I wish she had. But we just talked about kid stuff. School. How she likes living in a new town. She asked lots of good questions about being an artist. But nothing that will help find her."

His sigh came deep from his soul. "It was a long shot."

"If I think of something ..."

He nodded thanks. "I better get moving," he said, but he didn't budge.

"You look exhausted."

"The Creekhaven cops grilled me for hours last night. We searched Terri's house again, and the babysitter's and the school. Did a door-to-door in the neighborhood. Couldn't do much outside, not at night, not with this goddamn storm. But this morning they're mobilizing a search team. I've got to get back there, see what's developed."

Nick stacked the photos, the headshot on top. He gazed at his daughter's smile, then softly touched her cheek.

"I'm coming too," I said. "I want to help find her."

"Sure, but … you have work you need to get done." He gestured at the papers piled haphazardly on my desk, my glowing computer screen.

He was right. I had a ton of work. Background checks on prospective hires for one of our big corporate clients. An ongoing investigation of an insurance fraud scheme. A case where a man suspected his elderly parents were being swindled by a home-repair contractor. But none of them was a matter of life or death.

"None of it is as urgent as finding Amy." I straightened a stack of file folders. My hands were trembling.

"You know, there is one thing you could do."

"Name it."

"Spend time with Terri, okay? She needs support."

"Spend time … ?" In my mind I was already questioning every possible witness, scouring every square inch of woods …

"It would be a huge help."

"What about her family, her friends?"

"Her family's back east, and her dad's in poor health. Her mother can't leave him. As for friends, Terri doesn't have close connections in the Bay Area any more. The last few years, she's been up in Chico finishing her degree. She and Amy just moved to Creekhaven last August. Working, studying, caring for Amy— she hasn't had much time to build a social life. So if you could be there for her …"

"But … okay, if that's what you need, I'll do anything I can."

"Thanks. You can't believe what a nightmare this is."

Worse than a nightmare, I thought. When it's a bad dream, you wake up and find out the horrors weren't real.

Nick ran tense fingers over his neat, dark mustache. "There's another reason I want you near Terri. I need eyes and ears inside the house. You see, well, Terri's not the president of my fan club anymore. She doesn't like me much, doesn't trust me—hell, maybe she's got her reasons. And now, accusing me of ... Jess, I'm scared to death she's going to try to shut me out of this. I can't let that happen. I thought, well, you're a woman, you know Amy ... maybe you can get closer to Terri than I can."

"You've convinced her you didn't take Amy, haven't you? She knows you're not hiding her somewhere." I searched his face as I said this.

His expression didn't change; he didn't avert his eyes. But he hesitated before saying, "I hope so." Then, "You know I'd never do anything like that. I need you to stand up for me."

"Terri doesn't know me. She may not let me near her. If she thinks I'm your spy, or your girlfriend—"

"Terri and I have been divorced for three years. We should be past that kind of jealousy. Besides"—he gave an elaborate shrug—"she's engaged now."

"That's right. Amy mentioned it."

"But if you want to keep things clear, bring along that guy of yours, the photographer."

"Wish I could. But Kit's in Hawaii this week. He's shooting some big convention." I didn't tell him that Kit and I hadn't spoken since New Year's Day.

I scribbled a note about where I was going for Tyler, who'd gone to research property records at City Hall for a case involving a contested will. I flipped off the coffee machine and set the phone to be picked up by the answering service. Claudia, our office manager, was out with the flu that was running rampant. O'Meara would have to manage the business alone until Tyler returned.

"With the night you had, I'm surprised you came all the back this morning to this side of the bay," I said to Nick as I put on my raincoat.

He pushed himself to his feet. If I had been sketching him, I'd have chosen charcoal for its ability to smudge and shadow, using downstrokes to capture the way the strain was making his face and body sag.

"No choice," he said. "I had stuff to get ready for court tomorrow. I'm testifying and it's big time."

"The Moritz case," I said.

"Right. The frigging Moritz case."

The trial was front-page news. The whole city had been stunned by the crime: Robin Moritz, her fiancé and their baby had been gunned down on Haight Street in front of the bookstore where she worked. Haight Street was my neighborhood; I had known Robin and liked her. I still couldn't walk into the bookstore without feeling a pang of loss.

At first the triple murder had been put down as a random drive-by shooting. Then, several months later, came a second shock: Robin's father, one of the city's most prominent real estate investors, was taken in custody for pulling the trigger. Nick was the homicide detective who made the arrest.

Nick wandered over to the window. "I worked too damn hard for too many months to get that motherfucker behind bars. I want everything nailed down, airtight and solid. No screw-ups. If Carl Moritz skates on this, I might have to go out and kill him myself." With his finger he outlined a gallows in the condensation on the glass.

"God, what rotten timing. It's awful enough that Amy's gone. To have it happen just as Moritz is coming to trial ..."

"I've been thinking," he said. "Maybe it's not a coincidence."

"What do you mean?"

"My testimony's crucial to the D.A.'s case. Moritz has plenty of pull, even from jail. Suppose he got someone to arrange a little distraction to keep me away from the trial."

"You mean he hired someone to kidnap Amy?"

"Hell, it's probably wishful thinking. Like Terri wanting it to

9

be me." Nick leaned on the windowsill, staring out, as if willing Amy to appear on the other side of the pane. "Sounds strange, I know, wanting her to be in the hands of a murderer. But if she's a bargaining chip for Moritz, maybe they haven't … maybe they won't …"

He was choking on the words. I couldn't stop myself from mentally filling in the blanks: *rape, torture, kill.*

He turned to face me. "Could be they just want a simple deal. If I perjure myself or refuse to testify, and Moritz gets off, maybe they'll return my daughter safe and sound."

"Jesus, Nick. Have they contacted you about this?"

"Not exactly."

"What do you mean?"

"A note appeared at the Hall of Justice this morning. Nobody saw who delivered it. But it hints at a Moritz connection."

"What did it say?"

He stared at the ceiling as he recited: " 'Two of you have lost your daughters. Do the right thing for him, and maybe he'll help you find yours.' "

"You memorized it."

"Yeah."

"Moritz's name isn't mentioned. Are you sure it's for real?"

He crossed the room and plucked his soggy umbrella from the newspaper I'd spread out beneath the coat rack to catch the drips.

"Am I sure? Hell, no. We're already swamped with crank calls and weird messages and false alarms. I bet it's worse for the cops in Creekhaven. A kid disappears and all kinds of lunatics come crawling out of the sewer. But I've got a hunch about this one. There's something to it. I just don't know what."

I tossed O'Meara a dog biscuit, turned out the lights, took my keys from my purse so I could lock the office door.

"If it's Moritz's people," I said, "and they're offering that kind of deal, what will you do?"

"The right thing, of course. What could be easier?" Nick fixed me with bleak, haunted eyes. "Look at the options—let a slimebag get away with murdering his daughter, or give him an excuse to kill mine. Tell me, Jess, which would you choose?"

CHAPTER 3

I TUNED MY CAR RADIO to an all-news station. I had to wait through only one commercial break to hear a report on Amy's disappearance, full of hysterical words and wild speculation. The anchor team fanned the flames by recapping half a dozen of the Bay Area's most dramatic cases of missing children. Kids found imprisoned in vaults or car trunks. Kids found murdered. Kids never found at all.

Be all right, Amy, I willed. *Come home safe.*

Nick had given me his ex-wife's address. We would meet there. With the storm making hell of the Wednesday noon traffic, I couldn't count on following him. Rain sluiced down my windshield faster than the wipers could throw it off. I inched across the Bay Bridge and poked my way past Berkeley and Richmond on Interstate 80, dodging the spinouts, stalls and fender-benders that blocked the lanes.

The radio station's reports ran like a tape-loop—traffic, then weather, then another frenzied report on Amy. None of it was good news.

At one point the newscaster gave an update on the Moritz trial. Jury selection had finally been completed, and opening arguments were being presented today.

Then it was back to the insistent beat: *Amy … missing … Amy … kidnapped … Amy … gone.*

I couldn't stand it any more. I switched to a smooth-jazz station, hoping the music would help my stomach unknot.

12

I tried to imagine what Amy was experiencing, what she must be feeling. But the only mental image I could conjure was of whiteness—desolate, endless, unstoppable. Blinking hard, I forced myself to impose images on my mind's blank screen—Amy's face, and a bright splash of purple paint.

When my phone rang on New Year's morning, three weeks ago, I confess I'd been moping.

The evening before, Kit Cormier and I had treated ourselves to a fancy dinner at La Tavola and talked about what the coming year might hold for us. A shared household? Marriage? He hadn't actually uttered the M-word, but he was hinting about settling down, making noises about the benefits of having a family. I found myself backing away. I wasn't sure this was a direction I wanted to go, though I didn't understand why not. It wasn't Kit, I knew that. In the months we'd known each other, I'd grown confident of the strong bond between us. But some fear of moving forward was buried deep inside me.

At midnight, at my place, we popped the cork on a bottle of champagne, then moved on to a more intimate form of celebration.

In the morning he had to leave early so he could go home and organize his camera gear for a shoot of some politician's New Year's open house. He kissed me goodbye and then, in a moment of sudden passion, or whimsy, or insanity, he brought up the M-word for real, with a date attached.

"Two weeks from Saturday."

"But you're leaving the next day. You have that photo gig in Hawaii—"

"Exactly." He smiled, his eyes as blue and warm as tropical waters. "You'll come with me, and after the convention we'll stay awhile. Have a proper honeymoon."

"I ... I don't know what to say."

"Say yes."

My heart wavered on the brink. I was about to agree with his crazy plan when my clear-thinking head jumped in. "It's too quick, Kit. We need time to think about a decision like this."

And those words led to others, which grew increasingly heated until the door slammed behind Kit and I was left to wonder if I'd just made the worst mistake of my life.

Suddenly the holiday loomed bleak and empty. The new year was getting off to a rotten start.

I'd brought home some paperwork, but couldn't make myself concentrate on it. The football orgy on television was out of the question. And I was avoiding my studio. My current painting-in-progress hadn't been going right; if I tried to work on it now, I'd ruin it for sure.

So I curled up on my couch with three of the best comforts I know—a good book, a cup of tea and my dog. Scruff was O'Meara's son, the result of a clandestine love affair. I thought of him as a multicultural animal, a happy blend of Irish setter and Tibetan terrier. My little brother Teddy had named him based on his appearance as a pup. Scruff had been the runt of the litter, although you'd never guess it to look at him now—sleek amber fur, a head that reached my knee, paws that still didn't look like he'd grown into them even at almost two years old.

The tea grew cold. The pages of the book blurred through my tears.

The ringing of the phone set Scruff off on a frenzy of barking. I forced myself to answer it with a cheery, "Happy New Year!"

"Jess? It's Nick Gardino."

For an instant the name didn't register. Ours was a working relationship, not a social one. Our paths crossed on cases; Parks & O'Meara sometimes handled investigations for Stuart Weingarten, one of San Francisco's best criminal defense attorneys. Gardino had never called me at home.

"Hello, Nick."

"Jess, I know this is an imposition, being a holiday and all. You're probably busy, but ... see, my daughter is spending the day with me. She's seven, and she wants to be an artist. I mentioned I knew a real artist, and now she's clamoring to meet you."

This sounded like a fine way to brighten a dreary afternoon. "Sure, bring her over. I'd love to meet her."

They arrived carrying takeout Chinese, a six-pack of root beer and a bottle of wine. Gardino placed his arm around the little girl's shoulders and announced, "This is my daughter, Amy." The seven-year-old child I'd once been felt a tug of envy. I'd never had a father to introduce me with such pride.

At a nod from her dad, Amy extended her hand for me to shake. Her grip was firm. "I'm very pleased to meet you, Jess."

"I'm delighted to meet you too, Amy. And this is Scruff." I was hanging onto the dog's collar so he wouldn't jump. He'd probably knock her over. He loved kids and could be exuberant in expressing his affection.

"Hello, Scruff." Amy bent down and lifted his paw to give him a proper handshake too. His tail pumped wildly. She'd made a friend for life.

As we ate, Amy wandered around my living room, nibbling an egg roll and looking at the art on my walls with a connoisseur's eye.

"Did you paint all these?" she asked.

"Most were done by my friends in art school." I didn't point out that the majority weren't paintings, but drawings and prints. "Some of mine are in my studio. I'll show you when we've finished lunch."

She plopped the half-eaten egg roll on her plate. "I'm finished now."

I led the way to the sunporch I use as my studio. At the doorway Amy paused and softly said, "Wow."

Suddenly I was looking at the familiar space through a kid's fresh eyes. Daylight flooded in through tall windows on three sides. Drips and splotches of color speckled the floor. Canvases leaned against the walls, three and four deep. A half-finished painting stood on the easel in the middle of the room, a wintry swirl of snow and sky—azure, ice blue and indigo. Jars of brushes. Stacks of paper. Tubes of paint. Pencils and pastels scattered across the worktable.

Just one big playground.

Amy moved around the room, pausing to touch a brush's bristles, to run gentle fingers along the top edge of a blank canvas.

"Wow," she said again, her tone reverent. "This is so cool."

"Want to paint something?" I asked her.

"Oh yes!" She bounced on her toes. "Can I, Daddy?"

He gave his assent, so I moved my work-in-progress aside, tacked some poster paper to a board and set it on the easel.

Nick's phone buzzed and he went to take the call in the kitchen. When he came back Amy was smocked in an old denim workshirt polka-dotted with paint splatters. It hung almost to her ankles. I'd pinned up the dangling sleeves so her hands would be free.

"Look, Daddy, I'm dressed up like a real artist." She held up her arms and spun around as if modeling the latest Ucciello creation.

"You look beautiful, sunshine. But I'm afraid we have to leave. Duty calls. We've got to run over to the Hall of Justice for a while."

"But, Daddy! I was just getting started."

"We'll come back another time. I promise."

Her face fell. As her fingers fumbled with the buttons of the workshirt, she blinked as if warding off tears.

"Nick," I said, "how about letting Amy stay here? We'll have a good time painting, and you'll accomplish whatever you need to get done more easily if you don't have to worry about entertaining her."

Amy nodded, her eyes alight. "You know, Daddy, that's a very sensible idea."

It sounded like she was echoing something she'd heard her father say. Gardino laughed. "Okay, Jess, if you're willing to take on an art student for a couple of hours, that's what we'll do."

Amy proved to be a star pupil. I got out some tempera paints, and she was fascinated to discover how the colors could be blended to create new hues and tones. She wielded her brush with bold, expressive strokes—reminding me of the wonderful feeling of freedom that can be achieved by letting yourself go. I looked at the canvas I'd set aside. Was I becoming too timid? Too concerned with precision and perfection? That painting lacked energy, while Amy's creation abounded with it.

By the time we took a root beer break she'd completed a portrait of a dog who greatly resembled Scruff and a picture of a ballet dancer whose grace and fluid motion she'd captured with the skill of a much older child.

As we headed to the kitchen to fetch our drinks, Amy stopped and asked, "Who's that?"

She pointed to a painting on the hallway wall. A woman with dark hair, a gentle smile, a faraway expression as if her eyes were focused on an unattainable dream. She was in her early thirties, about the age I was now.

"My mother," I told her.

"She's pretty." Amy rose on tiptoes to peer more closely. "What's that writing in the corner?"

"My signature. It shows I'm the one who painted that picture."

"Did you make her sit very still?"

"What do you mean?"

"My dad said when you paint someone, they have to stay very quiet and not move till you're finished."

"Well, sometimes that's true. But I painted this from a photograph."

"Oh, that's a better idea. Does your mother like the way this picture turned out?"

"She never saw it. But I think she would have liked it."

17

"It's very good." Amy gave a decisive nod. "She'll like it fine when she sees it."

"I hope so." I didn't explain why Mom had never seen her portrait, or why I'd used a photo. I'd done the painting soon after she died. It was a way of expunging the awful memory of how she'd looked during her illness—the wasted flesh hanging from thin bones, the straggling remnants of hair, the tubes piercing bruised skin. I had wanted to restore her as best I could to her real self—vibrant, loving, a woman of determination and quiet strength.

"Come on," I said. "Let's get that root beer."

Back in my studio, I tacked up another sheet of paper while Amy sipped her drink. "I was wondering," she said thoughtfully. "Would a portrait make a good birthday present?"

"A super present. Are you thinking of someone in particular?"

"My mom's birthday is next month. Maybe I can paint a picture of her. I can use a photograph like you did and then it will be a surprise."

"Excellent plan. Your mom will love it."

Amy tilted her head to give me her best winning smile. "If it's going to be a surprise, I have to paint it in secret. So-o …"

I could guess where this was leading.

"Can I come back and paint it here?" When I didn't respond quickly enough, she added, "Please? Pretty please with sugar on it? Sugar and dog biscuits for Scruff?"

How could I refuse? When Nick returned we made the arrangements. Amy would come to my house every Saturday in January for an art lesson. I figured I'd learn as much as she did.

Nick watched while Amy finished one last picture: a careful arrangement of triangles, small green ones in the foreground, backed by tall purple ones capped in white.

"What's that, sunshine?" he asked as she printed her name with a flourish in the corner.

"Mountains," I guessed.

18

Amy said, "It's the pine land. See all the trees? Here, Jess, it's for you."

As they left, Amy and I shared a hug. Then she bounded out the door next to her father. The tails of the denim workshirt billowed below her parka. She'd refused to take it off.

Amy ... missing ... Amy ... kidnapped ... Amy ... gone ...

The mellow jazz on the radio failed to help. The beat of the crisis pounded in my head, synched to the rhythm of the windshield wipers. The knot in my stomach tightened.

Up ahead I saw one of the big electronic highway signs that warned motorists of traffic jams. They were also used to broadcast Amber Alerts, those be-on-the-lookout notices about abducted children. This sign, though, was dark and blank. The police didn't have enough information to make an alert about Amy worthwhile.

At last I reached the exit for Creekhaven, one of the suburban towns strung like beads along the East Bay hills. Getting off the freeway, I turned left, right, right again, and then followed the uphill curve of Blackberry Road, which paralleled the creek that gave the town its name. All along the street I saw soggy yellow ribbons fastened to trees, to mailbox posts, to porch pillars. Their streamers whipped in the wind as if beckoning Amy home.

Missing ... kidnapped ... gone ... gone ... gone ...

CHAPTER 4

I HAD TO PARK down the block. Up by Terri's house, Blackberry Road was clogged with vehicles—a Creekhaven police car, mobile news vans from three TV stations, sundry pickups and automobiles.

Nick's Mustang pulled in behind me. We climbed out of our cars into the rain, struggling to open umbrellas before we got soaked.

I started to walk up the street, but Gardino hung back.

"Nick?" I looked at him questioningly.

He sucked in a sharp breath and squared his shoulders. "I'm okay. Let's go."

As we splashed toward the house, doors flung open on the TV vans and some of the cars. Reporters and camera-hounds surged out.

"Look! There's the father!"

"Hey, Inspector!"

"Inspector Gardino! Coupla questions for you!"

"Is it true you've been accused of taking your daughter?"

The media in full whoop and cry.

They crowded around, brandishing cameras, microphones, notebooks and pens. Nick clenched his jaw, lengthened his stride and pushed through them.

Realizing I was with him, they turned their attention to me.

"Who's that?"

"Hey, lady!"

"Miss! Are you a relative?"

"Ma'am! A word with you!"

I pulled my umbrella down close to my red hair for protection and followed Nick to the house.

Amy's home was a small stucco bungalow, pale gray with deeper gray trim, as if it had been painted to match the rain. Three steps led up to a front porch. Its roof was supported by arches where Terri had hung baskets of geraniums, still green but no longer blooming.

A cop stood up from a lawn chair to inspect us. Despite the plastic raincoat he wore over his uniform, he looked chilled and miserable.

"I'm Amy's father." Nick pushed the doorbell. "Any developments?"

The cop shook his head. "Sure wish I could tell you there's good news."

A woman opened the door and abruptly froze, hands in the air, as if the sight of Nick put a halt to a frenzy of motion.

"Hi, Terri," Nick said. He nodded toward me. "This is Jess Randolph. She came along to help out."

Terri crossed her arms. "Volunteers are gathering at the community center."

The half-done portrait in my studio was a remarkably good likeness. Amy had arrived for her first Saturday lesson with a print of her mother's employee ID photo from SalesCom Technologies. She'd insisted on using "real" paints and canvas—no tempera and poster paper this time. She'd worked hard to capture the dark, loose curls that framed Terri's face, the high cheekbones and narrow chin.

In the photo, and in Amy's version, it was an attractive face. But right now it was blotchy from crying, gaunt with worry and grief.

"This is Jess," Nick repeated. "The artist who's giving Amy lessons."

"Oh. Of course." Terri shook my hand and I realized where

Amy's firm grip came from. "She loves the art lessons. Thank you for … for being so kind to her."

"It's easy. She's a wonderful student. More than that, a great kid." The compliment hung awkwardly in the air. I grappled for the right thing to say next. "I'm so sorry …"

"Come in, Jess." She pointedly left Nick out of the invitation.

"Terri," he said sharply. In a softer voice, he added, "Amy's my daughter, too."

Biting her lip, Terri turned and walked away from the open door. She was a couple of inches shorter than me, but her wiry build gave an impression of height and strength.

Leaving my umbrella on the porch, I followed her through a tiny foyer and into a living room that didn't seem much larger. A sofa, a pair of wing chairs, and a couple of small tables more than filled it. Terri had done a lot to warm and brighten the space. Quilted pillows were heaped on the sofa; a crocheted afghan was folded across its back. An array of ceramic pots contained glossy-leafed plants.

Normally, I thought, this room would be a peaceful haven. Not today. Perhaps never again.

No, Jess. I gave myself a mental shaking. Do not let yourself think that way.

Nick sank onto the sofa and watched his hands twist in his lap. Terri stood at the rain-streaked window, staring out. Another TV news van rolled up the street and halted in front of the house.

Silence hovered in the room like a ghost.

I went over to the fireplace, where pine-scented logs blazed, unsuccessful at lifting an atmosphere of gloom. I held out my hands, trying to dispel the chill I'd felt inside me ever since Nick told me that Amy was gone. No luck.

I turned and leaned against the mantel. From this vantage point I could see the dining room and a corner of the kitchen. A woman stood at the sink washing dishes; another was talking on Terri's landline phone.

A sandy-haired man came out of the kitchen with two steaming mugs. "Fresh coffee's ready," he announced. He handed a mug to Terri and carried the other out to the cop on the porch, who no doubt was grateful.

Nick stood up, stepped toward his ex-wife. "Terri …"

Instantly the blond guy was at her side. He put a proprietary arm around Terri's shoulders. "Afternoon, Inspector Gardino," he said.

"Hey, Philip." Nick acknowledged him with a dip of his head. Terri looked down at her coffee, avoiding the eyes of both men.

"Who's your friend?" With a polite smile, Philip nodded toward me.

"I'm Jess Randolph," I said.

"Jess, meet Philip Vandergriff. Terri's, uh …"

"Fiancé." Philip filled in the blank easily, giving Terri a squeeze as he said it. She gave him a look I couldn't quite read—surprise? Annoyance? No, most likely a reflection of the anguish she felt with her daughter missing. But Nick's scowl was unmistakable.

Philip Vandergriff was slim, with a loose, easy way of moving and an appealing boyish look. He was no kid, though; unlike his blond hair, his reddish mustache was shot through with silver. I guessed early forties. His eyes were probably hazel, but the blue sweater he wore pulled their color toward gray. Something about him seemed familiar, but I couldn't figure out what it was.

The phone in the kitchen rang. Everyone froze. I heard one of the women in the kitchen answer.

"Remember, I'm not talking to anyone," Terri called. "No more reporters, no more psychics, no more crazies. I don't care what their story is."

The woman appeared at the kitchen door, her hand covering the mouthpiece. "It's the police chief, Terri. Something about a press conference?"

Terri frowned, took the phone and disappeared into the kitchen.

Nick started to follow, then thought better of it. He sat at the dining room table, looking alone and sad. I moved to join him, for whatever comfort my presence might offer. But something about his expression told me to let him be.

I took a seat on the sofa. Philip settled across from me on one of the wing chairs.

"So, Jess Randolph. What's your story? Are you a colleague of the Inspector's? A cop? A friend?" He lifted his eyebrows on that last one.

I lifted mine back. "A friend of Amy's. I've been giving her painting lessons."

"Oh, you're the one. Amy's been thrilled. She's—" He bit off his words. "God, I have to watch myself. I keep rattling on as if nothing's happened. It's all so hard to believe."

The woman who had answered the phone edged her way over to us. "Hello, I'm Lacey Vandergriff," she said, extending her hand.

"My sister," Philip added, as if I couldn't tell. They shared a look—trim bodies, tawny coloring. Lacey was all tan and gold: khaki pants, matching shirt, and blond hair pulled into a ponytail. She was several years younger than Philip, closer to my age.

"Thanks for helping. Everybody's support means so much at a time like this," Lacey said, like a kid reciting lines in a school play.

"I hope Amy is found soon." I sounded just as clumsy. Sometimes I could figure out what to *do* in a crisis, but I never knew quite what to *say*.

"I'm sure she'll be okay." Lacey appealed to her brother: "Don't you think so? She has to be okay."

Philip looked grave. "We're doing everything we can. The cops are combing the neighborhood, and they've got a search team with dogs down in the canyon. If this damn weather ever breaks, they'll send out a helicopter with heat-sensing equipment. That FBI woman was here earlier, so the feds are involved. The volunteers are putting out flyers and—"

"And we're all praying for her." A new voice. The woman who'd been washing dishes had joined us, wiping damp hands on the apron tied around her plump waist. Her short-cropped hair looked undecided about whether to be blond or brown or gray.

"Yes. That's certainly helpful." I tried to say it with respect. I'd never been much for prayer myself, but it didn't make sense to rule out any possibilities.

"I'm Georgia Holcomb," she said, adding, "Hannah's mommy," as if that explained something.

"Hannah is Amy's friend," Philip said. "They go to the same after-school babysitter."

"She's in the bedroom watching TV," Georgia Holcomb said. "I didn't dare let her go to school. She's just getting over the flu, and she's so upset about Amy. Why, if they'd been together as usual yesterday, who knows … maybe both of them …"

Terri came back into the room, Nick trailing behind her. "Chief Doyle's holding a press conference at the Civic Center at three o'clock. Maybe then some of those creeps will get out of here." The living room grew dark as she yanked on the drapery cords, shutting the street and its media convention from view.

"Terri, something I need to tell you," Nick said.

Terri turned on a lamp, then another, keeping her back toward him. "So tell it."

"Please sit down, Terri. This is important. I'll inform Chief Doyle before the press conference, but I want to talk to you first."

She whirled to face him. "What? What is this? A confession? If you've got her after all, you bastard … If you've put me, and Amy, through all this …"

Philip went to her side. "Calm down, love. We'd better hear what he has to say."

He guided her to the wing chair he'd just vacated. When she was seated he perched on its arm.

"Go ahead, Nick." Terri pressed her hands together. She wore an engagement ring, I noticed, its showy diamond too large for the delicate gold band.

"You've heard of Carl Moritz," Nick began. He was pacing, not easy to do in the tight space. Lacey and Georgia hovered nearby, not wanting to miss a word.

"I don't think so," Terri said.

Philip nodded. "The guy who gunned down his family over in the Haight. You're the hero on that one, aren't you, Inspector? I heard you're the guy who brought him to justice."

I could tell Nick was biting back a sharp retort. He outlined his theory about Amy's disappearance being tied to Moritz's trial. Terri looked skeptical, dismayed, hopeful by turns. Having a theory—any theory—was more comforting than knowing nothing at all.

"Makes sense to me, Inspector," Philip said when Nick was done. "Sounds like an angle to go for."

"What are you going to do, Nick?" Terri asked.

"Talk to Chief Doyle. Then I'm heading back to the city. I'll find everybody with a connection to Carl Moritz and shake the truth out of them."

"What about the trial? Will you testify?"

Nick hesitated. "If Moritz's people haven't made specific demands by tomorrow, I've got no choice."

"But what happens to Amy?"

"I told you, this is mostly a hunch."

"But what if you're right? You're risking Amy's life."

"And if I'm wrong? Do I let Moritz get away with murdering three people?"

"What are you saying? You know how you can save her but won't do it?"

"No! For Chrissake, all I'm saying is it's a possibility. A maybe. A guess. If they *are* using Amy as a bargaining chip, they'll contact me before I get on the stand."

"And what if they don't? What if they don't, damn it?" Terri was on her feet, red-faced, yelling. "You should announce you're not going to testify. Tell the press. They're right out front. Tell the world. Make sure Moritz's goons hear it so they send Amy home."

Philip grabbed her fist, brought it to his lips for a kiss. "Calm down, love. He's right. He can't take action until he knows more. Look, I like your idea, Inspector. But suppose Moritz's people don't want a deal? Maybe they just want you too upset to testify. Then they can get some sort of postponement, right?"

"I hope not. The more delays there are, the more likely it is Moritz will walk. Evidence can get lost. Witnesses can lose their memories. Sometimes they die. If I don't hear from them, I have to assume they don't have Amy after all. And I get on that stand."

"I can't believe it!" Terri said. "You think you know where Amy is, but you're not going to do anything about it."

Nick's voice went suddenly soft. "Oh, Terri. I only wish I knew where she is. And I'm going to do everything in my power to … to …" He fell silent. After a long, tense moment he pushed himself to his feet. "Look, everybody—keep this among us. Not a word to those hyenas out there. I don't want Moritz's guys getting ideas from the media and claiming they've got Amy if they don't."

"You're leaving?" Terri asked. Her expression said *good riddance*.

"Gotta talk to Chief Doyle."

I walked him to the door. As we stepped onto the porch, the news vehicles sprang into action. Doors popped open, windows slid down, reporters jumped out into the rain. Nick sprinted down the walk, his open umbrella aimed straight ahead of him—useless against the storm, but a slight shield against the cameras and microphones.

A reporter spotted me on the porch and started up the sidewalk, only to be chased away by the plastic-wrapped cop on guard. A lesson my mother taught me when I was a little kid echoed in my head: *police officers are our friends*.

I breathed deeply, the cold damp air a relief after the stifling atmosphere inside. The rain made Terri's hanging plants smell like a forest. The cop and I chatted—he'd been on the Creekhaven force for three years. This was his first child abduction case and, he hoped, his last. I felt edgy and restless. Nick had asked for eyes and ears in Terri's house. What could I do here, really? How could I help?

A cry from inside the house: "Mommy! Mommy! Mommy!"

Amy! I dashed in, heart pounding.

A little girl was stumbling through the foyer, rubbing tears from her eyes with her fists. Her cheeks were flushed, small patches of hot pink. Silky golden hair had been brushed back from her face and caught at the crown in a barrette.

Georgia Holcomb gathered her up and sat with her on the sofa, rocking her and crooning, "I'm here, Hannah. Don't worry. I'm here."

"They showed Amy on telebision," the child sobbed. "They said a bad man took her away and she'll never come home."

"They don't know that, sweetheart. Lots of people are trying to find her. God willing, they'll bring her home."

"They said she got took from school. I'm never going to school again."

Hannah looked up. Her eyes widened as they fell on me. Making a small, choked sound, she hid her face against her mother's shoulder.

Georgia hugged her close. "No one will take you away. I'll never let anybody take you away."

Across the room, Terri was standing motionless. Tears slid down her cheeks. Philip reached for her, but she nudged him aside.

"Bow your head, sweetheart," Georgia said. "Let's pray for Amy."

"Our Father Who art in hebbin," Hannah chanted. "Make Amy come home."

Everyone in the room, even I, whispered *Amen.*

CHAPTER 5

"**G**OD, I LOVE THAT WOMAN," Philip murmured. He was speaking more to himself than to Lacey or me.

Through the kitchen window, we watched as Terri, in a yellow slicker, led the Holcombs across the backyard. Georgia had decided she'd better take her distraught daughter home. They'd left by the rear door, hoping to avoid the gantlet of reporters in front. Terri had told me a path ran behind the yards on this side of Blackberry Road, along the rim of the Blackberry Creek canyon. It ended at the school playground; kids used it as a shortcut to get to class.

Georgia was wearing a voluminous olive-drab rain cape. She had thrown it around Hannah, encircling the child within its shelter. They looked like a reptile-colored creature with four legs. A couple of times the smaller feet stumbled, as if Hannah were having trouble keeping up.

Terri opened the gate in the fence and let the pair through. She stood there for several minutes after mother and daughter disappeared. Eucalyptus trees grew tall on the slopes of the canyon, their dark gray-green shapes blurred by the falling rain. Against this backdrop Terri's yellow slicker was a small bright spot, like a sunflower, like a lick of flame.

"Should we go get her?" Lacey asked. She moved toward the door.

Philip put a hand on his sister's shoulder. "Let her be."

The phone rang and Lacey grabbed it; she seemed to be the official phone monitor. A recording device was rigged to the receiver. As Lacey talked, she scribbled in a logbook. I peered over her shoulder. For each call, she noted the number and name displayed on the Caller ID, the name of the person she actually spoke to, and the gist of the conversation. The list was long—neighbors, relatives, media people, a few that she'd labeled *asshole* or *jerk*. The latest caller was apparently the mother of one of Amy's classmates; Lacey explained how she could assist the volunteers at the community center.

"Come on," Philip said as she hung up. "I made all this coffee. Might as well drink it."

I picked up the empty milk pitcher to refill it and stopped short at the refrigerator door. Fastened to it with magnets was Amy's dancer, the graceful ballerina she'd painted at my house on New Year's Day. She'd signed it *Amy,* her name underscored with a bold swash of periwinkle blue.

The artist had been missing for twenty-two hours.

My fingers trembled as I poured the milk.

We carried our coffee mugs into the living room.

"Interesting idea the Inspector had there," Philip said. He sat on the sofa; Lacey and I took the wing chairs. "About Moritz, I mean."

"It's a hunch," I reminded him. "There may be nothing to it."

"He said there was a note."

"Probably from some crackpot—"

The kitchen door slammed, making us jump.

A moment later Terri appeared, mopping her hair with a dish towel. She had shed her wet slicker and shoes; the legs of her jeans were soaked. Philip pulled her down to the sofa. She curled up against him, burying her face in his blue sweater. But then she abruptly sat up straight, as if unwilling to allow herself too much comfort.

"What do you think Amy's doing right now?" she wondered aloud.

Philip kissed Terri's damp hair. "Try to be brave, love. We've got to trust she'll come home soon."

"She's fine," Lacey said, her voice betraying her doubt. "She just has to be."

Terri burst into tears. Her sobbing was quiet, almost silent, but the fact of it, the reason for it, filled the room.

Lacey went to poke the fire. As she knelt on the hearth the firelight touched the edges of her hair, transforming her into a shadowy angel with a halo of gold.

The flames hissed and crackled; raindrops pattered against the window and roof. None of us could think of a thing to say.

We were shocked when the doorbell buzzed. Dropping the poker, Lacey dashed to answer it.

A murmur of voices, then the cop from the porch came in with a flat white box. I smelled spices, cheese, tomato sauce.

"Who phoned for a pizza?" Lacey asked.

Blank looks all around. Philip took the box and set it on the coffee table. Behind Lacey I saw another face—the kid making the delivery.

"There's some mistake," Terri said. "No one ordered this."

Philip flipped open the top. The aroma intensified. "Pepperoni," he said.

"A money pizza," Terri whispered.

"No, there's no charge," the delivery guy said quickly. The rain had slicked down his hair, and his shiny black parka was sequined with water drops.

Terri used her dishtowel to whisk away a tear. "I meant … my daughter calls this a money pizza. Because the pepperoni slices look like coins."

The young man pushed past the cop into the room, a pen and pad in one hand.

"No charge," he repeated, fingering his small hoop earring. A white scar over his upper lip twitched as he spoke. "The pizza's on me. Just a few minutes of your time in exchange. To answer a question or two."

"You're a reporter?" Philip said.

"Well, yeah, you see—"

Philip placed a protective hand on Terri's shoulder. "You've got nerve, barging in like this."

The kid stepped forward. "Hey, you need publicity. Get the word out—it will help you find your little girl."

"Please," Terri said. "I can't. Not right now."

I slipped between them. "You'd better leave."

The kid sputtered a protest as the cop helped me hustle him out.

The phone rang again and Lacey ran to the kitchen to answer it. The tension in the room jumped higher. Would this be the call we were waiting for, the one with wonderful—or terrible—news?

She returned with plates and napkins.

"Who was on the phone?" Terri asked.

"Another reporter. All the way from San Diego." Lacey started to pass around slices of pizza. "Don't worry. I tell all the media types to go to hell."

"Don't tell them that," I said. "This trick was totally out of line, but the guy's right. You want Amy to be a top news story. The more the word spreads, the better the chance that someone will recognize her, or will realize they've witnessed something significant."

"Unless those Moritz people have her," Terri said with a shudder. "What is the trial about? Nick didn't say much about the details. The guy murdered his family?"

Lacey set down her pizza; she was the only one eating. "It happened over in the city, about a year ago. Really terrible—a whole family was shot to death on the street." She shoved her plate away. "You must remember it. It was all over the news."

Terri shook her head. "Amy and I were living in Chico then. I didn't hear about it. What happened?"

Philip said, "You don't need the gory details, love. The story doesn't have a happy ending."

"If these people have Amy, I need to know what I'm up against."

"The cops thought some guy was shooting for thrills, and they were in the wrong place at the wrong time," Lacey said. "But it turned out the girl's father killed them all."

"Her father?" Terri echoed.

I said, "The victims were Robin Moritz, her fiancé and their infant son. Robin worked in a bookstore on Haight Street, and they'd gone there to show off the baby to her friends. She was finally turning around her mess of a life. The whole thing was such a damn shame."

"You say that as if you knew her." Philip sounded surprised.

"I did, a little. The bookstore's in my neighborhood. I go in there a lot."

"Really? You live in the Haight? Where?"

"On Shrader, near Waller."

Philip grinned. "We're neighbors. I live on Belvedere."

Two streets away—my turn to be surprised. Seeing him around in shops, on the street—that would explain why he looked familiar.

"What do you mean, her mess of a life?" Terri prompted. "Please, someone—tell me what happened."

As Philip sketched out the story—toning down the bloody horror of it, thank God—Robin's image floated into my mind. High cheekbones, clear peach-toned skin, a ready smile. Her hair, glossy and dark, tumbled to her shoulders. Her fringe of bangs was trimmed just short enough to keep from masking her lively brown eyes.

Yes, lively, that was the right word for Robin. The experiences she'd endured would have left someone else beaten down or bitter, but she embraced life to the fullest.

She'd had the kind of childhood that to outsiders looks privileged. Her father, Carl Moritz, was the head of a prominent real estate firm and one of the richest men in San Francisco. Given how often I'd seen the Moritz Investment Group's name on for-lease signs, I figured he must own half the Financial District and a quarter of the city's residential rental units. He was a board member of the symphony, a major contributor to the city's pet causes, a prominent personage on both the business and society pages—and a man widely rumored to have underworld connections.

Twenty years earlier, Moritz's wife died in a traffic accident, leaving him two little daughters to raise. Bereft of her mother, and ignored by a father who was focused on making huge sums of money, Robin got into increasingly serious scrapes—stealing from classmates, dealing drugs, getting expelled from posh private schools.

Several times she ran away. Her father's cohorts would search her out and drag her home, once from a South of Market crackhouse, once from the apartment of a forty-year-old filmmaker who specialized in porn. Finally she disappeared, sinking below even Moritz's reach. He hunted for her to no avail. A year later a cop busted a scrawny, strung-out kid who was hooking on a Tenderloin corner. Robin had been found.

Moritz bailed her out of jail, pulled strings to hush up the headlines and booked her into a drug rehab center called New Dawn. She spent three months in residence, several months more in the outpatient counseling program. Nolan Aldridge, who owned Bountiful Books, had a son who'd been through the New Dawn regimen, and he felt it had saved the boy's life. His way of saying thanks was to give jobs in his shop to program graduates, which is how Robin came to work there. She held the job for three years, staying clean and sober the whole time.

I learned most of this after she died. At the bookstore, all I knew was that Robin was cheerful and friendly, and that she loved books.

Once she told me she planned to read her way around the store, starting with New Fiction in the front right corner and proceeding through Philosophy, Women's Studies, Cookbooks, Travel, Business, and all the others until she reached the front left corner with Humor and Art.

"That could take the rest of your life," I said.

"Yes," she agreed. "That's what's so great about it."

The bookstore was where she met her fiancé, Eric Nielsen. Her face lit up when she talked about him, and her pregnancy made her glow. A few weeks before giving birth, she quit her job, intending to devote herself to her new son.

When Michael was a month old, Robin and Eric brought him to the bookstore to show him off and invite the whole staff to their wedding. I heard later that it was a festive visit, with lots of coos and oohs and aahs and congratulations.

Then the new family walked out of the shop into a blaze of gunfire.

Witnesses agreed that the shots came from a Prius that rounded a corner and disappeared. Beyond that, no two people told the same story. Some said the car was silver, others insisted it was blue. Some said only the driver was inside, some swore there were passengers.

Three people had been slain on a crowded block in the middle of a sunny afternoon, and the police had almost nothing to go on.

For several days the stores on Haight Street were nearly deserted, and the whispered conversations within them focused on the bloody event. Then people began to forget.

Until six months later, when Carl Moritz was arrested for killing his daughter, his future son-in-law and his newborn grandson.

CHAPTER 6

"BUT WHY?" TERRI ASKED. "What could possibly have been his motive?"

Philip said, "Who knows? One rumor is that Robin was going to file a lawsuit against her father."

"A lawsuit? For what?"

I saw Philip hesitate, not wanting to plant pictures in Terri's head, lurid scenes in which she might visualize, not Robin, but Amy. I'd heard the speculations—abuse, molestation, incest—and Terri would too, if she started to follow the court proceedings.

"Nobody's sure," Philip said finally. "Maybe he didn't pay off on her trust fund. But the idea is, Moritz killed her to keep her from revealing something that could destroy him."

"Won't it come out during the trial?" Lacey asked.

"Not if the trial isn't held," Philip said. "If the Inspector's right about what's happened, that could short-circuit the trial, at least for now."

"If he's right," Terri said. "Maybe it's all a smokescreen. Nick could be trying to divert attention away from himself."

"Nick hasn't taken Amy," I said firmly. I was ninety-five percent sure of that. The other five percent I decided to ignore. "Why would he do such a thing?"

Terri twisted the diamond ring until it nearly came off her finger. "I don't know. Anger. Jealousy. I was the one who asked for the divorce. Nick didn't want it. And now that Philip's in the picture ..."

Philip took her hand and slid the ring back into place. "There's a note, remember. Pointing to Moritz. It's the best lead we have so far."

"The only lead," Lacey said.

"God, I can't stand this." Terri pulled her hand away and pressed her fingers to her temples. "I'm going down to the community center, see what's happening with the volunteers."

"You don't want go down there, love." Philip began to massage her shoulders. "The media will be all over the place."

"I have to get out of here." Terri stood. "I've breathed all the air in this house twelve times over. If the walls close in any more, they'll crush me."

Philip stood too. "Okay, then, let's go."

"No, I need you here. If Amy comes home ... Lacey's doing a great job screening phone calls, I'm really grateful. But Amy doesn't know her. She needs to be welcomed by someone she loves."

"You shouldn't be alone, love." He slid his arms around her. "What if—?"

Giving him a quick kiss, Terri pulled out of his embrace. "Please, stay here. I won't be gone long, I promise."

Quickly I said, "I'll come with you." When she protested, I added, "It makes sense for Philip to stay here, but it would be good for you to have company. I can be a buffer if you need one—say, if the media people get too pushy, or you run into someone you don't want to talk to."

She surprised me by saying, "Okay, come on."

Before she could change her mind, I retrieved my umbrella from the front porch, nodding to the cop.

Terri put on her yellow slicker. The only umbrella she could find was obviously Amy's, a child-sized one printed with Disney characters in bright blue and red. She looked like a paintbox of primary colors.

We went out the back door and through the gate, as Georgia and Hannah had done. The path along the canyon's crest was a thin dirt track edged by mashed weeds and grasses, trampled by scores of children's feet.

"This way," Terri said.

The wet air was pungent with the smell of eucalyptus. The rain had eased to that kind of thick drizzle that fills the air, making umbrellas pointless. So we lowered them and used them as walking sticks. I was glad I'd worn jeans and boots to work this morning.

Deep in the ravine below, we could hear a party of searchers thrashing through the brush along the creekbed, calling Amy's name.

Find her fast. I beamed the thought down to them. How long could a child, lost and afraid, last in this weather?

"They won't find her down there," Terri said, as if reading my thoughts. Her tone was bleak. "They think she might have gone exploring after school, or tried to walk home, and she got lost or she fell. But Amy wouldn't wander off on her own when knew she was supposed to go straight to Evelyn's. Someone grabbed her off the street. Maybe this Moritz guy Nick's worried about, maybe some psychopath, some pervert ..."

I tried to think of a good way to offer hope or provide answers. At last I gave up and said simply, "I'm sorry you're being put through such torment."

"You can't imagine it," Terri said. "This is what horror is. Stephen King hasn't got a clue." An oleander bush poked through someone's fence. She stripped off a handful of leaves and pulled them to shreds. "What's Nick up to, anyway?"

"Up to?"

"Bringing you here. Does he want you to spy on me? Or was coming here your idea? An excuse to check out the ex-wife, find out what she's like. Might as well see her at the worst moment of her life."

"I came for Amy's sake," I said. "I'm just getting to know her, but she's special to me."

The slicker's hood shadowed Terri's face. I could see little more than her eyes with their glisten of tears. "And you're special to Amy. She talks a lot about how much fun she has, painting. She … I … well, thank you."

We walked the length of another backyard. Children obviously lived in the house, and I saw Terri turn her head to avoid being confronted with the reminders: a swingset, a playhouse, a plastic horse suspended on springs.

I said, "Nick asked me to help. He's like you—something terrible has happened to his child, and he needs his friends."

"So what kind of friend are you?"

"Our work brings us into contact. I like Nick and respect him."

Terri said nothing.

"We're not lovers, if that's what you're wondering."

"Oh hell. It's none of my business anyway."

I paused. "Nick's upset that you've accused him of taking Amy."

She shoved back the hood, ran her fingers through tangled curls. "I wish I was right. Maybe then she'd be home now. Instead of … God knows where."

"Do you really suspect him?"

"What am I supposed to think? It's not like we parted friends." Her voice held an edge of anger.

"But the idea that he would kidnap his own daughter—"

She slammed Amy's umbrella against the fence. *Bang!*

"Don't give me that. Men do it all the time. I don't know Nick any more. I don't know what he's capable of. I've hardly seen him in the last three years. *Amy* has hardly seen him—what kind of man only visits his daughter a couple of times a year? Chico's not that far from San Francisco—what, a four-hour drive? If it were me, I'd have been on that freeway every goddamn weekend to see my child."

Bang! went the umbrella again.

"Then last summer—I graduated, finally got my degree, and Amy and I moved back to the Bay Area. Has that made a difference? Oh no. The super-dedicated cop. The one-man war on crime. The goddamn defender of truth, justice and the American way. He's just like he always was, never a minute for us. I don't know why he thought he was losing something when I took Amy and left. I'm surprised he even noticed we were gone. What did *he* have to be angry about? *I'm* the one who never had a real marriage. *Amy's* the one who might as well not have had a father. *Of course* you and Nick aren't lovers. The goddamn *Homicide Squad* is his lover. The Hall of Justice is his whorehouse. No woman can compete with that. No child can. You can't imagine what it does to a kid, not having her father there for her."

Bang!

"I can imagine," I murmured. "I met my own father for the first time less than a year ago." He had left Mom and me when I was a baby. All through my childhood he had existed only as a hollow place in my heart that I longed to have filled. How I would have cherished even what Amy had—occasional visits, phone calls, a card on my birthday. My mother rarely spoke of him, but if she had let herself, she would have sounded like Terri just now.

Terri broke stride and looked at me hard.

"Maybe that's why Nick asked me to help. Both of us with absent fathers—could be he senses a sort of kinship between Amy and me. Perhaps he thinks I can help him understand."

Terri scuffed her foot over a clump of weeds. "Don't make excuses for him."

"No excuses. It sounds like Nick's been a rotten father. But I think he wants to do the right thing now."

"A bit too late," she said bitterly.

"I hope not."

"Oh God, I hope not, too."

She fell silent, and I could think of nothing else to say.

We kept walking. The trail veered away from the houses and through a stand of live oaks.

"Almost there. Watch your step," Terri said. "The path gets steep here."

She led the way down the hill. The wind was kicking up again, the rain turning cold and sharp, like needles in our faces. I followed her across a softball diamond, then a blacktopped surface with hopscotch squares and game circles outlined in bright yellow paint, the same color as Terri's slicker. For an instant the scene created a painting in my mind: night color, sun color, the mother's desolate posture contrasted with the geometry of playtime.

We walked past the school and across a parking lot to the Creekhaven Community Center—a large, newish structure, redwood and plate glass, a showcase for civic pride. Through the wide windows we saw people milling about, heard the muted throb of activity.

Terri started to push open the door when the sight of the flyer taped to it stopped her.

MISSING—POSSIBLE STRANGER ABDUCTION.

Below the chilling words Amy smiled brightly. The same school photo that Nick carried.

Terri touched the glass, reaching for her daughter. "I can't tell yet if you're friend or foe, Jess. But I know this much: I hope you never in your life have to go through anything this hard."

CHAPTER 7

FOR A MOMENT Terri and I went unnoticed in the noisy turmoil of the room.

People were crowded around tables that had been shoved together in the center of the gleaming hardwood floor. They were stuffing envelopes, answering half a dozen phones, making big posterboard charts with labels like AREAS SEARCHED, ORGANIZATIONS CONTACTED, DONATIONS RECEIVED. The phones jangled again the instant they were hung up. In a corner a police radio chattered. Flyers had been taped to every available surface. No matter where I looked, I saw Amy gazing at me.

If Terri had hoped to escape the media by coming here, she'd been mistaken. TV and newspaper types were present in force, circling the activity in a macabre dance of notebooks, microphones and cameras.

Terri hung back by the door. I heard her murmur, "Maybe this was a bad idea."

Before we could retreat, a voice boomed out: "Terri!"

A tall, rawboned woman with steel-rimmed glasses and iron-gray hair strode over and grabbed both of Terri's hands. "I'm so sorry about Amy. I rushed down here the second I heard."

Terri gulped and nodded as she tried to pull away. "Thank you. I—"

"We're all devastated, of course, but I want you to know we're not giving up hope for a minute. Wait till you see how hard all these people are working to find her. Why, the support you've got in this community—"

"Pipe down, Verna," interjected a tiny bird-like woman carrying a clipboard, who had appeared at the tall one's side.

Every head in the room had turned toward us.

"We're shocked that this could take place in our town," the large woman yammered on. "I mean, if a child isn't safe on the nice, quiet streets we have in Creekhaven—"

"Verna, shut up." The smaller one rapped her on the wrist with a ballpoint pen. Amazingly, Verna released Terri's hands and fell silent.

The onlookers gathered around us. A camera's flash fired and the air exploded with light.

"Ignore her, hon." The tiny woman patted Terri's shoulder. "Verna means well. We all mean well." She sighed and turned to me, running her fingers through her feathery brown hair. "Have you come to volunteer? I'm Lillian Harwood. I'm helping to organize things here."

I introduced myself.

"Lillian's my next-door neighbor," Terri said. She looked shocked and pale. "And this is Verna, uh ..."

"Verna Spode," Lillian Harwood put in. "She was elected mayor last November, and she still hasn't climbed down from her soapbox."

"Don't be silly, Lilly," Verna said. "You know how important it is for the community to—"

A voice yelled out: "Mrs. Gardino!"

Terri turned toward the sound and winced as another camera flashed.

A thin, balding man stepped out of the crowd. "Terri, anything you need, let us know. We're here for you."

"Thank you, uh ... I'm sorry ... I ... I can't think of your name."

He didn't enlighten her, but said, "Come over here. We've got papers to set us up officially as the Find Amy Coalition and—"

He was jostled aside by a guy with a video camera balanced on his shoulder like a second head. He wore a drab Army jacket and two days' worth of whiskers. The woman with him, in elegant contrast, had a wine-red blazer, perfect makeup on her smooth, sepia-brown face and not one single black hair out of place. She carried a microphone.

"Mrs. Gardino?" she asked in her warm-honey voice. "Or is it Ms. Shawcross? I've been hearing both."

"Who are you?" Terri asked.

The woman looked surprised by the question. I was a little surprised myself. Hers was a well-known face; I saw it several nights a week.

"This is Paula Blakeney," I told Terri. "Channel Eight news."

"Will you make a statement for our viewers?" the reporter asked Terri. "The whole Bay Area is rooting for you and Amy. It would mean so much."

Other journalists pushed in, cutting us off from the Creekhaven neighbors. Cameras loomed. Microphones bristled in front of Terri; they looked like spikes aimed at her heart.

"You don't have to do this, Terri," I said.

She shot a glance toward the exit, as if yearning to flee. Then she pushed back her straggling hair and wiped a hand across her face, rubbing away her panicked look and replacing it with one of composure.

I admired her, and I ached for her.

Paula Blakeney stood next to Terri and nodded to her camera guy. "I'm at the Creekhaven Community Center," she intoned into her mike, "where friends and neighbors are helping to search for Amy Gardino. Yesterday afternoon, seven-year-old Amy left her school to walk to her babysitter's home two blocks away. She never arrived, and no one has seen her since. With me is Amy's mother." She gave Terri a smile of encouragement. "I know this must be a very difficult situation for you."

"Yes." The word caught in Terri's throat. "Oh my God, yes."

"We appreciate your talking to us. Is there anything—"

"I just want to say ... if someone took Amy: Please, please don't hurt my little girl. Please bring her back. And, Amy, sweetheart—wherever you are, Mommy loves you, darling. And ... Daddy loves you too." A tear slid down her face.

The newswoman held up a flyer and addressed the viewers-to-be. "This is Amy Gardino. If anyone watching has the smallest piece of information that might help to locate this little girl, or if you'd like to donate funds to help with the search, please contact the Find Amy Coalition or the Creekhaven Police."

With that, she signaled to her camera operator and lowered her microphone. "Okay," she said. "For that last part we'll fill the screen with Amy's photo and superimpose the web addresses and phone numbers."

She turned to Terri, who was hugging herself tightly, biting her lip. "Thank you. I know that was hard. If we're lucky, someone will see it who knows something, who can help bring Amy home."

Another photographer leaned close, his bright flash making Terri blink. He smiled smugly, as if savoring the impact his picture would have on some media website: the distraught mother, damp dark hair and stricken eyes above the yellow slicker, clutching the Disney umbrella as she pleads for her daughter's life.

A young man with a notebook popped up at Terri's side. He looked unpleasantly familiar—the scar over his upper lip, the gold hoop in his ear. His hair was drier now; a forelock flopped over his forehead. In his mid-twenties, I decided, older than I'd thought when he pulled the pizza ruse at the house.

"Hey, Terri," he said, "thanks for coming down. Better than hiding at home, isn't it?"

Terri spun away. "Let's get out of here," she whispered, and bolted for the exit.

"Sorry about the choice of topping," the Pizza Kid called. "I thought everyone liked pepperoni."

I glared at him and followed Terri into the vestibule.

The obnoxious twit was right behind us. "Is it true you suspect the girl's father of snatching her?"

Other reporters were crowding into the small space. I opened the exit door, letting Terri slip out into the rain. Then I turned to face the press.

"Leave her alone. Anyone who follows us, I'll make sure she never says one word to you."

The Pizza Kid started to protest.

"That goes double for you," I said.

He gave an exaggerated shrug. "No big deal. It's almost time for the top cop's press conference anyway." The scar twitched as he grinned. "Next time, how about sausage and mushrooms?"

I half expected Terri to be gone, but she was waiting at the corner of the building, huddled under a high redwood overhang.

"I'm glad so many people want to help," she said as I joined her. "But I couldn't stand being in there one more minute."

"I don't blame you," I said.

She pushed away from the wall and set out across the parking lot. I fell into step beside her. The sky was a tumult of grays. Fat raindrops began to pelt us, and we opened our umbrellas. The wind, gusting rough and cold, tried to yank them out of our hands.

I thought Terri would head toward the path on the canyon rim. But she cut across the main road to a street that angled off to the left. I glanced at the street sign: Hillwood Drive. It was lined with small neat bungalows surrounded by tidy lawns, like the homes on Blackberry Road. Lamps burned in occasional windows, fighting the gloom of the winter afternoon.

"This is the way Amy would have come yesterday," Terri said. "Evelyn lives two blocks down."

"Who's Evelyn?"

"Evelyn Talbot, Amy's babysitter. Every day after school Amy walks to her house and ..." She heaved a sigh. "Georgia and

Hannah live right there, third house from the corner. Any other day, Hannah and Amy would have been together. But yesterday Hannah was sick in bed. Georgia stayed home from work to take care of her, but when school was letting out, she was in the kitchen, at the back of the house. She never saw Amy. Never saw one damn thing."

This time Terri's sigh turned into a sob, and she abruptly stopped walking. Before I could say anything, she pulled her umbrella down to hide her face. Minnie Mouse and Pluto frolicked in front of my eyes.

A passing car slowed as the driver stared at us, then sprayed us with water as it speeded up again. Was that what had happened yesterday? A car came by and … I shivered. I saw that Terri was shaking, too.

Finally she lifted her umbrella and resumed walking. "I don't know what I think I'm going to find. I walked this route half a dozen times last night and found nothing. And the police have searched all along here—the yards and the gutters, even the storm drains." She kicked at some dead leaves that littered the sidewalk. "Even if there'd been any evidence—the rain would have washed it away."

"Something will turn up." I was conscious of how lame I sounded. "You've got to keep hoping."

"That's right. Philip says that too. Keep hoping." And she plodded on.

Soon she stopped before a brown-shingled house with a dark green door. The front walk was lined with rosebushes, pruned back for the winter to sticks and thorns.

"Here we are—this is Evelyn's. Somewhere in these two blocks, we passed the spot where Amy was taken. In front of every house I wonder, was it here? Or here? And I want to squeeze my eyes shut, as if when I'm standing in front of the right house, I'll get a picture. An car, or a face, or … or something. But the only face I ever see is Amy's, and she looks terrified."

A bright brass knocker ornamented Evelyn Talbot's door, but Terri pushed the doorbell instead. "We'll only stay long enough to warm up," she said. "If Evelyn's home, that is."

The door opened, and we were greeted by a short, sixtyish woman wearing a red turtleneck. Her hair looked like tarnished silver.

"Terri! What is it? Is there news?"

"No," Terri said. "We just needed a port in the storm."

"Well, you've always got one here." Evelyn ushered us inside. "Funny, I was about to leave for your house, to bring you something for dinner. Come in, come in."

Terri introduced us, and Evelyn greeted me warmly. She directed our umbrellas into a Chinese porcelain holder and Terri's slicker onto a Victorian coat tree. Then she led us down the hall. I glanced through doorways as we passed by. One room had been outfitted as a workspace with a sewing machine, shelves of fabric, and an old-fashioned dressmaker's dummy; Nick had told me that Evelyn earned most of her living by making custom clothes.

We entered a yellow-and-white kitchen full of delicious smells. A casserole dish and a cake pan sat on hot pads on the counter. In one corner, shelves were stacked with games and books for her after-school charges.

"Let me put water on. I'll make tea." She bustled with the preparations, filling a kettle, lighting the stove, taking cups from a glass-fronted cabinet. "Evelyn's famous catering service—I made you mac-and-cheese and an applesauce cake. I thought maybe some comfort food ..." Her determinedly cheery expression crumpled, and she gathered the younger woman into her arms. "Oh, Terri!"

They clung to each other. "Thanks for everything, Evelyn," Terri said when she pulled away.

"I wish I could do more. I feel responsible. If only I'd realized sooner that Amy was in trouble."

Evelyn poured the tea and set out a plate of gingersnaps. She was describing her plan to volunteer at the community center when the clock chimed in the hall.

"It's time for the press conference," I said. "Terri, would you like to go?"

Terri put down her cup. "I can't face those reporters again. Why don't you go, Jess, and tell me what happens?"

"Of course."

"Come back to my house when it's over." She was looking down, fiddling with her engagement ring. "I'd better get home."

"I'll drive you," Evelyn said. "I was coming over anyway with dinner."

We loaded the food and ourselves into Evelyn's car. They dropped me off at my Toyota. As the wipers swished the rain from my windshield, I watched them pull into Terri's driveway and dash for the front porch. The media encampment was gone, thank God. No doubt the reporters were all at the press conference. For a brief moment, Terri would be left in peace.

No, not peace, I reminded myself as I drove off. She wouldn't know peace until Amy came home.

CHAPTER 8

"AND YOU MAY BE SURE that no one in Creekhaven will rest until Amy is with us, safe and sound ..."

Mayor Spode was in mid-speech when I arrived at the City Council chamber and squeezed into the last empty chair in the back row. The big room was mobbed with journalists, search volunteers, concerned townspeople, the curious and the titillated.

A light tower had been erected for the TV cameras. The glare bathed Madame Mayor and the U.S. and California flags that draped from poles behind her. Taped over the town seal on the wall was the photo of Amy, blown up to triple lifesize.

" ... and the horrible person responsible is behind bars for good. Only then will we sleep in peace ..."

Two tables angled like wings from the podium where Verna Spode was holding forth. Each seat had its own microphone and a nameplate identifying the councilmember who usually sat there. But today the only person sharing the spotlight with the mayor was a beefy, reddish man in full cop regalia.

" ... we make this promise to our children: you will be able to play outdoors, to go home from school and feel safe ..."

A low, restless murmuring buzzed in the room. The air was steamy and stale, and it smelled of wet wool and damp, overheated bodies. I could hardly breathe.

" ... now I'd like to introduce our chief of police, Mac Doyle. Chief, will you please fill us in on what the police know at this point?"

Doyle's expression said he'd rather march to the guillotine. But he pushed himself to his feet and wiped a glisten of sweat from his forehead. "Right. Here's how it stands …"

I felt a jab on my shoulder and heard a whispered, "Hey, Jess."

Turning, I saw Nick Gardino in the crowd of standees behind me. He pointed his furled umbrella toward the door. I worked my way to the aisle, trying not to trip over too many feet.

"You okay, Nick?" I asked. He looked shrunken and gray.

"Yeah. Fine."

As he guided me out of the chamber, I glanced back, straining to hear the chief.

"Don't worry about Doyle," Nick said. "Basically, he's telling them the cops haven't got a clue. But he's couching it in lots of words so it'll sound like they're working hard. Which, Christ knows, they are."

"No progress, though." I sighed. "That's why you look so bleak."

Cold wind slapped our faces as we stepped outside. Creekhaven's Civic Center had been built to resemble a Spanish presidio. Adobe-style buildings ringed a plaza landscaped with flowers—lantana and spike-leafed agapanthus, both now bereft of blooms. In the center, a fountain splashed, adding its gurgly water music to the beat of the rain.

Nick sank onto a wooden bench near the doorway and leaned back against the rosy-tan wall. I sat beside him. A long balcony jutted out from the second floor, providing a little shelter.

"Glad I found you," Nick said. "How's Terri?"

"Frightened. Angry. Courageous. Strong. Those words come to mind."

He nodded. "Yeah. I'm sure they fit. They describe me too. The first two, anyway."

"You're all of them," I said.

He raked his fingers through his dark hair. "Moritz is probably counting against strong and courageous."

"Have you heard anything more?"

"No. I phoned my lieutenant right before showtime in there. No word from Moritz's people, not since the note this morning. But the timing is no frigging coincidence, I'll swear to it."

He shifted forward, planted his elbows on his knees. "I keep thinking about New Year's Day. It was a pretty day, sunny, remember?"

"I remember."

"After we left your place, Amy and I went to Golden Gate Park, the children's playground. She must have ridden that carousel fifteen times. She fell in love with this galloping white horse. Swirling golden mane, fancy red saddle. She gave him a name. Firecracker. 'He can fly, Daddy!' she told me. 'He flies me right into the sky! We go higher than angels!' "

"Nick ..." I groped for the right thing to say.

But he was watching raindrops splash into a puddle, not even aware of me. "I made a New Year's resolution. I promised this year I'd spend lots of time with my kid. Be a good father for a goddamn change."

Remembering Terri's outburst, I chose my words carefully. "You're the best father Amy has."

"Right. I'm the only father she has. But not for long, not if Vandergriff has his way."

"A stepfather's not the same thing." Based on my own experience, a stepfather could be better than the real one. But I didn't say that.

"That first Saturday I brought her for her art lesson? Hardly spent a moment with her. Dropped her off at your place, picked her up. Same thing the next week ..." He turned to look at me. "You're sure Amy didn't say anything to you that might be a clue to what happened?"

"I'm sure." A chill swept through me as a thought nudged my brain. Not about anything Amy had said to me, but what I'd said to her.

If we had lost her forever, could it be my fault?

"This last time, we were going to go out afterward, get burgers or something. But I caught a case early Saturday morning, that gang shooting in the Bayview district, so I had to cancel on Amy altogether. She was really disappointed, I could tell by her voice on the phone."

"I was disappointed too." I'd been surprised by the sharp sadness that knifed through me last Saturday when I learned Amy wouldn't be coming for her lesson. I hadn't realized how much I cherished our time together. Not just for the satisfaction of teaching, though I enjoyed both the role of mentor and the reality that I was the student, learning more from Amy than she was from me. Truth was, in the short time we'd known each other Amy had made herself essential to my life, filling a deep gap I hadn't even known was there.

Nick sighed. "And I haven't seen her since. She lives right across the bay, it's not like I've got to drive all the way to Chico anymore." He gave a snort that sounded like self-disgust. "But I get preoccupied. Frigging Moritz case. All the scumbags shooting and stabbing each other. The days slide away. Every night I say, 'I'll call Amy tomorrow.' And now—" He rose suddenly, kicked the terra cotta planter next to the bench. "Goddamn it to hell!"

The words vibrated in the air.

Looking defeated, Nick sat down again. I saw his gaze drift across the plaza to a row of windows blazed with yellow light. Behind them people bustled, looking determined and purposeful. Creekhaven's police headquarters.

"Cops never cry," he said. "It's part of the oath you take when they swear you in. Or so my old man used to tell me when I was a kid. He was a cop, too, I ever tell you that?"

"A good cop, I'm sure. Like you," I said. He didn't reply. After a few beats of silence I asked, "What did Doyle say when you met with him? He may be telling the media he has nothing, but that doesn't mean it's true."

"What, you think cops hold stuff back from reporters? Just because having them scream everything from the rooftops might jeopardize the investigation? Jess, I'm surprised at you. What about freedom of the press? What about the public's right to know? What about—"

"Okay, don't tell me."

"I'll tell you this much. Right before the press conference, Doyle interrogated a prime suspect."

"Really? Who—"

"Guy you happen to know. In fact you're looking at him."

"Nick! He can't really suspect you."

"Of course he does. Partly because Terri told him *she* suspects me. But mostly because I'm Amy's father. The family's always the first place you look. Plenty of times a parent has killed a kid, accidentally or on purpose, and then tries to hide it by yelling kidnap."

"You're right." A terrible idea to contemplate, but I knew it happened all too frequently. "But in your case—"

"He grilled me for hours last night too. It's okay. If he didn't come down on me hard, he wouldn't be doing his job. It was interesting in its way. I've dished it out plenty of times— questioning suspects, I mean. First time I've been the dishee. Gotta say I like the other way better."

"You convinced Doyle you weren't involved, didn't you?"

"Christ, I hope so."

"Did you tell him about Moritz?"

"Yeah. He found it an interesting theory. Promised to follow through with SFPD."

"You're SFPD," I pointed out.

"Yes and no," he said.

"What do you mean?"

"Remember I mentioned phoning in a moment ago? Seems I've been given a 'leave of absence.'" His voice put quote marks around the phrase. "Lieutenant's reassigning my cases. Except for

Moritz's trial, I'm off duty."

"Why? No matter what Doyle thinks, SFPD knows you better than that."

"In a way it makes sense, Jess," he said, although I could see hurt in his eyes. "What good would I be right now on a homicide investigation? All I can think about is Amy."

"It's a routine thing they do, then? When officers have crises in their personal lives?"

"You should have seen the way some people looked at me this morning at the Hall of Justice. The lieutenant, the Homicide Squad, they've been great. But some of the others—I could tell what they were thinking: 'Poor Gardino, too bad about his kid, you suppose he did something to her?' Christ!"

"Oh, Nick—"

"You believe me, don't you, Jess? You know I'd never, ever do anything to hurt Amy."

"I know that, Nick." It was what he needed to hear.

"So temporarily I'm not a cop. I've got cop skills, though. I can do cop work. I can find her, goddamn it, I've got to find her."

Nick lowered his head into his hands, covering his eyes. His body was trembling. If I hadn't known better, I'd have said Nick was breaking his father's oath.

To give him privacy, I wandered out into the plaza. I found a leftover agapanthus bloom, one the gardeners had neglected to remove once it faded. In the summer the plaza must have been brightened by hundreds of them—sprays of purple flowers on long green stalks.

Lilies of the Nile, people called them. We'd had some in the yard of the little house where Mom and I lived when I was Amy's age. She told me they were Cleopatra's favorite flower. I loved to play with them; they were scepters, they were magic wands.

This one was dry and brown, a blossom's skeleton. I broke it off at the base of its stalk, but couldn't think what to do with it.

Like Nick, I felt like crying.

The doors to the council chamber burst open, and people began spilling out. A guy with a notebook spotted us. "Inspector!" he yelled. He hustled in our direction, the media pack at his heels.

Nick jumped. "Oh shit. Let's scram." He hurried me toward the parking lot just ahead of the cresting wave of reporters. When we reached his Mustang, he said, "I've got to get back to the city. One last conference with the assistant D.A. on strategy before I take the stand tomorrow. Where are you headed?"

"Terri asked me to fill her in on the press conference. There's not much I can say, but I don't want her to think I forgot."

"Good. Tell her … no, I guess it's better if I tell her myself."

He unlocked the Mustang, got in and slammed the door as the first reporter raced up shouting, "Wait! Inspector!"

The Pizza Kid. I tried to make my own retreat, but he stepped in front of me. "Hey, it's you again. Who are you, anyway? Family friend? A relative or what?"

"Out of my way." I turned aside.

He maneuvered into my path again. "I know—you're shy because we haven't been properly introduced. William Paveleck, I'm on assignment with *Bay City Beat*."

An alternative weekly newspaper, known for its feistiness.

"William Pepperoni?"

"Cute. Look, here's my card. Sooner or later you're going to want to talk to me. What's your name?"

"Call me Cleopatra. Here's my card." I thrust the dead agapanthus stalk into his hand. As he stood there gaping, I fled to my Toyota.

CHAPTER 9

"I BET IT'S SCARY being a detective," Amy had said as she daubed bright red paint onto the paper I'd set up on my small spare easel. The dash of color set a banner waving on the roof peak of a merry-go-round.

It was her second visit to my studio, the Saturday after New Year's Day. The merry-go-round picture was a warmup for the birthday portrait she was planning for her mom.

"Why do you say that?" I was sitting at my worktable, sketching her as she worked.

"Because, you know, you have to chase bad guys and stuff." One hand on her hip, she cocked her head to study the painting.

"Not always." I captured the angles of her body with my pencil. "Your dad chases bad guys. He's very brave. But private investigators like me spend most of our time going through papers or looking things up on the Internet. Being an artist is scarier."

She turned to look at me. "That's silly. Being an artist is fun."

"Absolutely. But it's scary too."

"Why?"

"Because when you're an artist, you have to be adventurous. You have to take risks."

"What do you mean?"

"Sometimes you do something that frightens you a bit, and you're not sure you can do it well. But you try anyway because that's how you learn and grow. And you become a better artist."

"I see. Like me painting a portrait of my mom. I never did a real portrait before."

"Exactly. And your portrait's going to be very good. But suppose what you try doesn't work? You paint a picture you had high hopes for, and it turns out awful. Or you show it to someone and they don't like it. And then you might think, 'I'm no good, I'm a terrible artist,' and you're tempted to give up."

Getting into the spirit of it, Amy waved her red-tipped brush. "But you don't give up. 'Cause you're an artist and you're ad … ad … what's that word?"

"Adventurous."

"And you take risks. Even if you're scared." Red drops flew through the air to join the thousands of spatters on the floor.

"You've got it. You're becoming a real artist. Be adventurous. Take risks."

"Be adventurous! Take risks!" Wielding the paintbrush like a baton, Amy paraded around the studio. Scruff and I fell in behind, and he barked to accompany our chant:

"Be adventurous! Take risks!"

But, Amy, I meant when you're painting, I thought now as I drove away from the press conference. *I didn't mean you should get in a stranger's car, or go exploring the woods alone.*

Be adventurous! Take risks! My windshield wipers whispered the words.

My heart jumped when I saw a Creekhaven police car parked in front of Terri's house. Had they found Amy?

As I pulled to a stop, the car drove away. Raindrops veiled the windows, so I couldn't see who was in it.

A different officer was stationed on the porch, shorter and stockier than the one who'd had the duty earlier, but looking equally cold and miserable. Before I could ring the bell, the front door opened. I smelled something baking, a homey, all's-right-with-the-world aroma. Funny how deceptive perceptions can be.

Philip Vandergriff stood there, wearing a raincoat and bouncing a set of car keys in his hand. The light in the foyer behind him brightened his hair but shadowed his face, making it hard to read.

"Jess. I hope you bear good tidings." He remained squarely in the doorway. His sister Lacey hovered behind him.

"I came to see Terri. She asked me to drop by."

"Right. To tell her about the press conference. She mentioned that."

The wind whipped damp hair across my eyes. I brushed it back. "May I come in?"

"Terri's not here," Philip said. "You probably saw the police car. The cops just left. They took her with them."

"Has something happened? Is Amy—"

Lacey, looking frightened, edged up beside him. "No, they're just asking Terri more questions."

Philip frowned. "They interrogated her all last night. Now they want more blood. No way would Terri ever hurt that child."

I recalled what Nick had said about parents falsely claiming a child has been kidnapped. Could the cops be on the right track, questioning Terri? The thought made my heart clench.

"The police are doing what they have to do," I said. "Maybe Terri will give them some little clue, something she doesn't even know that she knows."

Philip wasn't mollified. "It's harassment, pure and simple. They're covering up their own incompetence. The inspector's got it solved—why aren't they following up on his theory? That guy on trial, Moritz."

"Phil, please." Lacey gripped his arm. They were a handsome pair. I was struck again by their close resemblance. The hazel eyes, the tawny hair. Both faces showed the strain of a grueling couple of days. "Go on down to the police station."

He nodded. "Yeah. I'm on my way."

"They won't let you in while they're questioning her," I said.

"I need to be there for her. I'll bring her home when they're through."

"What if they decide to interrogate you?" Lacey asked him.

"They already have. They know I was at work yesterday when Amy got out of school. Just like Terri was. In fact, we were in the same meeting when Evelyn called to tell us about Amy."

"You and Terri work together?" I asked.

"That's right. SalesCom Technologies. Terri's the star of our bookkeeping department."

"Do you crunch numbers too?"

"Among other things," he said, and Lacey snickered.

I looked from one to the other. "Did I miss a joke?"

"Phil owns the company," Lacey said. There was an odd note in her voice. Pride perhaps, or envy—I couldn't tell. "He built it up from nothing. SalesCom's got this software that's going to revolutionize the way companies handle sales on the Internet. Isn't that right, Phil?"

Philip brushed her comments aside. "Hey, we're not Microsoft yet."

The owner of SalesCom Technologies. Another reason why Philip looked familiar—I'd seen his photo in the business pages. SalesCom was a local legend, a firm that had grown and prospered on the wild rollercoaster of the technology sector's boom-and-bust cycles. Terri had found not only love but money too.

"Do you work there too, Lacey?" I asked.

She glanced at her brother. "Not any more."

"We were fifty-fifty partners in the earliest days. But she found better things to do and sold me her share." Philip cinched his raincoat tighter and turned up the collar to shield his neck. "Gotta run."

"Hurry back." Lacey sounded anxious. "We need to get into the city."

"Fast as I can. Depends on how soon they let Terri come home."

"The cookies are almost ready to come out of the oven. I was hoping we could leave right after that. You know we—"

She was speaking with her hands as well with words. Philip grasped them in mid-gesture. "What I know is that you need to calm down," he said gently.

She looked close to tears. "I'm so worried."

Philip circled his arm around her. "Hey, don't cry. You know everyone's doing our damnedest to bring Amy home safe."

She tugged at a wisp of gold hair. "Better be soon. I can't stand much more of this."

"We'll leave when I get back with Terri. We'll get Evelyn to come stay with her, take over the phone duty." Philip stepped out onto the porch. "I'll tell Terri you came by, Jess."

He hurried down the steps and crossed the lawn to his car.

"Do you live in San Francisco, like Phil?" I asked Lacey. "I'm driving back there now. I can take you home."

She smiled wanly. "I should wait for Phil. Thanks, though."

I heard a buzz. Lacey jerked up her head.

"That's the timer. Cookies are done."

"You made cookies?" It seemed like an odd way to spend her time under the circumstances, but I'd skipped lunch, and I was famished. "They smell delicious."

She didn't take the hint and offer me one.

"I hate sitting here idle, waiting for the phone to ring. I had to keep busy with something." In a despairing tone, she added, "They're for Amy when she comes home. Do you think she likes chocolate chip?"

"I'm sure she'll love them." For Amy's visits to my studio, I'd brought home chocolate chip cookies from Irma's, a deli near my office that makes the best cookies in town. It turned out that painting wasn't our only shared passion. But last Saturday, she hadn't been there to help me eat them. A little voice of fear spoke up to remind me: *Maybe never again.*

Lacey mumbled, "I need to get them out of the oven." She shut the door with a click of the latch, leaving me on the porch.

"Sad thing," said a voice from the shadows. I turned to the police officer. "I got a little girl of my own. Scares me to death, what can happen to kids these days."

"I hope nothing like this ever happens to your daughter." The rain was coming down hard again, driven by a brisk wind. I braced myself to get soaked. "Look, I'm going by the shopping center. Can I get anything for you? Coffee, a sandwich?"

"Thanks. I'm okay. Got a Thermos here. Maybe the lady'll give me a cookie. Don't get wet, now."

"I'll run between the raindrops."

I dashed toward my Toyota. Despite my umbrella I was drenched by the time I got in.

The dashboard clock told me it was almost five. Amy was twenty-six hours gone. More than one full day.

I thought I was going home, but at the Albany exit, I got off the freeway on impulse and navigated the steep, slick roads up into the Berkeley hills. Rounding a curve, I had a sudden sweeping view across the bay. I could make out the contours of San Francisco skyscrapers, the Marin headlands, the Golden Gate Bridge. Above the horizon the clouds had parted, opening up an unexpected sunset: ragged stripes of orange and magenta painted on the slate gray sky.

For the second time in half an hour I rang a doorbell, even though for this house I had a key.

The man who answered was gray-haired and comfortable-looking, and much more welcoming than either of the Vandergriffs.

"Jess! What a great surprise! You're in time for dinner." He took my umbrella and swooped me inside.

"Hi, Roger." I gave my stepfather a hug. "I'm not going to stay. I just wanted to see—are Keith and Teddy home?"

"Sure, they're in the den watching TV." He nodded toward the hallway, looking a little puzzled.

It was a hundred-year-old house, full of bookcases, cushioned furniture and ornately carved woodwork. Full of memories—this was where I spent my teenage years, having moved here with my mother when she married Roger Randolph. I was thirteen, and it was a wrenching change—all at once I acquired a new home, a new school and, for the first time in my memory, a father. At the time I wasn't sure I liked any of them. But I grew to love Roger. Good thing I did—he and my little brothers were now my only family.

The den door was shut, and I braced myself before turning the knob. The room was pleasant now, but whenever I walked in there, for a fleeting instant I saw the hospital bed that had been set up when my mother became too ill to make her painful way up the stairs. I'd flash on the anguish and helplessness of watching her die. Almost three years ago now. I took a deep breath and opened the door.

"Hi, guys!" I said.

Fourteen-year-old Keith was hunched in front of his laptop with a stack of open books on the desk beside him. As he looked up, his silky dark hair—our mother's hair—tumbled over his forehead to brush the top of his glasses frames. "Oh, hi."

Teddy, not quite twelve, sprawled on the sofa, reading a comic book, chomping on an apple and watching a *Star Trek* episode. Muggins, the ancient brindled cat, was curled in the crook of his knee.

"Hey, Jess!" Teddy waved the half-eaten apple at me. "Guess what! You know my friend Kyle? His dad's taking us skiing this weekend! Cool, huh? All this rain we're having, there's gonna be killer snow up there!"

I shivered. "Better you than me, Teddy-o."

He shook his head. "You're weird, Jess. *Normal* people like snow."

Roger had come in behind me. He said, "*Normal* people give their sister a hug. Come on, guys. She came here especially to see you."

With mock groans they stood up. When I wasn't with them, I still thought of my brothers as little kids. Yet Keith, I realized with a shock, now stood eye to eye with me. And Teddy, who couldn't even toddle when I moved out of this house, came up to my chin.

I gathered them both into my arms. "Why'dja wanna see us, Jess?" Teddy asked.

"Yeah, why?" echoed Keith.

"Because I ... because I love you." What else could I say? Because terrible things happen to kids out there. Because I needed to see with my own eyes that you're safe.

CHAPTER 10

I SLEPT BADLY that night.

I couldn't tell where nightmares left off and memories began. I was seven years old again. Lost in the Sierra. Stumbling around trees, scrambling over boulders, thrashing through brambles. Trying hard not to cry.

I yelled for my mother, for my Uncle Jack. A crow screeched. Wind rushed in the branches. But the only human voice I could hear was my own, bouncing off the canyon walls.

Rain started to fall, slowly at first, then harder. I found a shallow rock cave and huddled in it, soaking wet, shot through with cold. As I peered out, the rain turned into a white curtain of snow—the first snow I'd ever seen.

The terror I'd felt then gripped me now, made me toss in my bed as if I were fevered.

From the sun-sparkled pictures in my storybooks I'd imagined that snow had the fluff of feathers, the flavor of vanilla cream. Instead, a fierce and unrelenting whiteness filled the sky, blotted out the landscape, turned rocks and trees into ghosts.

Snow drifted across the entrance to my shelter, making the opening smaller and smaller. Before it could seal me in completely, I tugged off one of my purple mittens, pushed it onto the end of a stick and thrust it outside into the snow. A signal flag. The only thing I could think to do. I curled myself into a ball and ...

I jerked awake, my heart racing, a scream caught in my throat. When I dared to open my eyes, I discovered I was safe in my own bedroom. No longer seven years old. No longer lost, but trembling as if I were still that child. I forced myself to concentrate on the moment when the ranger had appeared, like an angel from the sky. He scooped me up in warm, solid arms and carried me through the snow to our cabin.

As I slid back to sleep, I tried hard to visualize a rescue like that for Amy. Prayer never came easily to me, but I sent out a plea to whatever gods might be listening: *Send her home safe.*

When the alarm blared, I was tangled in blankets, drenched with sweat, hugging my pillow hard. I reached out for Kit. No one there.

I was alone. The realization made me feel cold and hollow.

By this hour dawn should have been breaking, but my bedroom was still midnight dark. I could hear the whisper of raindrops at the window: *Amy's gone. Kit is gone. You're losing everyone.*

Damn it, Kit, I thought, why are you in Hawaii? I longed to tell him about Amy, to have him reassure me, cry with me, share the distress and fear. Have him convince me it wasn't my fault she was gone.

Be adventurous! Take risks!

I pictured Kit on a Hawaiian beach with his camera, warm sun on his bare back, the water as blue as his eyes. I painted the scene on the backs of my eyelids, filling my mind with gold, azure, aquamarine, trying to banish the empty whiteness of snow.

Why wasn't I there with him? I could have gone without giving in to an impulsive wedding. So often since New Year's Day I'd felt the urge to contact him, to fly to Honolulu so we could continue the slow but steady working out of our relationship. But I worried that as we relaxed in tropical climes, away from our usual rhythms and routines, I'd let my guard down—although what I was guarding so zealously, I couldn't say. So I'd never sent the text, never written the email, never picked up the phone.

On the other hand, neither had he.

I pulled the blankets over my head. Scruff padded over and gave me a get-up-lazybones nudge. He was surprised when I gathered him onto the bed and embraced him, but he rewarded me with a sloppy dog kiss. For the moment it would have to do.

I followed my usual get-the-day-started routine—showered and dressed, fixed a mug of tea, took Scruff for a quick, wet walk to the edge of Golden Gate Park. With every action, every step, Amy hovered like a shadow at the edge of my peripheral vision.

The rain stopped as Scruff and I returned from the park, and the leaden sky showed occasional small patches of blue. For a brief, bright instant, the sun broke through, and the world turned golden. But it would be a fleeting respite. The weather forecast showed several storms stacked up across the Pacific; the next one was expected to slam ashore this afternoon.

I thought of my rock cave, and wondered where—if—Amy had found shelter.

When we reached home, I phoned Terri. Fatigue and fear gave her voice a rough edge as she told me there was still no news. "How was the press conference?" she asked. In my mind's eye I saw her at the kitchen phone, recording my name and number in the logbook.

I told her about the few minutes of the conference that I'd attended, then said, "I'm on my way over. Any errands you'd like me to run on the way? I could pick up some groceries—"

"Don't come. I mean—it's such a long drive from the city."

"I'd like to help you out. It's the least I can do for Amy."

"Evelyn's here, she's holding down the fort. I—well, frankly I don't want anyone else around right now."

"I understand." And I did, but I felt discouraged and frustrated all the same.

"There is something you could do for me?" She lifted her inflection, making the sentence a question.

"Anything you need," I assured her.

"Nick claims that Amy ... that this is all connected to that Moritz trial. He's supposed to testify today—do you think he'll go through with it? I mean, if those people do have Amy ..."

I'd wondered about that myself. "He won't do anything if he thinks it might put Amy at risk."

"He told me he's not allowed in the courtroom until he actually goes on the stand, and that might be for a while. I wondered—could you go there and look around? You know, watch people, see if anyone looks suspicious?"

"Good idea," I said.

"I don't know what you'd look for exactly. But I'd feel better, knowing I had reliable eyes and ears on the scene."

Eyes and ears. The same words Nick had used when he asked me to spend time with Terri. I wondered if the phrase was a habit they'd picked up from each other. A tiny link between them, one they weren't even aware of.

"All right. I'll bring you a report later today."

"Thank you. Oh, God, this is awful. I was awake all night, listening for Amy. I kept thinking, if I could just listen hard enough, I'd hear her voice. She'd tell me where she is. But I heard nothing. Nothing at all. When is this nightmare going to end?"

I had no answer.

When we hung up, I checked to see how much time I had before the trial started for the day.

Eight o'clock. Amy had been missing for forty-one hours.

"Do you swear to tell the truth, the whole truth and nothing but the truth?"

"I do."

"Please state your name and occupation."

"Nolan Aldridge. I'm the proprietor of Bountiful Books on Haight Street."

The courtroom was packed; I'd been lucky to snag a seat. There were almost as many reporters here as at the press conference. I half expected to see William Paveleck, the Pizza Kid. In Creekhaven he'd been in my face every time I turned around.

Aldridge was the prosecution's first witness; yesterday's opening arguments had consumed the whole day. Nick might not testify until late this afternoon, if at all. I opened the sketchbook on my lap and occupied myself with scribbling a portrait of the man on the witness stand. Tall and thin, white-haired and bearded. He looked like Santa Claus might if the jolly old elf were into aerobics and a sensible diet plan. Instead of a red suit, he wore a tweed jacket and horn-rimmed glasses, which gave him a professorial air.

"Mr. Aldridge, were you acquainted with Robin Moritz?" the prosecutor asked.

"Yes, I was."

"Would you please explain in what context you knew her?"

"Robin worked for me at my bookstore."

I knew the prosecutor, Joe Buchanan. He'd questioned me when an embezzlement case I investigated came to trial. He was sharp, thorough and fair, genial when that was called for, fierce and tenacious at other times. He led the bookseller through the details of his association with Robin Moritz—a hopeful tale of a troubled young woman finding her way. As Aldridge told it, you could almost forget it didn't end happily ever after.

"How long did she work for you?"

"Just over three years."

My seat was a few rows behind the defense table, where Robin's father sat stiff and straight, flanked by a brace of high-priced defense attorneys. His wide back and shoulders were sheathed in expensive-looking fabric, navy with pinstripes, and his shiny black hair had been carefully coaxed over a tonsure of bare scalp. I couldn't see his face because he stared straight ahead, never venturing a glance around the courtroom.

It was easy to believe this man was a real estate magnate. But did he look like a murderer—a man who could kill his own daughter, his newborn grandson? Someone who would mastermind a plot to steal another man's child to keep himself out of prison?

I could almost hear Nick chiding me: "Come on, Jess. You know you can't tell the bad guys by their looks."

Buchanan asked the witness, "How did you come to hire Robin?"

"She was recommended by the counselors at New Dawn," Aldridge said. "I've hired several of their graduates."

"What is New Dawn?"

"It's a drug rehabilitation program."

"Don't you feel there's some risk involved in hiring drug addicts to work in your store?"

"They're not using drugs any more. And if I give them a chance at a meaningful job, they're more likely to stay clean. Everyone I've hired from New Dawn has worked out fine. Especially Robin Moritz."

"You got involved with New Dawn because of a situation in your own family, is that correct?"

"Yes. My son John. He got involved with drugs and—we nearly lost him. When New Dawn took him in, he was out on the streets, so far down they had to scrape him off the pavement. Now he's at San Francisco State, studying computer science, getting A's. New Dawn saved his life. My way to thank them is by extending a helping hand to its graduates."

Under Buchanan's skilled guidance, Nolan Aldridge described Robin's duties at the store, her helpfulness to customers, her love of books. I could have backed up his testimony had anyone asked. For three years, every time I went into Bountiful Books, Robin had greeted me. After the shooting I was one of many people who laid flowers on the bloodstained spot in front of the store where Robin, her fiancé and their baby were slain.

"Mr. Aldridge," Buchanan said, "did Robin ever talk to you about her father?"

Aldridge shifted in the witness chair, looking uncomfortable. "A little. Not much."

"Did she ever discuss how her father treated her as she was growing up?" The prosecutor was alluding, I assumed, to the rumors of abuse.

"She, uh—nothing specific, no. All I can tell you is that she seemed to be afraid of him."

Buchanan nodded and moved on. He'd opened the door. No doubt he'd call later witnesses to pursue the idea that Robin planned to file a lawsuit against her father, and the horrible reasons why.

Tension built in the courtroom as Nolan Aldridge's tale reached its climax—the young family's last moments of life.

Buchanan steadied himself with a sip of water from a glass on the prosecutor's table. He asked: "Did you see Robin that day?"

"Yes. At my store."

"But she was no longer working for you."

"No. She left right before her baby was born."

"So why was she there that day?"

"She and Eric—her fiancé—they came to show off their new son. Everybody wanted to hold him. They passed him around from one person to the next, cooing and clucking, and Michael smiled and smiled."

"It was a happy moment, then?"

"Oh, yes," Aldridge said, his voice filled with sadness.

"How long were they there, Robin and Eric and Michael?"

"About twenty minutes."

"And what happened when they left?"

Aldridge was visibly shaking. "They had just walked out the door. And then I heard … gunshots. Gunshots like thunder. Then Robin screamed her baby's name. 'Oh God!' she screamed. 'Michael! Michael!'"

At the defense table, Carl Moritz did not so much as twitch. Of course I couldn't see his face; perhaps he was tearful, like the woman next to me, who was dabbing a handkerchief at her eyes.

The prosecutor asked, "What did you do, Mr. Aldridge, when you heard the gunshots?"

"I ran outside to see what had happened."

"Why? Weren't you frightened?"

"When I heard Robin scream ... I hoped I could help her. My cashier was already calling nine-one-one, but ... it was too late."

"Tell us what you saw."

"Blood. So much blood. Oh Lord, that little baby. Flung from his mother's arms into the gutter. Robin was lying on the sidewalk, reaching out for him. Eric was crumpled against the building. All of them bright red with blood. I knelt beside Robin, my hands got covered with blood."

Aldridge held up his hands, turned them slowly, as if the blood could still be seen.

Directly behind Moritz, in the first row of spectators, a young woman gave a sharp cry. She half rose from her seat, then sank down again as a bailiff started to move in her direction.

Robin!

For an instant my heart stopped. It was Robin, attending her own murder trial, returned from the dead to avenge herself.

Of course it couldn't be. But she was the right age and the right size; she had Robin's long dark hair, with the same bangs falling over her forehead.

Then I remembered. Robin had a sister named—Sharon? Sheila? Shanna, that was it—who was a year or two older. She'd been at the bookstore one day when I was there, and Robin had introduced us.

The young woman covered her face with her hands. How awful this must be for her—her sister murdered by their father's hand.

One of Moritz's attorneys asked to approach the bench so he could quibble about a point of law. Was he the one who'd dropped a discreet word to some thug who owed Moritz a favor? Had this man arranged for an untraceable payment to be made once Amy was stolen and a mistrial declared?

Or was it someone else in the courtroom? Gazing around, I saw no one who looked obviously sinister. Not even anyone, other than his lawyers and his daughter, who I could say for certain was connected with Carl Moritz. Reporters, yes, and plenty of trial junkies—people who hung out in courtrooms, savoring a trial like a real-life soap opera. Behind the prosecutors' table sat a somber woman whom I guessed to be the mother of Robin's fiancé. She looked wispy and dry, as if the rigors of mourning had wrung all the life fluids out of her.

Joe Buchanan joined Moritz's lawyer at the bench. The opposing attorneys spoke in hushed voices so the jurors couldn't hear, but their emphatic gestures made the heat of their wrangling clear.

With a bang of his gavel, the judge declared a short recess. Instantly the courtroom buzzed with conversation and activity. As I stood and stretched, I saw Shanna Moritz dart down the aisle. Leaving my sketchbook and umbrella to hold my seat, I hurried after her.

In the corridor Shanna dodged several reporters and ducked into the ladies room. I went in too, slipping into a stall while I considered how best to approach her. When I emerged she was at a sink, smearing gooey green dispenser soap on her hands.

"Shanna?" I said. "I'm Jess Randolph. We met at the bookstore." There was no reason why she'd remember, but it was the only opening I could think of.

She gazed at me in the mirror, her dark eyes wary. Up close she looked less like Robin—her features were sharper, her skin less rosy, her hair more lank. Most of all, she lacked the spark of animation that Robin always had. Of course, this wasn't a day when she'd be at her best.

When she didn't reply I continued: "I'm sorry about what

happened to Robin. I liked her a lot. I'm sorry for all you're going through."

Shanna rubbed her hands under the spout of water. "Yes. I'm sorry too."

"Mind if I talk to you for a minute?"

She shrugged. "Seems to me you're talking already."

"Yes, well ..." I wasn't sure how to bring up what was on my mind. "Have you heard about Amy Gardino?"

"No." She grabbed a paper towel and dried her hands. "Wait—you mean the cop's kid? The one that's missing?"

"That's right." I turned on the faucet at the next sink and washed my own hands. When I pumped the soap dispenser, nothing came out.

"I saw it on TV last night. It's weird—the same cop who investigated Robin. I mean, the killings and ... and everything." Shanna was avoiding my eyes. So far she'd addressed all her remarks to my reflection in the mirror.

"Yes, it is weird. I heard some people suggest there might be a connection."

"A connection? To what?"

"To your father. This trial. They're saying Amy was kidnapped to keep Nick Gardino from testifying. I wondered if maybe you'd heard something—anything at all that might help us find her."

Shanna took a brush from her purse and ran it through her hair.

"Are you saying my father's involved? That's crazy, he'd never—and even if he would, he's been in jail for months." She sounded bitter.

"Maybe an associate thought he could make points with your father. One of his employees, or—"

"What are you anyway, a cop or something? A reporter?"

"No. A friend of Amy's family."

Shanna aimed her back toward me as studied her face in the mirror. She dug into her purse and took out a lipstick.

"Amy's just a kid, " I said as she daubed color onto her lips. "Only seven years old. She must be terrified. No child deserves to be a pawn in grownup disputes."

Shanna's eyes in the mirror were suddenly bright with tears. "I'm sorry about the child," she whispered. For the first time, she turned to face me. She looked slightly grotesque, half her mouth a purply red, the other half pale. "Look, I don't know about the little girl. Honest. I can't imagine my father—I hope she'll be okay."

"I hope so too."

"Tell you what, give me your phone number or something. If I hear anything about … her name's Amy? I'll let you know."

"Thanks." I gave her my artist's business card instead of the one from Parks & O'Meara. Finding out I was a private investigator might make her skittish about calling.

The restroom door whooshed open and a woman came in, notebook in hand. Her face brightened when she saw us.

"Aren't you Shanna Moritz?" she chirped, her pen poised. "I'd like to ask you a few questions."

"Never heard of her," Shanna mumbled. She spun away from the mirror and fled.

CHAPTER 11

SHORTLY BEFORE NOON, the prosecutor and the defense attorney got into another squabble at the bench. The judge took the opportunity to adjourn for lunch.

As people pushed out of the courtroom, Carl Moritz stood and turned to watch the crowd. Staring at the back of his head all morning, I'd guessed at his features from the rearview evidence, then sketched a speculative portrait. What would evil look like straight on?

I hadn't done too badly. His face was broad, as I'd expected, in keeping with his hefty frame. I'd also been right about the high forehead under the thinning black hair, and the hawkish nose. He had no horns, but I decided not to erase the ones I'd drawn.

The real Moritz was better-looking than my version on paper. What kept him from being handsome was the heavy ridge of brow that capped his eyes like a lid. It was impossible to see any light in them.

Shanna Moritz rose from her seat in the first row. She leaned toward her father across the wooden barrier that separated the spectators from the lawyers and crooks. Perhaps she said something; I couldn't tell. Moritz reached out as if wanting to touch her. But his attorney whispered to him, and Moritz, his expression suddenly sad, shook his head and allowed himself to be led away. Shanna watched him go. Then, head lowered and shoulders hunched, she shuffled down the aisle.

I left the courtroom too. The marble corridor rang with the

chattering of voices and the clicking of heels. Shanna was nowhere in sight.

"Jess! Hey!"

The sudden summons came from behind me. I spun around and was surprised to see Philip Vandergriff.

"Philip," I said. "I didn't expect to see you here."

His clothes suggested a man at ease: khaki pants and an open-necked shirt, topped by a jacket of tan leather that looked so soft I had to fight the urge to stroke it. But his shoulders looked weighted down and his face appeared pinched by stress.

"Terri asked me to come and take a close look at this guy Moritz. If the Inspector's right and he's got Amy... well, we need to get a firsthand perspective."

Interesting. She'd asked me to do the same thing.

People jostled us as they came out of the courtroom. We started walking down the corridor.

"How's Terri this morning?" I asked.

"Not good. It breaks my heart, seeing her in such pain."

"Someone should be with her. Is your sister there?"

"No, Lacey had things to take care of here in the city. But Georgia Holcomb—remember, Hannah's mom?—she came by with the prayer group from her church."

"Will Terri find that comforting?"

"Well, Georgia's brand of religion isn't really Terri's style. But Georgia means well. We can use all the good wishes we can get, whatever form they come in."

Amen to that, I thought.

We rounded the corner to the elevator lobby. "There's the Inspector," Philip announced.

Nick Gardino stood in the crowd waiting for the elevator. His partner was with him. Ray Beschke, stubble-haired and jowly, had always reminded me of a bulldog, in both appearance and manner. Philip trailed me as I made my way toward them.

"Hey, Nick. Hello, Ray," I said.

Beschke gave me a military-style salute. "If it isn't Ms. Ace Detective."

I tried not to bristle. Although Beschke and I had met only a few times, we'd found right away that we had something in common: we each got on the other's nerves.

He glanced over my shoulder. "Who's your friend?"

I introduced Philip. With the slightest of scowls, Nick added, "This is Terri's, uh, fiancé."

Beschke extended a beefy hand for Philip to shake. "I'm sorry about the little girl. Hope she turns up safe real soon."

"So do I," Philip said. "So do I."

He turned to Nick. "I expected to see you on the stand this morning, Inspector."

Something about his tone made me wonder: had he told me his real purpose for being here at the Hall of Justice? Maybe Terri had sent him to keep on eye not on Moritz but on Nick.

"That won't happen today," Nick said. "Maybe not tomorrow either. They haven't finished with the bookstore owner, and there's three, maybe four, other witnesses on the list ahead of me."

I couldn't tell from his expression if the delay was good news or not. Exhaustion and worry had smudged bluish shadows under his eyes, sharpened the tension lines around his mouth.

Nick echoed the question I'd asked a moment ago: "How's Terri doing?"

"She's a strong lady, Inspector," Philip replied. "I really admire her, the way she's holding up."

The two men exchanged wary glances. I was struck by how similar they looked. They were both compactly built, and within an inch of the same height. Both had long, straight noses and cleft chins. They each had a mustache, and they even parted their hair on the same side. The one big difference was their coloring—Nick was dark, Philip fair. Terri was going to marry a blond version of her ex-husband.

"So what will you do now?" I asked Nick.

"Ray and I are heading upstairs to review our open cases, since he'll have to shoulder them alone for a while." The homicide department was on the fourth floor of the Hall of Justice, one flight up from Superior Court where we were now. "Then I'm going to talk to anybody who ever exchanged three words with Carl Moritz and get my daughter back."

"Any word from Moritz's people about what they want?"

"Not exactly," Nick said.

"What do you mean?"

"Someone dropped off another note with the guard downstairs this morning."

"What does it say?" I asked.

"Not enough, unfortunately," Nick said. "This one mentions Amy and Moritz by name, gives a couple of little details. But there's nothing specific that will help us find her."

"Just the fact that you got it is good news, right?" Philip said.

Both Nick and Beschke were shaking their heads.

"But—isn't it good? A lead, finally?"

"It's a fake," Beschke stated flatly.

Philip looked disappointed. "How can you tell?"

"It doesn't ring right. Nick wants to believe there's something to it, but two cases like these, lots of publicity—I think some wacko decided to tie them together, hoping for a little thrill."

"I'd like to see the note—"

Beschke stopped him with a cold smile. "Sorry, Vandergriff. You must watch cop shows; you know we gotta hold something back that only the asshole who's guilty would know."

Philip gave a little shrug of acquiescence. "But if the note's a fake, do you still think Moritz is behind what's happened to Amy?"

A chime announced an elevator's arrival. The UP arrow lighted above the door.

"Yeah, I do," Nick said. "Only ... oh hell, I don't know. I frigging don't know what to think."

"What I think"—Beschke thrust an arm forward to hold the door open—"is we better get moving. Sooner we're done upstairs, the sooner we get back to looking for your little girl."

The two cops were the only people to enter the elevator. A moment later a car going down arrived. The rest of the crowd, including Philip and I, shoved into it.

Philip kept pace beside me as I left the Hall of Justice and headed down the wide front steps. The promising patches of blue were gone; the sky was a solid expanse of gray. Darkness at noon, I thought.

"Nice running into you." Philip turned to leave.

Seize the moment, Jess.

"How about joining me for lunch?"

Nick had given me a mission—keep Terri and those around her from shutting him out of the search for Amy. Getting better acquainted with Philip Vandergriff would be a good place to start.

"Lunch?" Philip glanced at his watch—hesitating, or pretending to. "Why not? I've got some thoughts about what's going on. Might be good to bounce them off someone. I know a good place. How about Dandelion?"

"Dandelion? That's all the way over in the Haight."

"Well, where is there to eat around here? Bernie's Bail Bond Cafe? Besides, I need to run some errands in the Haight this afternoon."

Actually, it made sense for me too. I'd planned to go back to the courtroom, but I couldn't see how sitting there any longer would lead us to Amy. I could go home after lunch, make some notes and phone calls, give Scruff the unaccustomed treat of a midday walk.

"Okay," I said. "Meet you at Dandelion in twenty minutes."

CHAPTER 12

"WOW! LOOK at that guy!"

January wasn't tourist season, but the trio at Dandelion's window table were clearly out-of-towners. Mom, Dad and a boy of about eleven who reminded me of my brother Teddy. Several things gave them away: their neat haircuts, their camera gear, the son's ESCAPEE FROM ALCATRAZ T-shirt and the way all three were gawking at the passing Haight Street scene.

"That is so totally cool!" the boy exclaimed.

I looked up from my Caesar salad in time to see the object of his admiration whiz by—one of the Haight-Ashbury regulars, a kid in his late teens who called himself Atom. He was tall enough to play pro basketball, and the inline skates he habitually wore added a couple more inches to his height. Yet I'd have been surprised if his weight topped one hundred thirty pounds. Every time Mrs. Fiorelli, my landlady, saw him on the street, she invited him home to dinner. I'd personally seen him pack away three homemade pizzas and a quart of ice cream at one sitting.

What probably intrigued the kid at the window, however, wasn't Atom's whippet-like frame, or even his skates, but his hair. Both sides of his skull were shaved, leaving a three-inch-high ridge of hair that ran from his forehead to the nape of his neck. Today the strands had been gelled into spikes and colored bright turquoise.

I was glad it was Atom and not me out skating on this cold, gloomy afternoon. Dandelion, with its steamy warmth and

81

tantalizing smells of garlic and sourdough, was a much better place to be. The room was painted a cheerful yellow—substitute sunshine. The owner had decorated the walls with a decade's worth of posters for the annual Haight Street Fair. Each year a contest was held to choose the new poster design. I'd entered five times; last summer I finally snagged an honorable mention.

Across from me, Philip Vandergriff brushed back his sandy hair with one hand. I had a sudden image of him wearing a turquoise-tipped mohawk and almost laughed. I covered it by asking, "You told me Terri works for your company. Is that how you met?"

Philip sipped his coffee before answering. He'd barely touched his fettuccine. "That's right. Terri joined SalesCom in September, right after she moved down from Chico. She's in collections."

"Last night you said bookkeeping."

"Collections is part of the bookkeeping department. Terri calls customers with overdue accounts and gets them to pay up. She's great at it, best we've ever had."

"Sounds exciting. Good use of her accounting degree."

Philip detected the sarcasm in my tone. "It may seem dull, but it takes real skill. Psychology. Problem-solving. Maybe the wrong product got shipped, or an order got shipped twice. Maybe a returned item didn't get logged in properly. Maybe a payment got credited to someone else's invoice."

"Or maybe the customer is a deadbeat."

"That too." He nodded. "On Terri's first day, one of the admin assistants was touring her around, introducing her to people. When they stopped by my office, I looked up from my desk and fell in love."

"The feeling seems to be mutual."

I could see why Terri might cast her lot with this man, aside from his physical resemblance to Nick. He had a boyish appeal coupled with take-charge energy, and being the CEO of a successful company couldn't hurt. Especially after bitter years of struggling to hold down a job, keep up with college classes, and not neglect a young daughter. That was my own mother's story, too. Except Nick sent support money, stayed in tenuous touch—far more than my father ever did.

"Well, the attraction wasn't quite so instantaneous for Terri. It took me awhile to convince her she loved me in return."

"Meet in September, engaged at Christmas. Sounds pretty quick to me."

"Commit to your course, then take action—that's my motto. If I decide something's right for me, I go for it."

"Be adventurous, take risks," I murmured.

"What was that?"

"Nothing. Go on."

"I'll tell you, the happiest moment of my life was when I put that ring on her finger."

I glanced at my hands, bare of jewelry. If I said yes to this marriage thing, would Kit want to give me a ring? Nothing as extravagant as Terri's glittering bauble, I hoped. Maybe I could talk him into something unconventional, like amber or jade—if we ever spoke again.

"When's the wedding?" I asked.

"Next June."

"Ah, the traditional marriage month."

"I was pushing for sooner. But Terri wants to wait until school's out. We'll have a weekend honeymoon, then take a nice long vacation, all three of us. That is, if ... God, I hope Amy's all right."

"So do I. I can't tell you how much."

He pushed the fettuccine around on his plate. "This tragedy will bring us closer, Terri and me."

The three syllables wrenched my heart. "Tragedy? Do you think Amy won't be found? Or that ..." I couldn't bring myself to say: *She's not alive.*

"No," Philip said quickly. "Bad choice of words. We're going to find her."

"You sound pretty certain."

He shoved his plate away. "Oh hell. I'm not certain at all. But like I keep telling Terri—we have to think positive. We have to believe we'll find Amy, she'll be okay, and we can get on with being a family."

"I hope you're right."

"Amy's such a sweetheart. Some men resent a package deal, but I think it's a bonus—getting a wife and a daughter all at once. I can't wait until Amy calls me daddy."

I didn't point out that she already had a daddy. Philip's marrying Terri wouldn't change that. It had been different for me. Roger Randolph came late into my life, but he was the only dad I'd known. When I was seven I would have given the world to know who my father was, to have an occasional visit, a birthday card. To know what he looked like or recognize the sound of his voice. Amy had that much, at least.

Philip dipped a chunk of sourdough bread into the dish of olive oil. "I've told you our story, Terri's and mine. What's yours with the Inspector?"

"No story. We're friends, that's all. Our paths have crossed on cases. Nick plays tennis sometimes with my boss." I deflected the conversation back to him. "You said you had ideas about what's happened to Amy?"

He looked toward the window where the tourists sat, probably collecting his thoughts. Turning back to me, he said, "At first Terri was convinced that the Inspector took her."

"But she can't still feel that way. She must see that Nick's going through agony, just like she is."

He lifted one shoulder, a half-shrug that left Terri's opinion open.

"Nick would never do anything like that," I persisted. "Why would she think he's remotely capable—"

"I don't know. But there are a lot of old wounds there."

"Is that the theory you wanted to bounce off me? Some wild

conjecture that Nick grabbed Amy and hid her somewhere to get back at Terri for hurting his feelings?" I banged my knife on my plate. "Is he planning to flee the country? Am I involved? Would you like to search my flat?"

"Hey, calm down. I'm not accusing anybody of anything. We're all in this together."

I became aware that my face was hot, my voice was shrill, and the patrons at other tables were staring. Not a good way to get answers to my questions. I grabbed my water glass, mumbled "Sorry" into it, and took a long swallow.

"It's okay," Philip said. "All of us are stressed out."

Yes, but I hadn't realized how close to the edge Amy's disappearance was pushing me.

"What makes sense to me," Philip went on, "is the Inspector's theory about this trial. The Moritz Investment Group happens to be a SalesCom customer. I asked the sales rep who handles their account to give me the name of someone there to talk to. She referred me right to the top—Creighton Oliver, who's running the show now that Carl Moritz is, well, unavailable. So first thing this morning I stopped in to see Oliver."

"What did he say?"

"She—Ms. Creighton Oliver. She denied knowing anything about Amy—was shocked at the very suggestion. Too shocked, in fact. The lady doth protest too much if you ask me."

"You think she's involved?"

"Let's just say if anyone in the company's involved, Creighton Oliver could shake things loose. She's in charge, so she knows who to lean on. What's the matter? You're frowning."

"I hope your going to see her hasn't put Amy in greater danger."

"What do you mean? I'm trying to find Amy. To rescue her."

"If the kidnappers think someone's closing in, they might—" A shudder jolted through me.

"Look, Jess, a favor, okay? I know Nick's wary about sharing information with Terri and me. But we need to know what's going on. If you hear anything about what Nick or the cops are thinking, let me know. For Terri's peace of mind."

He pulled out a pen and a business card, flipped the card over and scrawled something on the blank side. "Call me any time, day or night."

I took the card. The SalesCom Technologies logo and Philip's contact information were printed on the front. On the back he'd written two phone numbers, labeled *home* and *cell*, in thick, angular penstrokes.

"All right," I said, not sure that I meant it. We all had a common objective: to find Amy. Why was I beginning to feel caught between two sides in a battle? I slid the card into my purse.

There was a moment of commotion as the family at the window table stood up and pulled on raincoats. Atom zipped by again, heading in the opposite direction, and the boy bounced on his toes with excitement. His father put a restraining hand on his shoulder and they headed out the door.

"Thank you." Philip grasped my hand, gave it a quick squeeze. "Think positive. Something tells me things will break soon."

Rain spattered our faces as we left Dandelion. Philip and I walked along the street in silence. Half a block down, in front of Bountiful Books, we both stopped, as if by some sort of agreement.

I hadn't witnessed the deaths of Robin Moritz, Eric Nielsen and baby Michael. I hadn't seen the bodies on the sidewalk or the chalk outlines drawn by the police. Yet every time I walked past this spot I felt their presence. I could see again the brownish traces of bloodstains, the brilliant colors of the flowers placed there by friends and neighbors.

Philip was staring into the bookstore window at a display of children's books. They were stacked like a house of cards, with a clown doll sitting on the topmost one. The merry effect was spoiled by the flyer taped to the inside of the glass—the picture of Amy. MISSING—POSSIBLE STRANGER ABDUCTION.

"You know, Jess," Philip said, "I think—"

I turned toward him and saw disaster coming.

"Philip, look out!"

Atom, skating too fast and out of control, skidded into him. The impact knocked them both off their feet.

"Jesus!" Philip moaned. He lay sprawled on the sidewalk. "Watch where the hell you're going!"

"Are you guys all right?" I helped them untangle various limbs.

"Hey, man, I'm sorry." Atom pushed to his knees, then extended himself to full height, balancing carefully on his wheels. "You okay?" He bent down to offer Philip a hand.

Philip ignored it and stood up on his own. "Crazy punk! You should be arrested, careening down the sidewalk like that."

As he brushed himself off and straightened his jacket, he gazed at Atom, taking in the black denim attire, the miniature skull dangling from an earlobe, and the tattooed snake peeking out from a sleeve. Not to mention the turquoise spikes of hair, drooping under a sudden onslaught of rain.

"I didn't mean to hit you, honest. You aren't hurt, are you?"

"Goddamn menace," Philip muttered.

"I'm sorry," Atom said again. "It's just, the sidewalk's so slick. Some lady bumped me with her umbrella, I hit a puddle, it's not my fault."

Philip made Atom give him his name and address—whether to report him to the police or sue him for damages, I wasn't sure. His name was Pete Best, Atom said, and he lived at 1201 Ashbury. Apparently satisfied, Philip nodded curtly at Atom, said goodbye to me and walked off.

"What a grouch," Atom grumbled. "I said I was sorry."

"He's under a lot of stress," I explained.

"No excuse for acting like a—"

"Hey, Atom," I said.

He was avoiding my eye. "Grownups freak when kids don't show 'em manners, but they think they've got some kinda rudeness license so they can be assholes whenever they want."

"Atom ..."

He made an elaborate show of looking around. "Say, where's good ol' Scruff?" He and my dog were friends.

"Atom, there's no 1200 block on Ashbury Street. The numbers don't go that high."

"Is that right?" He made himself look all wide-eyed and innocent—not an easy task.

"And wasn't Pete Best the Beatles' first drummer? The one replaced by Ringo Starr?"

"Yeah, well, I kinda get a charge out of, you know, ancient history." He grinned. "Hey, thanks for not giving me away."

CHAPTER 13

WHEN I CAME THROUGH my front door Scruff rushed down the stairs and hurtled himself at me, nearly knocking me over.

"Hey, kiddo, no jumping. Where are your manners?"

Perhaps my tone wasn't stern enough. Or maybe the hug I gave him spoke louder than the words. Instead of acting chastised, he danced a jig that sent him bouncing from wall to wall. Easy to do—the walls were close together. The foyer of my flat was hardly wider than the door, and no deeper than it was wide. Opposite the door, a flight of stairs ascended to the living space on the second floor. Amy had laughed when I described my home as a peanut butter flat—the middle unit in a stack of three, like sandwich filling between two slices of bread.

I took Scruff's leash from a coat peg. By the time I clipped it to his collar, his tail was spinning almost in circles. One day it was going to lift him off the ground like a helicopter. I would hire him out to a radio station to do traffic reports.

I opened the door and Scruff zipped out, dragging me behind. The rain didn't faze him. His tail rode high as we trotted down the sidewalk. Just as I was getting into the rhythm of his pace, he halted and I nearly fell headlong. He stuck his face into the tangled weeds beneath a street tree. Some other dog's bathroom, no doubt. Scruff took a deep, soul-satisfying whiff and left his own mark.

Watching him, I thought of the search dogs that had been set on Amy's trail. If Amy was lost in Blackberry Canyon, the dogs stood a chance of locating her, but could they do it in time? She'd been gone two nights—two cold, stormy nights. My mind flashed to my Sierra shelter. Was there a rock cave in the canyon, a place where she might have found refuge?

Grim as it was, Amy's being lost seemed like the most hopeful scenario. The dogs would never reach her if she'd been snatched by—whom? A Moritz hireling? A prowling pedophile?

The rain suddenly felt icy.

I guided Scruff down Frederick Street to Belvedere. Last night I'd looked up Philip Vandergriff's address, and I was curious to see where my newfound neighbor lived. Most of the Haight-Ashbury was a congenial hodgepodge of small houses and three-story flats, populated by an energetic mix of artists, entrepreneurs, activists and unreconstructed hippies. Belvedere, though, was upscale. Large Victorian and Edwardian homes were arranged in neat rows on either side of the tree-lined street.

I stopped across the street from Philip's house. It appeared freshly painted. Ivory-colored walls, elaborate scrollwork in forest green, highlights of gold that would shine in the sun, if the sun ever came out again.

Was this the home that Philip, Terri and Amy would share? It would certainly be a great step up from the cramped gray bungalow in Creekhaven. Or would they buy a different house, start their lives together afresh, in a place that was unburdened by memories? I hoped they'd stay here. I liked the idea of Amy living so close to me.

If she came back.

I made myself rephrase it: When she came back.

"Come on, kiddo," I said to Scruff. "We're cold and wet. Let's go home."

I took a few steps, but a tug on the leash brought me up short. Scruff, pursuing another delicious scent, had wrapped the leash around a tree. He sat on the sidewalk, looking proud of himself.

When I finished untangling him, I saw a woman standing in

front of Philip's house, watching us. She wore a raincoat with a hood over her hair, and it took me a moment to realize who she was.

"Lacey?" I called.

She looked startled, then recognition dawned for her, too. "Oh, it's you. Terri's detective friend."

Terri's friend, Nick's friend—I didn't correct her.

Lacey crossed the street to join us. The rain had eased, and she let her hood slide off, revealing her blond mane.

"Looking for Phil? He's not home."

"No, I'm walking my dog. This is Scruff."

She let him sniff her hand, then patted his head. A tan tote bag hung by its loops from her other arm. Scruff poked it with his nose and I pulled him back. "Scruff! Behave yourself."

Lacey lifted the bag out of reach. "Nothing in there for you, Scruff. Sorry I can't offer a bone." She turned to me. "I remember now. You said you live in this neighborhood."

"That's right. Do you share this house with Philip?"

"I live in L.A. I came up to help out however I can until we get Amy back. I'm going to Terri's house soon and take another turn answering the phone."

"This must be hard on you. Are you and Amy close?"

"Actually, I've never met Amy. Or Terri either, until yesterday. I was planning to come for Christmas, but Phil decided to take Terri and Amy to his place in the mountains. That's when he popped the question, you know. Gave Terri the diamond. It was all kind of sudden."

"What do you do in Los Angeles?"

She answered with a rueful laugh. "Well, when I went down there I had visions of giving Scarlett Johansson a run for her money. Much more fun than boring high-tech stuff, don't you think?"

"Absolutely."

"Even as a kid I wanted to be an actress. But I got sidetracked into computer programming. A much more practical line of work, my family insisted."

"Practical isn't everything."

"They were right, as it turned out. Phil and I started SalesCom, and I designed the software that turned out to be the company's biggest moneymaker. Then the technology sector began to take a huge dive. I decided, better cash out while I can. I sold my half of SalesCom to Phil. That gave me a nest egg, so I headed to Hollywood." She hugged her tote bag to her chest. "Little did I know that right after that, the demand for SalesCom's software would explode."

"How have things worked out in L.A.?"

"Well, Scarlett's not losing any sleep over me. I'm doing commercials mostly, some voiceover work. But my time is coming."

A sudden gust of wind flung raindrops into our faces. The drizzle became a downpour.

"Better go in," Lacey said, and she dashed across the street. I hoped her words were an invitation but she shut Philip's door behind her almost before Scruff and I had a chance to move.

Back at our front porch, I unhooked Scruff from the leash and he shook himself with vigor. As water drops flew in all directions, I rang the bell of the first-floor flat. My landlady lived there with an ever-changing assortment of foster kids. Davy, now ten, had arrived at Mrs. Fiorelli's place the same week that Scruff, then a raggedy runt puppy, arrived at mine. Sensing each other as fellow waifs, they instantly became great pals. I paid Davy two dollars a day to walk Scruff after school, though I knew he'd have done it for free.

A toddler with streaks of jam on her cheeks opened the door. Mrs. Fiorelli was right behind her, wiping floury hands on the apron that covered the front of her short, square body.

"Walk time already?" she said. "Davy's not home from school."

"Doggie," said the child, pointing. Scruff licked her fingers and she giggled.

"We just got back from a walk," I said. "I wanted to tell you there's no need for Davy to go out in the rain. I'll pay him anyway." I shivered as I pictured Davy trudging through the storm. Cold, wet, vulnerable. Easy prey, even with Scruff for company and protection. It was worth far more than two dollars to know he'd be safe and warm at home.

Upstairs in our flat, Scruff beelined to the kitchen, expecting a snack. I took out a wedge of swiss cheese—his favorite treat—and cut him off a chunk.

Closing the fridge, I gazed at the two paintings held by magnets to its door—a landscape featuring mountains and pine trees, and a sketch of me, with my eyes emerald green and my hair a bright scarlet. Both were signed *Amy*. I'd planned to frame them, imagining how delighted she'd be to see them properly displayed in my gallery of friends' art.

I felt unsettled, restless. I went into the bedroom and changed out of my damp clothes. I wandered into the living room, picked up the mail I'd set on the table, then dropped it, still unopened. I drifted back into the kitchen, put the teakettle on to boil, changed my mind and turned it off. Scruff padded after me, puzzled by my behavior.

I wound up in my studio. Rain racketed against the expanses of window glass, graying the light and blocking the view as effectively as if I'd drawn the bamboo blinds. The painting on my easel was the one with an array of winter blues. The near-white blue of ice. The cerulean of shadows on snow. Azure for the bright noon sky, deep teal blending to indigo for dusk darkening into night. I picked up a brush, fingered its bristles. It would be good to paint now. It would calm me, focus me.

But it wouldn't find Amy.

In the corner stood the smaller easel with Amy's half-finished portrait of her mother, the small photo of Terri clipped to the top. A hard lump settled in my chest as I remembered bending over Amy, showing her how to sketch the contours of the face. She'd been fascinated by the concept of proportions—spacing the eyes one eye-width apart; aligning the eyes with the tops of the ears; dividing the face into three equal zones, from hairline to eyebrows, from eyebrows to the tip of the nose, from the tip of the nose to the chin.

"You're good at art, aren't you?" Amy had said as she began to fill in the guidelines we'd drawn.

"So are you," I told her. "It's just that I've had more training."

"I've decided something. You should be my mother too."

"You have a mother already," I pointed out.

"I know that, silly. But I'm going to have two fathers, Daddy and Philip. So why can't I have two mothers? You can be my art mother."

"Thank you, but one mother is enough. If you adopted a second one, your mom's feelings might be hurt."

"Hmm … that's not a good idea." Looking thoughtful, she applied a blush of pink to Terri's painted cheek.

"I know!" she said after a moment. "You can be my sister. I always wanted one. Do you have a sister?"

"No. I always wanted one, too. I have two brothers, but no sister."

"Sisters are better." She asserted this firmly, as if speaking from a vast experience of comparative siblinghood. "And one person can have lots of brothers and sisters, right? It's not like parents where you just get one or two."

"That's right. I'd be honored to be your sister, Amy."

"Good. That's settled. Should we make Mom's dress green or blue?"

We chose green. Later, I poured root beer into wineglasses, and we clinked them ceremoniously, sealing our new relationship with a toast.

Now, looking at her painting, I debated whether I should load it into my car, take it to Creekhaven. Maybe Terri would find a bit of comfort in it. If—*when*—Amy came home, we could bring it back to the studio so she could finish it.

No, I decided. Let it be waiting here. Let Amy pick up where she left off, let her complete it as a joyous surprise for her mother. Leaving the painting in place would be a testament to hope, to the bond she and I had established.

It was true—I had always wanted a sister. Now that I'd found her, the thought of losing her terrified me.

Philip had mentioned going to see Creighton Oliver, who was running Carl Moritz's business now that he was in jail. Could Moritz really have allies so loyal that they would steal a child to help him get away with murder? If we pressed her from several directions, maybe she'd slip and reveal what, if anything, she knew.

I went to my computer. Moritz Investment Group was located in the Financial District, not far from P&O. I'd check in at my office, then pay Creighton Oliver a visit.

"Good afternoon. Parks and O'Meara."

As I came through the door, Claudia McFarlane was speaking crisply into the phone. I was glad to see her. Though her fair skin was even paler than normal, she looked like she'd finally shaken the flu that had laid her low.

Officially Claudia's title was receptionist and administrative assistant—the job I'd had when I joined P&O almost a decade ago. In reality she functioned as glue, holding the office together. Right now she was pressing the receiver to her ear with one hand; with the other, she twisted a pencil through her curls. She had lots of curls, mahogany with chestnut highlights, although she insisted on describing her hair as mud brown.

"I'm sorry," she said. "You've got the wrong number."

For my benefit Claudia knit her brow and drooped the corners of her mouth in an exaggerated frown.

"No, really, I can't give you extra cheese. This isn't Formaggio's. You've got the wrong—"

She pulled the phone away from her ear. I could hear someone yelling on the other end of the line.

"No, I don't need your address for the delivery. You've got the wrong—oh, what the heck. Sure, corner of Green and Larkin. Half an hour. That's right, if it's late, it's free."

She rolled her eyes as she hung up. "Do you have any idea how miserable my life has been since that pizza place opened with the phone number just one digit off from ours?"

I nodded. "I fielded their calls all week while you were out sick. Do you always pretend to take the pizza orders?"

"Only when people are rude and refuse to listen. Stupid jerk, I hope he starves waiting for his deluxe mega-combo to show up. Oh, speaking of pizza ..." She handed me a pink message slip. "You had a call this morning from some guy with an odd name. William Pepperoni?"

O'Meara, waving his tail, wandered in from the other room, apparently drawn by the talk of food. I bent down to scratch him under his chin.

"I know who he is. A reporter doing a story on Amy Gardino." William Paveleck, the Pizza Kid. I hadn't given him my name. How had he tracked me down?

"You think he has news about her?"

"More likely he's sniffing for news, not handing any out."

"It's so terrible, what's happened. Is there any way I can help?"

"They've got volunteers stuffing envelopes and putting up flyers. I'm sure they could use extra hands if you want to go over to Creekhaven after work. Check in at the community center. The woman in charge is Lillian Harwood."

"Right, the place I saw on TV last night. That Channel Eight reporter interviewed Amy's mother. She looked strong and brave, yet so sad. I felt really sorry for her."

Claudia gave me the rest of my messages. A couple of them would have been urgent two days ago, but now they seemed trivial. What was important in the world had shifted.

I went into the big office I shared with Tyler Parks, debating whether to call Creighton Oliver or just show up.

Tyler was working at his computer. He beckoned me over. "Hey, Jess, look at this."

"What are you doing?" I sat in his visitor's chair and brushed aside the fronds of the immense Boston fern on his desk so I could see the computer screen.

"We've launched a website for the Find Amy Coalition," Tyler said. "Last night Nick helped me scan in the photos and info. I'm linking the site wherever I can. I've set up social media accounts for the cause too."

"That looks like an ad for a concert."

"Yep, a benefit tomorrow for the coalition. The Andante Quartet has volunteered to play. Apparently they've got quite a following. Their cello player lives in Creekhaven."

"I've heard them. They're terrific. Very eclectic. A cross between classical and jazz, with a dash of rock."

"Good. Something for everybody. It's at the Powder Hill Mansion. You know where that is? Edge of Creekhaven, on a hill overlooking the bay. Lillian talked the East Bay Historic Trust into letting us use it for free. You'll come?"

"Of course. But I hope by tomorrow night this will all be over. Amy will be home and there'll be no more need for the coalition."

"You sound discouraged."

In the reception room, the phone rang, and I heard Claudia pick it up.

"Do I? Maybe I am. It's what, three o'clock? Amy's been gone for forty-eight hours. The longer she's missing, the worse the chance gets that she—"

Claudia appeared in the doorway. "Jess, phone for you."

"Mr. Pepperoni again?"

"No, it's Nick Gardino."

I picked up Tyler's phone. Please let this be good news.

"Jess?" Nick's voice sounded frantic. "Have you seen Terri today? Or talked to her?"

"A brief phone call this morning." My stomach clenched with fear.

"Something's come up. I'm at Terri's, but no one knows where she is. She's not answering her phone. Did she say anything to you about where she might have gone?"

"What do you mean, something's come up?"

"It arrived in the mail. And to make things worse, a TV crew's coming."

"Slow down, Nick. What are you talking about?"

"Can you get over here? Help us retrace Terri's steps? We've got to find her."

"I'm on my way. Nick, what came in the mail?"

"God help us, it's a ransom note. One hundred thousand dollars and they'll give Amy back."

CHAPTER 14

"ONE HUNDRED THOUSAND dollars! Jesus Christ!"

Nick paced like a caged tiger in the cramped space between Terri's dining table and the window. Daylight was fading, and raindrops drummed against the panes. "Where the hell am I supposed to come up with that kind of money?"

I had no answer, and certainly no cash to offer. A magic wand, that's what I needed. Wave it and materialize a mountain of money. Better yet, make Amy herself appear. Bring my sister home, safe and smiling.

I was sitting at the table with two other women. Nick had introduced one as Carmen Aguilar, head of the FBI team that Creekhaven's police chief had called in to assist with the search for Amy. The other was Amy's babysitter, Evelyn Talbot; this morning Terri had asked her to come over and answer the phone while she went "out for a while." When I came in, a half-smile of welcome flitted across Evelyn's face and disappeared.

Terri hadn't returned.

The ransom letter lay in the middle of the table, protected in a clear plastic evidence bag, looking white and stark against the dark oak. Another bag held a manila envelope, its ragged edge showing how Nick had ripped it open. A third held chilling proof that this was not a prank, not the product of some twisted mind unconnected with the real crime—Amy's leather cord with its two house keys, one to her own home and one to Evelyn's.

"One hundred thousand dollars," Nick repeated. "I don't have money like that. Terri sure as hell doesn't have it."

Evelyn was wearing a soft blue cardigan. It looked warm, but she was hugging herself as if she were freezing.

"The Find Amy Coalition?" she ventured. "They've been collecting donations. Maybe—"

"The bastards might as well ask for a million. One hundred million!"

"We might not need the money," said Carmen Aguilar. She jotted something in a large notebook. She was slender and probably tall, although the way she was slouching in her seat made it hard to tell. Strands of her black hair stuck out askew because she kept raking them with her hand. "We'll try to come up with a plan that will let us recover Amy and nail her kidnapper without turning over any cash."

"They wanted money, they should have snatched some rich kid. Not Amy. Oh Christ, why Amy!"

"Terri's gone too," Evelyn moaned. "What if the same people took them both?"

Nick dropped into the last vacant chair and lowered his head into his hand. Before his fingers could cover his eyes, I saw tears forming.

One hundred thousand dollars. $-1-0-0-0-0-0. A dollar sign, a one, then five empty zeros strung in a row.

I'd half expected to see that the numerals had been clipped one by one from a magazine and glued on a ragged scrap of paper. But the ransom letter had been produced by a computer printer on an ordinary sheet of white bond. The label on the envelope, directed to THE PARENTS OF AMY GARDINO, had been addressed the same way.

"Why are these here?" I wondered aloud. "Shouldn't they be at a forensics lab?"

"Someone from the county crime lab is coming by for them soon," Carmen Aguilar said.

"How can they figure out anything from this?" asked Evelyn. "It's so ... so anonymous-looking. No handwriting to compare with some suspect's, no typewriter with a chipped S or a crooked E to give it away, like in the old movies."

Aguilar ruffled her hair. "They'll check for fingerprints. Fibers and dust in the envelope, things like that. And they'll examine the cord and the keys, see if they've been used for ... well, anything that might have left traces."

"Do you think they'll have any luck?" Evelyn's eyes pleaded for a positive answer.

"I hope so," Aguilar said. "But the snatcher hasn't left diddly-squat for clues so far. No reason to think he'll start now."

Nick said, "According to the postmark, it was mailed yesterday in San Francisco. What with the people who live there and the ones who work there and the ones who are passing through, that narrows it down to a few million possibilities."

My fingers itched to pick up the sheet and read it again, just to give myself the illusion that I was doing something. But there was no need. I knew the short text by heart:

Dear Mommy and Daddy,
I want to come home. They will bring me home if you give them $100,000. They will let you know where to take the money. Please do it soon. I miss you very much. And don't tell anyone. They say if there is any police except Daddy, I can't go home after all.
LOVE AMY XOXOXO

Black laser printing. An ordinary serif typeface. Nothing to distinguish it.

Except for the last line. The bold capitals had been carefully drawn with a periwinkle-blue crayon and underlined with a swash. Just like on the ballerina drawing that was proudly displayed on Terri's refrigerator door.

"We need a plan for responding to this," I said.

Aguilar nodded. "We're having a strategy meeting tonight. Eight o'clock at the Creekhaven police station, Chief Doyle's office."

I looked at my watch. Four-thirty. "Why wait?"

"That's the soonest the chief can be available. Small-town force like this, they're short of detectives. He's running down some of the registered sex offenders who live nearby."

As she spoke the last phrase, Nick made a strangled sound. Rising abruptly, he pivoted to stare out at the blackness beyond the window—or perhaps at the gruesome images the words painted on the canvas of his mind.

Aguilar continued, "Hopefully by then we'll have heard from the kidnappers again, gotten more details."

"Why Doyle's office?" I asked. "The note says no police."

Nick turned back toward the room. "Jess is right. I'm not happy about getting Doyle involved."

"Don't worry, he'll keep things quiet. And he'll help us think clearly. We need plenty of brainpower on our side." Aguilar gave me an appraising look. "Nick says he wants you there, too."

"Right," Nick said. "You're an experienced investigator, but not a cop. Which is why you'll be helpful." He picked up the letter in its plastic sheath. "Damn it, where could Terri have gone?"

"I should have insisted she tell me her plans," Evelyn fretted. "First Amy, now Terri ..."

"What did she say to you this morning?" I asked.

"Just that she needed to get out of the house for a couple of hours. That was at nine o'clock. She should have been back long ago."

"We've put out a be-on-the-lookout for her car," Aguilar said. "She'll be spotted soon. We'll bring her back."

"Damn well better—"

The kitchen phone rang. With a sharp in-drawn breath, Evelyn hurried to answer it.

"Turn on the speaker." Aguilar rose to her feet. "And don't

forget to write down the number."

We all crowded into the kitchen. Evelyn said, "Hello?" and punched the button to activate the speaker-phone. I logged the incoming number that showed on the ID display.

A voice floated into the room, tinny and hollow. "Is Inspector Gardino there?"

"This is Gardino." Nick's voice was gruff.

"Philip Vandergriff, Inspector. I just heard your voicemail. What's this about Terri? Is she all right?"

"We don't know. I was hoping you'd know where she is.

"I haven't talked to her since early this morning. She was at home then."

"Damn it. Where the hell is she?" Nick rubbed the furrows in his brow.

"What are you saying, Inspector? What's happening?"

"There's been a—a development Terri needs to know about."

"You mean Amy?" Excitement, or fear, pitched Philip's voice higher. "Have you found Amy?"

"No." Nick shifted his weight from one foot to the other. "Not yet."

"Then what kind of development? Some word from Moritz's people?"

"Look, Philip, that fancy company of yours—can you raise some quick cash?"

"Please talk sense, Inspector. You better tell me what's going on."

Nick sighed. His voice sounded as if it came from a smaller man. "Terri's gone out. No one knows where. A letter came in the mail today. A ransom request. I'm asking you if SalesCom can put up some money to help us get Amy back."

"A ransom note! Someone sent a ransom note?"

"We only need the cash long enough to lure the snatcher out of hiding and make sure we recover Amy safely."

"I don't get it. What did the note say? How much ransom?"

"One hundred thousand dollars."

"Jesus. I can't believe this."

"I know it's a lot to ask. Maybe SalesCom can't supply the whole amount, but we've got to tap into every possible source. Once we grab this bastard, you'll get every penny back. My personal guarantee."

"Why would Moritz ask for a ransom?"

"How the hell should I know? Maybe it's not Moritz. What's important is getting Amy back."

"Maybe it's a fake."

Nick glanced back through the dining room door. From where he was standing he'd be able to see Amy's leather cord with its keys.

"It's no fake. That's certain."

"Hell of a lot of cash to come up with on short notice," Philip muttered. Then, louder: "When and where does the money get delivered?"

"They're supposed to let us know. Are you with us or not?"

"One hundred percent, Inspector. I'll talk to my financial officer right away, see what I can work out. I'll try to cover the whole amount. Count on it, we'll get Amy back."

Aguilar moved close to the speaker. "Mr. Vandergriff, this is Carmen Aguilar. FBI. Please don't speak to anyone about this. Especially not the media. If word about this ransom demand gets out—"

"Don't worry," Philip cut in. "I won't do anything stupid to jeopardize Amy. Count on that. When Terri shows up, have her call me."

Static crackled. The line went dead.

Silence hung heavily over the kitchen. Then Aguilar spoke.

"I can't believe you told him about the letter."

"What was I supposed to do?" Nick said. "He's got money. He can help."

"Do you really want to knuckle under to a ransom demand?

That may not be the wisest tactic."

"What I want, goddammit, is to get my daughter back."

"Amy's the top priority. We agree on that. But we don't want to handle this in a way that could make things worse for her." Aguilar's fingers shot through her black hair. "A lot of parents wouldn't understand what's at stake here. But you're a police officer, you know the risk."

Nick shook his head. "All I know is, if the money will bring her home safe, then by God we're going to pay it."

"Can you trust Vandergriff to handle this discreetly?" she asked. "What happens if word about the ransom gets out and the kidnapper panics? Or—"

"I have to trust him. What choice do I have? In a few months he'll be Amy's stepfather. If he can't be trusted to do what's best for her—"

The doorbell buzzed. "Evelyn, answer that," Aguilar said. "Should be the forensics guys. But I'd better get that letter out of sight just in case." She loped into the dining room on her long legs.

We followed her. Nick was moving like an old man.

Aguilar started to pack the evidence bags into her briefcase, but Nick took the one with the letter out of her hand.

"X-O-X-O," he muttered. "Kisses and hugs."

Evelyn appeared in the archway. "It's the Channel Eight news crew."

"Christ!" Nick said. "I forgot all about them."

"Don't mention the ransom," Aguilar warned.

Nick hurried into the living room, lifting his shoulders and straightening his spine to gain a look of being in control. Standing behind him, I saw people come bustling in—the reporter Paula Blakeney, the camera guy who'd been with her yesterday at the Community Center, and a couple of techs carrying cables and lights.

"Thanks for coming." Nick strode toward Paula Blakeney,

extending his hand. "But it turns out that this isn't a good time."

"Why?" Paula asked. "Has something happened?" She grasped his hand in both of hers, her face showing deep concern. As always, she looked crisp and polished. Today she had on a copper-colored jacket that flattered her sepia-toned skin. Raindrops glistened on her black coiffure like jewels.

She looked around. "Where's Ms. Shawcross?"

"Uh ... Terri had to go out. She, well, some errands are taking longer than she expected. We appreciate your help, the publicity and all, but—look, your station is sponsoring the concert tomorrow night, right? We'll give you an interview then."

Paula Blakeney started to protest, but changed her mind. "Tomorrow then."

With a shooing motion she herded her crew out the door. Nick sank on the sofa and leaned back, and pressed his hands to his eyes.

Hearing a muffled sob behind me, I spun around. Evelyn Talbot was leaning against the jamb of the kitchen door, picking at the hem of her blue cardigan sleeve.

"Are you all right?" I asked.

"Of course I'm not all right." She choked out the words. "If only ... it's all my fault. If I hadn't been so wrapped up in sewing that skirt, I might have noticed sooner that Amy hadn't shown up on time. They say every minute counts ... and now Terri's gone too."

"Would you like a cup of tea?" I asked, remembering how Evelyn had offered tea in response to Terri's crisis. I drew her into the kitchen, closing the door so we'd have privacy.

She nodded. I filled the kettle that was sitting on the stove. "Are you sure, Evelyn, that Terri didn't give you any clue about her plans? What were her exact words?"

"Only that she wanted to get away for a while. She asked if I'd monitor the calls until she got back."

I placed the kettle on a burner and lit the flame.

"I asked where she was going," Evelyn went on. "Wherever she could find calm and quiet, that's what she said. She—"

The phone rang. We both froze.

Then I grabbed the log to record the number while Evelyn greeted the caller with a trembling "Hello?"

The voice that came over the speaker sounded electronic, a robotic monotone.

"Listen carefully. This will only play once. Here are your instructions. Remember, pay close attention if you want to see Amy alive …"

CHAPTER 15

M AC DOYLE, CREEKHAVEN'S chief of police, had pulled off a
neat trick with his complexion—he looked florid and ashy
at the same time. In my head I mixed paints, imagining the colors
I'd choose to capture his appearance on canvas. Vermilion red and
cerulean blue. Chalk white, a dash of ocher.

At yesterday's press conference he'd been dressed in full
uniform, projecting a strong, reassuring cop image for public
consumption. Now he was wearing a rumpled shirt, collar open
and sleeves rolled up. A necktie snaked across the papers on his
desk, and a sports jacket hung crookedly on the back of his chair.
Doyle was thickset, square-shouldered, graying at the temples.
Laugh lines bracketed his eyes, but he looked as if he didn't expect
to laugh again for a long time.

"What have we got?" Nick asked. He was fidgeting in his seat,
and I could feel the sparks of his nervous energy.

Doyle had pulled four chairs into his office. Nick, Carmen
Aguilar and I occupied three of them.

The empty chair was for Terri.

Ten hours she'd been gone. No word from her, no contact at
all. She wasn't answering her phone, hadn't responded to
voicemails or texts.

Her absence was like a physical force in the room. It seemed to
have a shape; it seemed to breathe. We all kept our eyes averted
from the vacant seat. Evelyn was waiting at Terri's house, with
instructions to send her to police headquarters the minute she

came home.

If she came home. If something terrible hadn't happened …

"What have we got?" Doyle repeated, glancing at his scribbled notes. "Not much. The call came from an outdoor pay phone near Golden Gate Park."

"Amazing the son of a bitch found one that worked," Nick muttered.

"Probably the last one in the city," Doyle said. "SFPD dispatched officers, but by the time they got there, the caller was long gone. They questioned people in the area, but no one noticed anybody using the phone."

Nick asked, "Where was it exactly?"

"Intersection of Haight and Stanyan. There's a McDonald's on one corner, a supermarket on the other. Lots of people coming and going."

"Yeah," Nick said. "And across the street, that edge of the park, is where all the druggies hang out. Too brain-fried to see a damn thing."

I clutched the sketchbook on my lap. "The Moritz connection."

Carmen Aguilar leaned forward. She had her notebook open too, a pen poised over the page. "What do you mean, Jess?"

"Haight and Stanyan. Bountiful Books is a couple of blocks down Haight Street. And didn't Robin and Eric live in an apartment on Stanyan?"

Nick nodded. "One of her father's buildings."

"What does that tell us?" Aguilar asked.

"Nothing," said Doyle. "Looks like you've been on the wrong track with this Moritz thing, Gardino. This ransom letter points us in a whole new direction."

"Hell, I don't know what to think." Nick's fingers drummed a rhythm on his knees. "Those two notes that came to the Hall of Justice—they hint that Moritz masterminded the whole thing. They seem valid, more than you'd expect from some random low-life seeking attention."

"Valid how?" Aguilar asked.

"The first one came yesterday morning, before Amy's disappearance hit the news. And the second one … whoever wrote it knows Amy, knows little things he must have made her tell him. Her birthday, her teacher's name."

"I can buy that someone close to Moritz might've taken your little girl to throw a wrench into his trial," Doyle said. "The case against him kinda falls apart without your testimony, isn't that so?"

"The evidence is pretty strong. But, yeah, convicting him gets a lot tougher if I don't take the stand."

"So if that's their goal," Doyle said, "why ask for a ransom?"

"Lots of possible reasons," Nick said. "Maybe Moritz wants the cash to pay off whoever he hired to take Amy. It's hard to run an expense like that through the corporate books."

Aguilar tapped her pen on the corner of Doyle's desk. "Maybe the kidnapper's gone rogue. He isn't satisfied with what Moritz is paying so he's decided to go after some extra money. Give himself a bonus."

"Or some Moritz flunkie could be acting on his own," I surmised. "He figures he'll help his boss out of a big jam and do himself a favor at the same time."

Doyle looked skeptical. "My guys have talked to Moritz's associates. SFPD has too. Nothing solid has turned up so far."

Nothing solid. Try nothing at all.

I doodled a squiggly line in my sketchbook. I hadn't managed to take many notes. A few scattered words, a string of dollar signs. The name *Amy* over and over, the word *sister* once. I shivered, even though Doyle's office was overheated and stuffy. It smelled of stale coffee and grease; he'd been gulping down a takeout burger when we arrived—his first food since breakfast, he'd said.

"Are we convinced this ransom demand is genuine?" I asked.

"The keys." Nick rubbed his neck as if Amy's cord were hanging there. "You saw it—the leather string with the keys.

Evelyn Talbot swears it's Amy's, and it sure looks like the one I've seen her wear. Whoever sent that letter has Amy."

"And now Terri's gone too." I shifted my gaze to the empty chair where Terri's ghost seemed to hover.

"She left on her own, right?" Doyle said. "She told her friend, Mrs. Talbot, that she was going out for a while."

"For an hour or two, that's all," I said.

"Look, it's not like Terri hasn't done this before," Nick said. "It's her way of dealing with stress. When we were married, she often went off for a day by herself when—well, when things got tense. A mental vacation, she calls it. She'll be back any minute, I'm certain of it." But the look on Nick's face betrayed his doubt.

"She wouldn't stay away this long when Amy is missing. She'd be home, waiting by the phone ..."

"Suppose there's any chance"—Doyle spoke slowly, as if reluctant to drag the words from his mouth—"that she's somewhere with her daughter?"

"With her dau—" Nick half-rose from the chair. "What the hell are you suggesting, Doyle?"

"Hey, take it easy. It's just—well, it wouldn't be the first time a mother engineered the disappearance of her own child."

"Not Terri. She'd never hurt Amy. She—no, I don't believe it." Nick sank back down, folded his arms tight across his chest. But his eyes looked wide and frightened, as if seeing some horror he hadn't imagined before.

The word *Terri* drew itself on my sketchbook page, with a big question mark through the middle of it. I couldn't believe it either. But how well did I know Terri really? Hardly at all.

"What makes you think she's involved, Chief?" I asked.

"Just covering the bases. This ransom—the fiancé's rich, right?"

"Well, comfortable anyway," Nick said grudgingly. "Terri will be living a fancier lifestyle than I gave her, that's for sure."

Doyle nodded. "But they haven't set a wedding date. From

talking to them both, I've gathered he's hot to trot down the aisle, but she's putting him off."

Nick shrugged. "News to me."

"Okay, for argument's sake, let's say she's changed her mind about the fiancé but not about the better lifestyle. So she hides Amy somewhere and sends a ransom note. She collects the money and brings Amy back. Now she has herself a nice bankroll without having to go through the bother of getting married."

"No way," Nick insisted.

"You went straight to Philip for the ransom money, Nick," Aguilar pointed out. "Maybe she was counting on your doing exactly that."

"Christ, this is crazy. First, Terri accuses me of stealing Amy. Now you're accusing—"

"Good point," the chief said. "Maybe you're the one looking to upgrade your lifestyle."

"Goddammit, Doyle, I ought to—"

I tugged at Nick's sleeve. "Gentlemen, please. Until we know otherwise, let's assume the ransom demand is for real."

"Right," Aguilar said. "How are we going to respond—that's what this meeting is about."

Doyle pinched the bridge of his nose. "Sorry. Maybe I was out of line. It's been a long day."

"Long day for all of us," Nick agreed.

He turned his eyes to the empty chair. I wished again for a magic wand, so I could touch the chair seat and make Terri appear. Terri and Amy and the answers to a whole lot of questions.

"Okay, let's get back to work." Doyle pushed aside a crumpled napkin and a coffee mug and picked up one of the papers on the desk. "We transcribed the recording you made of the call. Ms. Aguilar here is sending the tape to her lab for analysis."

"For what it's worth," Aguilar said, "the phone call seems to have been prerecorded using some kind of voice-distortion device. So we've got a recording of a recording of a fake voice. It's going to be hard to get anything helpful from that."

"Here's what the transcript says." Doyle cleared his throat and began to read: "'Listen carefully. This tape will only play once. Here are your delivery instructions. Pay close attention if you want to see Amy alive—'"

Nick waved a hand to stop him. "I know what the frigging thing says. I've listened to it, what, fifty times? One hundred thousand dollars. Small bills, of course. Deliver it at one p.m. Saturday to the Japanese Tea Garden in Golden Gate Park. Put the money in a bag from the Tea Garden gift shop. Follow the path under the bridge that connects the pagoda and the Buddha statue. Hide the bag between the trash can and the ... and the ..."

He started to choke on his words. I finished for him: "The bush with the gold-dust leaves."

I'd listened fifty times, too.

"Right. The bush with the frigging gold-dust leaves."

"Whatever that means," Doyle said.

"They've given us"—Aguilar looked at her watch—"forty-two hours. There are some financial institutions that are prepared to work with us in situations like this. I'll make some calls ..."

Nick shook his head. "Bad idea. Moritz's tentacles extend into the banks. What if the wrong person gets wind of what you're doing? That could blow the whole thing."

Aguilar pursed her lips. "Well," she said slowly, thinking out loud, "we can prepare some bundles that look like cash, a few bills on top. Stake out the site—I'm sure SFPD will help out. Then we'll—"

"No!" Nick said.

"You don't think your own force will help?" Doyle asked.

"Of course they will," Aguilar said. "We've always had excellent cooperation from the San Francisco force. And since Amy belongs to one of their own—"

"Damn it, the caller said no police." Nick's voice was tight. "I'm going to do this exactly according to the instructions. The full amount of money. Vandergriff said he'd come up with it."

"Some of it," I said.

Nick ignored me. "We'll deliver it at the right time to the right place, and we won't interfere until we've got Amy back. That's all that counts, you understand? Getting Amy back."

For a moment no one spoke. I heard the wind clamoring at the window, the insistent whisper of the rain.

Then Aguilar murmured, "Right. That's all that counts."

Doyle wiped a hand across his brow. "What about Terri? Assuming for now that she's not involved. As the child's mother, she should have some say—"

Nick cut in. "She's not here. I wish to God I knew where she was. But we can't afford to wait."

I drew a frame around Terri's name on my page. "I agree, but I'm worried about her. I know there's an alert out for Terri's car. What else is being done to find her?"

Doyle said, "I've got an officer talking to her neighbors and coworkers and the Find Amy volunteers, in case Terri mentioned her plans. And we're checking local hospitals and accident reports. It's only been a few hours. If this fits her behavior pattern, like you say, Nick—well, let's play it your way for now."

"We'll do what we can to help you raise and package the money," Aguilar said. "But who's going to deliver it?"

"I am," Nick said.

She shook her head. "Not the best plan. You could be recognized. The last thing we need is to have some reporter spot you and tag along to see what you're up to."

"I'll get a volunteer from my department to make the drop," Doyle offered. "Or someone from SFPD."

"No way," Nick protested. "The instructions said no police except me. Just by telling you two about the ransom, I've gone too far."

Aguilar said, "If you attract attention, that could foul up everything."

"I'll shave my mustache, I'll wear a frigging disguise—no one will know it's me."

"Nick, be reasonable—"

"I'll do it," I said.

They all looked at me as if they'd forgotten I was there.

Aguilar pursed her lips. "We can't let you. Too much risk for a civilian—"

"I'm perfect for the job. I'm a private investigator; I can handle the risk. But I'm not a cop, so we'll be playing by the rules that have been set up."

Nick's expression had brightened, but Aguilar was shaking her head.

"Look," I said, "I know the Japanese Tea Garden well. I live close by, and I go there a lot. I can picture the exact spot they're referring to."

"The trash can?" said Aguilar skeptically. "The gold-dust leaves?"

Don't blow it with the FBI, my inner voice warned.

"The point where the path goes under the bridge," I said, striving for patience. I wasn't sure why, but it felt important—essential—for me to be the one to do this task. I leaned forward, the better to make my argument. "Nick might be recognized, but no one will know me. After I make the drop, I can hang around, keep an eye on what happens."

Aguilar jacked up her dark bangs with her fingers. "No, don't do that. You'd be too obvious. We'll put officers on the tea shop terrace. They'll be inconspicuous—just tourists enjoying their jasmine tea and fortune cookies."

"You can't see under the bridge from the tea shop," I said. "I'll take my folding campstool and a sketchbook and set up where I can see the spot under the bridge."

"Suppose they're watching. They'll make you as the person who did the drop."

"I'll change how I look. After I leave the money, I'll slip on my Art Institute sweatshirt and stick my hair under a cap. I'll mutter about unfair grades and unreasonable professors. They'll think I'm an art student hustling an end-of-term deadline."

"It could work." Nick's voice held more hope than conviction.

"Unless it's pouring rain." Doyle pointed up; we could hear the storm still drumming on the roof. "No artist would be out there in weather like this."

"In that case," I said, "I'll go to Plan B."

"And what's that?" Aguilar asked.

"I don't know," I admitted. "But I'll figure one out by Saturday."

No one spoke as Nick drove us back to Terri's house, where Aguilar and I had left our cars. The only sound that broke the silence was the swish of the windshield wipers. Headlights of oncoming cars spangled the raindrops that the wipers couldn't reach at the edges of the glass. I glanced at Nick; his face would go bright as traffic approached, then subside into shadow. He stared fixedly ahead, his jaw clenched. I wondered where his thoughts were. With Amy? With Terri? With the kidnappers, and what he'd do when they were caught?

I ached for him, and for myself too. Amy, with her charm and good cheer and offer of sisterhood, had begun to blaze a trail into a corner of my heart, to stake a claim to a small hollow place whose emptiness I had always carefully guarded. From what I'd observed of life, the bonds between husband and wife, parent and child, were precarious at best—full of love sometimes, but all too often fraught with hurt, fear, anger, disappointment. Best to keep such bonds to a minimum, that's what I'd always thought. Perhaps that's why I'd fared so well with my stepfather and half-brothers—the family tie we shared was set at one remove. It came with fewer expectations, demands and obligations. Fewer promises to fulfill, less heartbreak to suffer or inflict.

Nick turned onto Blackberry Drive and followed the yellow

ribbons up the hill. Getting Amy back is all that counts, he'd said. Amen to that.

What would my own father have done if one day I had vanished? He lived in New York, three thousand miles away, had lived there for almost all of my life. Until last year, we'd had no contact at all; our relationship now could best be described as an uneasy friendship. Yet all those years, he had kept in regular touch with our family friend Jack Emerich, the man I thought of as my Uncle Jack. My father knew what I was doing, how I was progressing in school, while I knew nothing of him at all. Had Jack told him about the time I was lost in the mountains? If so, how had he responded? What would he have felt if he had lost forever the daughter he'd never bothered to know?

It wasn't the same, I reminded myself. Nick knew Amy. Not as well as he should, but clearly he loved her. And Amy—the thought was as close as I ever came to prayer—surely Amy was not lost forever.

Nick pulled to a stop in front of Terri's house. "Her car's not here," he said, making the words sound matter-of-fact.

We got out of the Mustang; the slamming of the doors reverberated in the quiet of the night. As if summoned by the sound, a large male figure opened Terri's front door and stepped out onto the dark porch.

"Who the hell's that?" Nick muttered. I saw Aguilar's hand go to her purse, where, I was sure, she carried her gun.

The man waited as we warily approached through the slanting rain. "Hey, Nick," he called when we were halfway up the walk.

His bulldog-like build and face registered on Nick half a beat before they did on me. "Ray! What are you doing here?"

"Figured you'd come back here. Mrs. Talbot said you needed to bring the ladies back for their cars." Beschke nodded at me. "How ya doin', Ace?"

"Hello, Ray." I climbed the steps to the shelter of the porch.

Aguilar looked at him through narrowed eyes and stuck out a

hand. "Carmen Aguilar, FBI."

Beschke cocked his brows as if in disbelief; in my dealings with him, I'd gotten the impression that his concept of female cops began and ended with meter maids. But he shook her hand. "Ray Beschke, SFPD Homicide. Nick's partner. We better go inside." He ushered us through the door. "Heard from Terri yet, Nick?"

"No," Nick said. "Ray, what's up?"

"You want to sit down?" Beschke gestured at the couch where Evelyn Talbot in her blue cardigan was already seated. She looked as though she'd been crying.

"No, I don't." Nick remained standing in the middle of Terri's living room. Aguilar and I kept back in the foyer archway. I didn't know about hers, but my heart was pounding and my stomach was balled like a fist.

Beschke gazed down and rubbed a spot on the carpet with the toe of his shoe. "I don't know, maybe you better sit …"

"Spit it out, Ray. You didn't come all the way over here to make sure I was comfortable."

"Oh, hell, Nick. You know this is one of the toughest parts of this job. Breaking the news—"

"What news?" Though Nick's voice was low and even, it sounded more tense than a scream.

"We had a homicide in the Haight tonight. McCabe and Rovinsky caught it, but I thought I'd better come tell you myself. Man was shot in a studio apartment on Cole Street." Beschke glanced from one of us to the next, looking profoundly uncomfortable. "I was hoping Terri'd be here so I'd only have to tell it once. Victim's a friend of hers. Philip Vandergriff."

CHAPTER 16

"FIRST TIME," NICK MURMURED. We pushed through the throng that had gathered in spite of the rain and wind.

"What's that?" I said.

"All the homicides I've worked, this is the first time I've known the victim in advance."

We started up the steps to the apartment house where Philip had been murdered.

The building was at the corner of Haight and Cole Streets, close to Dandelion and Bountiful Books, and just a few blocks from both Philip's home and my own flat. It was a late Victorian structure, three stories high, and in need of paint. Two storefronts on the first floor faced Haight Street; we were at the Cole Street entrance, which led to a warren of tiny apartments on the floors above.

At the top of the steps I looked back. Police vehicles clogged the street. A couple of TV news vans had arrived, and another was rounding the corner. I recognized some faces in the crowd—proprietors of Haight Street shops, street people Scruff had befriended on our walks. I spotted Atom's head above the crowd, his height boosted by his Rollerblades. His turquoise-tipped Mohawk gleamed wetly under the streetlights. He looked my way; when he realized who I was, his face registered a jolt of surprise.

The uniformed cop who guarded the door widened his stance and crossed his arms, barring our way. Nick flashed his badge, and the cop peered at it closely.

Margaret Lucke

"Gardino. You're the one with the missing girl. I'm sure sorry about that. Hope you find her okay."

"Thanks. Me too."

The cop gestured for Gardino to enter, but he stepped in front of me. "Sorry, lady. Tenants can't go in and out without an escort."

"She's with me," Nick said. "I brought her to answer some questions for the guys upstairs."

The officer frowned but stood aside. "Third floor."

"What questions?" I asked Nick as we mounted the inside stairs. Faint scents hung in the air: Pine-Sol, garlic, marijuana. Competing kinds of music—jazz versus rap versus rock—pounded in the walls.

"You saw Vandergriff today, right? Had lunch with him. Trust me, they'll want to talk to you."

Several doors on the third floor were cracked open, and I felt eyes watching us as we walked down the hall. No mistaking which apartment was our destination—its door was open wide; bright light spilled out onto the thin carpet of the corridor. A strand of yellow crime-scene tape had been thumbtacked across the empty doorway, and another uniformed cop was stationed beside it. After a word with Nick, she handed us latex gloves and paper booties, which we put on. Then she unfastened one side of the tape and held it so we could enter.

A short passage led us past a kitchen to a larger room.

"Oh my God!" I whispered. Nick sucked in a sharp breath.

I had expected the body to be gone. But Philip Vandergriff lay twisted on his side on a threadbare rug.

Blood reddened the front of his white shirt and stained the rug beneath him.

Blood covered his face and streaked through his sandy hair.

Blood pooled in one eye. The other was open and staring.

The police photographer stood over the body. The camera flashed. She crouched down. Flash again. She aimed the lens right into that blood-blind eye. Flash! Flash!

120

My stomach churned. Swallowing hard to quell the nausea, I retreated into the kitchen. I started to brace myself against the counter, but my inner voice warned *don't touch*. Even with gloves on, I didn't want to risk smudging possible evidence. I stood in the middle of the room and closed my eyes until I felt steady.

The kitchen was dreary: scuffed linoleum floor, dark wood cabinets streaked with grease, a mottled counter surface so scratched and marred it would never look clean. Fast-food wrappers and wadded papers overflowed the trash can. A mug in the sink held an inch or so of coffee. A glass had a ring of milk in the bottom. A cookie tin sat on the drainboard, empty except for a litter of crumbs. I bent and sniffed. Chocolate. The aroma mingled with the smell of death, making me queasy again.

Nick appeared in the doorway. "Jess? You okay?"

"I'm fine." I hoped saying it out loud would make it true.

I came back into the main room and made myself look anywhere but at Philip.

This room, plus the kitchen, a closet and a tiny bath, made up the entire apartment. The furnishings were sparse—a pair of cots with skimpy mattresses, a card table with three mismatched folding chairs, a TV on top of a packing carton. Nothing in the way of decoration—no pictures, no photos, no framed certificates. But the walls were dotted not only with blood spatter but with staples and bits of Scotch tape, some of which held torn corners of cheap white paper. I reached out to feel one, then remembered and jammed my hands in my pockets.

When I turned away from studying the wall, Philip's body was still there, seeming to fill the entire room. People buzzed around it like flies: the photographer snapping pictures, three crime-scene techs collecting evidence with tape measures, notepads, tweezers, and little bags.

Taking care where I stepped, I drifted over to the tall, narrow window. Through a gap in the sagging floor-length drapes, I could see across a light well to the window of the unit next door. The curtains over there had been yanked aside and the tenants were gaping out, their faces avid, trying to get a glimpse of the excitement.

A dash of color caught my eye, a small object resting against the baseboard, half hidden by the drape. I squatted to examine it.

"Jess!" Nick beckoned me over. He was talking with a man in a motorcycle jacket and a woman in a gray blazer. As I crossed the room to join them, I caught the eye of the nearest tech and pointed to the floor beneath the window.

"This is Jess Randolph," Nick said. "Jess, meet Matt McCabe and Anna Rovinsky, Homicide Division."

Rovinsky gave me an appraising look, so I gave her one back. She was on the short side, with dark blond hair to her shoulders and glasses that kept slipping to the end of her small nose. "Nick says you had lunch with this guy today."

"That's right. Just a few hours ago, and now ... I can't believe this. What happened?"

"He was shot," said McCabe, a tall man whose thinning hair was a red much brighter than mine, almost orange; as a kid he'd probably been called Carrot-Top. "At pretty close range, I'm guessing. Maybe the shooter came in the front door, maybe he was hiding in the kitchen, who knows? Fired two shots at least. One hit our friend here, one went wild. We found the slug in the far wall." He pointed, and I could see the scar, high up between the closet and bathroom doors.

"Who found him?" I asked.

"Neighbor in unit thirty-eight says he heard people yelling, then loud pops that must have been the gunshots. This was around eight o'clock, maybe a few minutes after. A stereo was blasting down the hall, so it didn't register on him what had happened. Half an hour later the guy headed out to get a beer. Saw the door here was ajar, which struck him as odd. He remembered the noise and peeked in to make sure everything was all right." McCabe gestured at Philip's corpse. "Turned out things were all wrong."

"Did he know the people living here?" Nick asked.

"No. The apartment had been empty. A new tenant moved in last weekend. The guy didn't know any more than that."

Rovinsky pushed her glasses up the bridge of her nose. "What did you and Vandergriff talk about at lunch?" she asked me. "Did he give any indication of where he was going after you left the restaurant? Or why he might have come to a dump like this?"

"He said he had errands to run. But—"

I was interrupted by the crime-scene tech I'd signaled to earlier. "Hey, look at this." He handed McCabe an evidence bag.

"Crayons," McCabe said.

"One crayon," corrected the tech. "Two pieces, but the same crayon. The broken ends fit together."

"Periwinkle," I murmured.

"What's that?"

"The color. It's called periwinkle. It's the color Amy used to sign the ransom note."

"Christ, you're right," Nick said.

Suddenly I realized what I'd seen in the kitchen. "On the floor in there, by the trash can—there's a crumpled paper with that color on it."

The tech ran to fetch it and returned with the wrinkled sheet dangling from his tweezers. It appeared to be the same kind of inexpensive white bond as the fragments fastened to the walls. The same kind as the ransom letter.

"Looks like we had an artist here," Rovinsky said softly.

It was a drawing in crayon and pencil. A white horse, red saddle, bright yellow mane and tail. Galloping into a periwinkle sky. Beneath the horse, there was a square topped with a triangle, striped blue and orange like a circus tent.

A child's drawing, clearly, yet the horse's movement was captured with uncommon skill.

"Oh my God. Firecracker." Nick had gone pale. A sheen of sweat dampened his forehead.

"What do you mean?" McCabe said. "It's a horse."

"Right. Firecracker—the merry-go-round horse Amy fell in love with when I took her to Golden Gate Park on New Year's."

"Of course." I peered more closely at the drawing. "He's flying in the sky. The shape with the pointed roof—that's the carousel."

Nick was trembling now. "She was here. Amy was here. Philip found her and they shot him and they're gone. He found her, goddammit, and now ... oh Christ, what's happened to her now?"

He whirled around and slammed his fist into the wall.

CHAPTER 17

THOUGH I LIVED only three blocks away, Nick insisted on driving me home.

"People kill people in this neighborhood," he said. "Let's not take chances."

We'd driven our own cars into the city, and I'd scored a parking place almost in front of my door. I'd walked to Haight and Cole for our rendezvous. Now I craved a solitary hike home, a time to sort out my jumbled thoughts and feelings.

But I realized he needed a way to put off being alone. We got into his Mustang, which was parked among the police and press vehicles that cluttered Haight Street.

He lowered his head until his forehead was touching his hands on the steering wheel. The blow he'd given the wall must have made his knuckles sore. He was lucky he hadn't broken some bones.

I touched his shoulder. "You okay?" I knew he wasn't; neither was I.

He pulled himself upright. I saw that his cheeks were wet.

He maneuvered the Mustang out of the tangle of cars and vans and headed up Haight Street. The streetlights gave the rainy street a surreal orange shine.

"I can't stand it," he said. "Amy was there. She drank milk from that glass. She slept on one of those frigging cots. We got so close."

I closed my eyes, hoping to shut out the vision of Amy in that blood-soaked apartment. Had she witnessed the killing? Experienced the horror of seeing Philip shot to death before her eyes?

"At least we know she's alive." I bit my lip; the lame remark had slipped out before I could stop it.

"*Was* alive. Maybe as recently as four hours ago. But now—we don't know jack shit about now."

"Philip must have known something. He hinted about it at lunch. I thought he was just doing a think-positive act."

"What did he say exactly?"

I'd already described my lunch with Philip to Nick and also to McCabe and Rovinsky. Tomorrow morning I had an appointment with them at the Hall of Justice when we'd go over it again. "Philip went to see Creighton Oliver, the woman who's running Moritz's company now that he's in jail. Maybe she let something slip."

"Beschke talked to her this afternoon. She claims total ignorance about Amy."

I wracked my brain trying to reconstruct every detail of the conversation. So much had happened since lunchtime; the interlude at Dandelion seemed like days ago. And I was exhausted way beyond the point of clear thinking.

"Philip might not have known anything for certain at lunchtime. But looking back, he seemed to think he was on Amy's trail. He mentioned plans to run errands. If we could only find what they were."

"Damn him anyway. If he figured out where she was, he should have told us. Why did he have to go off half-cocked on his own?"

Nick swung left onto Shrader. This street was darker. Instead of stores and restaurants, it was lined with two- and three-story houses—Victorians and Edwardians, some single-family and some, like mine, divided into flats. It was past midnight. Most windows were dark, though a few showed lamplight or a TV's flickering glow.

"Another thing," Nick said. "Vandergriff was going to arrange to get the hundred thousand out of that business of his. How the hell are we going to get the ransom money now?"

"I have a couple of ideas about that. I'll check them out first thing tomorrow."

"Ideas? Such as?"

I tried to sound confident. "I'll let you know once I've got something solid. Meanwhile, follow up on any possibilities you can think of."

We had reached my place. Nick pulled to a halt.

"Hell of a cop I am. Can't even find my own daughter." He wasn't looking at me. "Christ, what's this going to do to Terri? First Amy ... now her fiancé gets blown away. What if Terri ..."

He left the thought unfinished. I supplied my own endings: *What if Terri killed Philip? What if Terri has been murdered too?*

To my surprise, Nick gave me a hug. "Thanks, Jess. For—well, for helping."

"Whatever I can do. You know that." Fat lot of help I'd been so far. I sighed and opened the car door. "I'll let you know what I find out about raising the money."

I got out of the car and climbed the front steps. I opened the door, flicked on the light and accepted several wet kisses from Scruff. I hadn't heard Nick's engine start, so I turned and waved—a signal that at least one person he knew was safely home.

The instant Nick's taillights disappeared, I realized I was wrong—being alone was the last thing I needed.

I ached for human company. Scruff tried hard, but he couldn't dispel the shadows that persisted in the corners of my flat even after I turned on every light.

I'd known Philip Vandergriff for only two days. My memory of the living Philip probably would fade quickly. But the image of his bloodied corpse would be part of me forever, stamped on my soul.

Where was Terri? Had she gone for what Nick had called a mental vacation, a break for a few hours from the intense stress she was under? Or was she in danger, or in hiding? Was she still alive?

And Amy. Oh, Amy. So close, and then ...

Fifty-seven hours gone.

A cup of tea had been my mother's choice of solace whenever she was troubled, and she'd passed on the habit to me. I went to the kitchen and put the kettle on.

Scruff nosed his empty dish over to the stove so I'd be sure to step in it, then he barked once to say: "I've had no dinner and I'm starving to death." But I knew he was faking. I'd called Mrs. Fiorelli before the meeting in Chief Doyle's office and asked her to send Davy up to feed Scruff and take him for an extra walk. Davy had left a note saying he'd accomplished this mission.

Still, Scruff's thespian skills merited a reward. I put two chunks of swiss cheese in his dish. When they were gone—half a second later—I let him out the back door to visit the yard.

The kettle shrilled. Mom liked to make tea right—warm the pot first, use loose leaves, pour the brew through a silver strainer into a bone-china cup. Tonight I had no heart for the ceremony. I tossed a teabag into a mug and poured hot water over it. Then I got out the bottle of brandy a client had given me and added a strong dose.

I carried my drink into the living room, flopped onto the sofa and got out my phone, hoping for a distraction from my dark thoughts. I sent out messages about tomorrow night's concert to my network of friends. Then I noticed I had missed a call while at the murder scene.

Oh, please, I thought, let it be Kit. I felt a sudden huge longing to talk to him, a desire so intense that all my nerve ends tingled.

Fingers crossed, I retrieved the voicemail.

A telemarketer.

I felt like an empty shell. It had been more than three weeks since Kit and I had spoken—what made me think he'd pick tonight to call? Or any night? There was no reason I couldn't be the first to reach out. It was ten-thirty Hawaii time—not too late. I went to my contacts list and pulled up his number.

But was this the state I wanted to be in for our first conversation in too long a time? Incoherent, on the verge of tears? I put down the phone and went to let Scruff inside.

When I crawled into bed I did two unusual things: I enticed Scruff up onto the bed with me so there'd be a warm, breathing being close at hand, and I left the bedside lamp burning.

I shot awake, jerking upright, straining to hear again the noise that had roused me.

If there had been a noise. If I hadn't been wakened by a bad dream—a nightmare vision of Philip Vandergriff's ghost, the imagined sound of gunfire and Amy's screams.

I listened, unmoving, my body tense. Silence all around me.

Then a low doggie moan from Scruff, twitching on the blankets beside me, and in the distance a siren.

I looked at the clock. Four-twenty-three. I lowered myself to my pillow and put my face against Scruff's fur. Finally my thumping heartbeats returned to normal.

But sleep eluded me. Eventually I gave up, got out of bed and shuffled out to my studio.

This was perhaps my favorite place in the world, the place where I felt most at home. There was something soul-soothing about the speckles of color on the floor, the canvases stacked against the walls beneath the windows, the smell of paints and turpentine.

For a while I simply sat and stared at the bamboo blinds, studying the skinny stripes they made against the window—the beige lines of wood cutting across the black of the night outside. Then I decided to put my uneasy wakefulness to good use. I squeezed various blues onto a palette and applied a dab or two to my winter wonderland. But the result looked clumsy. Afraid I'd ruin the painting, I set the palette aside.

I spread a sheet of vellum onto my worktable and began to sketch. A child in charcoal, smudgy, her outlines vague. Myself as a kid, I thought, until I recognized Amy's grin.

I bent my head over the picture and started to cry.

CHAPTER 18

I MUST HAVE DOZED OFF, because when I lifted my head from the worktable the stripes made by the blinds had reversed: The bamboo matchsticks looked dark, and the slivers of sky between them had lightened from black to dreary gray. The clock on the shelf said six-forty-five.

I looked down at the sketch I'd made of the little girl—half me, half Amy. The charcoal was smeared, blotched by tears. I crumpled the paper and flung it in the trash.

Sixty-three hours. That's how long it had been since the last time Amy was seen. Unless a miracle had occurred during the night.

Some miracle, my inner voice retorted. Philip Vandergriff dead in a pool of blood. And Terri—where was she? Murdered too, her body lying undiscovered in some hidden alley or dark, unfurnished room?

Sensing that I was awake, Scruff crawled out from under the worktable, yawned mightily and shook himself until the tags on his collar rattled. I stood up and stretched. Sleeping in that awkward position had put kinks in my neck and shoulders. And my mind, of course, was a tangled mess.

"Come on, kiddo," I told him. "We'd better go for a walk and work out these knots."

Fine with him. I pulled on jeans under the T-shirt I'd worn to bed, shrugged into my jacket, grabbed Scruff's leash and my umbrella.

We ventured out into a cold rain, which suited my mood. Gusts of wind yanked at the umbrella. Scruff didn't care; I suspected he'd inherited a few seagull genes along with his Irish setter and Tibetan terrier blood. He pulled me along at a trot, tail at full mast, wrenching to a stop from time to time when some compelling odor demanded his attention.

At the corner of Haight and Shrader, we encountered half a dozen damp, unhappy-looking souls huddling under the awning of Frank's Liquors, waiting for the bus. Most of the shops along Haight Street were closed, their windows fortressed behind metal grates. A couple of doorways served as improvised bedrooms, and I felt sympathy for the inhabitants rolled up in their scraps of blankets. My worktable wasn't the most comfortable spot for a nap, but at least I'd been warm and dry.

We reached the building where Philip Vandergriff died. In front of the Cole Street entrance a police car was double-parked—the only sign that someone had been murdered in the building a few hours earlier. I expected more—a shudder in the air around the building, a moan in the wind, bloodstains seeping under the windows and door.

Had Amy really been hidden inside? Had Philip died trying to rescue her? Once more I replayed yesterday's conversation in my head, trying to recall if he'd dropped any hint …

The front door flew open and a uniformed cop trotted down the steps. I moved toward him, calling "Excuse me!" to get his attention.

Narrowing his eyes, he glanced from me to Scruff. "Need help, miss?"

"I'm working with Amy Gardino's family. Has anything more turned up in there? Anything that might help us find her?"

"Sorry, can't answer those questions." He strode across the sidewalk, opened the police car's door.

"Wait—I was up there last night with Nick Gardino, after the body was found. I'm a private investigator and—"

"Then you know better than to interfere with a homicide investigation." He got in, slammed the car door and fired up the engine.

A nose nudged my leg. "You're right, Scruff, " I replied. "We have things to do."

We turned back to Haight Street, where one of the stores in the building's first floor was an oasis of bright lights. La Pasticceria Magnifica. A customer came out, along with comforting aromas of coffee, cinnamon, sugar and yeast.

"My turn to check out the smells," I told Scruff. I started to loop his leash around a newspaper box out front, but the proprietor caught my eye and waved us both in.

"Nice puppy. You not leave him outside. Too cold, too wet," she said as we entered. "Come in, get warm. You stay just a minute, health department never know."

"Thanks, Mrs. Ying," I said. I'd never asked her how a Hong Kong immigrant came to choose Italian pastries as her life's work. I simply was grateful that she'd picked my neighborhood as the place to pursue her calling. I ordered a caffe latte and a cannoli to go. Then changed my mind and made it two cannoli, feeling a twinge of guilt—usually I tried to go swimming every couple of days, but I hadn't made it to the pool all week. Several times, such as now, I'd been soaking wet, but unfortunately you don't burn calories by getting drenched in a rainstorm.

Mrs. Ying handed me a white paper bag full of goodies, a steaming cardboard cup, and a broken chunk of biscotti. "Here, for the nice puppy. What's his name?"

"Scruff," I told her. I shook cinnamon and cocoa onto the foam top of the latte. The nice puppy set his muddy forepaws on the front of the display case and put out his tongue as if he planned to lick up panettone and anise cookies right through the glass. "Come on, kiddo, be polite," I scolded, and pulled him back until all four feet were firmly on the floor. Only then did I give him his treat.

"Maybe I get a dog," Mrs. Ying said. "Watchdog, for protection." She shook her head. "All sorts of craziness around here."

I took a napkin and wiped Scruff's muddy pawprints off the glass. "I hear you had a lot of excitement in this building last night."

"Yes, a man is murdered, can you imagine? I am thinking, maybe I close down here. This building, I think it has—what is the word? A jinx. Too much blood."

"What do you mean? Have there been other killings here?"

"Not here, but …" She leaned over the counter and lowered her voice, as if sharing a secret. "The owner, my landlord? He is a murderer."

"Really?" I jostled my cup as I tried to clamp on a plastic lid, and coffee slopped over the rim.

"He is having his trial right now. Yesterday I see it on the TV news."

"You don't mean Carl Moritz?"

She nodded sagely. "Yes, it is true. Terrible thing—the man shoots his own family, just down the street."

Philip had been killed in a building owned by Carl Moritz.

Amy had been hidden there. A small captive, kept busy with crayons. Until she'd witnessed a murder and been moved to—where? Where was she now?

I mulled the question over as Scruff and I sloshed toward home. I didn't like the answers that crossed my mind.

Fortified with caffeine and cream, I felt a little better. Time to get ready to face a difficult day.

My fragile mood shattered when I saw myself in the bathroom mirror. Mrs. Ying had politely pretended not to notice how awful I looked. Hair ravaged by wind and rain. Face tear-streaked and charcoal-stained, just like my discarded sketch. If I looked too close, I would see Philip's bloody body imprinted on my eyes.

I jumped into the shower and tried to scrub away the horror of last night. Gradually the water worked its soothing magic. Amazing how much more pleasant it was to have water pelt your body when it's hot and you're naked than when it's cold and you're wrapped in soggy clothes.

I stood at my closet for a long time, debating what to wear, given the weather and my plans for the day. If you wanted something from someone, I'd discovered, it helped to look like you belonged in their world. Wearing the right clothes, like speaking the right jargon, created a bond of understanding and trust—or at least the illusion of a bond, which could be just as useful.

I would find Jack Emerich wearing pinstripes and a power tie. He was an accountant and financial advisor; clients liked it when the people who handled their money look conservative and rich. But I'd known Uncle Jack since my diaper days. I could wear my sloppiest sweats or a gown worthy of an Oscars ceremony—either way he'd welcome me warmly. For my appointment at the Hall of Justice, simply being clean and neat would win me points, considering the dismal sartorial condition of many of the people that homicide inspectors had occasion to see. But my visit to the Moritz Investment Group had me stumped. I had no idea what their corporate culture might be.

I finally opted for a casual-Friday look: black leather boots for the puddles, black jeans, an cream-colored shirt and a camelhair blazer. Then I pinned on a brooch that had belonged to my mother—a two-inch silver dagger, its hilt studded with amber. She had considered it a good-luck charm. Maybe it would conjure some good luck for Amy.

The rain was falling harder so I loaded a canvas bag with extra shoes, socks and a sweater, just in case. As I opened the trunk of my Toyota to stow the bag inside I discovered a length of black electrician's tape angled across my left taillight.

A shiver ran up my spine. I'd used the trick myself—the distinctive stripe of tape made it easier to spot the taillight in traffic at night. Easier to keep track of the car.

I looked around quickly. No one in sight. The windows of the vehicles parked along the block were dark, streaked with rain. Impossible to tell if anyone was inside keeping watch on my house and my car.

I ripped off the tape, and paid extra attention as I pulled away from the curb. No movement anywhere.

But sometime recently—last night?—someone had been following me.

CHAPTER 19

CREIGHTON OLIVER, executive vice president of the Moritz Investment Group, tapped out a rhythm on her desktop with the end of her pencil as I spoke. The eraser tip, I noticed—she wouldn't want to gouge the gleaming rosewood surface. The desk was vast; I pictured a dinner party of twelve seated around it, eating foie gras and truffles from gold-rimmed porcelain. The whole office was opulent—top-of-the-line computer system, a jewel-toned Persian rug layered over thick carpeting, a collection of Chinese vases lined up like soldiers in a bookcase against the far wall.

Ms. Oliver laid the pencil on a stack of papers, looked at me sitting in her soft leather visitor's chair and carefully arranged her lips into a smile.

She looked as glossy as the rosewood. I wondered if her hair—deep brunette, russet highlights—had been dyed to match her desk. Her complexion was so smooth and so artfully tinted, it was hard to believe she had real skin under the makeup. Her black suit jacket had mother-of-pearl buttons, flared white lapels and a deep V-neck. I'd been wrong—nothing casual about Friday around here. Even in my camelhair blazer, I felt decidedly underdressed.

Creighton changed her mind about the smile, switching to a look of sympathy and concern.

"Of course I feel sorry about the little girl who's missing, Ms. Randolph. Everyone in our company does. We all hope she returns safely. But her disappearance has nothing to do with us."

"You can understand why people might think so," I said. "Amy's the daughter of the homicide detective who arrested Carl Moritz for murder. And just as the trial gets underway, she's kidnapped. A pretty incredible coincidence."

"The police are wrong about Carl," Creighton said firmly. "He would never kill anyone. And they're wrong about this, too. I don't understand why we're being harassed."

"Harrassed?"

"First that cop for SFPD. What was his name? Inspector, uh—" She flipped through a pile of business cards on a small silver tray. "Beschke. Then that other man showed up, the girl's stepfather. And now you. What are you after?"

"Amy doesn't have a stepfather," I said, though I knew whom she meant.

"He told me he was. No, wait, about to be her stepfather is what he said. Her mother's fiancé."

Nothing in Creighton's expression or tone suggested she knew that yesterday's visitor had been shot to death a few hours later in a building owned by her firm, or that Amy had been held captive there.

She ran a finger over a perfectly arched brow. "I'll tell you the same thing I told them. No one from the Moritz Group, no one who's in any way associated with Carl, would do so horrendous a thing as kidnap a child. And certainly not to throw Carl's trial into disarray."

"What makes you so sure?"

"You mean besides the fact that it's immoral, illegal, vile, reprehensible—"

"Besides that."

"Because Carl's not afraid of this trial, that's why. There's no way the jury can convict him. He did not kill Robin." *Tap*, went the pencil. "He did not kill Eric." *Tap*. "He did not kill the baby." *Tap, tap, tap.*

"I've heard the case against him is pretty solid."

She dismissed the case with a wave. I noticed she wore a diamond solitaire; the stone was nearly the size of an apricot pit. It reminded me of Terri's ring.

"All circumstantial," she said. "Why would he kill them? His own family."

As if that never happened. Robin was hardly the first person to discover to her sorrow that her own family members were the ones to fear most.

"I knew Robin through the bookstore. I had the impression she and her father weren't on good terms."

Creighton pointed the pencil at me. "Okay. I'm going to explain to you about Carl and his family. But you need to do something in exchange."

"What's that?"

"Get the girl's family and their cop friends to back off."

I nodded, biding time. What approach would be in Amy's best interest? I needed whatever information Creighton could give us; best to stay on her good side until we knew where Amy was. But an equal concern—what I really had come for—was getting cash for the ransom.

"I appreciate anything you can tell me," I said finally.

"And you'll make the police stop hassling us?"

"Tell me about Carl. After that I have a request to make. Then I'll do what I can."

With a sigh, Creighton turned and gazed out the huge picture window. We were twenty-seven stories up in a Financial District highrise. On a clear day she'd have a spectacular view, but this morning the visibility was about six inches; we were looking straight into a cloud.

I wondered why she was here, not attending the trial to provide moral support to Moritz if she was so concerned about him, so certain of his innocence. Then the answer occurred to me—she was probably on the witness list, so she wouldn't be admitted to the courtroom until it was her time to testify.

My phone buzzed. I silenced it, letting the call go to voicemail.

Creighton turned her attention back to me with a poignant version of her smile.

"You can't imagine what a struggle it's been, keeping the firm going with Carl in jail. No one wants to do business with someone who's accused of murder. Whatever happened to 'innocent until proven guilty'? Thank God the vacancy rate in San Francisco is so low; otherwise we'd never find tenants. Once Carl's acquitted everything will be fine. But right now, it will kill us to be associated with this kidnapping. A seven-year-old girl, for God's sake. Her pretty little face gazing out at people everywhere they look."

"Tell me about the Moritzes," I prodded.

Creighton twisted her diamond ring. "Carl's first wife, Lydia, died twenty years ago."

"First wife? He remarried?"

Her smile became surprisingly soft and sweet. "Not yet. But as soon as the trial's over …"

"Ah. Congratulations."

She bit her crimsoned lip and continued, "The girls were small when Lydia died. Shanna was seven, Robin only five. Carl was overwhelmed with grief. He handled it in that foolish way men do, by closing himself off emotionally. He put all his energy into building up his real estate holdings and getting involved with good works. He's a major contributor to the symphony, you know. The opera too. And he's on a lot of nonprofit boards."

"Yes, I've heard that."

"Unfortunately, the girls got the short end of things. I don't mean they were neglected or anything. They had nannies, they went to the best schools. Music lessons, camp every summer. But Carl couldn't deal with his own grief. He wasn't equipped to help two little children work through theirs. So it's not surprising if there were some … resentments."

"And Robin expressed hers by running wild." If you asked me, getting involved in drugs and prostitution would suggest that her resentments were pretty strong.

"Robin's troubles are no secret. Carl's never claimed he was a perfect father. But he did get her into that New Dawn program, and he was so pleased when things started going right for her. The bookstore job, meeting Eric, having the baby. You should have seen Carl when she died. It was like losing Lydia all over again."

"Was Shanna a wild kid too?"

"Shanna handled her mother's death like Carl did, by bottling up her emotions. She didn't get angry, she never got in trouble, but ..."

"But what?" I prodded.

Creighton brushed an invisible speck off her desktop. "I worry about Shanna, frankly. Such a sad little waif. She has no friends, and she's never found a sense of direction, just drifts from one dead-end job to another."

"Sounds like signs of serious depression. Has anyone encouraged her to get help?"

"A couple of years ago Carl was paying for her to see a therapist, and I thought they were making good headway. She brightened up a lot, she was cheerful and upbeat. But then ... suddenly she crashed back to earth. Lower than earth, even."

"Having her sister murdered can't have helped."

"This was before that happened. But Shanna did take Robin's death hard. Carl became very solicitous of her. I think he finally realized the value of family. That's when he asked me to marry him." Creighton touched her diamond to her cheek, then rubbed the stone with a finger, probably wiping the makeup off.

"But then he was arrested." Too bad he hadn't realized the value of his family before he decided to murder some of its members. I felt no sympathy for him.

"Unjustly arrested. Shanna was devastated all over again. Mother dead, sister dead, now her father's in jail—who does she have left? Daddy's fiancée?" She gave a harsh laugh.

141

"You two don't get along?"

"I'm very fond of Shanna. I wish she returned my feelings. When she gets her father back, things will be better for all of us."

"What if the worst happens and Carl is convicted?"

"He won't be. What kind of evidence do they have? Carl owns a car similar to the one the shooter was driving. So do lots of people. Priuses are common around here."

Very true. Nick told me this was one reason it took him six months to tie the murder to Moritz. Robin's father had been questioned early on, of course—all the victims' family members had—but there were no solid leads to the shooter. The investigation crawled to a dead end, but Nick kept on it, pursuing new angles whenever he could steal a moment from his caseload of more recent crimes. Sifting through the parking tickets written in the Haight around the time of the murders, he found half a dozen that had been issued to the same Prius over the preceding month—one of them the day before the murders. But from that date on, there were none. It was as if the car had disappeared from the neighborhood. He checked the license number on the tickets; it was registered to Moritz Investment Group.

"And the car's all they have for evidence," Creighton said. "They tried putting Carl in lineups—not one witness could say he was in the car when the shots were fired."

I knew the D.A. had more than Carl's Prius to make the case, though it seemed to me the car might be enough. Confronted with the tickets, Moritz had produced his Prius, one of several cars he owned. It was red, not blue or gray as the witnesses had described. But the crime lab discovered it had been painted; the red concealed a factory coat of blue underneath. Nick made the rounds of auto body shops until he turned up the one that had done the paint job—just a week after the murders.

Then there was the blood. The victims had been shot at close enough range that spatters would have hit the car. Despite the new paint, when the Prius was tested with Luminol, traces of blood showed up on the tires and windows. Further tests linked the blood to Eric and Robin.

Creighton must have known all this. But it wouldn't serve my purpose to argue the evidence with her.

"I'd like to see the best outcome for everyone," I told her. "If Carl is innocent, he certainly shouldn't go to prison. And none of you should suffer from unfair suspicions that you're involved with Amy's kidnapping." If the suspicions really are unfair, I added silently.

"What are you suggesting?"

How to phrase it? I ran my finger along the smooth, curved edge of the desk, tracing a streak of red grain through the dark wood. I wanted to ask flat out: Give us the money to buy Amy back. But the ransom demand hadn't been made public, so I had to skate around it.

"We'd like your help—financial help, I mean—for the search for Amy."

She frowned, creasing her impeccable face. "Financial? What's this, some kind of extortion?"

"No, no," I assured her. "I'm talking about a goodwill gesture, something you can use as a public relations tactic. A contribution to the Find Amy Coalition."

"Is that all?" She reached down and I heard a drawer glide open. She brought a black leather pocketbook into view, flipping open its gold clasp. "I'll write you a check myself."

I took a deep breath and touched the amber on my dagger pin for luck. "A sizable donation. Something in the order of, say, one hundred thousand dollars."

She stared at me as if I'd gone crazy. Maybe I had. "You can't be serious."

"We need seed money for our search and our fundraising campaign. A substantial commitment from a firm like the Moritz Investment Group would go a long way toward convincing other corporations to contribute too."

Creighton started to interrupt, but I pushed on over her words.

"You can't imagine the expense of mounting a search like this. Once Amy is home safe, any money that's left will go toward setting up a foundation to find other missing kids—to help kids in trouble, like Robin was."

"Carl will—"

"Carl would want to do this, I'm sure. A memorial to Robin and Eric and baby Michael. It will remind people what a philanthropist Carl is, keep them from connecting the Moritz name with crime. And you could be helping to save Amy's life."

She leaned back in her chair. I could see her starting to consider the idea. It was outrageous to hope for the whole hundred thousand. But if she came up with twenty or thirty, we'd be that much closer.

"The thing is," I said, "it's urgent. The Find Amy Coalition has nothing at all, just volunteers with a lot of heart. And every minute counts. If we could get the money today—"

Her phone rang. Damn. Just as I was getting warmed up. Just as she was beginning to look enthusiastic.

She picked up the receiver and told it her name. The caller's response clearly upset her.

"What? Calm down, Rick. Are you sure it's one of our buildings? God, Cole and Haight, wouldn't you know it."

Giving me a grim look, she covered the mouthpiece, mouthed the word "Sorry" and waved me toward the door.
Pretending I didn't understand, I sat back and studied the pattern on the Persian rug while I waited for the call to end.

"I can't believe this," she said into the phone. "That man was actually here in this office yesterday. God, this is all we need—being connected to another murder." She glared at me and pointed again at the exit. "Wait a minute, Frank. There's someone here in my office I need to get rid of."

I thought about Mrs. Ying's saying her building was jinxed: *Too much blood.* I decided not to wait and see what Creighton might mean by "get rid of."

I rose from the soft leather chair and let myself out the door. I'd come so close. If the phone hadn't rung for five more minutes, I'd have had a check in my hand.

No way I'd get any Moritz money now.

CHAPTER 20

DODGING UMBRELLAS, puddles and the dirty spray kicked up by passing cars, I walked the three blocks from the Moritz offices to Uncle Jack's accounting firm. Every few minutes I glanced back over my shoulder. On the crowded downtown sidewalk, I couldn't tell if I was being followed. But I felt an uneasy itch between my shoulder blades, as if somebody's eyes were laser-beamed on that spot.

Don't be paranoid, Jess. I ticked off the cases I was working on—couldn't think of one where someone might gain an advantage by tailing me.

Amy's kidnapper? Possible, but why? I was on the fringe of the investigation, not a central player. If the kidnapper wanted to know what the plans were, what the cops or the FBI were thinking, he had any number of more promising taillights to slap his tape on.

Lost in this speculation, I almost walked past the entrance to Jack's building. Turning abruptly to go in, I nearly collided with a man dashing down the sidewalk, a newspaper over his head as a makeshift umbrella. I sidestepped him and bumped into a woman in a Burberry raincoat and high heels.

"Sorry!" I said as she wobbled. I took her arm to help her regain her balance.

"Goddamn bitch!" she shrieked. "Watch where the hell you're going!"

"Well, excuse me!" I ducked into the building lobby, finally safe and dry.

I took out my phone to see who had called while I was in Creighton's office.

"Hello? Jess Randolph? This is Shanna Moritz, remember? We met at the courthouse yesterday. I want to talk to you. Could you call me? I'm at work so I'll give you that number. I Found My Heart in San Francisco—that's the name of the shop. It's at Pier Thirty-Nine."

"Really? You did that painting over there?"

Jack's new receptionist had introduced herself as Caitlin. We chatted while we waited for him to get off the phone. She was very young but had an air of seasoned competence—the product of a neat wash-and-wear haircut, short unpolished nails, and the tortoiseshell glasses that perched on her snub nose.

"Yes. When I was in school," I said. "Hope you like it, since you have to stare at it all day."

"I think it's great. Honest. It reminds me of hiking in the mountains. Those browns and that olivey green. And the dark corners—like shadows under trees, or night falling. It's peaceful."

"It is?" Peaceful was the last thing I'd felt when I painted it. I'd just had another huge battle with the man who in those days—before I came to my senses—had held my heart and shared my home. I'd painted fast, churning with anger, slashing at the large square canvas with my brush. Yet through some miracle, the lines and shapes and colors had come together into a satisfying whole. The painting transcended the pain that had inspired it. That kind of magic was one of the things I loved about art.

"Yes, totally," Caitlin said. "My boyfriend and I went camping near Lake Shasta last October and the forest looked just like that. Everything serene and natural. I mean, I know the painting's abstract and all, but the feeling's the same. Oh, Jack's off the line now."

While she let Jack know I was there, I studied the painting

again. Peaceful. She was right, it was peaceful if you looked at it in a certain frame of mind. A line from a song I'd sung with Amy drifted through my head. *Deep peace of the quiet earth to you …*

Caitlin summoned my attention. "He says go on back."

I thanked her and went into Jack's big corner office.

"Jess!" He rose from his chair as I entered. "I was just wishing for sunshine, and here you are."

I smiled; I'd always found it easy to smile at Jack, a big man with warm eyes and a ready laugh. He was in his fifties now. What was left of his hair, just a fringe around his ears and the back of his head, almost matched the gray suit jacket hanging on his coat rack.

"Hello, Jack. Thanks for letting me burst in on your busy day."

He came around his wide walnut desk and enveloped me in a bear hug. "I'm never too busy for you, honey. Here, have a seat."

I took the armchair that faced the desk and the window behind it. Like Creighton Oliver's, Jack's office was a large, elegantly furnished space with an impressive view on sunny days. But this room resembled a country-house library rather than a palace dining room.

"Want some coffee?" Jack asked from his credenza. "I put in my own coffee maker, saves me from running back and forth to the kitchen. Wait, you're a tea drinker. I'll go put the kettle on."

"No need. I'm in coffee mode today." No point in putting Jack to extra trouble—at least, not more trouble than the favor I was about to ask of him.

He poured coffee into two ceramic mugs and handed me one. "It's a designer brew someone gave me. Hazelnut flavor. Hope it's not too frou-frou."

I took a sip and let the warmth flow through me. "Delicious," I said, and it was.

He returned to his chair. "Heard from your father lately?"

He wasn't referring to my stepfather, Roger. He meant Allen Fraser—the man who had given me my red hair and lean build. Who had dutifully married my mother when she got pregnant, and walked out of our lives when I was one year old. One night last spring, to my great shock, he phoned me. After a rocky beginning, we had worked out sort of an uneasy long-distance friendship, consisting mostly of texts and phone calls between San Francisco and New York, where Allen lived.

"We talked over the holidays. Merry Christmas, happy new year, the usual thing."

Jack nodded. He probably knew this already. A friend of my parents in their college days, he stuck by my mother after the divorce and became my honorary Uncle Jack. When I was little, before Mom met Roger, I'd wanted her to marry Jack, but their close friendship never evolved into a romance. What neither Mom nor I knew was that Jack had also remained friends with Allen Fraser. When Allen contacted me, I discovered Jack had been keeping my wayward father up to date on his daughter all along.

Jack interrupted my thoughts. "Jess? You're looking pensive."

I steadied myself with another swallow of coffee. "You're probably wondering why I'm here."

He smiled. "Because I'm a charming host?"

"Besides that. You've heard about the child who's missing? The homicide detective's daughter?"

His expression sobered. "Of course. Amy Gardino. Are you working on that?"

"Amy's father is a friend. He asked me to help. And Amy—well, she's sort of like family to me." I recounted the events since Tuesday afternoon when Amy vanished, sixty-seven hours ago—what we knew, what we speculated, what we hoped and feared. I described Philip's murder.

Then I told Jack about the ransom demand. "I'm swearing you to total secrecy on this. You can't tell anyone."

He raised his right hand and placed his left on a pile of papers. "I swear on a stack of profit-and-loss statements, I will not tell the truth, the whole truth, or anything resembling the truth."

"The thing is, I need your assistance."

149

"Of course. What would you like me to do?"

"I'm hoping you might be willing … I know you have some clients who are very wealthy …"

"Ah. You need someone to put together money for this ransom."

"Well … yes."

"Only I have to do it without telling anyone why I'm asking them to give thousands of dollars on a moment's notice."

"You can tell them why, just not exactly why." I stood up, bracing my hands on his desk. The speech I'd practiced on Creighton Oliver tumbled out in a rush. "Explain it's for the Find Amy Coalition. They need to raise a lot of money to conduct a comprehensive search. The police have limited resources, and you can't imagine how costly it is to mount the kind of effort that's needed. And time is of the essence. Every second counts if we're going to get Amy back—"

"Whoa! I get the idea. I think I can handle it."

"You mean … you'll do it?" I'd been prepared to argue and cajole.

"I'll do my best. Without letting on about the ransom."

I moved behind his chair and kissed the crown of his shiny head.

"I knew I could count on you."

He looked embarrassed. "Hey, that's what friends are for. Here, let's have some more coffee."

"Who will you ask?"

"Not telling. You swore me to secrecy. That's part of the secret." He went to the credenza and refilled our mugs. "Do you remember the time we rented a little cabin in the Sierra? You and your mother and me? You were about Amy's age—what is she, seven?"

"That's right."

He brought the coffee over. I was standing by his window, watching rivulets of rain run down the glass.

"We were hiking on a backwoods trail. All of a sudden you

were gone. Your mom and I went crazy. We searched everywhere, yelling your name. Nothing. It was like the sky had reached down and snatched you, or the earth had swallowed you up."

"I remember. I had a nightmare about it the other night."

"It got dark and cold. Started to rain, then snow. Finally, thank God, we found a ranger, and he organized a search party. Hours went by. We didn't know if we'd ever find you. Or if you were found, whether you'd be alive." He set down his mug and put his arm around my shoulder. "I have never in my life, before or since, been as frightened as I was that day."

"Me either ... I was so scared."

A field of frozen whiteness moved across my vision, obliterating Jack's face, the rain-streaked window, the entire world.

"I found a rock cave, a shelter," I whispered, more to myself than to Jack. "I hung a purple mitten outside on a dead stick. Thank God the ranger spotted it. A few minutes more and it would have been buried."

I could see the mitten now, vivid as a bloodstain on the ice. I began to shiver and couldn't stop.

"Jess, are you okay?"

"I'm fine." I stood up straighter, forced a smile. Sipped the coffee but this time it didn't warm me. "When I first saw the ranger, he had snow on his jacket. It looked like a white robe. I thought he was an angel who'd come to take me to heaven."

"An angel." Jack chuckled softly.

"What's so funny?" I asked.

"That's the other thing I recall about that trip. Angels. We ended up snowbound at the cabin for several days, remember? Your mom and I had a hard time enticing you outside to play. We tried building a snowman and staging a snowball fight, but what finally won you over was making snow angels. We made a whole flock of angels all around the cabin."

"Snow angels. It's odd, I hadn't thought about them in years. But I was telling Amy about them just the other day."

Amy and I had been working in my studio, our easels side by side. She was intrigued when I told her I was painting a snow scene. "But there's no picture in it," she said. "It's just colors."

"Winter colors. See how that pale, pale blue looks like snow out in the open? And the dark blue suggests how it looks in deep shade. The sky's in there too. Can you find it?"

"Right there!" She pointed to a patch of deep cerulean, the sky on a sunny January afternoon. "And look, there's the lace Jack Frost painted on the window."

I examined the pattern she pointed to, a tracery of thin white lines over a dark background. "You know, you're right. I hadn't seen it that way before."

"It surprised you, didn't it," she said with delight.

"Yes, indeed. Art can be very surprising sometimes."

"I want to paint a snow scene too."

So we took the portrait of her mother off her easel and I set up a clean sheet of poster paper. She whisked her brush across the surface, making mountains and trees appear. The painting was similar to one she'd done the first time Nick brought her to my house—the picture of the place she called the pine land, now tacked up on my studio wall. This time, though, the triangular shapes weren't purple and green, but assorted shades of blue.

While she painted we shared stories of our adventures in the snow. I told her about my sojourn in the mountains when I was her age. I didn't mention getting lost but talked instead about toasting marshmallows in the fireplace and building a fort and making snow angels.

"What are they?" Amy asked. "Are they like statues?"

"No, more like pictures you draw on the ground, only instead of a pencil or paintbrush, you use your body."

"How do you do that?"

I lay down on the floor to demonstrate. "Pretend you're lying in the snow. Now move your legs like this." I pushed my legs outward. "That shapes the angel's skirt. Then wave your arms up and down like this to make the wings. Then get up very carefully"—I eased myself to my feet—"and presto! There's an imprint of an angel in the snow."

"My turn! I want to do it," she said, clapping her hands. She spread out on the floor and flapped her arms and legs. I grabbed a stick of charcoal and drew the outline of an angel around her, then helped her stand up.

"Look," I told her, "you made an angel. See, there's her head, and her skirt, and her wings—"

"What about the halo?"

"I don't think snow angels have haloes."

"Of course they do. Angels always have haloes." She screwed up her face in the way that meant she was thinking hard. Then: "I know! We can make one out of illumine foil."

"Illumine? Oh, you mean aluminum foil."

"Isn't that what I said?"

"Not quite. But I like your word better. It's like illuminated, which means something bright with light. A good description for a halo."

"Do you have any?"

"Illumine foil? There's some in the kitchen. Let's go get it."

So we twisted a strip of foil into a halo. When the chalk outline wore off the floor, I hung the halo on the post of her easel. It was still there.

When I finished telling him this story, Jack picked up the phone. "Caitlin," he said into it, "please reschedule my appointments for the rest of the day. And hold my calls. An emergency project has come up."

I stood up to leave; I was due soon at the Hall of Justice to give a statement to the cops in charge of investigating Philip's murder.

"Thank you, Jack. You don't know how much your help means. I know you're busy, and—"

Jack raised a hand to stop me. "This is important, and I want to help. I can understand, a little bit, what Amy's parents are going through. I was lucky. When a little girl I loved disappeared, I got to see her come back and make snow angels. I hope they'll be as fortunate."

The rotten weather had brought out the worst in my fellow drivers, who were blowing horns, jumping lanes and running red lights. Traffic was near gridlock. I drummed on the steering wheel and cursed the clock as the Toyota inched along.

I kept one eye on the rearview mirror, scanning the vehicles behind me. I couldn't spot anyone trying to tail me, but in these conditions who could tell? I shrugged my shoulders, trying to shake off the itchy feeling of being watched.

By the time I reached the Hall of Justice the rain slackened to a drizzle. Good thing, too, since the only parking place I could find was four blocks away.

Inside the building, I joined the long, slow line of lawyers, petty criminals, prospective jurors, witnesses and parking ticket protesters waiting to clear the security checkpoint. Our progress came to a halt when a greasy-haired man set off the metal detector, then angrily refused to submit to a further search. Two guards hustled him, still yelling, out the front steps. The rest of us resumed our shuffle forward.

Finally I joined the crowd waiting for the elevator, which took its sweet time to arrive. We jammed ourselves in. I was pinned against the far wall, with an oversized woman's soggy jacket pressed into my face and her wooden clog on top of my instep.

By the time I sprinted into Homicide, I was frustrated, tense and twenty minutes late. I sputtered an apology to Matt McCabe and Anna Rovinsky.

The two detectives ushered me into one of the small, stark interrogation rooms. Bare walls, dreary furnishings. Nothing to brighten it except McCabe's persimmon-colored hair.

I asked, "Did anything more turn up in the apartment that could lead to Amy?"

"Nothing obvious." Rovinsky gestured me into a hard chair that seemed designed for slumping, not sitting, then perched on the scarred wooden table that filled most of the room. She fiddled with a strand of her dark blond hair. The brown eyes behind her glasses looked tired. She and her partner had probably been up all night.

McCabe set up a recorder and announced the date, the time, and everyone's name. "Okay, Ms. Randolph. Tell us when you first met Philip Vandergriff, and what the circumstances were."

"Wednesday," I said. "Day before yesterday. I went to Amy's house in Creekhaven—"

"Why did you go there?"

"To find out what was happening with the search. And to see her mother—Nick Gardino asked me to help Terri out if I could. Philip was there when I arrived."

They led me through the course of my brief acquaintance with Philip Vandergriff—my impressions of him that first afternoon, our encounter yesterday at the Hall of Justice, our lunch at Dandelion. I told them everything I could recall of the conversations we'd had, and what little I'd observed of his interactions with other people—Terri, Nick, his sister Lacey. Even though the recorder was running, McCabe took notes on a pad of paper, his pen almost invisible in his big hand.

"While we were at lunch, Philip told me he was intrigued by the idea that Carl Moritz engineered Amy's kidnapping to derail the murder trial. So yesterday morning he went to Moritz's office and confronted the firm's executive VP."

"Just what we need," McCabe muttered. "Amateurs trying to do a cop's job."

"What did the guy say?" asked Rovinsky.

"Not a guy," I said. "A woman named Creighton Oliver." They both nodded; I wasn't telling them anything they didn't know. "Philip said she acted shocked at the accusation. But it's significant, don't you think, that Moritz owns the building where Philip was killed?"

McCabe and Rovinsky exchanged glances; I couldn't tell whether this was news or not.

"How do you know that?" McCabe asked. I explained, and he scribbled on his pad.

"Do you know whose apartment it is?" I asked. "Who rented it, I mean?"

"Not yet. We're checking," McCabe said.

"Apparently a new tenant moved in last week," Rovinsky added. "Didn't move in much, though—you saw yourself how empty the place was."

I nodded. "As if whoever rented only wanted a place to keep Amy."

"Could be," she agreed. "Did Vandergriff say anything that might indicate how he ended up there? Or where he was going after you finished lunch?"

"He said he had errands to run in the neighborhood. But he lived nearby, so that wasn't odd." I closed my eyes to conjure the scene at Dandelion. Sunny yellow walls, aromas of basil and coffee and sourdough. The family of tourists by the window, and the kid's excitement when Atom and his turquoise hair zoomed by on his Rollerblades. The soft look on Philip's face as he talked about Terri. The way he squeezed my hand when he said—

"'Something tells me things are going to break soon.'" I opened my eyes, sat up straight.

"Sure hope you're right." Rovinsky slid her glasses up the bridge of her nose.

"No, that's a quote. Something Philip said to me at lunch. He commented that he was trying to find Amy and rescue her. Then he said, 'Something tells me things are going to break soon.'"

McCabe snorted. "Provocative opening like that, and you didn't ask him what he meant?"

"I tried. He wouldn't elaborate."

"Pretty clear what he meant." Rovinsky pushed herself off the table. "Somehow he figured out where Amy was and tried to be a goddamn hero."

Rovinsky and McCabe took me through my encounters with Philip again and yet again. To everyone's frustration, including mine, I couldn't come up with a reason why Philip had gone to that particular apartment, or what made him he think he might find Amy there. Finally Rovinsky walked me to the elevator.

On the way down I detoured to go by the Moritz courtroom. Maybe the proceedings had reached the point where Nick was testifying. But the room was empty. I glanced at my watch. Past noon. Lunch recess.

The down elevator, by contrast, was packed. When we arrived at the first floor, passengers wanting to go up began elbowing in before the outbound riders could get clear. I was so busy avoiding being jabbed by umbrellas, I almost missed noticing the woman with the loose dark curls.

Then I realized who she was. I whirled around, yelled and waved.

"Terri! Terri!"

But the elevator door slid shut and she was gone.

CHAPTER 21

WHEN THE NEXT ELEVATOR came, I rode it back up, my mind racing. Thank God, Terri was alive. But where had she been all this time?

The Homicide Squad, I guessed, was her destination now. McCabe and Rovinsky would want to talk to her about Philip's murder. I wondered how she'd taken the news. How could she bear up with two such dreadful events happening in her life at once?

Maybe she's bearing up fine, whispered my inner voice, always suspicious. *Maybe she's responsible for those events herself.*

It took forever for the elevator to get to there fourth floor. The corridor was empty.

I went into Homicide. The clerk on duty looked puzzled to see me but smiled anyway. "Hello, weren't you just in here?"

"Yes. Did a woman come in? A brunette, about my height?"

"I can't really say." Though her glance at the door of the interrogation room told me what I wanted to know. "Privacy policy."

"Please. I really need to talk with her."

The clerk pointed to a chair. "If you want to wait, I can get one of the homicide inspectors to speak with you about your concerns. But it might be awhile before one's available."

I was tempted to stay. I was burning with curiosity about where she'd gone and why. Had she learned anything about Amy? Had she—there was the little voice again—sent the ransom note?

But sitting here and fidgeting wouldn't help the situation. I'd catch up with Terri later.

I thanked the clerk and slipped out the door.

A gusting wind whipped the blue-and-white banners on the flagpoles at the entrance to Pier 39. It was colder here by the water, and I wished I'd taken the time to put on the sweater I'd stashed in my car trunk. The rain had turned to a thick mist, the kind that soaks you through and makes an umbrella useless.

In her voicemail message, Shanna Moritz had asked me to call her, but I'd decided to see her in person. The more insight I could get into her and her family, the better. Ransom demand or no, I wasn't convinced we could rule out a connection between Moritz and Amy's kidnapping.

I checked the carved wooden directory board. The shop called I Found My Heart in San Francisco was located at the far end of the pier.

Most days I would have had to jostle my way through a horde of tourists to get there. I'd read somewhere that this faux fishing village, full of cutesy shops and expensive restaurants, was the second most popular attraction in California—after Disneyland, I assumed, although the article didn't say. I couldn't believe this place would outpull natural splendors like Yosemite, or Point Reyes up the coast. In tourist-speak *attraction* must have meant manmade, an artificial environment designed expressly to promote the exchange of amusement for money. If so, Pier 39 was the place, all right.

Today, there were just a few hardy stragglers. My boot heels clacked loudly on the wooden planking as I strode past the video arcade, the cappuccino kiosk, the Cinemax theater where tourists could experience the safe thrill of a simulated earthquake. And the double tiers of specialty shops, each one purveying nothing but music boxes, or gadgets for left-handed people, or wind-up toys, or refrigerator magnets. How could stores so limited ever sell enough to stay in business?

The carousel at the end of the pier was grinding out tinny music when I reached it. A man hunkered into his raincoat as he watched a little girl screaming in delighted fear as she clutched the pole of a white horse with gold mane. Just like Firecracker, the horse in the drawing we'd found in the Cole Street apartment. Amy's favorite horse.

Seventy hours she'd been gone.

I turned away from the merry-go-round and realized I was standing in front of the shop I was looking for. A pink sign over the door announced I FOUND MY HEART IN SAN FRANCISCO in bright silver letters. My suspicions about the store's merchandising focus proved correct. Almost everything—from Mylar balloons to rhinestone earrings, from lollipops to porcelain bowls—was heart-shaped, or had hearts emblazoned upon it. It looked like a Valentine factory had exploded.

Shanna Moritz was alone inside, sitting listlessly on a stool behind a glass display counter, her elbow propped on the counter and her head in her hand. A chime bingbonged as I entered and she glanced up.

"May I help—oh wait, you're her, aren't you? Jess Randolph." She pulled herself up straight. Pinned to her pink polo shirt was a heart-shaped badge displaying her name in elaborate script. "I was expecting you to call. You didn't have to come all the way here."

"I was in the neighborhood." A little fib surely wouldn't count against me if anyone was keeping score. "Thought I'd stop by."

She hooked a strand of limp brown hair behind her ear. I was struck again by how much she resembled her sister. But Shanna lacked some vital spark. Watching her was like seeing Robin in a faded, slow-motion film.

"I'm glad you came in, actually," she said. "Things are dead around here. When the weather sucks like this, I'm lucky if there's even seagulls to talk to."

"It should be high season for this store, with Valentine's Day next month."

"You'd think. But if the tourists aren't out, who's going to buy stuff? Locals don't come here. When was the last time you shopped at Pier 39?"

Good point. I looked around to see if there was anything worth buying. Make a purchase, get her on my side. Would Kit like a purple silk necktie embroidered with chartreuse hearts? Would I have reason to buy him a Valentine gift at all?

"What did you want to talk to me about?" I asked Shanna.

"Just that ... hey, you mind if we go outside? I think the rain's stopped. This place gets on my nerves sometimes. And I could use a nicotine break."

She taped a well-worn BACK IN 5 MINUTES sign to the door, then led me out of the shop and through a covered passage to a walkway beside the water.

Originally sailboats and pleasure craft had been moored on both sides of Pier 39, and this walkway had provided access to the boats on the west. Then a colony of sea lions invaded the marina, lumbering onto the boats and making themselves at home. The boat owners objected to the noise and the foul droppings and the fact that their expensive vessels were sinking under the creatures' weight. After trying to evict the pests, the pier management noticed they were drawing in tourists in droves. I'd been rather pleased when the boats went and the sea lions stayed.

When Shanna and I emerged from the passage, the stench of the beasts smacked our nostrils. Dozens of them were draped over the docks and floating platforms. They greeted us with a chorus of honks, barks and groans. Or a few did—most seemed to be asleep, lying around like fat brown slugs.

We stood by the railing overlooking the water. The mist had lightened, but the salt-flavored wind was strong. My blazer offered scant protection against the chill. I felt sorry for Shanna in her thin short-sleeved shirt.

Cupping her hand around the lighter flame, she lit a cigarette and inhaled a lungful of smoke.

"I like to watch these guys," she said when she'd blown the smoke out again. "They sort of remind me of—well, of me."

"The sea lions? In what way?" A brown-speckled pup slithered off a platform and splashed in the murky water.

She leaned both elbows on the railing and gazed at the animals. "I don't know. They're so out of place here. They belong out in nature somewhere but they're stuck in this people environment. Yet they go along trying to make the best of things." She took another drag. "At least they have each other."

I wasn't sure how to respond. I ventured, "You don't feel like you belong in the city?"

"Or anywhere else." Her voice was soft, as if she weren't really talking to me. "I never have."

I decided to wait, let her bring up whatever else was on her mind in her own way. Beyond the sea lions, an excursion boat bounced across the choppy water, ferrying die-hard tourists to Alcatraz. My stomach was happy not to be on board.

Shanna flipped her cigarette butt over the railing. "I've been thinking about what you said yesterday. About the little girl." She fell silent again.

"What about her?" I prompted.

"Everyone thinks my father is this awful person. But they're wrong. He didn't kill Robin or anybody. He'd never kidnap a child."

Her voice was flat, emotionless. She was looking at the sea lions, not at me. A couple of bulls had gotten into a tussle. They thrashed at each other, bellowed and shrieked. Their companions ignored them.

"So I can't help you that way. With any information, I mean, like some friend of my father's is hiding her in the basement or something. Because it's just not true."

She tilted her head and looked at me like she was trying to

gauge if I believed her. I wasn't sure I did.

"Are you sure?" I said. "I'm not saying you're part of it, but maybe—"

"No! Whatever's happened to that girl has nothing to do with any of us, okay? Nothing!"

Back off, Jess. If I could build a rapport with her, that might serve Amy best. I lifted my hands in a peacemaking gesture.

Shanna brushed a strand of wind-tossed hair out of her eyes. "But I want to help you find her."

"Help me? How?"

"Any way I can. That's why I called—to find out how. Search the woods, talk to people, put up flyers, whatever. Last night I couldn't sleep, thinking about her being lost. I felt so sad. So scared for her." She hugged herself with goosefleshed arms; she must have been freezing. "I thought, maybe I could come along with you and—"

"Come with me?"

"Sure. I'll do whatever you need. There must be some way I could be, you know, useful."

"Right now, I'm going to my office. But it's great that you want to help. There's a group that's coordinating volunteers—the Find Amy Coalition."

"I heard about them. Only I thought maybe they wouldn't want me around."

"Why wouldn't they?"

"Well, these rumors and all about who took her … since my name is Moritz …"

"They'll be delighted to have you. Here, I'll give you a number to call. The woman in charge is Lillian Harwood." I took out one of my artist's business cards and wrote down the phone number. I'd memorized it from the ubiquitous flyer.

"Yeah, okay." Shanna tucked the card into a pocket of her jeans.

"There's another way you could help," I said.

"How?'

"The Find Amy Coalition needs money, and—"

"Hey, so do I. Who doesn't? Look, I can donate my time, I really want to do that. But I don't have any spare cash. I need every cent I can get and then some, believe me. Everybody thinks because your father is rolling in money, you must have plenty yourself. But with some families, it doesn't work that way. You think I'd be working in that stupid shop if I had a choice?"

I hastened to reassure her. "I didn't mean money from you. You're very generous, giving your time. The thing is, I was talking to Creighton Oliver this morning about having the Moritz Investment Group make a sizable donation. You know, seed money to fund the search for Amy. But we were interrupted and I had to leave. Maybe you could put in a good word—"

"With Creighton?" Shanna's face puckered with distaste. I could see why the two women might not get along. Creighton Oliver, polished to an elegant gleam, was probably puzzled and a little repulsed by Shanna's slipshod look and manner. And no doubt Shanna was jealous and resentful of her stepmother-to-be—partly for having a brand of self-assurance that Shanna, the perpetual waif, probably never would. And even more for winning the love that her father had never seen fit to give her.

I expected a quick and emphatic no. But Shanna surprised me, saying, "Okay, I'll see what I can do."

I gave her heartfelt thanks. "It would be great if we could have a check this afternoon. This man is coordinating the contributions." I jotted Jack's name and number on another business card. Before leaving his office, I'd put Jack in touch with Nick and they'd worked out Jack's role. I had no idea how Jack would convert checks to cash by tomorrow's ransom deadline, but he'd assured me he'd find a way.

"It will help my father if we do this, won't it?" Shanna said. "I mean, if his company helps you out, then everyone will stop suspecting him arranging for this girl to get snatched?"

I phrased my response carefully. "I'm sure a lot of people will see it that way."

"Do you think ..." She left the words hanging.

"What?"

"Nothing. I better get back to the shop. Keep the mob of customers from beating down the door." She half-laughed, then said, "Thanks for coming by. I'll try to talk to Creighton. And maybe I'll see you at this coalition place."

She turned and walked back through the passage. Head lowered, shoulders slumped, she looked like a lost child herself.

CHAPTER 22

"Hey, Jess!" Claudia greeted me when I arrived at Parks & O'Meara. "You've been keeping secrets from us."

"Secrets?" I leaned my umbrella against the wall behind the coat rack.

"I thought you were still hot and heavy with Kit. But come to think of it, he hasn't been around lately."

"He's in Hawaii on an assignment." I stepped behind her desk so she couldn't see any flicker of pain in my face, and flipped through the basket where she put my mail. A copy of a client report, an invoice I needed to approve, an invitation to an art show. True, I'd kept quiet about the abrupt halt of my love life. Not to keep secrets, but because I didn't want to be asked questions when I hadn't figured out any answers.

Claudia grinned mischievously. "Ah, but now we know what's going on."

"Claudia, what are you talking about?"

She swiveled around in her chair to face me. "A handsome guy who brings you food and flowers, that's what."

I stared at her. She brushed a tangle of mahogany curls back from her forehead. The grin remained in place.

"The stress of this job is getting to you, Claudia. Or did the flu addle your brain?"

"No, honest. He came in about an hour ago. He was real disappointed you weren't here. Go look on your desk."

I went into the office and stopped cold. Sure enough, there on

166

my desk was a tall vase with half a dozen fading agapanthus blooms, long stalks capped with bundles of purple flowers. Damn. Next to the vase was a square flat box of white cardboard. The scent of the cheese and tomato filled the room. Damn again.

O'Meara stood next to my desk, tail waving. He'd assigned himself guard duty and was valiantly prepared to protect the pizza from invading Mongols and Huns.

Claudia had followed me. "Eccentric choices. Most guys go in for roses and chocolates."

"Hi, Jess," Tyler greeted me from his post at his computer. "We were hoping you'd show up. Didn't want to devour your goodies without you."

I lifted the box lid. Sausage and mushrooms. No pepperoni this time.

"Your friend said to tell you he was sorry he couldn't wait," Claudia said.

"He's not a friend. He's not a secret admirer. He's just a kid, a journalist wannabe."

Tyler wandered over to my desk. "He did seem a little young for you."

"That doesn't matter," Claudia said. "My Aunt Camilla says it's good for couples when the guy's younger. The wife's less likely to be left a widow. Not to mention that men and women reach their sexual peaks at different—"

"Enough!" I put up my hands.

"Well, if you don't want him, pass him along." Claudia plucked a tidbit of sausage off the pizza and fed it to O'Meara.

"Have you two had lunch?" I asked. "Might as well warm this thing up and enjoy it."

"Thought you'd never ask." Tyler picked up the box and carried it out, with Claudia and O'Meara at his heels.

I lingered behind, touching one of the purple petals. Lilies of the Nile bloomed in summer; where had the Pizza Kid found these that still had color in January? He must have gone to every florist and raided every park in the city. A gift-enclosure envelope was taped to the vase, with a handwritten name: *Cleopatra*. I peeled it off and pulled out a card:

Dear Cleo,
A little floral tribute, somewhat fresher than the one you gave me. Hope you like this pizza better than the last one. Contact me. We need to talk.
— Mark Antony

Right, I was really going to jump to call him. I knew getting publicity was good, would help us find Amy. But this guy rubbed me wrong. He had enclosed a business card—just name, phone, and email, plus the word *Journalist*. No company affiliation.

So William Paveleck was freelance, not on staff with *Bay City Beat* or anywhere else. He could be a stringer, though, assigned to Amy's story. I phoned the *Beat* office and spoke to the editor. She had never heard of him. Somehow I wasn't surprised. Next I put his name into Google. Maybe I could turn up his byline on articles he'd written for other publications. The search yielded no results.

Claudia appeared in the doorway and announced, "Lunch is ready."

I joined the gang in the big space that did triple duty as kitchen, library and conference room. Tyler put a slice of pizza on a plate for me.

"Here, you look like you need sustenance."

"Thanks." I took a bite, surprised at how hungry I was.

"At least the guy's got good taste," Tyler said. "He got this from Formaggio's. Best pizza in the city."

"Even if I do go crazy fielding their phone calls," Claudia grumped. "Wish they'd get a new phone number that wasn't so close to ours."

"Maybe we can work out a deal with them," Tyler said. "One free pizza for every ten of their calls we get by mistake."

"Every five calls."

I changed the subject. "What happened to the client files that were on my desk? They're gone."

"I've got them," Tyler said. "Thought I'd do the follow-up work so you can concentrate on helping Nick."

"I've taken off two days already. I don't want to leave you in the lurch."

"Don't worry about it, okay? Our contribution to the cause. Besides, I won't have to spare you for long. Amy's going to turn up any minute."

"How can you be so sure?"

"Hope. Faith." He pressed his hands together as if he were praying. "We have to think that way. Because if she doesn't turn up soon, what's the alternative?"

Neither Claudia nor I wanted to answer that.

It was seventy-two hours since Amy was last seen.

With each hour that passed, her chances grew dimmer.

My appetite vanished as quickly as it had come. I set down my pizza and put the kettle on. A cup of tea would be warming. Soothing. Or so I hoped.

Tyler broke the silence. "Someone out there will spot her. The Find Amy website is already getting thousands of hits. We're linked to a bunch of other sites as well. And I've been researching Moritz's connections. Nick told me his theory the other night when we set up the website."

He didn't seem to know about the ransom demand. I'd keep that to myself.

Claudia took up the litany. "We'll find her. There are flyers all over the place, and I heard on TV that the Find Amy hotline's getting hundreds of calls. And they're conducting a door-to-door search in Creekhaven, and running checks on the whereabouts of sex offenders and parolees—"

"And they've got dogs combing the woods," I said glumly, "and they're dragging the creeks and the bay. Somehow this discussion is not making me feel better."

The office phone rang. I grabbed the extension before Claudia could, glad for the excuse to do something … anything. "Good afternoon, Parks and O'Meara."

The caller asked for me, and I recognized Nick Gardino's weary voice. I sat up straight and alert.

"This is Jess, Nick. What is it? News about Amy?"

"No. But no news is good news. At least I hope so, damn it. I wanted to let you know about the fundraiser tonight."

"The concert? Tyler told me about it. I wouldn't miss it."

Hearing Nick's name, Claudia and Tyler had looked up expectantly. At the word *concert,* they turned their attention back to the pizza.

Nick said, "Might be tough, pulling in people at the last minute like this."

"The Andante Quartet should be a big draw."

"We were lucky to get them."

"How are you getting the word out?" I took the kettle off the burner before it could shrill, and poured hot water into my mug.

"TV, radio, word of mouth. All of the volunteers are posting, tweeting and sharing on social media."

"I did that last night."

He thanked me, then said, "Terri's next-door neighbor, Lillian Harwood, is organizing the thing. The woman's amazing. She's got Channel Eight behind this big time. Paula Blakeney's going to do a live feed, and the station is sponsoring a special pledge line to collect money from viewers who can't make it to Creekhaven."

"Great idea. The money goes toward the, uh …" I glanced at Tyler and Claudia, not wanting to arouse their curiosity by saying the word.

"The ransom, right," Nick confirmed. "We're not announcing that publicly, of course. Frankly, I don't know if it'll do much good. We'll encourage the ticket buyers at the door to pay cash, but the pledge-line donations will all be check or credit card. Not much help for tomorrow."

"Rely on Jack Emerich," I told him. "He'll come through."

"Yeah, thanks for bringing Jack on board. He persuaded a nonprofit organization he works with to serve as the fiscal agent for the Coalition so donations can be tax-deductible. And he's hopeful about coming up with some big cash in time for the deadline."

Nick, on the other hand, didn't sound hopeful at all.

I wasn't sure I was, either, but I said, "Try to be optimistic. Jack can do it if anyone can."

"Optimistic. I'll have to remember that. See you tonight."

"Nick, wait," I said to stop him from signing off. "Terri's back. I saw her at the Hall of Justice."

A pause and a sigh. "Yeah. She showed up here this morning, thank God."

"Here?"

"I'm at her house."

"Not at the Hall? What about the trial?"

"Didn't you hear? The judge recessed it until next week. Said this little matter of Inspector Gardino's missing daughter was proving too much of a distraction to all concerned, but maybe by Monday it will have resolved itself. Christ, I hope he's right."

"How did the defense attorneys react to that?"

"Hell, it was their idea. In fact, they want him to declare a mistrial. There's no way the jurors can avoid hearing the news about this unfortunate and regrettable situation, sympathy for the father of the missing child will prejudice the jurors against their scumbag client, blah, blah, blah."

"And now there's Philip Vandergriff's murder to complicate things further."

"That hasn't come up yet at the trial. But I sure as hell hated being the one to tell Terri he was dead."

"You broke the news?"

"Yeah. I came back and stayed here last night. Figured someone should be here, just in case. I was here when Terri got home."

"Where had she been?"

"Out. What was she doing? Nothing. That's all I could get out of her. But I'm hardly her number-one confidant."

"But she's okay? She looked all right, but—"

"Yeah, she's fine. That's the good news."

"What's the bad news?" I asked, not sure I wanted to hear it.

"The bad news is," he said, "Terri doesn't have any alibi for the time when Vandergriff got himself killed."

CHAPTER 23

I LEFT THE CITY around seven, expecting clear sailing to Creekhaven. It was past commute time and the rain finally had stopped. But I'd forgotten it was Friday, which meant all traffic bets were off. Friday rush hours started early and ended late as people sneaked out before quitting time to get a jumpstart on the weekend, or lingered downtown for happy hour.

Friday. Amy had been missing since Tuesday afternoon. Three days. Seventy-six hours. It's the first forty-eight hours that count, experts said. After that the chance of finding a missing child safe get—

No. I wouldn't let myself think about the alternatives.

At eight o'clock, time for the concert to start, I was still crawling along Interstate 80 in a fume-ridden sludge of cars, vans, trucks. I was fuming myself, at the lack of progress. Hundreds of almost immobile taillights and headlights sketched red and white patterns on the surface of the night. Many of the eastbound vehicles had ski racks on top. Winter storms meant rain in the Bay Area but fresh powder in the Sierra. My brother Teddy was probably in one of those cars, headed for the slopes with his buddy Kyle's family. Better him than me. Ever since I was seven, the idea of romping in the snow had made me shudder.

At last I reached the Creekhaven exit. I took the road that led to the Powder Hill Mansion. The extravagant Queen Anne house was named not for snow, but explosives. I'd gone to a wedding there once, and picked up a pamphlet describing its history. High on a bluff overlooking the bay, the house was built in the late 1800s by the owner of a dynamite plant, who courted scandal by staging wild parties for the high-society set. But the factory blew up once too often, the business went bankrupt, and the dynamite king died of heartbreak when his fancy friends deserted him. Years later, his heirs donated the mansion, with all its towers and gables and gingerbread, to the East Bay Historic Trust.

The paved lot was full; parking had spilled over onto an adjacent field. Mud sucked at my boots as I hurried to the house, and the wind shook raindrops from tree limbs into my face. But the clouds overhead had thinned, and a silvery smudge of moonlight was seeping through. In the west, above the dark expanse of the bay, a hole had opened in the tattered covering, revealing a sprinkle of stars.

Yellow ribbons flapped from the mansion's lampposts. As I climbed the front steps I heard lilting notes from a violin. The music grew louder when I opened the door. I let in a gust of wind, which riffled the program flyers stacked on the table just inside. Lillian Harwood, behind the table, grabbed them before they could blow away.

"Tickets are ten dollars." She spoke softly to avoid disturbing nearby concertgoers.

I gave her a twenty and waved away the change.

"Thank you," she said. "Every dollar helps. There might still be a few chairs in the back."

The setup crew had pushed open the double pocket doors that separated front parlor, back parlor and dining room, creating a long, spacious recital hall. Rows of folding chairs, filled with people, faced a makeshift stage. No empty seats. I slipped in behind the last row and leaned against the flocked wallpaper.

The man standing next to me gave me a nod—one of the Creekhaven cops who'd been stationed on Amy's front porch. There'd be lots of police here watching for someone to act the least bit suspicious. I surveyed the crowd myself, but saw no one whose

forehead was obligingly stamped with a bright scarlet
K—*kidnapper, killer.*

Gradually the music eased my edginess, and I settled in to
listen. The musicians—two men and two women, all dressed in
tuxes—were making their instruments sing. Even from this
distance, I could see they were perspiring under the bright lights
set up by Channel Eight. They played Brubeck and Bach and
Broadway, striking a careful balance between cheer and solemnity.
Too lighthearted would demean the occasion, too somber would
distress an audience that was already tense and worried.

Then one of the quartet traded his viola for a clarinet and
announced the next number: "We're told this is one of Amy's
favorite songs. The words are a traditional Gaelic blessing."

The cellist stood, tossed back her blond hair and began to sing
in a clear, sweet soprano voice.

"Deep peace of the running wave to you ... "

Sadness engulfed me like a wave crashing on shore.

"Deep peace of the flowing air to you ... "

When Amy came to my house for her second art lesson, I put
on a Richard Stoltzman CD for background music. This song
started playing as Amy was putting the finishing touches on a
portrait of Scruff with bright orange fur.

"Is this a Christmas carol?" she asked.

"No," I said. "What makes you think so?"

"In Christmas carols they're always singing, 'Peace on earth.' "

"This is different," I said. "It means the kind of peace you find
in your heart. Like when you do something that make you feel
good about yourself."

Her face lit up. "I get it. It's a song about art."

"Art? Well, not exactly—"

"Sure it is." She dipped her brush in purple and gave Scruff an
eye with curled lashes. "Being an artist makes me feel good and
peaceful in my heart. Don't you feel that way?"

"Yes, now that you mention it, I do."

She made me play the song again, then again, and several more times before the afternoon was over. I sent her home with the CD.

"Deep peace of the gentle night to you ... "

Wherever you are, Amy, I hope you're having a gentle night.

A saxophone blared, tuning me back into the concert. The quartet finished their first set with an upbeat Gershwin medley that had people humming. The lights changed, and Paula Blakeney bounded onto the stage. The camera operators moved in close.

"Wasn't that splendid?" Blakeney said in her best television voice. She led a round of applause.

"The Andante Quartet will be back in twenty minutes. We thank them for donating their time and talent to this cause. And we thank all of you, whether you're here at the Powder Hill Mansion or watching at home, for your loving concern for Amy Gardino." She leaned toward one of the cameras. "I peeked outside a moment ago, and the skies are actually clearing. I'm taking that as a sign that we'll find Amy soon—safe, sound and healthy."

More applause, louder than before.

"Let's check in with the studio. Joel, what's the latest count on the Find Amy Pledge-a-thon?" A two-beat pause as she listened to her headset. "Fantastic! Ladies and gentlemen, the viewers at home have pledged ten thousand dollars! And we're only halfway through."

Ten thousand. My spirits sank. Barely a dent in what we needed to come up with for the ransom. I could only hope that Jack was meeting with success in his quest for funds.

Blakeney announced that coffee, wine and pastries were available in the solarium, and named the companies that had donated the refreshments. "Their generosity means every penny you spend goes to the Coalition. So indulge yourselves. You'll be helping Amy."

Following the audience into the hallway, I spotted the bobbing head of Creekhaven's mayor, Verna Spode, and the plumpish figure of Evelyn Talbot, Amy's babysitter. A few steps in front of me, Georgia Holcomb steered her daughter Hannah through the crowd, her hand resting on the child's spun-gold hair. Hannah wore a blue sweater and a red barrette; she had a wispy quality that reminded me of Renoir's "Girl with a Watering Can." Twisting around to shake off her mother's hand, she caught sight of me. Her eyes went wide and her mouth dropped into a round O of startled recognition. She faced front quickly, grabbing Georgia's sleeve.

No sign of Nick, or Terri.

The solarium was a huge semicircle of glass, with a terrazzo floor and a ceiling that rose to a peak against the main house, like half a circus tent. White-clothed tables had been arranged around the circumference and set with wine bottles, coffee urns, glasses and cups.

I got in a line and purchased a glass of cabernet. As I stepped away from the table, someone jostled my arm and I nearly spilled the wine.

"Oops, sorry." The speaker wore a grin under the white scar on his upper lip; his face revealed not one hint of remorse.

The Pizza Kid. Also known as William Paveleck.

"You again," I said. Of all the people I could have run into.

"Ah, the lovely Cleopatra. Did you get my message?"

"Yes. O'Meara sends thanks; he loves pizza. For him, though, you should have stuck with pepperoni. How did you know where I worked?"

"Wasn't hard." He looked much too pleased with himself. "I asked around at the community center. It's not like you were using a fake name or anything. Say, now that we're friends—"

He was interrupted by a woman carrying two glasses of white wine.

"Will? It's chardonnay. Is that okay?"

I had to look twice to recognize her. The polo shirt with the heart-shaped badge had been exchanged for a lilac silk blouse. The limp brown hair was pinned up in a French twist, and the sallow cheeks now had an attractive blush.

"Shanna! You two know each other?"

Shanna gave a radiant smile. "Not until today. After you left I called the Find Amy Coalition. They said they could use help setting up for the concert, so I locked up the shop and came right over." She looked warmly at Paveleck, who had taken one of the glasses and was gulping down the wine. "Will was here. He helped me put out all the chairs."

"Watch out," I said, only half in jest. "He's a journalist, you know. You're likely to find all your secrets under his byline on page one."

"Hey," he protested, "just because I see a story here doesn't mean I'm not a decent guy. I want a happy ending."

Just then I spied Nick and my Uncle Jack talking by a ficus tree on the far side of the room. A chance to escape. "Excuse me, I see someone I have to talk to."

"Be sure to stick around," Shanna said. "There's a surprise coming up."

I turned back to face her. Did she know something about Amy after all?

"What surprise?"

She giggled, enjoying her secret. "You'll see. You'll like it. Won't she, Will?"

"Even better than she likes pizza." He saluted me with his glass. "Ciao, Cleo."

I wanted to ask more, but he guided Shanna away, his hand at her waist. Leaving them to get better acquainted, I pushed through the crowd to the ficus tree. But when I reached it, Nick and Jack were gone.

"Jess! Over here."

My brother Keith, waving from a nearby refreshment table. Roger was paying for their purchases—wine for himself, while

Keith had grabbed a can of Coke and a brownie as big as a paperback book. I headed over to join them.

"I'm glad you came," I said. We exchanged quick hugs.

Roger said, "Wouldn't have missed it. It's a good cause. Besides," he added good-naturedly, "I never skip a chance to expose Mr. Hip-Hop here to real music." He leaned toward me and stage-whispered, "He's fallen in love with the blonde who plays the cello."

Keith made a show of rolling his eyes. "Don't be weird, Dad." But his face had turned beet red. To distract me he held out the brownie. "Want some, Jess? You look like you could stand a little nourishment."

"Thanks." I broke off a chunk. "You're right, I could. It's been a rough few days." Amy's disappearance. Philip's death. The search for ransom money. I felt bone-weary. I bit into the brownie, and the scent of chocolate hit my nose.

Suddenly I was back in the Cole Street apartment. Cookie crumbs in the kitchen. Philip's body on the floor. The stench of blood sharp in the air. Amy's crayon, broken and forgotten.

So close. Philip had been so close. What made him go there? I replayed our conversation at Dandelion. If only I'd said the right thing, asked the right question—would he still be alive? Would we have Amy back?

My head was spinning. For a second everything went black.

A voice in the distance: "Yo! Earth to Jess."

Keith waved his hand in front of my eyes. "You in there?"

Frankly, I wasn't sure. Then the lights blinked again, and from the main part of the house I heard instruments tuning up. We were being summoned back for the second half of the concert.

CHAPTER 24

THE IMPROMPTU AUDITORIUM darkened, then the stage was awash in light. This time I wedged myself into a standing-room spot right up front, in the opening that connected dining room and hall.

The TV cameras pulled forward to focus on Paula Blakeney.

"An update, everyone!" she announced. "The Find Amy Pledge-a-thon has now reached twelve thousand dollars!" She led the applause, then said, "But much more is needed. The toll-free number is on your TV screen. If you haven't called, pick up your phone right now."

Yes, I thought, everybody call in. Make pledges. Bring sacks full of cash so tomorrow we can pay the damn ransom.

"We have an incentive for you," she went on. "A Bay Area company is offering to match every dollar you give. Please welcome Creighton Oliver of the Moritz Investment Group."

Aha! Here was Shanna's surprise.

Creighton stepped up to the stage and struck a regal pose. When we'd had a chance to admire her rosewood-dark hair and flawless makeup, she launched into a speech:

"I'm pleased to announce this challenge grant on behalf of the Moritz Investment Group. You know us as San Francisco's premier real estate firm, but more important, we're people who understand what it means to lose loved ones in horrible circumstances. Our contribution to the Find Amy Coalition is a testament to our faith that there will be a good outcome—not only for Amy and her family, but for our company and its founder. The travesty of justice that's currently underway—"

"Thank you, Ms. Oliver!" Paula Blakeney cut in smoothly and urged Creighton offstage. "And thanks to the Moritz Investment Group. All of you, open your wallets. Remember, your donation will be matched dollar for dollar by—"

"Wait!"

Lacey Vandergriff dashed into the spotlight. The tan leather jacket she wore was too large for her—Philip's, the one he had on when I saw him yesterday. I was touched by her effort, however futile, to keep him close.

"I want to do this, too." Her hair looked windblown and disheveled. "I have a donation."

A man in a Channel Eight T-shirt hastened to give her a microphone. Paula Blakeney appeared delighted by the drama; she stepped aside to give Lacey center stage.

Lacey tapped the mike nervously. Ordinarily I'd have expected more composure from someone who earned her living in front of a camera making commercials. But under the circumstances I was surprised to see her here at all. She took a deep breath and began.

"My name is Lacey Vandergriff. The gift I'm announcing comes from SalesCom Technologies. My brother's company. Well, mine now, I guess. He … he died last night. I went there today—to his office, I mean—and the board took a vote. We're making this contribution as a memorial to him. Goodbye, Phil. We love you."

Handing Paula Blakeney the mike and a large brown envelope, she slipped away as abruptly as she'd arrived. The audience was silent for a moment before bursting into applause—tentative at first, and then heartfelt.

Paula took charge again. "Our sympathy to you, Lacey, and our deep appreciation to SalesCom Technologies. All right, everyone, follow this great example! Make your pledge now and make it large!" She waved Lacey's envelope high in the air.

"In a minute we'll resume the wonderful music by the Andante Quartet. But first there are two more people I want to introduce. I know you've been wanting to see them, so you can offer them your love and hope. Amy Gardino's mom and dad. Terri, Nick, please come on up."

She beckoned, and they emerged from nearby shadows. Paula reached for Terri's hand, Nick touched the small of her back and together they guided her onto the stage.

Nick and Terri stood close together, almost touching, as they faced the TV cameras and the crowd of well-wishers, neighbors, friends. I was struck by what a well-matched couple they made. Dark hair and eyes, compact builds and similar shapes to their faces. They looked comfortable together in a way that Terri and Philip had not. You'd never guess they were divorced, barely speaking—that this was the man Terri had accused of stealing her child.

They were dressed for mourning, Nick in a sober suit and tie, Terri in a plain navy blue dress. Lapel mikes were their only ornaments. Terri put up a hand to shade her eyes. The harsh TV lights bleached the color out of her face, flattened it, made her look ghostly. When she lowered her hand, her eyes seemed to glitter with panic.

"This ordeal has turned into a double nightmare for the family," Paula Blakeney intoned. "As his sister Lacey told you, Philip Vandergriff, who was Terri Shawcross's fiancé, died suddenly and tragically yesterday. Terri, we all offer you our condolences, and we admire your courage."

Nick gave his ex a taut smile of encouragement. Terri looked longingly at the exit.

"Th-thank you," she said. The words barely made it past her teeth. She cleared her throat and began again, louder. "Thank you for coming here and ... and being so supportive. People watching at home, too. I'm grateful to all of you and ... so is Nick. And Philip ... I'll miss him. If only he could be here. And Amy—oh my God, Amy! I love you, sweetheart."

Suddenly she spun around, stumbled from the stage. Whispers rippled through the crowd as she pushed past me and fled the room.

I turned and went after her. Behind me I heard Nick's voice, low and steady, as he picked up the interview and tried to restore calm.

Terri opened a tall oak door and disappeared. I followed, entering an old-fashioned butler's pantry outfitted with wooden shelves and glass-fronted cabinets. She collapsed onto a chair and buried her face in a stack of crisp white tablecloths. From the kitchen beyond came the bustle of people washing glasses, loading wine bottles into recycling barrels.

I gently placed my hands on Terri's shaking shoulders. She looked up, regarded me blankly with reddened, tear-stained eyes.

"Are you okay?" I asked. Dumb question. "What can I do to help?"

"N—nothing. I'm fine. Really. I'm—" And she was overwhelmed by a fresh burst of sobbing.

There was another chair in the corner. Pulling it over, I sat there, holding Terri's hand. She wasn't wearing her diamond ring. Music drifted in from the makeshift concert hall.

After a while I got up and went into the high-ceilinged kitchen, half stainless steel and modern appliances, half Victorian charm. An urn of coffee had its ready-light glowing. I poured some into a cup. Not knowing if she liked sugar or cream, I decided to leave it black. Then, not sure that caffeine would be the best medicine, I filled a wineglass with mineral water.

When I returned to the butler's pantry, Terri was dabbing her eyes with a tablecloth hem. I held out the two beverages. "I wasn't sure which you'd prefer."

"What I'd prefer is a draught of hemlock."

"I trust you don't mean that." I tried to say it lightly.

"I guess not." She took the water, then changed her mind and reached for the coffee. "A belt of brandy in this would be nice, though."

"You've been going through hell. I'm sorry about Philip—about all of it."

"Hell doesn't begin to describe it." She held the coffee to her nose and inhaled the rich aroma. "I keep trying to focus on little things. Coffee—it smells the same as before. The rain still turns the dirt outside to mud. My lungs keep working—air in, air out, just like always. How is that possible? The planet has been knocked out of orbit, yet things go on as if nothing's happened."

She sipped the coffee. Before I could think of anything soothing to say, she spoke again.

"When Amy vanished, when we didn't find her right away ... I thought, the world has ended, life can't possibly get worse. But I was wrong, wasn't I? Dead wrong. This morning when Nick told me ... about the ransom ... about Philip ... oh, Lord, I can't stand this any more."

"Things will get better. We're going to find Amy." I said it as much to convince myself as to reassure Terri. The words sounded hollow.

"Philip found Amy, and look what happened. He's dead. And my daughter's still gone."

Terri folded herself up, arms across her chest, hands on her shoulders, head bowed. "I should have walked out into the ocean when I had the chance. Let the tide carry me away. It would have been so much easier."

I heard applause from the main part of the house. The quartet began playing something livelier, jazzier, with a saxophone part.

"Is that where you went yesterday? To the ocean?"

"Yeah." She looked up, brushed limp curls away from her pallid face. "I went to the cabin. I thought, maybe he's hidden Amy there. I had to go see. I had to do something besides wait around and go crazy."

"What cabin?" I asked.

"Don't you know about it? Up on the coast in Mendocino. His dad owned it, an old fishing lodge. Nick inherited the place when his father died."

"You still think Nick took Amy?" I thought she'd given up that idea, had been convinced by the fear and love Nick displayed for his missing child.

"Not any more, with this ransom demand. Nick knows I haven't got money. There's no way he could profit from this. Unless ..."

"Unless what?"

"Well, what if it was a way to extort money from Philip? From SalesCom. Maybe he thought he could get Philip to pay."

Exactly what Nick had tried, I realized with alarm.

Nick could not have killed Philip. If McCabe and Rovinsky had reconstructed the crime correctly, Nick was walking into Chief Doyle's office last night with Carmen Aguilar and me when the fatal shots were fired in the Cole Street flat.

But Nick did ask Philip for cash to pay the ransom. What if he had staged Amy's abduction, hidden her in that dreary apartment in the care of a confederate, and faked the ransom note? Suppose Philip discovered the scheme and went there thinking he could overcome Nick's ally and bring Amy home.

Who could the ally be? And how could Nick be capable of such treachery?

My brain was spinning—there were so many theories about Amy's disappearance. I tried to steer the conversation back to what I hoped was safer territory. "Tell me about your trip to the cabin. We were worried—you were gone a long time."

"Yeah, longer than I expected," Terri said. "The rain made the driving slow. Then I got lost trying to find the place. Nick always drove when we went there; I never paid attention to the landmarks. I didn't get there until late afternoon. I remembered where the key was hidden, so I let myself in. It was freezing inside, all musty and dark. No Amy, no sign that anyone had been there in months."

She put the coffee cup to her lips. I felt a chill in the room, as if I were standing in the winter woods, peering into the shadows that lurked inside a damp, empty cabin.

"I felt so alone. And, well, defeated. I hiked down to the beach and walked for hours. Let the crash of the surf drown out my thoughts. I didn't even feel the rain and the wind. Of course I got soaked to the bone, and frozen. I went back, built a fire in the fireplace so I could thaw out. There were some supplies in the kitchen and I found a bottle of wine. I sat there staring at the flames and drinking wine, while outside it got darker and darker. Finally I decided I'd better go home."

She looked at me, shamefaced. "This part's embarrassing. When I stood up—well, I couldn't stand up. I knew I had no business driving. I dug out some blankets and curled up on the lumpy old sofa with its broken springs and didn't have another conscious thought until dawn."

"Why didn't you let anybody know where you were?"

"I meant to, but there's no phone there, and I forgot my cell phone. Before I left home, I called Philip to tell him where I was going. I got his voicemail. I thought he'd hear the message and spread the word. But he never … he never …"

I remembered Nick saying that Terri had no alibi for the time Philip was killed. "Did you see anyone while you were up in Mendocino?"

"No, I—" She was interrupted by another burst of applause, this one louder. She rose from the chair. "I've got to get out of here."

"The concert's almost over," I said.

"That's why I need to go now. Before I have to face all these people, and try to keep from screaming while they make sympathy small-talk and wonder if they dare to smile."

"They mean well."

"I know. I appreciate it. But they all have their families safe and sound. And I can't bear it."

"Come on," I said. "If you like, I'll drive you home."

"Thank you. I rode over with Nick, but he'll figure out where I've gone."

I led the way into the kitchen. The cleanup crew gave us curious glances as we stole out the back door into the windswept night.

"Br-r-r." Terri rubbed her arms.

"Where's your coat? I'll run back and get it." I was fighting shivers myself.

"A coat won't help. I feel like the cold is radiating out from the marrow of my bones. Come on, let's go."

Just enough light spilled from the windows to let us see our way. We scuffed through wet grass as we rounded the house. When we reached the front, I thought we'd made good our escape. But Georgia Holcomb and Hannah, both in thick parkas, were coming down the steps.

"Terri!" Georgia exclaimed. "I was so distressed to hear about Philip. I want you to know I'm praying for his soul."

Terri looked ready to bolt. But she managed to say, "That's good of you," and make it sound gracious. More than I could have done under the circumstances.

Hannah stared at me and pushed against her mother's side.

Georgia locked her hand on Terri's arm. "Such a tragedy when someone young like that passes. But the Good Lord has His plans for everyone, even though to us they're a mystery. God must love Philip especially well to bring him home to heaven while he's still in his prime."

"Please, Georgia—"

Trying to shake loose, Terri stumbled into me.

"Will you excuse us?" I said. "We need to leave. Terri's had an awful day."

"Mommy!" Hannah tugged on Georgia's jacket.

Georgia was blocking our way. "And Amy—there's no news?" She sighed as Terri, looking frantic, shook her head. "Well, Jesus loves the little children best of all. I'm sure He's watching out for Amy. I know—let's offer a prayer. Right now, all of us together. Our voices in harmony will rise to heaven and—"

"Mom-mee!" Hannah's voice was louder, more urgent.

Georgia gave her daughter a small, not quite gentle shove. "Not now, Hannah. Mommy's talking. Excuse her, Terri, she's getting over this flu. That's why I'm taking her home early. I don't want her to get overtired—"

"Mommy, listen!" Hannah jumped up and down. "Don't you 'member what I told you? 'Bout the lady with red hair? You know, when Amy got took."

She pointed a mittened hand at me.

"Mommy, don't let her get away!"

CHAPTER 25

H ANNAH HOLCOMB, LOOKING TINY, sat in a chair facing police chief Mac Doyle's big oak desk. Her mud-stained sneakers dangled above the floor. The red barrette had slipped, releasing wisps of hair to fly around her face. Two bright pink patches burned on her cheeks. I couldn't tell if the flush was a remnant of her flu or came from some intense emotion.

Doyle crouched in front of her, bringing his florid face to her level. "Now, little lady," he said in a kindly voice, "what did you see?"

Hannah didn't answer but fixed her eyes on me.

Periwinkle, I thought. Hannah's eyes are periwinkle blue. The color of the crayon we found in that horrible bloodstained apartment.

The other eyes in the room turned to stare at me—Nick's, Terri's, Georgia's. I squirmed in the heat of their gaze. My chair had been placed next to Doyle's desk like the witness box beside a judge's bench. Only here, I was the accused. I was not guilty of anything, but I felt defensive, angry and small.

Doyle glared the hardest. He hadn't wanted me present at this late-night questioning of Hannah. But Nick and Terri had both insisted, though for different reasons. Nick argued that I had a right to face my accuser, that Hannah's charge was nonsense, that the sooner we cleared this up, the better. But Terri's attitude toward me had abruptly turned cold. *If Nick and Jess are working some scheme together,* she'd told Doyle, *I want to know it now.*

In the end he'd relented, if only to keep Hannah, me and the whole situation out of the media's clutches. A few departing concertgoers had overheard Hannah's dramatic announcement, and the rumor that the kidnapper had been caught on the front steps had raced through the Powder Hill Mansion like a fire ignited by the dynamite the house was named for. We'd been chased to the police station by the Channel Eight news crew, two *Chronicle* reporters, William Paveleck and a pack of media types waving notebooks, cameras and microphones.

"Hannah?" Doyle tried again. "Can you tell us what you saw?"

Hannah chewed on her pinkie—a habit for comforting herself, I guessed. She turned to Georgia, who sat next to her daughter with both of their parkas bundled in her lap. "Do I have to, Mommy?"

"Must we put her through this, Chief?" Georgia demanded. "She's only six years old. It's very late, way past her bedtime, and—"

"If Hannah has information, Mrs. Holcomb, we need to know it."

"She doesn't know anything. Ever since Amy ... since it happened ... Hannah's imagination has run wild. Indulging her fantasies just makes her fearful. She—"

"Stop it, Georgia," Terri snapped. "Your daughter is fine. She's right here in front of you, alive and healthy. You can see her and hug her. While my daughter—"

She choked back a sob. Nick placed a steadying hand on her shoulder, but she shrugged it off. When she spoke again, her tone was softer. "I'm sorry. The tension is getting to me. Please—let Hannah tell us what she knows."

Yes, I agreed silently. What she knows, or what she imagines. Let's straighten out this mixup.

Georgia folded her hands atop the jackets. "You're right, Terri. I must count my blessings." She managed to sound both contrite and smug.

Doyle was still in his crouch. "Hannah, you want to help Amy, don't you?"

The spun-gold hair rippled as Hannah nodded. "Uh-huh. I prayed to God to bring Amy back."

"Good. We want her back, too. If you tell us what you saw, that might help us find her."

"Is it okay, Mommy?"

"Yes, honey." Georgia sounded resigned. "Remember, don't make anything up."

"Well, I saw that lady in a car." Hannah pointed at me.

"You mean Jess," Doyle said. "This lady here."

I started to protest, and was frustrated when Doyle waved me to silence.

"When was this?" he asked Hannah.

"When Amy got took. I was watching from my window."

Nick jumped in. "Whoa! You saw someone put Amy in the car?"

Georgia tapped Hannah's hand. "What did I say about making things up?"

"I'm not!" Hannah twisted toward her mother. Her whole face matched her flushed cheeks. "I saw Amy and I saw the car and I saw the lady and—"

Doyle rocked back on his heels. "Tell you what, Hannah, let's start at the beginning. Why were you at your window?"

"Cuz I got sick. Mommy called Amy's mother and said I wasn't going to school in the morning. 'Member, Mommy? 'Member how I asked to talk to Amy?"

"That's right," Georgia said. "This was Monday evening, Mr. Doyle. The night before this awful thing happened."

"Yes," Terri agreed. "The girls talked for quite a while." Her gaze drifted to a corner of the room. In her mind's eye, I was sure, she was seeing Amy chatting on the phone—such a normal, ordinary activity—and she was wondering if she'd ever see Amy do that again.

Hannah continued her story. "Amy said for me to watch from my window when school gets out, and me and her can signal each other. I stick one arm up"—she stretched her right arm high to demonstrate—"and that means I still feel bad. But if I stick up both arms like this"—she aimed her left arm toward the ceiling—"it means I feel better. And Amy can raise her arms and tell me how school went."

"I see," Doyle said. "A sensible system. So you were looking out your window last Tuesday afternoon, watching for Amy to come by."

"Uh-huh."

"Did you see her?"

"Yes. She raised up both arms and so did I."

"Was anyone with her?"

"No, she was all by herself. Most days me and her walk to Evelyn's house, but I couldn't cuz I was sick." Hannah's lips quivered. "Amy was all alone and she got took by a bad person."

Georgia brushed a strand of hair from Hannah's forehead. "Don't cry, honey. It's not your fault. You're being a big help. Mr. Doyle, you see how this is upsetting her. We'd better—"

Doyle ignored her. "What time was this, Hannah? Do you know?"

"What time did I see Amy?"

"That's right."

"Well, school gets out at three aclock. Mommy told me when it was time. I went to the window, and I waited, and then Amy came."

Doyle lumbered to his feet. Grimacing, he rubbed the small of his back. "You were home?" he said to Georgia.

She looked offended. "Of course. My daughter was sick. I had to take the whole week off work to care for her."

"But you saw none of this."

Georgia busied herself with straightening the sleeves of Hannah's parka. "I was in the kitchen making chicken soup. It's at the back of the house. You can't see the street from there."

Doyle groaned and cracked as he stooped down again. "Okay, Hannah, you and Amy signaled each other. What happened after that?"

"Amy waved goodbye and went away." Hannah swung her feet back and forth in a walking rhythm. Left, right, left, right. "She went down the street where it curves. I couldn't see her any more."

"But you stayed at the window."

"Uh-huh. Buster was out running in his yard. I stayed and watched him."

"Ah." Doyle's face brightened at the thought of a witness. "Who's Buster?"

Georgia sighed. "Buster is the poodle who lives across the street."

The chief looked as disappointed as I felt. "Darn," he said. I suspect he would have chosen a different word had a six-year-old not been present. "Guess he won't be able to tell us much."

"Course not, Mr. Doyle," Hannah said. "Dogs can't talk!"

"Okay, you were watching Buster. And then what happened?"

"A car came *zoom* down the street, really fast."

"What direction did it come from?"

Hannah swept her arm from right to left. "Like that."

"Like it was coming from Evelyn's house?" Georgia prompted.

"Uh-huh." Hannah nodded.

"What did the car look like?" Doyle asked.

"It looked sort of like Reverend Moyer's car, you know, Mommy, at church? Only it was gray."

"A Buick," Georgia said. "Reverend Moyer drives a red Buick Regal."

Nick said, "And you saw the driver, is that right, Hannah?"

"Uh-huh. It was her." Each time Hannah pointed at me, I felt it as a sharp jab. Terri was looking at me with eyes of ice.

"I'm sorry, Hannah." I tried to keep anger from creeping into my voice. "It wasn't me."

"It was too! You got red hair."

"It's easy to make a mistake when people have the same color hair. But the driver was someone else." I looked from her to the grownups. "I was in my office that afternoon. With witnesses."

"Tell the truth, Hannah," Georgia warned.

Hannah sat up as straight as she could. "I *am* telling the troof!" Then she crumpled and stuck her pinkie in her mouth. My frustration warred with an urge to comfort her with a hug.

"Don't get upset, honey," Georgia told her. "Close your eyes and ask the Good Lord to help you."

The little girl scrunched her eyes shut. Georgia bowed her head. The rest of us stayed silent. I couldn't even hear breathing. Maybe a prayer wouldn't hurt; I offered up one of my own to whatever gods might listen.

"It was fluffy," Hannah said at last.

"Fluffy," repeated Nick.

Hannah opened her eyes. "It was more fluffier than this lady's hair. It kinda stuck out." She put her hands against her head, spreading out her fingers like spikes.

"Okay, good." Doyle shifted in his crouch and gazed up at me, as if assessing my hair's fluff potential. "What else did you notice about the driver, Hannah?"

"She was going too fast. You woulda said so too, Mommy. You woulda said, *these maniacs 'dangering little children, they oughta frow drivers like that in jail.*" Hannah stuck her fists against her hips and put a nasal whine into her voice. A spot-on imitation of her mother. Doyle covered his mouth with his hand to hide his chuckle. I had to suppress one myself.

"Are you sure the driver was a woman?" Terri asked.

Hannah's face fell. "I ... I think so. Cuz of her hair. And men are bigger."

"Great," Terri said. "We've got a woman or a small, fluffy-haired man. That sure narrows it down."

"Or maybe a big bald guy," Nick put in. "Wearing a wig and

slouching down behind the wheel."

Doyle pulled himself up, gripping the edge of his desk for leverage. "We've got a possible car. That's more than we had before. Now, little lady, you've been a good, brave girl. What else did you see? Was Amy in the car? Was anyone else?"

"No. Just the lady driving." Hannah bobbed up and down in her chair. The flames in her cheeks burned brighter. "But what if she locked Amy in the trunk? Or knocked her out and hided her on the floor? Or made her lie down on the backseat and tied her up so she couldn't move—"

"Enough, Hannah," her mother cut in. "You're getting over-excited. Here, put on your jacket. Mr. Doyle, I'm taking my daughter home. She's been sick, and I don't want her to have a relapse. I'm sorry, Terri, I thought she might have something useful to say. But as usual she's letting her imagination carry her away."

"I'm not carried away," Hannah protested. "It's Amy that got carried away. I'm right here."

"Of course you are, honey. Let's go home. Mommy and the Good Lord will keep you safe."

"Why didn't the Good Lord keep Amy safe?" Hannah asked. But Georgia hustled the child out the door, so we didn't get to hear her explanation.

Chief Doyle slouched in his chair and ran his hand over his reddened face.

"Gotta ask, Jess," he said. "What kind of car do you drive?"

"An ancient Toyota," I said. "Honey beige. It doesn't look one bit like a gray Buick Regal."

"And Tuesday afternoon you were in your office, you say."

"Come on, Mac," Nick protested. "We know Jess didn't take Amy."

"I was in my office," I repeated. "In a meeting with a client that went from two to four. Our receptionist was there all afternoon, and around three my boss Tyler Parks came in with O'Meara. They'll all be happy to give you statements."

"Except O'Meara," said Nick. "He's an Irish setter."

"And as we were just informed, dogs can't talk." Doyle permitted himself a small smile. I hoped it signaled that I was off the hook. "Terri, you're awful quiet. Does what Hannah said mean anything to you? Know anyone with fluffy red hair? Man or woman?"

Terri was staring blankly at the litter of files and papers on Doyle's desk.

"What? I can't think of anyone who—no, it means nothing to me. I'm sorry. I wish it did."

The chief pushed himself out of his seat. "Okay, go home, try to get some sleep. Big day tomorrow, what with this ransom business. When and where is that meeting to get all our ducks in a row?"

"Eleven o'clock," Nick said. "Jack Emerich's office in the city. He's the accountant who's helping us out on this thing."

Doyle jerked his head toward me. "I'm not so sure about the plan to have *her* make the drop. Especially if this brouhaha made the news tonight. That means her face is known, and—"

"Jess is right for the job," Nick insisted. "I have total confidence."

"You would," Terri said. "The two of you have been together in this from the beginning."

"Hey, what do you mean?" Nick said. "You can't still be suggesting—"

Time to interject myself and stop the fray. "I thought we had this settled. I'm making the delivery, and that's that. I'll disguise my appearance somehow. And Nick and I aren't in anything together, except wanting Amy home."

Terri bit her lip and looked down at her arms, which she'd folded across her chest. I thought she might elaborate on her suspicions, but instead she said, "What about the money? Even with those two big donations, the concert couldn't possibly have raised enough."

Nick's posture sagged. "I haven't heard the final tally. But most of it's pledges, not cash."

Doyle snorted. "You can bet the kidnapper doesn't accept pledge cards."

Terri rubbed her finger where her engagement diamond had been. "That wretched pawnshop didn't give me anywhere near what my ring was worth. But no one else would give me cash."

"You pawned your ring?" I exclaimed. "Oh, Terri!" How sad that she'd had to give it up. Now that Philip was dead, the ring was the only thing she'd ever have of their dreams of a life together.

"What's important is Amy. The ring is just—" She dipped her head and whispered: "I was thinking of giving it back anyway."

Neither Nick nor Doyle reacted; I must have been the only one who heard.

"We've got twelve hours," Nick said. "We'll come up with something." He sounded more optimistic than he possibly could have felt. "Come on, Terri. I'll take you home."

As they went out the door, he put his arm across Terri's shoulders. This time she didn't resist.

I started to follow them, but Doyle stopped me. "Not so fast. I've got a few more questions for you, Jess. Maybe you didn't drive that car, but we have plenty to talk about."

I was exhausted when I finally left Mac Doyle's office. He'd grilled me about my work as an artist, my career as an investigator, my friends, my love life, my financial situation, my attitude toward kids, and every scrape I'd gotten into from kindergarten on. He made me spell out every detail of Amy's art lessons. He dug especially hard at my connection with Nick, and what I knew about Nick's relationships with his daughter and ex-wife. Doyle's manner roved back and forth between genial to gruff, and I couldn't tell if he believed a single word I said.

No one was around when I crossed the Civic Center plaza. The media horde had given up. I glanced at my watch. Past two o'clock. Eighty-three hours since Amy was last seen.

Eighty-three endless hours.

The plaza fountain was silent. The clouds had pushed east, leaving the sky half clear. Puddles glistened with reflections of moonlight. I spotted an agapanthus stalk pushing up from its spiky leaves. Thin stem, sparse blooms, struggling but alive.

When I reached the parking lot, I had to walk behind my Toyota to get around to the driver's door. Something on the taillight caught my eye.

A strip of black electrician's tape.

Whoever had been following me was trying again.

CHAPTER 26

WHAT WAS THAT NOISE?

At first I thought it rose out of a dream. A siren, a fire alarm, my mother's moans in the pain of her final days, a child's voice calling from a hollow tomb. Amy's voice.

Then Scruff barked and I jerked awake.

My cell phone.

Kit, calling from Hawaii? I fumbled the phone from the bedside table and murmured, "Aloha."

"Jess? Did I wake you?"

Damn. Not Kit. My sleep-fuzzed brain groped to recognize the voice. I pushed up from my pillow into a sitting position, rubbing my eyes.

The clock showed eight-fifteen. Damn again.

"No," I said to whoever it was. "I've been up for a while." That had been my intention anyway.

"Good news. We've accomplished our mission."

"Your—Jack?" Suddenly I was wide awake. "You got the money?"

"We pulled it off."

"The whole hundred thousand?"

"Every penny."

"Fantastic! You're a miracle worker."

"I had help. Nick arranged with Lillian Harwood to let me take charge of the concert proceeds. I'm now the official treasurer of the Find Amy Coalition. I don't know how one handles ransom

199

payments in the financial records of a nonprofit group, but we'll figure it out."

"But the concert couldn't have brought in near enough cash."

"More than I would have thought," Jack said. "The grant from Moritz won't generate any funds in time, but the SalesCom donation really helped. That envelope of Lacey Vandergriff's contained more than ten thousand dollars, all in cash. Terri and Nick each scraped together something from their personal funds. And I managed to come up with the balance."

"Where did you get it?"

"Ah! Trade secret."

"Come on, Jack. Tell me." A thought struck me. "Is it your own money?" Jack enjoyed a successful career, and I was sure he'd made wise investments, but I'd never thought of him as the kind of man to keep stacks of spare currency lying around the house.

"Well, I did shake a few pennies out of my piggy bank."

"Thank you."

"But most of it came from a client of mine."

"Who?"

"Not saying. She insists on being anonymous. I'll tell you this much. She's one of the richest women in the city, and she's terrified of earthquakes. She's convinced that when the Big One hits, the whole city will collapse and the banking system will be thrown into disarray."

"She could be right."

"Yes indeed. In addition to canned goods and drinking water, her earthquake kit contains large sums of cash that she stockpiles under the proverbial mattress—against my advice, I might add. She wants to be ready when disaster strikes. She agreed that Amy's disappearance qualifies as a disaster."

"You didn't tell her about the ransom, did you?"

"I pitched it as a donation to the coalition. But she may have guessed."

"She's an angel," I said.

"I told her that. She said she hopes she won't become an angel for many more years."

"Thanks so much, Jack. You deserve wings and a halo too."

"You can deliver them at the strategy meeting. See you at eleven o'clock."

As I hung up the phone, Scruff pushed his head under my free hand so I could scratch his favorite spot by his left ear. I surprised him by grabbing him in a huge hug.

I went downstairs and grabbed the *Chronicle* from the porch. The Bay Area section had an article about the fundraising concert for Amy, but there was no mention, thank goodness, of a suspect—me—being nailed there and hauled off for questioning.

I was too restless to read the rest of the paper, and breakfast was out of the question. My stomach was in knots at the thought of the task I was taking on. Yes, I was thrilled that we had the money. But what if I were stepping into a trap? Worse, what if I screwed up?

My gaze fell on the calendar on the kitchen wall. A Christmas gift from Kit, featuring a dozen of his photos. January, showing now, was a Sierra snow scene. That was snow the way I liked it—on paper, confined within a twelve-by-twelve-inch square.

In the date block for every Saturday, Amy had printed her name in neat red capital letters. If this were a normal Saturday, the one we'd planned, she'd be ringing my doorbell at one o'clock, ready for her art lesson.

Instead, at that precise hour I would be in the Japanese Tea Garden delivering the ransom.

Maybe I wasn't the right person to do this. I could call Nick, beg off, tell him to let one of his police colleagues handle the drop.

"I'm going to write my name on every Saturday for the whole year," Amy had said, red pen in hand, when we scheduled her lessons.

"How about just for January," I suggested. "You may find better things to do with your Saturdays."

"What could be better than painting?"

"Well, I like painting best, but you might want to try something else."

"Not me," she said. "Painting is forever."

Three letters printed in red. Amazing how something so simple could bring tears to your eyes.

I didn't dare back out. I was haunted by the idea that I'd inadvertently urged Amy to some kind of risky behavior. And I still felt frustrated that I was overlooking an important detail that could make a difference.

Be adventurous, take risks.

Delivering the ransom was one risk I could take that might really help Amy.

Sunshine greeted Scruff and me as we set out for our morning walk. Its sharp light glinted off houses and cars, giving the cold air a diamond brightness. The storm had scrubbed the sky clean and blue. To the east I could see a few straggling clouds, but the breeze from the ocean would soon blow them away. No sign remained of the fierce weather except puddles, and Scruff, his tail wagging, splashed through every one.

The pedestrians on Haight Street had light steps and cheerful smiles. I tried to match the general buoyant mood, but I was uneasy. I kept an eye on shrubbery and recessed entryways where a person trying to tail me might hide. Every few yards I glanced over my shoulder in case someone was lurking half a block behind.

Last night, driving back to the Haight, I hadn't been able to pick out any vehicle sticking too close. The closest parking place I could find was a block and a half from my flat. When I left the car I seized my heavy flashlight from under the seat in case I needed a weapon. I jogged the whole way home.

A weapon. Should I take one today? Go by P&O and pick up my gun from the office safe?

Back on Shrader Street, Scruff and I passed my Toyota parked at the curb. I checked the taillight where I'd ripped off the tape. There was residue from the adhesive, but otherwise the red lens was bare.

Scruff left a trail of muddy prints on the front stairs. I made him wait on the porch while I nipped into the foyer to grab the paw-wiping towel from its coat peg.

When I came out again, the door to Mrs. Fiorelli's flat opened and Atom burst through, shoeless, his skates in his hands.

As usual, Atom was dressed collar to socks in black, in contrast to the turquoise ridge of hair centered along his otherwise shaved scalp. Scruff yipped with joy and planted two still-unwiped paws on his thighs.

"Hey, Scruffle Duff! How ya doin', man?" Dropping the skates, Atom crouched to give Scruff a proper two-handed rub. "How 'bout this weather, hey? Bet you're glad to see the sun." In no time he was lying on his lumpy backpack while Scruff licked his face.

I grabbed Scruff's collar and backed him off—not that Atom minded the affection. The boy sat up, wiped his face with his hand, and grinned. "Hey, Jess."

"Hey back to you. What's going on?"

"Breakfast." The grin widened as he jerked a thumb toward Mrs. F's door. "I ran into Davy on Haight Street this morning. Mrs. F sent him out to get maple syrup. He invited me back for blueberry-pecan waffles. An offer I couldn't refuse."

"That would be foolish in the extreme," I agreed. Mrs. F's waffles were legendary in the neighborhood. So were her cookies and her minestrone and her pasta with puttanesca sauce and her homemade pizza and ...

For the briefest instant I was starving; then my stomach clenched. Nerves, I told myself. Jitters. Everything would go fine, we'd have Amy back this afternoon. If I repeated that mantra often enough, hopefully it would come true.

Atom rocked to his feet and stretched to his full height. He brushed at his clothes in an ineffectual effort to remove the muddy traces of Scruff's ardor.

"Gotta run," he said, adding nonchalantly, "Cops are after me."

"Atom! What for? Are you in trouble?" The question probably should have been: *What are you in trouble for this time?*

"Me?" He put his hand over his heart and jumped his voice an octave higher. "I didn't do nothin', officer. I swear I'm innocent."

"Only until you're proven guilty," I said, faking sternness.

He reverted to his normal tone. "You remember the guy that bumped into me the other day? In front of the bookstore?"

"The one Pete Best knocked down." My God, had Philip Vandergriff reported the incident to the police? Surely they didn't suspect Atom of killing him.

"Yeah. Well, talk about weird—that very same night, the dude gets murdered. Say, didn't I see you there? Going in the building with the cops? What was it like to—" He put his hand to his mouth. "Oh, jeez, I'm sorry. Was he your boyfriend or something? I should give you, what is it, condolences, right?"

I remembered noticing Atom in the crowd that had gathered outside the murder scene. "I knew him, but we weren't friends. What do the cops want with you?"

"Well, you know the old dude that owns the bookstore? Turns out he was at the door and saw the guy take his tumble. So he tells the cops, and they come and, like, drag me off to jail. I had to spend all yesterday afternoon talking to them. And they want me back today." Beneath his whine of complaint I detected a clear note of boasting.

"They took you to jail?"

"Well, the Hall of Justice. This creepy little room where they give people the third degree. Don't worry, I did you a favor and kept your name out of it."

That sounded ominous. "Kept my name out of what, exactly? It's no secret that I went to the murder scene."

Atom sat on the top step and shoved his feet into his skates. "Yeah, but the cops don't know you were part of the bookstore thing, right?"

Actually they didn't, I realized. I'd told McCabe and Rovinsky about the lunch I'd had with Philip, but I'd neglected to mention the run-in with Atom—probably because I'd learned nothing from it except that Philip could be a bit of a self-righteous prick.

Atom went on: "I told them about the other woman, though."

"What other woman?"

"The black-haired chick. I saw him go in and out of there with her a few times. I'm glad he wasn't your boyfriend or nothing, because if he was, he was cheating on you."

"Wait a minute. You saw Philip Vandergriff go in and out of where? The building where he died?"

"Yeah. He lived there, didn't he?"

"When did you see him?"

He shrugged one black leather shoulder. "Dunno. Couple days ago."

I tried not to sound exasperated. "Could you be a little more specific?"

"Well, one time was in the morning. I was on my way to the bakery, the one that's in that same building? I wanted to see if I could talk Mrs. Ying into giving me some doughnuts, ya know, like on credit. He and this lady were coming out of the door that leads to the apartments."

"Which morning, do you remember?"

He rubbed his cheek while he thought. It was covered with reddish fuzz, as if he'd skipped his once-a-week shave.

"Wednesday maybe? Or Thursday. Another time, I saw 'em

going in. The same day, I think, only it was night, like ten o'clock, eleven maybe."

"What did the woman look like?"

"Black hair, like I said. Shortish, kinda curly. She looked hot for an old chick."

"How old was she?"

"I dunno. Your age at least."

"What? You think I'm an old chick?"

"Well, not old old. Just kinda—"

I didn't find out kinda what, because Mrs. Fiorelli's front door banged opened again. Davy, the eldest of her foster children, came out, holding a black nylon wallet. He was ten but looked smaller, a scrawny boy whose dark eyes were almost hidden beneath a thatch of brown hair.

"Hey, Atom. Look what you forgot!"

"Whoa! Wouldn'ta got far without that. Thanks, dude." Atom stuffed the wallet into his backpack. As he finished lacing up the skates, Mrs. F appeared at the door. From the depths of her flat I heard a couple of the other kids raising some sort of ruckus.

"Here you go, I fixed a doggie bag. But it's not for you, doggie," she told Scruff, who was sniffing eagerly at the brown paper parcel. "It's for Atom. A sandwich for later, chicken with roasted peppers. This boy is too skinny, Jess. He needs filling out."

Atom accepted the lunch with thanks and a wave, then skated off. Davy and Scruff watched him until he reached Haight Street.

Mrs. F must have decided that I needed filling out too because she said, "Come on in, Jess. All these youngsters I fed, and I still got waffle batter left. Help me put it to good use."

Any other morning, I would have accepted. "Thanks, Mrs. F, but I have something I need to do this morning. By the way, did you happen to see the TV news last night? Was there anything about Amy—the missing girl?"

She pulled Davy next to her, ran her hand over his thick hair. "Such a sad thing. I feel bad for that girl's family. The news said there was a concert to raise money to help search for her. I'm going to send a check."

"It will be appreciated. Did they mention a suspect being spotted at the concert?"

"No! You mean they know who did it? Have they found her?"

"I guess it was a false alarm." Good—nothing in the paper, nothing on TV. I wanted to remain unknown, a shadow at the edge of the case. That would improve my chances of delivering the ransom this afternoon without a hitch.

And tonight, if all went well—if it pleased the gods, if I didn't make some tragic error—we would welcome Amy home.

CHAPTER 27

A
S I DROVE DOWN Haight Street a short time later, my mind was going crazy trying to make sense of Atom's information. Several times he saw Philip Vandergriff outside the building where Amy'd been held and Philip was murdered. Had Philip been scouting the place, trying to figure out how to rescue Amy? If so, how had he found her? And the woman he was with—a woman who was my age, who had curly black hair ...

A good description of Terri.

I caught a sudden movement in the corner of my eye. I jammed on the brakes just in time to miss hitting a greasy guy in a camouflage jacket who'd bolted into the street from between two parked cars. He slammed his fist on my hood and raised a menacing finger at my windshield. I returned his salute as a horn behind me blared.

I jumped into the first empty parking place I saw and tried to deep-breathe myself back into calmness. Then I got out, fed the meter and walked to my first destination, Bountiful Books.

The flyer with Amy's picture was still posted in the bookstore window. *Take heart, Amy,* I whispered. *We'll be with you soon.*

I found Nolan Aldridge kneeling on the floor of the mystery section slotting new paperbacks onto the bottom shelf. With his red sweater and snowy beard, he looked like a skinny Santa tucking presents under a Christmas tree.

When I greeted him he stood and dusted his hands on his trousers. "If you ever write a book," he said, "choose a pen name in the middle of the alphabet. Then you won't have to crawl around down there with all the Y's and Z's to find it."

"I'll keep that in mind," I said.

"I'm sorry, I know you're a regular customer, but I'm not coming up with your name. Art books, right? Contemporary fiction. And didn't you buy that wonderful fat album of John Pearson's nature photography at Christmastime? A gift for someone special—I seem to recall wrapping it in the paper with the silver stars."

"Yes. Someone very special." I felt a pang at the memory of the holiday just past. Kit and I spent the morning at my place exchanging presents and making my mother's traditional chocolate velvet pie. In the afternoon we went to Berkeley for dinner with Roger and the boys. This was our third Christmas without Mom, and the first where we'd allowed a stranger to intrude upon our awkward, sorrow-tinged celebration. I'd been nervous about inviting him, but Kit's presence took an edge off the sadness. He helped Keith set up his new electric keyboard and added his off-key baritone to our impromptu carol choir. He took Teddy up to Tilden Park to try out his new skateboard. He chopped onions and simmered cranberries and blended a perfect lump-free gravy. Not a stranger, I thought as we ate the pie in front of the fireplace. Kit is one of us. There's something real here. Something strong and permanent that I can build a future on.

But when he'd offered me that future, I'd balked. Now Kit was in Honolulu, frolicking on the beach. And I was here alone.

"What can I help you with?" Nolan Aldridge asked, cutting through my momentary fog.

I told him my name and why I was there—to find out what he'd seen of the collision between Atom and Philip Vandergriff and what he'd told the police.

"Terrible situation," Aldridge said, shaking his head. "The second time in a year that this store has been touched by murder. You can imagine my shock when I heard about it, having just seen

Mr. Vandergriff that afternoon. A customer, a neighbor. I knew the police would be interested in his activities on the day he died, so I told them about Atom running him down."

"That had nothing to do with his death."

"Well, I don't want to get the boy in trouble if he doesn't deserve it."

"He doesn't," I said. "Not about this anyway."

Aldridge nodded. "I see him around a lot, and he seems like a decent enough kid, for all his show of being tough and wild. He has too much time on his hands though, for a young man that age. What's his home life like, do you know?"

I remembered Atom's giving Philip a false address. "No. I don't even know where his home is."

"Or if he has one." Aldridge looked thoughtful. "It's rough growing up these days for a lot of kids. My own son can attest to that. So could Robin Moritz. Did you know her?"

"Yes. I liked her a lot. You were close to her, weren't you?"

"She'd become family. She lived with my wife and me for a while after I hired her. She'd just finished the New Dawn program and was struggling to make it in the real world, clean and sober, with a straight job. Her own family—well, talk about dysfunctional. What happened to her certainly demonstrated that."

Looking suddenly fatigued, he leaned against the tall bookcase full of mysteries. "I testified at her father's trial this week. That brought it all home again—three people gunned down right in front of my store! I'd just returned from court when I saw the incident with Atom and Mr. Vandergriff. Next thing I know, the man has been murdered." He took off his glasses, pinched the thin bridge of his nose. "Too damn much violence in this world. It's hard to understand how the human race manages to survive the horrific things we inflict on each other."

"Why do you suppose Moritz killed Robin?" I asked.

"I don't know. Robin refused to talk much about her father. I could tell she didn't like him, didn't trust him—she was afraid of him, I think. New Dawn encourages its clients to deal with people who've wronged them, and I had the impression that Robin was working up the nerve to confront her father about something. But I don't know if she ever did."

"Whatever Moritz's motive, it seems strange that he'd kill three people in such a brutal, public way."

Aldridge plucked a paperback from a stack on top of the bookcase. I caught a glimpse of the cover. Blood-red lettering above a garish arrangement of gravestones and guns.

He said, "I wondered at first if Eric might have been the target. The police looked into that, I'm sure. But his life seemed so straightforward. No problems with the law, no reason to have enemies."

"He and Robin seemed happy together?"

"Getting together with Eric was what really turned Robin's life around. They met here in the bookstore, you know. I was with Robin behind the counter that day when her sister came in. What was her name ... Sandra?"

"Shanna," I said.

"That's it. Sad little mousy thing." He scanned the shelves, then shoved the book into place. At eye level, I noticed.

"That author's name starts with L," I said.

"What? Oh, right. You see how it works." He smiled wanly. "Anyway, Shanna stopped by sometimes to say hello, maybe to join Robin on her coffee break. This time she had Eric in tow. She'd brought him expressly to meet Robin. She clearly has a gift as a matchmaker. I saw the spark ignite between Robin and Eric right away. Next thing I knew, she was moving out of my place and into his."

"How long were they together before—"

"Before tragedy struck? Not long enough. They should've had many happy years in which to enjoy each other and their child. But that's not what you meant. Shanna introduced them a couple

211

of years ago. They were killed last January, almost exactly one year ago. They were planning their wedding for Valentine's Day."

"I wonder why they hadn't already gotten married. If they loved each other and had a baby on the way ..."

"That's easy," Aldridge said. "The trust fund."

"Robin had a trust fund?"

"Eric did. He came from wealth. His mother's family owns a restaurant empire. Her father set up trust funds for his grandchildren. Quite hefty sums, as I understand it. Eric's money would go to him on his twenty-fifth birthday, but only if he was still unmarried. The old man had a foolish alliance in his early youth and he didn't want his grandkids making the same mistake."

"I see. So if they were planning a wedding on Valentine's Day, Eric's birthday must have been February thirteenth."

"The tenth, actually. They figured if they'd waited that long, what was four more days to achieve the proper romantic moment." He picked up another book, its cover adorned with a noose.

"What happened to the money, since Eric died before he could claim it?"

"It got distributed among the rest of the grandchildren, I suppose. It's a large family. Each one's share of Eric's fund couldn't have amounted to much. Certainly not enough to kill for."

Aldridge slid the book into its home. I used to devour mystery novels like candy. Lately, though, murder was losing its appeal as a form of entertainment.

"Follow the money," Aldridge said. "For a long time I thought that's where the answer would lie. But then they arrested Carl Moritz. Turned out I was wrong."

The mention of money made me glance at my watch. Ten-thirty—time to get to Jack's office. I thanked Nolan Aldridge and went out into brilliant sunshine. I hoped the fine weather was a good omen.

Today I'd be following the money myself. Or more accurately, carrying it to the Japanese Tea Garden where—I crossed my fingers—it would lead us to Amy.

CHAPTER 28

"**N**O." NICK HAD STEEL in his voice. "No cops."

"The kidnappers'll never know," said his partner, Ray Beschke. "It's all set up, Nick, a very discreet operation."

"I said no." Nick crossed his arms, resolute. "The instructions were clear. No cops but me."

None of us spoke. The tension in Jack Emerich's conference room tightened another notch.

There were seven of us gathered around the teakwood table. My companions' faces looked grim, fatigued, worried. So did mine, most likely.

I gazed at the wall clock. Eleven-thirty. Less than an hour and a half to go.

To steady my fluttering nerves, I reached for my mug. The tea had gone cold and tasted bitter.

When we arrived, one by one, Jack had shown us into this room. As soon as everyone was present, he laid out the money he'd collected, provided a list of the serial numbers and reported on where the cash had come from. Then he withdrew to his office, leaving us to hammer out the details of the ransom delivery.

So far, we weren't having great luck.

Mac Doyle drummed his thick fingers on the table. "Come on, Nick, be reasonable. We were up the whole damn night arranging things."

"That's right," said Anna Rovinsky, Nick and Ray's homicide colleague. "We've got our people filling in for the Tea Garden

214

staff, and a few playing tourist. There's a command post next door in the de Young Museum, in an office, out of the way. And a video camera mounted on the underside of the footbridge that goes over the spot where the drop is to be made."

"It's mostly guys off-duty, Nick." Beschke rubbed his hand over the unshaven stubble on his bulldog jowls. "Volunteering their free time."

"I appreciate it. Really. But this is my little girl we're talking about." Nick shot a glance at Terri, seated next to me. "*Our* little girl. I won't do one damn thing to jeopardize getting her back safe."

"Jesus, man," sputtered Doyle, his face reddening. "You think for one second we'd do anything to put her in danger?"

"It's a clean operation, Nick." This from the FBI agent, Carmen Aguilar. "We've thought it through and—"

Nick jumped to his feet. "No! How many times do I have to say it? The more people there are, the bigger the chance of a screwup. Not to mention it'll piss off the kidnappers. We don't know what kind of crazies we're dealing with here."

"Having backup's a good idea, Nick," I said. Personally, I felt reassured by the notion of having a police team behind me. But the question was, what would be best for Amy?

"The creeps will never know we're there. Swear to God," Beschke said. "Terri, talk sense into the man."

Terri refused to look at any of us. She stared down at the coffee mug clutched in her hands. Her face was drained of color, so pale it looked translucent, and she was holding herself rigid. If she moved, I was afraid she would shatter like blown glass.

When she spoke, her words were so faint I could barely hear them. "I want Amy back. That's all that matters."

"Since it's all in place, I say leave it," said Carmen Aguilar. "If everything goes right"—she knocked on the polished teak—"then nobody will have to make a move, except Jess when she drops off the money, and Nick and Terri when they hug their daughter. If something goes wrong, God forbid—well, then we're prepared."

"She's right, Nick," Doyle said. "You know that. If you use your professional judgment—"

"Professional judgment," Nick muttered. He sank back into his chair, his face contorted with anguish. My heart ached for him. "You know why I wanted to be a cop, one of the main reasons? Because I thought cops had answers. But you know what? In my professional judgment, not one of us has got the least frigging clue."

"Nick?" Terri ventured. She was spinning her mug around on its paper coaster. I could see the sheen of tears in her eyes. "Maybe they're right. Maybe we should play it this way."

Nick lowered his head, pressed fingers tight against his temple.

"Last week, if I was talking to the father of some kid who'd gone missing, I'd have said the same things you guys are all saying. But this isn't *some kid.* This is Amy!"

Anna Rovinsky took off her glasses and rubbed them on her sweater sleeve, as if clean lenses might help her find the answers that were eluding Nick. Eluding all of us.

"You would've been giving that father the right advice, Nick," she said. "So let's forge ahead and do the best job we can."

"Christ, I don't know. I just don't know—"

"Recovering Amy is priority one, we all agree on that," Rovinsky said. "But remember, there's been a homicide too. What goes down this afternoon could help us get a handle on finding Philip Vandergriff's killer."

Terri made a strangled sound.

I touched her arm. "Are you okay?"

Her reply was not at all what I expected.

"Such a small amount of money," she murmured.

She pointed to the center of the conference table.

The ransom cash. Three neat stacks of bills in rubber bands, not much higher than my tea mug.

Terri shook her head in disbelief. "One hundred thousand dollars. Somehow I thought it would be bigger. At least as big as Amy is."

"Me too," I agreed.

When I first saw the money I'd been shocked at how paltry it looked. And relieved. In my dreams last night I'd carried a sack of cash so huge I could barely get my arms around it. Its surface was lit with neon dollar signs that flickered and flashed. All the low-lifes in San Francisco hovered around me like feral cats stalking a fallen bird.

"Okay," Mac Doyle said. "Let's load this stuff up. We don't have much time left. You ready, Jess?"

My skin felt clammy, my stomach queasy.

"Absolutely."

Doyle gave me a look I couldn't quite read. He'd been brusque toward me this morning, as if he still suspected I was guilty of being the red-haired lady Hannah Holcomb saw. No doubt he'd called Tyler Parks first thing this morning to verify my alibi for the time Amy was taken.

"It's not too late. You can back out," he said.

"I'm not backing out."

"Beschke can handle the drop. Or Rovinsky here."

"Damn it, I thought we'd had this settled. I'm going to do this. I went to the Tea Garden late yesterday afternoon, before the concert in Creekhaven. I scoped everything out. I found the right trash can, the right bush—"

Beschke broke in. "The bush with the gold-dust leaves?"

"Yes. The leaves are variegated. Green with yellow spots. Look, I'm ready. I know what to do."

Terri gripped the edge of the table and sat up straight.

"Let me do it," she said.

All eyes turned to her.

"That's a noble offer, Terri," Anna Rovinsky began. "But I don't think—"

"I'm her mother, I should be the one. I need to do something. I need to help bring Amy back."

Doyle frowned. "It makes much more sense to have a cop—"

Nick slammed his fist on the table. "I said no cops! Not for the drop. Christ, at least give me that much. They'll be watching, we can count on it. If they see we're not playing by their rules—"

"What rules?" Beschke demanded. "Who gave the scumbags the right to set the rules?"

Carmen Aguilar stood up and banged a spoon against her coffee mug. "Everyone! Stop it!"

We all froze as if a bolt of electricity had jolted the room.

"That's better," she said. "Jess will make the drop, like we agreed. Let's not rewrite the script while the curtain is going up. That's asking for disaster."

"What about Amy?" I asked. "Once we've done our part, do we know how and where she's going to be released?"

"A stone lantern," Terri whispered.

Rovinsky looked puzzled. "A what?"

"A call came this morning," Nick said. "The voice was distorted like before. The caller said instructions for finding Amy are taped inside a stone lantern in the Tea Garden."

"Jeez, what kind of idiot scheme is that?" Beschke said. "Suppose someone finds it first, some kid maybe—"

"What if we do a sweep?" offered Rovinsky. "The team in the Tea Garden can check the lanterns. We might not need to leave the money after all."

Nick waved the idea away.

"They're watching, I tell you. I'm supposed to look for the note when the ransom's been dropped. They said if anyone else finds the note first, the whole deal's off."

He glared at his colleagues in turn: Doyle, Beschke, Rovinsky and finally Aguilar.

"Don't worry, Nick," Carmen Aguilar said. "We'll leave the task of retrieving the instructions to you, like they asked."

"Yeah." Beschke nodded. "We're here to help. We're not gonna screw things up."

Aguilar's fingers pushed her dark bangs askew. "All right, then. Let's get started."

Silence fell over the room. We all eased forward in our chairs. My nerves were zinging.

Mac Doyle picked up a stack of bills and snapped the rubber band.

"Earthquake phobia," he muttered, recalling Jack's account of where the cash had come from. "Who would have believed it?"

Aguilar set two white plastic bags on the table. No flashing neon dollar signs. They were adorned with black brushstrokes of calligraphy and a red circle for the sun. Emblazoned beneath the image were the words JAPANESE TEA GARDEN.

She began taking things out of the bags.

"What's all this?" Beschke asked.

"I had to buy stuff at the souvenir shop to get these. If I asked for empty bags, someone might remember."

She laid out her purchases: postcards, fortune cookies, a San Francisco guidebook, a delicate doll in an elaborately embroidered kimono.

"For my niece," but she held the doll close to her chest as she spoke. I suspected it was going home with Aguilar herself. "Someone open the cookies. Let's make sure luck is with us."

Beschke ripped apart the cellophane wrapper, removed a cookie and sent the package around the table. When it reached Terri, she hesitated, then shook her head and passed it to me.

I took one. A bit of flour and sugar folded around a secret. My heart pounded as I broke it open. Don't be silly, Jess, I told myself. It's your standard generic fortune, worded to apply to anyone. Means less than a newspaper horoscope.

I pulled out the little slip: *You are in a position to do a friend a great favor. Use your power wisely.*

"Ha!" Beschke said. "Mine says, 'You will handle a great

fortune.'" He snorted. "Doesn't say it's my fortune. Maybe it means I should deliver this money instead of Ms. Ace Detective."

I started to protest.

Nick said, "No. We'll stick with Plan A."

Beschke put up his hand, a *stop* gesture. "Hey, a joke, okay?"

Aguilar loaded the rubber-banded cash into one of the white bags. The postcards and guidebook went back into the other. She kept the doll aside.

Doyle checked his watch. "Almost noon. Time to roll. Jess—you know where to go, what to do, right?"

"Right," I said.

"Nick, you're going to the Tea Garden too, but stay away from Jess until after the drop is made. When you find the instructions for recovering Amy, contact us the minute you think it's safe. You have everyone's cell phone numbers, and the guys posted in the park have radios."

Nick asked, "Who's in charge of the Tea Garden team?"

"Dal Humphreys," Beschke told him.

"Good man," Nick said.

I nodded in agreement. I knew Humphreys; a good choice.

Aguilar said, "Depending on what happens, you might actually appreciate having some fellow cops there."

Nick stiffened. "Don't worry. I'll handle things."

Doyle continued, "The rest of us, including you, Terri, will station ourselves at the museum in the command post."

Nods all around.

"Okay, let's go."

We scrambled to our feet.

"Nick and Jess first," Aguilar said. "The rest of us should stagger our departures. Better we don't all leave at once, in case they followed one of us here and are watching the building. We'll meet at the museum."

She handed me the plastic bags. I pushed them into the tote bag I'd brought.

Jack met us in his reception area and saw us to the door. "Good luck, honey," he whispered to me.

"Thanks for everything." I kissed him on the cheek and left the safe confines of his office.

Going out onto the street, I clutched the tote bag tightly. It was surprisingly lightweight, yet it was one of the heaviest burdens I'd ever carried.

When I reached my Toyota, I checked the taillight. Thank God, no black tape. I decided to consider that a good omen.

CHAPTER 29

BREATHE DEEP, JESS, I told myself. You can do this.

Usually a visit to the Japanese Tea Garden wove a spell on me, making me feel calm, at peace. Not today. My heart thumped madly as I approached the tall wooden entrance gate. A tumult of emotions—hope, dread, panic—threatened to spin me out of control.

Since moving to Shrader Street I'd been coming to the Tea Garden regularly. I followed the meandering paths to find inspiration for my paintings, or to regain my balance when life knocked me off-center.

I loved the idea of a work of art in four dimensions. With a painting you created a world on a flat surface. With sculpture you brought the work out into space; you could walk around it and touch it. The Tea Garden added the element of time. You were invited to linger inside the artwork, marveling at the masterful arrangement of pines and cypress, rocks and water, wind-tossed green leaves and flashing orange-and-silver koi. At each hour and in every season, the garden offered a new experience.

My favorite time there was when the fog drifted in, softening the colors, blurring the treetops and the spire of the pagoda. I tried to visit in the early morning or late afternoon, when the crowds were small. That's when the magic worked best.

Today all the magic had disappeared.

Hoisting the tote bag to my shoulder, I joined the long line of restless people queued up to get in. Buses out front spewed exhaust. Babies fussed in strollers, and shrieking kids ran up and down the sidewalks. Despite the cold, it was a brilliant Saturday afternoon, the sun shining for the first time in a week—everyone who hadn't gone to the ski slopes was flocking to the park. The Tea Garden had the jangled energy of Pier 39 at its touristy worst.

Or maybe I was the one who felt jangled.

My job was simple. Drop the white bag full of cash in its assigned place, then get out of the way. And don't call attention to myself in the process.

The guy inside the ticket booth looked like a college kid, not a cop, but I knew better. As I paid the admission fee, he gave no sign, not so much a lifted eyebrow, to indicate whether he knew who I was. Once through the gate, I took the path to the right that led to the restrooms. Inside a stall, I opened my tote bag and took out the plastic sack full of cash. It felt hot to the touch; it seemed to vibrate and burn.

Keep the brakes on your imagination, Jess. Stay focused. Don't get carried away.

I took another deep breath and sauntered out, clutching the tote to my side but swinging the white bag in my hand. Just another tourist with souvenirs for the folks back home.

Ten minutes to one.

I wandered to the terrace where the tall bronze Buddha presided, stopping to pay my respects. *Please make this go right,* I whispered. Buddha sat impassively on his lotus flower, hand upraised, eyes closed, head haloed by a circle of tarnished green. I couldn't tell if he heard me or not.

From there I stepped onto the Long Bridge and peered over the side. Beneath me I could see the square pebble-surfaced trashcan and the bush with the gold-dust leaves. Big glossy leaves, dark green mottled with bright yellow patches, as if someone had splattered them with paint. Three denim-clad teenagers came along the path; one of them tossed a candy wrapper at the trash can and missed. They walked on, oblivious, carefree.

Scanning the scene, I spotted nothing amiss. Even at midday, the January sun angled sharply, creating patterns of intense light against harsh shadow. The azaleas bore a few brave, early blossoms, punctuating the landscape with dots of red.

Nearby, the wooden Drum Bridge arched over the water, a perfect semicircle. At its base stood Dal Humphreys, who was in charge of the team in the park. Casual in jeans and a fleece jacket, he didn't look like a man running an intricate police operation. He was watching a gaggle of laughing kids who could have been his own—same frizz of black hair, same coffee-hued skin—as they climbed the ladder-like sides. A small boy reached the top of the bridge and raised his arms in triumph. Amy and Hannah's signal for a good day.

On the far side of the pond I saw Nick stooping at a squat stone lantern, reaching inside as instructed, trying to find the kidnappers' word on when and where he would at last retrieve his daughter.

Five minutes to one.

Heart in my throat, I crossed the Long Bridge and strolled down a path that curved back under it. When I reached the trash can I ducked into the bushes and thrust the white plastic bag deep among the gold-dust leaves.

Then I yanked its twin, with the postcards and guidebook, out of my tote bag. To anyone watching, I'd look the same walking away from the spot as I had walking toward it.

Mission accomplished. I realized I was holding my breath. I let it out in a deep sigh of relief as I pushed along the path against a sudden surge of tourists—first a rush of young people chattering in German, then a tour group of name-tagged senior citizens, most of them carrying white gift-shop bags.

I resisted the urge to look back.

Nick and I were to rendezvous at the tea house. All of the tables beneath the open-sided roof were taken; I was lucky to snag an empty one outside on the terrace overlooking the sun-dappled pond.

I ordered tea for two. The kimono-clad waitress—a cop?—brought it in a blue-and-white china pot. I poured some and curled my hands around my cup to warm them while I inhaled the flowery jasmine scent.

Checking the crowd, I saw a girl sitting with a man at a table close to the service counter. Brown hair. Around seven years old.

"Amy!" I jumped to my feet and called the name without thinking, then instantly was awash in remorse. Had I just blown the kidnappers' plan? Put Amy in danger?

All of the tea house patrons, including the girl, turned to stare at the crazy woman who'd yelled.

She didn't look remotely like Amy.

I pulled my knit hat down over my ears and wrapped my scarf tighter around my neck. They'd been in my tote bag. After making the drop, I'd gone to a remote corner of the tea garden and put them on. I shed a bulky jacket of Nick's, which I'd worn over my own, and left it behind, along with the tote bag and the extra gift shop bag. Dal Humphreys would retrieve them. With my profile thinner profile and my red hair covered, I looked quite different from the person who'd left the sack of money by the bush with the gold-dust leaves.

Nick arrived ten long minutes later. He did a double-take at my appearance, and then sank onto the stool opposite mine.

"Good job of changing your look," he said.

I nodded. "Did you find the note?"

"Wasn't one." His voice was so low I could barely hear the words.

"What? But, Nick, they promised instructions, information …"

He rubbed a hand over his weary face.

"I checked every stone lantern in the whole damn park. And

there's too frigging many of them, let me tell you. Nothing. You made the drop okay?"

"Yeah. I left the bag and walked away, like we agreed." I poured tea into the other cup and handed it to him. "What do we do now?"

"I wish I knew. Oh God, I wish—"

His phone rang. He grabbed it from his pocket and growled his name. Then listened for a long time.

Finally he ended the call.

"The distorted voice again," he said. "They're bringing Amy to the playground here in Golden Gate Park. To the carousel, for Christ's sake. Three o'clock." He looked at the phone screen. "One hour and forty-two minutes from now."

"The carousel. Of course. Firecracker." I thought of the crumpled drawing we'd found in the apartment where Philip had died.

Nick gulped the tea, then looked surprised to find a cup in his hand.

"Yeah. We'll get to the playground and there'll she be, riding round and round on that horse, laughing like nothing happened."

"I'm coming with you."

"Instructions say only her parents. I'll call Terri, get her to meet me there."

"Might be good to have a witness. Or extra hands. Just in case."

"Can't risk it. What if they think you're a cop?"

"I'll stay in the background. Pretend I'm babysitting some kid on the play equipment.."

He drummed his fingers on the tabletop. "I don't think—oh hell, why not."

"What about Beschke and Doyle and the rest of them?"

Nick stood up, shifted his weight from foot to foot. The tables were packed tightly together—no room to pace. "Christ. They'll want to be swarming all over the damn place."

I stood too. An older couple, swaddled in sweaters, suddenly moved toward us. We froze, holding our breath, until we realized they just wanted to claim our table.

"I'm not even going to tell the rest of the team about the call," Nick said as we walked out. "Not until we've got Amy."

Nick and Terri fell into step beside me as I walked past the carousel.

"That's Firecracker." Nick pointed. "That one there."

The white horse on its gleaming brass pole was frozen in mid-gallop, its head tossed back, golden mane streaming in a make-believe wind. A small boy shrieked with delight as he bounced in the red saddle.

"Just like Amy's picture," I said. Amy had done a superb job of depicting the carved animal's spirit. I pictured her bending over a sheet of paper, crayon in hand, a captive in that barren Cole Street apartment. It made me profoundly sad to think what she might have been feeling. Loneliness ... abandonment ... pain ... fear.

Terri murmured something, but I couldn't hear her words over the brassy music.

Putting a hand on her shoulder, Nick turned her away from the carousel. "Quarter to three," he said. "Come on, let's sit down. In a few minutes this will all be over."

"I hope so," Terri replied, but then she shook her head. "Not all of it. Philip ..." She raised her hand, pretending to brush a wisp of hair from her eye, but I could tell she was rubbing away a tear.

Nick's voice sounded gruff, perhaps from the cold. "I'm sorry about Philip, Terri. Truly I am. You know I would have wished you two every happiness."

The look Terri gave him said she knew nothing of the kind.

We parted, pretending our encounter had been a chance meeting of strangers. They found a bench near the carousel's entrance and settled in to wait.

Tugging down my hat to make sure it hid my hair, I went to the play area and found a bench of my own. I set down the sketchbook I'd rescued from my abandoned tote bag and sat on the edge of the wooden slat. I felt tense, nervous, ready to spring to action if needed. In front of me, kids with mittens pinned to their sleeves were clambering over an elaborate structure of poles and ramps and ladders. I gazed at the adults who were watching the children. Nothing suspicious about any of them.

I picked out a child to keep an eye on as if she were my babysitting charge—a girl about kindergarten age who was holding her own in a climbing contest with two bigger boys. I heard one of them call her Jenna. Quick smile, dark eyes, brunette curls that peeked from under a yellow stocking cap—she could have been Amy's younger sister.

"I know! You can be my sister. I always wanted one."

"I always wanted one, too. I'd be honored to be your sister, Amy."

I opened my sketchbook, wishing that drawing could distract me from the chill in the air and the bleak thoughts in my head. The minutes took hours to tick by.

Three o'clock.

The moment at last. I sat up straight, heart hammering. Electricity surged along my nerves.

Over by the carousel, I saw Nick look at his watch. Terri was scrutinizing the nearest road, which ran along the hillcrest above the playground. She was watching for a car to stop and let Amy out.

Five past three. Ten past. Three-thirty.

The shadows lengthened. The sunlight grew thin. Cold seeped through my jacket and boots. A few moms gathered their kids to head for warm homes. Cozy fireplaces, cookies and cocoa—I shook away the mental pictures. Jenna and her pals moved to the lawn for a vigorous game of tag. Their breath made white puffs that hung in the air.

Four o'clock.

The carousel music floated in the cold air. On their bench Nick and Terri moved together, huddling close for warmth and encouragement. I wanted to go over to them but didn't dare. Someone might be watching.

The sky's color deepened toward indigo, and a star or two winked on. To the west, clouds were building—smoky orange, sooty magenta. We were in for another storm.

Too dark to draw. I closed the sketchbook. Did some jumping jacks to force my blood to move.

A woman called to Jenna and her friends—time to leave. They made ritual protests but seemed happy enough to be herded off to supper. Only a couple of kids remained, halfheartedly digging in the sandbox.

Security lights blazed on, and the carousel music abruptly ceased. Firecracker and the other animals whirled to a halt.

Five o'clock.

Ray Beschke had found Nick and Terri; Nick must have called him. They were deep in conversation. I drifted in their direction, pretending my attention was focused on the kids dismounting from the carousel.

" ... no sign of anything," Beschke was saying. "Might as well go somewhere warm to wait."

Terri protested. "The caller said Amy would come here."

"They also said three o'clock," Beschke pointed out. "We got guys posted. Anything happens, you'll know right away."

"Come on, Terri," Nick said. I had never seen his expression look bleaker. "We won't help Amy by freezing to death."

Terri bit her lip. It was blue with cold. She hugged herself tight. "But I ... I can't go far. I have to get back here right away if—"

I decided it would be okay to join them. "My place," I suggested. "It's only five minutes away."

Terri hesitated. "Five minutes ..." She gazed at the road on the hill above us. A car passed, its headlights sweeping by. It didn't stop. "All right. Let's go. What else can we do?"

CHAPTER 30

"I'LL NEVER SEE AMY again, will I?"

Terri stood in the bay window of my living room, her back to Nick and me, speaking to her reflection in the black pane of glass. Outside, the wind was rising.

Nick moved to her side. "Terri ... you can't let yourself think like that."

He tried to put his arm across her shoulders but she shrugged it off.

"I wanted to believe you took her," Terri said. "Then she'd be safe. You've ignored Amy plenty, Lord knows, but you'd never hurt her."

Nick's hands dangled helplessly. "No. Never."

Terri came back to the sofa and sank onto it. She picked up her wineglass from the coffee table and twirled it by its slender stem. She'd asked for the wine when we arrived, but she had yet to take a sip.

My glass was half-empty, and I'd already replenished Nick's scotch. I'd set out a plate of food—cheese, crackers, apple slices—which no one had touched. As soon as we'd arrived at my flat, discouraged and fearful and frozen to the bone, I'd turned on all the lights and bumped up the thermostat setting. But a chill still permeated the air, and shadows lurked at the edges of the room.

"Terri ..." Nick sat beside her, close but not close enough to make her pull away.

"The thing is, it's not your style, this ... this elaborate charade.

Collecting the ransom, then not bringing her back. That's what convinced me. You might have taken Amy and run, but you wouldn't pull this clumsy, ridiculous ... horrible scheme."

She set down the glass and put her face in her hands. Scruff, with his unerring instinct for knowing who needed the most comforting, pushed between them and planted his paws in Terri's lap.

"We gave them their money," she said in a choked voice. "So why won't they bring her back? The only thing it can mean is she's—"

Nick pressed his finger against her lips. "Don't say that. It's not true."

"How do you know? Damn it, how do you know it's not true? Philip is dead and Amy is dead and I wish I was dead too."

"Oh, Terri, Terri ..." Nick gathered her into his arms. This time she didn't resist. She laid her head on her ex-husband's shoulder.

The dog padded across the room to where I was slumped in the blue easy chair that had belonged to my mother. It meant solace to me—when I was tiny, we sat together in this chair and she'd do what she could to soothe my hurts. It was one of the few things of hers I'd asked Roger for after she died.

My mind flashed to a moment on New Year's Day—Amy flinging her arms around Scruff and squealing as he turned his head to give her a sloppy dog kiss.

"Philip's gonna make Mommy get me a puppy," she'd confided. "I want one just like Scruff. He's special."

"I think so too," I told her. "What makes him special to you?"

"His tail." She gave a decisive nod.

"His tail?"

"Sure. See how floofy it is? You could use it for a paintbrush. That makes him the right kind of dog for artists like you and me."

Just as I felt tears threatening, the doorbell buzzed. We all jumped, thinking: *Amy!*

I ran to answer it. Thank God, something simple and useful I could do.

Scruff beat me to the bottom and shivered expectantly while I peered through the peephole.

Ray Beschke. Alone. Damn it, he was alone.

I led him upstairs. We found Terri and Nick sitting stiffly apart on the sofa. Terri was dabbing at her damp, reddened cheeks with a handkerchief.

"News?" asked Nick quickly.

"Not much," Beschke said. "Nothing about Amy. I'm sorry."

"Nothing?" Terri moaned.

Beschke looked more haggard than he had when we parted ways at the playground. "It's, what, not even an hour since you left the park. Way too soon to quit hoping."

He looked around for a place to park his bulky body. I gestured him into Mom's chair and offered him something to drink.

He pointed to Nick's glass. "Better give me a splash of that. Hell of a day."

In the kitchen, as I tumbled ice cubes into a glass, I heard Terri's tight voice: "You said 'not much' news. Does that mean you have something to tell us?"

"Thought I'd fill you in on what went down at the Tea Garden."

"They got the money. You told us that much back at the carousel."

"Yeah," Beschke said. "We watched the action on the monitor we set up at the museum—you know, from the camera mounted under the bridge. We saw Jess drop off the bag just fine. Thanks, Jess." He was responding to the glass of scotch I handed him, not my sterling performance this afternoon.

"Few minutes later," he went on, "some senior citizens group came along that same path. Thirty or forty of 'em. Lots of confusion, people jostling around, tossing stuff into that trash can. And most of 'em had gift shop bags—must have cleaned the damn place out."

"But did you see who took the money?" Terri pleaded.

"Well, hard to tell for certain." Beschke wouldn't look at her. He twirled the ice in his glass with his finger. "But it looked like one of the geezers grabbed the ransom bag."

"And did what with it?" she asked.

"We don't know."

Nick jumped to his feet. "You don't know? Jesus, Ray."

"The guy disappeared."

Nick's sharp exhale of breath sounded like a muttered curse.

Beschke said, "When the group moved on, the ransom bag was still in place, or so we thought. So maybe we didn't act as quick as we should have."

I pulled out a chair for myself from the oak table by the bay window. "What do you mean: 'or so we thought'?"

"We believed it was the bag with the money. Figured the kidnapper was taking his time to retrieve it. After the Tea Garden shut for the night and all the visitors were gone, we yanked it out. Turned out someone, maybe the old guy, had grabbed it the money after all. Pulled a switch and left an identical bag behind."

"So he'd look the same before and after," I said. "The exact trick I used."

"Yep." Beschke swigged his scotch.

Nick fetched the bottle from the kitchen, topped up Beschke's glass and his own. "So what was in the frigging bag?"

"Nothing."

"Nothing at all?"

"Crumpled newspaper. We were hoping for something good. Instructions for finding Amy, or at least a traceable clue. No such luck."

Terri was clenching and unclenching her fists. "I can't believe it. You just let the man get away?"

"We tried to find him." Beschke said. "We radioed Dal Humphreys in the Tea Garden. Gave him the description of the geezer we saw on the monitor—small guy, jeans, red jacket, gray hair, black slouch cap. By the time Dal caught up with the group, they were streaming out the exit, back to their bus. Some damn church group from Arkansas. We held the bus, but nobody there looked like our guy. Dal inspected all their damn gift shop bags anyway. Nada. Zilch. Postcards, tea sets, shit like that."

"So what did you do?" Terri demanded. "There must have been other old men in the Tea Garden. Didn't you stop them and question them? Couldn't you seal off the entrance and search everyone inside? How could you let someone get away with taking the money and not bringing Amy back?"

Nick dropped back down onto the sofa beside her. "They did right, Terri. The instructions said no cops, remember? Start searching people and you might as well put up a neon sign announcing the place is swarming with police. Christ, why not fly a plane overhead towing a frigging banner?"

"Plus," Beschke added, "you start that, and in two minutes you've got the media crawling all over the damn place."

Terri twisted in her seat. "But you would have caught him! If you arrested whoever took the money, he'd lead you to Amy. This hell would be over. I'd have my daughter back. Or at least I'd know if ... I'd know what happened."

"More likely," Beschke said, "we woulda spooked his accomplices. No telling what they'd do then."

"You don't know there's more than one."

Nick said, "It's probable though. The ransom note said 'they.'"

"I guess so." Terri reached for her glass and took her first sip of wine. "Philip was strong and smart. It must have taken two people to overpower him."

No one challenged her statement, though it was clearly not true—one individual with a gun outmatches an unarmed person any time. But we were all willing to let Terri clutch at any meager straws of comfort she could find.

Finally Nick said, "Our best bet was to play by their rules. Keep from alarming them. Doyle wanted to put a transmitter in the bag so we could track whoever picked it up, but I vetoed that. No way they wouldn't find it, and it would only make them angry." His face contorted. "Maybe I was wrong, Terri. Maybe we should've done that."

She reached out her hand, pulled it back, then placed it on his shoulder. "When things this awful happen, how can anyone know what's the best thing to do?"

Beschke drained his glass and heaved himself to his feet. "I'm gonna head back, check out the latest developments. We've got guys searching the Tea Garden, could be they'll find something. And someone's watching the playground too. Just in case."

Nick nodded. "Thanks for the update."

"Yes," Terri whispered. "Thank you."

Beschke looked downcast as he ran his hand over his stubble of hair.

"Next time," he said, "I'm gonna do my damnedest to bring you good news."

No one had much to say when I returned from letting Beschke out. After a few half-hearted attempts at small talk, we gave up and sat there listening to the gusts of wind rattling the windowpanes.

Eventually Terri got up and circled the room, stopping in turn at each artwork on the walls.

"Did you do all these, Jess?" she asked.

"Only the seascape above the sofa. The rest are by friends."

"Amy loves to paint and draw. I think she has incredible talent." She bit her lip, and her face crumpled. "But what do I know? I'm only her mother."

"She has a gift," I agreed. I debated showing Terri my studio, the birthday portrait in progress. Not the right time, I decided. If—no, Jess, say when—when Amy came back, she wouldn't like it if I'd spoiled the surprise.

I could see Terri was trembling. "This waiting is driving me crazy," she said. "I can't stand it any more. I've got to get home before I fall apart."

Nick stood. "Terri, let me—"

"The problem is, I rode into the city this morning with Chief Doyle. Could ... I'm sorry to have to ask, Jess, but could you give me a ride home?"

"I'll do it," Nick said quickly, before I could answer.

"And you'll make sure I know the minute anything happens."

"Of course," he said. "Let's get your coat."

I had tossed our coats on my bed. I brought theirs out, and Nick was helping Terri shrug into hers when the buzzer sounded again.

Terri froze. "Please, God ..." she murmured, and then I couldn't hear her, but her lips kept moving as if in a silent prayer.

Scruff and I went downstairs to see who was at the door.

More cops. Matt McCabe and Anna Rovinsky from Homicide, both with grim faces. I felt a shiver of foreboding.

"Is Terri Shawcross still here?" Rovinsky asked. McCabe was looking at his shoes, avoiding my eyes. Scruff gave a low growl.

"Upstairs." I pulled the door open wider. "What's wrong? Is Amy—"

"This isn't about Amy," Rovinsky said. Flashing a paper in my direction, they pushed past me and up the stairs.

Nick and Terri had come into the hallway above us, coats on, ready to leave.

"Oh, no," Terri whispered.

Nick frowned. "What's going on?"

McCabe and Rovinsky halted at the top of the stairs, blocking anyone from going up or down. I stopped, Scruff next to me, a couple of steps below.

"Sometimes I hate this job," McCabe said. "Terri, we've got a warrant."

"What?" She shot a bewildered glance at Nick.

He said, "Not funny, Matt."

"It's no joke, Nick," Rovinsky said. She drew out her handcuffs. "I wish it were."

McCabe took a deep breath. "Ms. Shawcross, you're under arrest for the murder of Philip Vandergriff."

"No!"

McCabe focused his eyes on a painting on the wall beyond Terri's shoulders. "You have the right to remain silent."

Terri pulled away, but Rovinsky clamped a cuff around her wrist. "Wait a minute, what's happening? You can't think I killed him!"

"Anything you say can and will be used against you in a court of law."

Nick grabbed Rovinsky's arm as she reached for Terri's other wrist. "Christ, you guys, what is this frigging nonsense?"

"I'm sorry, Nick," Rovinsky said. "We hate like hell doing this, all the trouble you're going through."

"Then don't, damn it."

"The evidence points right at her. We had no choice but to get the warrant."

"Don't cuff her, for Chrissake," Nick said. "She's not running anywhere."

"What evidence?" Terri cried. "What evidence could there possibly be?"

"Evidence that says you and Vandergriff colluded to stage the kidnapping," Rovinsky said. "And you had a falling-out."

Terri struggled to escape Rovinsky's grasp. "What? You think I kidnapped my own daughter?"

"Fingerprints." McCabe grabbed her shoulder. "You left fingerprints on objects in the apartment where Vandergriff was killed."

Rovinsky snapped on the other cuff. "And we have a witness who places you at the building that night."

"But I wasn't there! I was up in Mendocino County. At Nick's cabin. I told you."

The two cops hustled her downstairs. Scruff growled again as they went by. I hooked my hand on his collar.

"Nick!" Terri yelled.

Nick caught up with them at the foot of the stairs. He grabbed Terri in a quick, awkward embrace.

"Oh, Christ. Terri, don't say a word to them. Not one word."

McCabe pulled Nick back. Rovinsky opened the door.

Nick raced out after them. "I'm right behind you, Terri. I'm calling Stuart Weingarten. A defense attorney, a damn good one. Everything will be okay."

The last sentence had a hollow sound.

No phone calls. No more visitors. No word about Amy, or about what Terri was going through at the Hall of Justice. I paced through the flat, listening to my footsteps echo.

Scruff shadowed me. Occasionally he whined, asking what the problem was, but I had no satisfactory answer. When I fed him, he wolfed down his dinner, but I couldn't muster an appetite. I picked at the crackers and apple slices on the plate on the coffee table. They tasted like sawdust and dead leaves.

I went into my studio, set a fresh canvas on the easel, squeezed paint onto my palette. After a few slashing strokes—umber, midnight blue, an angry streak of scarlet—I had to quit. My stomach churned; the brush in my fingers was shaking.

I couldn't believe it—Terri arrested for Philip Vandergriff's murder.

How could it be true? But the police wouldn't act on a whim—especially not in this case, which involved one of their own.

Colluded to stage the kidnapping, Rovinsky said. But why? What reason could they have had?

Terri's distress, her grief, were genuine—I was certain of it. Almost certain, anyway.

And the biggest question of all—where was Amy?

I phoned the Hall of Justice. No answer on Nick's direct line or the Homicide squadroom's number. Whoever answered the main number for SFPD couldn't, or wouldn't, tell me anything. I called the press office, posing as a reporter, but the harried voice I reached there would only confirm the arrest.

Finally I took Scruff for a walk. The wind was blowing hard from the north, shaking the branches of the street trees, tossing bits of trash along the sidewalk, whirling up grit that stung my eyes. Clouds paraded overhead, silver-edged ghosts backlit by the nearly full moon. Our brief respite from storms was over. Tomorrow the sky would be gray; we'd have rain before nightfall.

When we returned home I spotted Terri's purse at the top of the stairs. She must have dropped it during the confusion of her arrest. I fetched a handkerchief to avoid smudging fingerprints or adding my own, then sat on the sofa to examine the contents. I felt vaguely guilty when I opened the clasp.

I laid out Terri's things in orderly rows on the sofa. Maybe arranging them precisely would yield insights that might otherwise elude me.

A lipstick, a hairbrush, a pen, a notepad with blank pages. A wallet that held forty-four dollars in cash, a driver's license and a couple of credit cards. A copy of Amy's school portrait, the image that had become so familiar to me and the entire Bay Area thanks to the missing-child poster. A snapshot of mother and daughter with sunlight gilding their faces, bending toward each other so that their heads touched. Seeing it broke my heart.

Not one thing that could shed any light on Terri's guilt or innocence.

I tried again to reach Nick for an update, with no more success than before. I left messages and then, totally drained of energy, I flopped onto the sofa and punched the TV remote. Some sitcom was playing. I left it on, pretending that canned laughter would lighten my mood. Scruff curled up beside me and we drifted, half-dozing, for most of an hour.

Until a news anchor's voice startled me awake.

" … a shocking development in a case that has gripped the hearts of Bay Area residents."

Martina Valdez, Channel Eight. Behind her was Amy's face, larger than life.

"Terri Shawcross, mother of Amy Gardino, the Creekhaven seven-year-old who disappeared last Tuesday, has been arrested for the murder of her fiancé, SalesCom Technologies CEO Philip Vandergriff. Our reporter Paula Blakeney has more."

A close shot of Blakeney. Her appearance was flawless, as always. "Martina, at the Hall of Justice tonight San Francisco police were keeping tight-lipped about this dramatic turn of events."

Cut to a video clip of a frowning Inspector Anna Rovinsky, looking tense and tired. "Yes, we do have a suspect in custody. However, we cannot go into the evidence at this time. The child is still missing, and we don't want to say anything that might jeopardize her safety."

Back to Paula Blakeney, a wider shot this time. "Right now I'm live on scene in the Haight-Ashbury district. Behind me is the house where Philip Vandergriff was killed and where, some sources are saying, Amy may have been held for a time by her abductors. One of the key witnesses in this case is here with me."

The camera pulled back farther to reveal the witness. He towered over her, teetering on his Rollerblades.

I felt a jolt of dismay.

They made an odd pair—the impeccably groomed reporter with the sepia-toned complexion and the pallid street kid with his tattoos and piercings.

"This young man is a neighborhood resident. Atom, you say you've seen Ms. Shawcross at this building?" Blakeney had to lift the microphone above her head to catch his reply.

Closeup on Atom, who grinned into the camera, high on the attention he was getting.

"Yeah, for sure. Same lady, black hair and everything. The cops showed me a bunch of pictures and I picked her right out."

"And you saw her here on Thursday, the fatal night."

"Absolutely. Well, maybe more like, you know, late afternoon. But Thursday, definitely. Other times too. Walking right up these steps here."

Back to Paula Blakeney. "Some sources have suggested that if Terri Shawcross was here several times, she may in fact have known that her daughter was being held in this building."

Atom leaned down, putting his face next to hers and forcing the camera operator to widen the shot. "Dunno about that. I never saw a little girl or anything. But wouldn't that be a trip, if her mom knew all along where the kid was." He chuckled, then apparently thought better of it and composed his face into sadness. "I feel real sorry for the little girl. I hope they find her soon, even if her mom is a murderer."

Blakeney winced. "Alleged murderer. She's innocent until proven guilty, of course."

"Of course." Atom nodded sagely.

"It was good of you to come forward, Atom. Many witnesses don't show your courage. Now back to—"

"Oh, I'm not afraid. Besides, I want to, like, do my duty as a whatchamacallit, a citizen and stuff. But you know what I think? I—"

"I'm sorry, Atom, we're out of time. Back to you, Martina," Blakeney said, a hint of desperation in her voice. Atom waggled his fingers, signing off with a little wave to his fans.

Bet that was the last live feed Blakeney would try for a while.

I punched the remote button to shut off the TV and sat there feeling depressed. Terri was in jail. Amy was still missing. And Atom, God help us, was reveling in his fifteen minutes of fame.

I was about to give up and go to bed when my phone rang.

"Jess? It's Evelyn Talbot. I've got to speak to Terri but she's not answering her phone. Is she still there? She called earlier, said she was with you."

241

Evelyn must not have been watching the news.

"Not anymore. Evelyn, you won't believe this, but she's been—"

"It's urgent, Jess. I have to get hold of her."

"That would be hard right now. She—"

"I've been here at her house all day, just in case. And finally—only a few minutes ago. A phone call, listen, I'll play the tape."

I heard a hum, then Evelyn's amplified voice: "Hello?"

Followed by a childish treble: "Mommy?"

My heart leapt into my throat.

Evelyn's voice: "Amy? Oh my God—Amy!"

"Mom, is that you? I'm sorry, Mommy. Please come help me."

"Amy, honey, it's Evelyn. Where are you, sweetheart?"

"Uh-oh! Gotta hang up." And Amy was gone.

CHAPTER 31

VIOLET, I DECIDED. Violet and indigo; maybe a touch of viridian green. If I were painting Nick Gardino's portrait this morning, those were the colors I'd need to capture the shadows haunting the hollows beneath his eyes.

I probably didn't look much better.

"Morning, Nick," I said. I left off the *good*—that was still an open question.

Nick had been at the Hall of Justice all night, dealing with Terri's arrest and Amy's phone call. After several futile tries, I finally got hold of him an hour ago. We arranged to meet at The Alibi, a coffee shop across from the Hall of Justice, so I could give him Terri's forgotten handbag. I had debated turning it over to McCabe or Rovinsky, but I couldn't see how that would help matters.

I'd found him waiting at a rickety Formica-topped table by the window. Both hands were wrapped around a coffee cup; his head was bowed as if in prayer.

On this dreary Sunday morning Nick and I were the sole customers.

At my greeting, he raised his head, tried a smile. "Hey, Jess. Grab a cup of something and sit down. I could use a little friendly company."

Handing him Terri's bag, I went to the counter, where I interrupted the pudgy teenaged clerk from his scrutiny of his cellphone screen. A glass dome covered a plate of stale-looking doughnuts, and the kid was busily stuffing one in his mouth. Chocolate-frosted with sprinkles. From the look of him, I suspected he made a habit of helping himself to the merchandise.

I ordered tea, which he delivered with a deep sigh of annoyance. Lipton—you wouldn't find Earl Grey or English Breakfast or exotic herbal blends here. The Alibi was a no-frills establishment. Grime-streaked plate glass windows, scuffed linoleum floors, walls painted institutional green. Harsh-tasting coffee in flimsy paper cups. A far cry from the upscale espresso bars on Valencia Street or the jazz-and-java joints in North Beach. But this ambiance suited the neighborhood. It's hard to put on airs when you're shoehorned in between two bail-bond shops.

Nick was flipping through the purse as I slid onto my chair. "Nothing in here that's going to help," he muttered.

"Or hurt," I pointed out. "That's good, anyway."

"Wouldn't make much difference either way. Too many weak links in the chain of custody. Oh, Jesus ..."

He had come upon the snapshot of Amy and her mother. He laid it on the table. "At least we know Amy's alive. Thank God for that." His voice was flat. He was probably thinking the same thing I was: *She was alive last night. But a lot can go wrong in a few hours.*

"Any luck tracing her phone call?" I asked.

"Dead end so far."

"Don't say that word."

"You're right. Bad choice." He braced his elbows on the table and leaned heavily on them, as if his chair wasn't strong enough to bear the great weight of his despair. "Amy called on Philip Vandergriff's cell phone. Kidnappers must have snagged the phone off his body before they fled."

I fished the teabag out of my cup. "Have you found out where the call originated?"

"Apparently the GPS was disabled. We've got the cellular service people trying to track down which towers bounced the call around, but no luck so far. And of course no one answers when we call the number. Damn phone's probably in a garbage can somewhere.

"How's Terri holding up?"

He rubbed a finger along his upper lip. I hadn't noticed before, but gray was creeping into his mustache and there were thin threads of silver in his black hair.

"I don't know. They won't let me near her."

"They? McCabe and Rovinsky?"

"Yeah. My colleagues. My so-called friends." He shook his head. "They're right, of course. It's what I'd do. You bring in a suspect on a homicide, you've got no business letting her ex-husband hang around trying to call the shots."

"Does she have a lawyer?"

"I phoned Stuart Weingarten. He spent half the night in there with her."

"Good. Stuart's one of the best."

"Yeah. Christ, I never thought I'd find myself on the same side as a defense attorney."

"Are you on Terri's side?"

"I'm on Amy's side."

He rubbed his eyes as if trying to clear away years of accumulated pain. Burnt umber, I thought. That was the shade I'd use to paint his eyes. Normally Nick's eyes were bronze-colored, but the stress and the dull clouds outside the window made them look tarnished.

"Of course I'm on Terri's side, too," he added. "Hell knows, we've had our differences, but I've never believed she's anything but good and honest. She works hard for what she wants, she's caring and compassionate. Exactly the kind of mother I'd want a kid of mine to have. There's no way she's the killer type."

"Nick," I said gently, "I can't believe she killed Philip either. But there is no killer type."

"Yeah. Don't I know it. Better than anyone. But Terri doesn't have it in her."

"What evidence do McCabe and Rovinsky have? They wouldn't arrest her on a whim."

"Terri insists she's never been in the apartment on Cole Street, didn't even know the place existed until she heard about Vandergriff's murder. But her fingerprints are on things there, like the cookie tin in the kitchen. And they've got an eyewitness, some jerk kid, who claims he saw her go in the building Thursday a short time before Vandergriff got shot."

"I know the eyewitness, Nick. I wouldn't call him the most reliable—"

"There's more. According to the rental agent, a woman fitting her description signed the lease. And here's the kicker—the name on the lease is Theresa Shaw."

Damn. "Theresa Shaw. Terri Shawcross."

"Exactly." He gulped the last of his coffee.

"The rental agent—Nick, that building is owned by Moritz."

"Right. A bit much for coincidence, wouldn't you think? But the woman who handled the rental contends it was a routine transaction. Nothing set off alarm bells. McCabe questioned her at length yesterday, says she seems straightforward enough. An underling—she barely knows Moritz by sight."

"So it's random chance that the kidnappers picked one of Moritz's buildings?"

"He owns enough of them. Anyone looking for a place to rent stands good odds of hitting one of his."

"I don't get it. What's supposed to be the scenario? Last night, Rovinsky said something about collusion."

"My esteemed colleagues are operating on the hypothesis that Terri staged the kidnapping herself. Told Amy it was some kind of game, or a joke they were playing on Philip."

"That makes no sense. Why would she do that?"

"The same reasons most people do stupid things. Love and money. Or lack of love in this case. Terri decided she didn't want to marry Philip after all, but she did want a little of the easy life he'd promised her. She figured she'd fake a kidnapping and scam the ransom out of Philip. After Amy came home, she'd play the part of the smitten and grateful fiancée for a suitable time, and break things off before a wedding could happen. That's the theory anyway."

The same theory that Mac Doyle had posited. "I don't believe it."

"Of course the whole thing went horribly wrong. Philip wasn't supposed to die."

"What do McCabe and Rovinsky say happened?"

"In their version, Terri didn't go up to Mendocino on Thursday, she was right there on Cole Street with Amy. Philip learned about the scheme somehow and showed up at the apartment to confront her. They got into a fight and—*boom*." He fired a finger-gun at me.

My heart jumped. I could almost feel a bullet slamming through it. "But what happened to Amy?"

"The million-dollar question. If Terri knows, she's not telling."

"She doesn't know. You saw her last night at my place. She wasn't acting. She was really distressed. Grief-stricken. It was genuine."

"Yeah. Looked that way to me, too. Of course I've been fooled before."

"And the ransom—someone took it. Do they think she had an accomplice? Who would it be?"

"For all we know she grabbed it herself and stashed it somewhere. Assuming some tourist didn't stumble on it by accident and decide it was his lucky day."

"That's crazy. Terri was with the police in the command center at the museum when I made the drop."

Nick looked pained. "Actually, she wasn't. She told them she was going to the ladies room, went off and didn't come back. She says she needed to be by herself, so she wandered around the museum looking at the pictures. Another mental vacation. But no one can verify that. The next time anyone saw her for sure was when I met her at the playground."

"Oh, hell," I said.

"Exactly."

We lapsed into silence. I was trying to sort through a jumble of thoughts and emotions. Nick tore his empty paper cup into strips.

After a few minutes he lumbered to his feet. "Want a refill?" I shook my head. He went to the counter, where the clerk was chowing down on another doughnut, and bought a fresh cup of coffee.

Back at the table, he tore open a packet of sugar and dumped the contents in.

"There are a lot of things I'm going to miss about being a cop," he said, "but having a front-row seat to violence isn't one of them."

"Nick? What are you saying? You told me the brass put you on leave, but isn't it temporary?"

"Yeah. But I've had it, Jess. I'm not going back." He stirred the coffee, took a sip and made a face.

"But … why not?"

"There's no point. We've lost. The criminals, the assholes, the stupid jerks—they've won, Jess. They've taken over the world. No use pretending the rest of us have a chance. I'm sick and tired of tilting at goddamn windmills."

"Don't say that. We need people like you on the force, Nick."

"Right. We need losers and fuckups."

"Nick, it's frustrating and discouraging, I know that. But it's important work, and you're good at it. When this is over, when Amy's back—"

"Jess, face it. It's been five days. Almost one hundred and twenty hours. Every second that passes makes it less likely she'll ever come back."

One hundred and fifteen hours, I wanted to say but didn't. It won't be a full five days until three o'clock this afternoon. Don't give up yet.

"Remember the other day, I told you my father was a cop? What I didn't say was, he was killed in the line of duty. Whoever shot him got clean away, was never caught. I was fourteen. I went to his funeral, hundreds of cops there with black tape on their badges, paying him tribute. Right then I decided I'd join the force when I got old enough. If I locked up enough bad guys, maybe my father would be avenged; his soul could rest in peace. Of course it doesn't work that way."

He slouched deeper, no easy feat on the hard, narrow chair. He ripped open another sugar packet, stirred the white grains into his coffee. I wondered if he'd forgotten he'd already sweetened it.

"At least for me it doesn't," he said. "I can't achieve justice for my father, I can't send a frigging slimebag like Moritz to prison … I can't even protect my own daughter. If any kid's ever safe, it should be the cop's kid, right? I mean, that's her father's profession—protecting people, rescuing them, fixing things that go wrong. She's only seven, for Christ's sake. You shouldn't need protection if you're only seven. Your life should be good, and fun, and easy. What kind of world is this?"

I had no good answer, but I attempted one anyway. "It's a better world for having you on the police force, Nick. Don't you think—"

Nick put up a hand to say *stop*. "I'm through, Jess. What's the point of banging my head against the wall forever?"

He gulped his coffee and grimaced as his cell phone rang. I couldn't tell if he was reacting to the call or the oversugared brew. He barked into the phone: "Gardino." Then: "Yeah, Mac." He looked at me and mouthed the name *Doyle*. "What's up? … Christ, not another one … Crackpots, every damn one of them … Okay, tell me."

Nick fumbled at his pockets, then extracted the pen and notepad from Terri's purse. "Mountain Guy's, Route Fifty, got it … Wants his name in the newspaper, that's my guess … Not cynical, Mac, just realistic … Yeah, I'm on my way … I'll pick you up in Creekhaven ... Supposed to be another storm coming, we better move."

He signed off and pushed himself to his feet.

I felt my pulse race. "What did Doyle say? What's happening?"

"Hotline just got a call. Fellow who runs one of those store-and-cafe combos on the way to Lake Tahoe. Someone stopped there last night with a girl in the car who looked like Amy. The shopkeeper didn't make the connection till he saw the eleven o'clock news. Then he spent the whole goddamn night making up his mind to call."

I was afraid to feel hopeful. "There've been lots of sightings, right?"

"Yeah. So far Amy's been seen in Anchorage, Savannah, Amarillo—Singapore, even. Can't keep track of them all."

"But none have panned out."

"Mac thinks this one could be for real. We're going to go talk to the shopkeeper, see what's what."

I stood up too. "I'm coming with you."

His phone rang again. "Now what?" Nick answered it, and then didn't speak for a while.

Finally he said, "I'll be right over. Thanks for telling me." He stuffed the phone in his pocket.

"Who was it?" I asked.

"Ray Beschke. They've got the gun that shot Philip."

"Really? Where did they find it?"

"In a dumpster behind the Cole Street building. Underneath a load of bakery garbage."

"Isn't that good news?"

The look on his face said it wasn't. "God help us, it's Terri's gun."

"Oh, Nick, no."

"It gets worse. The gun's still registered in my name. I bought it for her back when we were still married." He snatched the photograph from the table, dropped it in Terri's purse and slipped his arm through the strap. "Case I was working on, the suspect was making threats. I wanted her to have a way to protect herself and Amy if something came down when I wasn't home."

"It's got to be a mistake."

"Christ, I hope so. I've got to go check it out."

I grabbed my purse. "Wait for me."

"Call Doyle, will you, Jess? Tell him I got delayed, I'll be there quick as I can. Tell him to get the county sheriff on it."

Before I could move he was out the door. The kid behind the counter snickered at the sight: Tough cop, running fast, swinging a purse.

CHAPTER 32

I DASHED OUT OF THE ALIBI and crossed the street to the Hall of Justice. Nick had already disappeared inside.

Most likely he'd gone to Homicide, so I took the elevator to the fourth floor. No Nick, and if Beschke, McCabe and Rovinsky were there, they were behind closed doors. The clerk on duty stonewalled my inquiries. I tried phoning Chief Doyle, but he'd gone on an emergency call; I left a message about Nick's delay. Finally I went upstairs to the jail and asked to see Terri, but visiting hours hadn't started and my request was denied. I left feeling angry. By the time I reached my car, the anger had turned into a perverse moroseness.

Be adventurous! Take risks!

As I drove home, the refrain kept beating in my head, the way a half-heard melody lodges in your brain and drives you crazy because it won't let go.

Be adventurous! Take risks!

I tapped out the rhythm on my steering wheel. It wasn't my fault that Amy had disappeared, yet I felt like I was to blame. Nothing I'd said to her, or failed to say, had placed her in harm's way—I told myself this, over and over, but I wasn't convinced. Nor had I missed any subtle hints in things she'd said to me. She'd never mentioned a stranger hanging around the schoolyard, or an acquaintance who made her uncomfortable, or any incident that left her angry or scared. I'd replayed our conversations in my mind a dozen times and they contained no clue.

Or did they? Maybe I was being stupid, or blind, or ...

No! I gave myself a mental shaking. It was sheer bad luck that calamity struck so soon after she came into my life and we adopted each other as sisters. We weren't really family. I had no right to compare my grief and loss to Nick's, to Terri's.

Assuming their grief and loss are genuine, my inner voice chided. I flicked the thought away.

I'd brought Terri trouble too. The minute she set foot into my home, she was arrested for Philip's murder.

And Philip—I was one of the last people to see him alive. I should have noticed the angel of death hovering at his shoulder while we ate lunch at Dandelion. I should have warned him, should have saved him ...

Damn! I felt like a jinx. Come on, everybody, hook up with Jess and you too can experience disaster and violence.

Be adventurous, take risks, fail and die.

When I put my key in the front-door lock, I expected to hear the scampering paws of my welcome committee.

Silence. Feeling uneasy, I pushed open the door and hurried upstairs. "Scruff! Hey, kiddo!"

No answering bark, no glimpse of furry, amber-colored ears or tail. The flat was empty and still, as if all the life-energy it contained had settled onto the floor like dust and no living creature had ever ruffled the air with breathing.

On the coffee table I found a piece of paper folded like a tent. I grabbed it up. A note from Davy. Mrs. Fiorelli was taking the kids to the beach—no doubt she wanted to let them run off their excess energy before more storms slammed onshore, keeping them housebound and crazy—and they'd borrowed Scruff to join the fun.

Too bad, I thought. Not for Scruff, who loved the beach, but for me. I needed his company. I felt housebound and crazy myself, and I'd been home less than five minutes.

I needed to do something useful. I went into my studio and spread out a large sheet of paper on my worktable. I would make lists, draw lines, diagram connections and try to map out some answers.

Moritz's associates—he had allies and enemies all over the city. I had no doubt that he could easily pull strings from prison, but to whom were they attached? Creighton Oliver, obviously. His daughter Shanna. Lawyers, employees, tenants, his fellow members of the symphony board.

Terri's friends, acquaintances, distant cousins—if she staged the kidnapping, whom had she enlisted to help her? She and I had shared strong emotions over the last few days, which made me feel like we'd forged a bond. But that was an illusion. I really didn't know her at all.

And you don't know Nick either, my inner voice pointed out. I called him a friend, but I had scant details about his personal life. He played tennis, his dad was killed in the line of duty, he had a little girl whom he ignored for too many years. I had no idea what dark motives he might be concealing deep in his heart, or who would assist him in seeing them achieved. What if Terri was right all along?

The paper, like my mind, stayed blank.

My eye drifted to Amy's half-finished portrait of Terri on my small easel, which still bore its halo of illumine foil. Then to the big easel, with the angry scarlet-streaked canvas I'd taken my frustrations out on last night. I set that painting aside and put back the one of winter snow, with its ice blue and indigo. It was nearly done, but looking at it now I could see that it hadn't really come together.

Winter snow. I remembered Mac Doyle's call to Nick at The Alibi—the storekeeper who'd seen a child like Amy in a customer's car. Mountain Guy's, Route 50, up in the mountains.

The timing was right; someone grabbing the ransom money in San Francisco at one o'clock could reach the Sierra by nightfall.

Until Nick and Doyle could get there, they would leave chasing the lead to the county sheriff's department—good people, no doubt, but without any real connection to the case, just doing a favor to fellow cops.

Be adventurous, take risks, prompted one inner voice. *Butt out, jinx,* insisted another.

With luck, I could make it to Mountain Guy's before sunset.

Better take Kit's car, I decided. For a winter trip into the Sierra, his Jeep Cherokee had advantages my Toyota didn't—four-wheel drive and a set of tire chains. Another plus—whoever had been taping my taillight wouldn't know Kit's car, wouldn't connect it with me.

I had a ring of Kit's keys in my jewelry box. Neither of us had asked to have our keys back, or other personal items returned; we'd taken no action that would sign and seal the end of our relationship.

Kit hadn't told me I could use his car while he was in Hawaii. On the other hand he didn't say I couldn't. Maybe that was because we hadn't spoken at all for a couple of weeks before he left. But under the circumstances I was sure he'd endorse my driving it.

Besides, chances were good he'd never know.

No tape on my taillight when I left home. I drove to South Park, where Kit lived, with one eye on the rearview mirror, but saw no signs that I was being followed.

I began my search for the Cherokee in front of the woodframe Victorian cottage that housed Kit on the second floor and his photo studio on the first. The place was dark.

I cruised for twenty minutes without spotting his car. I began to worry—could he have driven it to the airport instead of taking the shuttle? Leaving his car in a long-term lot would cost a fortune but if the conference sponsor was paying his expenses …

Ah, there it was, in the middle of a block on Second Street.

I found a free space at the corner and parked my Toyota. Grabbing my heavy jacket from the front seat, I went back to Cherokee, unlocked it and climbed in. A couple of minutes later, I whispered thanks to Kit and was on my way.

As I crossed the Bay Bridge, the sky was low and flat, like a painted ceiling. The water below was nearly the same dull gray as the cloud cover, but rippled with white caps. Out toward Alcatraz, a single sailboat pitched and yawed, fighting the waves. With heavy rain predicted, most Sunday sailors had had the good sense to stay home. When the storm moved east and reached the mountains it would turn to snow—a lot of snow, if we could believe the forecasters. A foot of fresh powder, snow level down all the way to three thousand feet.

Up I-80, past Berkeley, past Richmond. At the Creekhaven exit, I pulled off the freeway, so I could stop at the community center and pick up a fistful of flyers with Amy's photos. The only picture of her I had was the sketch I'd made while she'd painted in my studio. If you knew her, it captured her look and her spirit, but it wouldn't identify her to strangers.

The atmosphere in the community center was much more subdued than it had been on Wednesday when I came here with Terri. The phones sat silent. The chattering police radio was gone. The reporters with their cameras and microphones were absent. Just five days since Amy vanished, and already the excitement was bleeding out of her story. With no progress in the search to report, the media were turning their attention to new thrills, more recent disasters.

In a corner, a small boy was listlessly building a tower of blocks. A toddler slept in a stroller, a pink bunny pressed to her cheek. In the hush of the big room I could hear the click of the blocks and the little girl's raspy breathing.

Then I became aware of the murmur of conversation. A group of adults was clustered around the pulled-together tables in the middle of the space. Lillian Harwood, Evelyn Talbot, Creekhaven's mayor Verna Spode, three or four others I didn't recognize.

Everyone's attention was focused on a woman with wire-rimmed glasses and a frothy perm which looked like it had been styled with an eggbeater. She was scribbling in a spiral-topped notebook.

Looked like I was wrong about the media. At least it wasn't the Pizza Kid.

"If the police think Terri shot that man," Lillian Harwood was saying, "they've got no more sense than rabbits."

"Think about it, Lily," said Mayor Spode. "She's a stranger here. We don't know her. She only moved to town last August—"

"She's a quiet one," said a man with thinning gray hair. "You know what they say, it's always the quiet ones."

"I know her," Lillian said firmly. "I live right next door, and you couldn't ask for a better neighbor."

"But her own child. Her fiancé," said a woman I didn't know. "How could she do such awful things to people she loves?"

"Love," another woman grumbled. "The people who claim they love us are the ones we should worry about most."

The reporter looked up and saw me approaching. The others followed her gaze. When I greeted them, I got hellos from Lillian and Evelyn, but everyone else stayed silent. Mayor Spode pursed her lips and looked away. The reporter appeared puzzled until Evelyn whispered an explanation: "A friend of Terri's."

Gripping her pen, Ms. Eggbeater sat up straighter, looking bright and expectant.

Before she could speak, Lillian offered a hello. "Have you come to help?" she asked.

"I just want to pick up some flyers."

"You're a friend of Terri Shawcross? What's your name?" the reporter asked with an ingratiating smile. "What do you think about Terri's arrest?"

I shook my head. "There's nothing I can say."

Lillian snorted. "A wild-goose chase, that's all it is. Terri didn't shoot him, and arresting her doesn't put us one step closer to bringing Amy home."

Mayor Spode leaned forward, gripping the edge of the table as if it were a speaker's podium. "I say, where there's smoke, there's fire."

"That's right," the balding man agreed. "They wouldn't have arrested her if they didn't have evidence."

A couple of the others nodded. Evelyn dabbed at her eyes with a handkerchief.

Part of me longed to tell them about the phone call from Amy, the possible sighting—take heart, keep searching, we heard her voice, she's alive. But if the news became public, that might jeopardize Amy. I didn't know what had made her abruptly cut short her call.

Ms. Eggbeater was taking notes. "The shocking news of the arrest has taken the spirit out of the search. Would that be fair to say?" She sounded as if she hoped it were true; was it a juicier story that way? "There's only a handful of you here this morning, whereas yesterday—"

"Nonsense. It hasn't dispirited me," Lillian insisted. "Or any of us. We're going to find Amy and—"

"There he is," announced the mayor. "Finally." She pointed at Mac Doyle, who was walking into the community center. Clad in jeans and a dark blue parka, he looked ready to leave for the mountains the minute Nick arrived.

Ms. Eggbeater stood up, eager to pounce. "Chief Doyle! You're just in time to answer a question or two."

Doyle came to a halt next to me. His eyes were gray hollows in his florid face, and the square shoulders sagged as if the weight of the world rested on them.

"You're here again? Damn if you don't keep turning up like a bad penny."

"Did you get my message, Chief?" I asked.

"About Gardino being delayed? Yeah, I got it." He fixed me with a look; if his eyes had been power drills they'd have bored twin holes into my skull. "Let me give you a word of friendly advice, Ms. Randolph. Whatever game you're playing, don't think you can get away with it."

"No game, Chief. I'm just trying to help my friends find their missing child."

He folded his thick arms across his chest. "Find her or hide her?"

Count to ten, Jess, before you answer. "What are you saying?"

Ms. Eggbeater moved toward us. "Chief Doyle?"

Doyle waved her away. "Let's step over here, Ms. Randolph." He steered me to a corner of the big room, out of earshot of the table.

"If you have something to say about this case," he said, "a good time to do it would be now."

A chill went through me. "What are you talking about?"

He leaned closer, forcing me to step back. I smelled coffee on his breath. "I'm asking you to tell us where Amy is. Now that Terri's been apprehended, there's no point in hiding her any longer."

"God, if I knew where she was—"

"Her mother must have had help pulling off a scheme like this—faking the kidnapping, collecting the ransom cash. I'm not saying you were involved in Vandergriff's murder, that could be Terri's own doing, but—"

"I can't believe you're saying this." I made my voice as icy as I could to damp down my anger.

"The child's gone. The ransom money's gone. It would have

been easy for you to carry the cash out of the Tea Garden and leave behind a bag full of old newspaper. I wondered why you insisted so hard on being the person to handle the money. And then there's the eyewitness who places you near the scene where Amy vanished—"

"What, you mean Hannah? All she saw was a car driving down the street."

"A car with a redheaded woman at the wheel."

"We went through that, Chief. At length, on Friday night."

"That was before the latest developments."

"I'm not going to continue this discussion without my lawyer present." Not trusting myself to say more, I grabbed a stack of flyers and strode toward the door.

Doyle didn't stop me, but Ms. Eggbeater jumped up and gave chase. "Wait! I need to talk to you."

I could almost hear her thoughts. *Wow, a possible perpetrator. A real scoop—much better than another round of no-comments with the top cop.*

I quickened my pace and got out of there.

CHAPTER 33

M Y NERVES AS TAUT as a steel wire, I crossed the Carquinez Strait and veered east. The hills, golden brown most of the year, were turning green from the persistent winter rains. When I reached the broad Central Valley, the landscape flattened. Spatters hit my windshield and quickly turned into a steady shower.

Outside Sacramento, I picked up Highway 50. Soon I was climbing into the foothills. Traffic in my direction was light, but trucks, SUVs and cars sporting ski racks jammed the opposite lanes, pushing to reach home before the storm hit full force.

At Placerville the rain stopped, though I was sure the lull was temporary. I was in the Gold Country now. Placerville had once been a wild outpost known, for good reason, as Hangtown. As a fourth grader studying California history, I'd been intrigued that a town would be named for the fate of its least welcome citizens. Now, even that tiny hint of violent death made me shudder.

I stopped to fill the gas tank and look for Kit's tire chains so they'd be ready if I needed them. The backseat was folded down, turning the whole rear area into cargo space. Kit had spread a tarp over the contents to protect them from the view of curious thieves. I pulled it away, revealing his car-repair tools, the plaid blanket we used for picnics, the big plastic storage box he'd packed with survival gear in case of an earthquake.

Where were the chains?

Maybe I'd been wrong and Kit didn't have chains after all.

No, there they were—behind the driver's seat, hiding under a

California road atlas. At the top of the stack was a spare camera tripod, the three legs telescoped down to make it compact. An image flashed in my mind—a day we spent tasting wine in the Napa Valley last autumn. Kit was carrying this tripod as he took pictures of grapevines, their clusters of lush fruit awaiting harvest.

I put the tripod back in place and brought the map book and chains up front with me. Then I pointed the Cherokee toward the mountains.

Beyond Pollock Pines the road narrowed to two lanes, which ran beside the rain-swollen south fork of the American River. Whitewater surged along the riverbed. Steep, forested hills rose on both sides. Passing the four-thousand-feet marker I noticed the first patches of snow, lying in sheltered spots under trees or rocks. Before long snow was everywhere—in a thick cottony blanket that covered the ground; in white bunting that festooned dark evergreen branches; in dirty, crusty piles that had been plowed off the roadbed and now lined the route like a misshapen wall.

Most people would have found the wintry vistas beautiful, but the sight of so much snow tightened my nerves another notch.

Half a mile past a sign warning of chain controls ahead, I saw a mini-billboard advertising the attractions of Mountain Guy's: GAS, FOOD, HOT COFFEE, SUPPLIES and of course TIRE CHAINS.

Rounding the next bend, I spotted the place itself—a large log cabin with a deep porch across the front and a steeply pitched roof covered with snow. Smoke drifted up from a metal chimney.

A wide parking area full of cars separated Mountain Guy's from the highway. Handwritten signs stuck on sticks in the snow by the road gave one reason why the place was so popular. Young men clad in boots and thick jackets were conducting a booming business—putting tire chains on for the city slickers or removing them, depending on which direction the customer was traveling. I pulled into the lot, and the Cherokee's tires crunched across frozen slush and patches of rutted ice.

Opening the car door, I stepped down to the ground. I inhaled a deep breath, expecting mountain freshness, and was shocked by the frigid air that slammed into my lungs. It had been cold in San Francisco, but that weather was balmy compared to this. I was grateful I'd brought my heaviest jacket. I took a few tentative steps. My smooth-soled leather boots were great for rainy city sidewalks but I didn't trust them to handle the treacherous conditions currently under my feet.

As I picked my way across the parking lot, I watched people come and go, and figured out the location of my important first stop—the ladies room, in a small outbuilding behind the main structure. I moved there as fast as I dared and joined a line of impatient women who were stamping their feet for warmth and puffing breaths of steam into the air.

When I got back to the parking area, I was astonished to see two people standing behind the Cherokee, heads bent low. They appeared to be fiddling with the rear door, trying to break in.

A surge of adrenaline carried me, half trotting, half sliding, across the icy parking lot.

"Hey!" I yelled. "What are you doing?"

They turned toward me.

Damn. That idiot reporter, William Paveleck. The Pizza Kid, black parka, gold hoop earring and all.

Next to him was Shanna Moritz, shivering in a thin windbreaker, her cheeks stung scarlet by the cold. Looked like their romance was blossoming.

The Kid flashed a grin. He probably intended it to look sheepish but it barely concealed the underlying smirk. "Whoops. Caught in the act." He flourished scissors in one hand, a roll of black electrician's tape in the other. "If it isn't the lovely Cleopatra. I like your new barge, Cleo."

"You! You're the one who's been taping my taillight! You've been following me."

"In the line of duty," he said self-righteously.

"Duty! What 'duty'?"

He bowed low, a burlesque of gallantry. "Gotta get that story."

Shanna fingered the fresh black stripe on the taillight. "Isn't this a cool trick? Will learned it from a spy movie."

"But—this isn't even my car. How did you pick up my trail?"

"Oh, it was easy," Shanna said.

"Easy?" In my head, I replayed my steps—leaving home, trading my car for the Cherokee. I'd been so careful, so watchful. Damn it, Jess, how could you not have noticed them?

A gust of wind teased a strand of limp brown hair into Shanna's face. She brushed it away. "I mean, it wasn't the original plan. We went to the community center in Creekhaven to talk to people about the latest news. Did you hear? The missing girl's mom has been arrested for murder!"

"Quite a twist to the story," the Kid said. "My thought was, local gossip would add color to my writeup. But while we were parking, you dashed out of there like the building was on fire. We decided to see where you were going."

"We had no idea you were coming so far." Shanna was hugging herself for warmth. The windbreaker hung loosely on her, much too large; it probably belonged to the Kid. At its neck, the edge of a lilac silk collar poked out—the blouse she'd worn to the concert. My guess was she hadn't been home since Friday.

"Well, you can go back to San Francisco now," I told them.

"So what's happening?" the Kid demanded. "What brought you up to the mountains? Let's go inside. We'll get warm, have some coffee. You can tell us about—"

I curled my frozen hands into fists inside my jacket pockets. "What are you really after, William Paveleck? You're not doing any story. They've never heard of you at *Bay City Beat*."

"They have too!" Shanna pressed herself tightly to her new

love's side. "He's doing this huge article. How a big case like this is investigated, the effect on the family and all. Isn't that right, Will?"

"You bet." The Kid patted her hand, but the gesture turned out to be merely a way to give her the scissors. He then draped his arm around me. "You're not really angry, are you, Cleo my love?"

"If I'm not angry, then you're not an insincere, incompetent fraud."

"All right! I knew you weren't mad at me."

He kissed my cheek.

My impulse was to slap him, but I had a feeling that was exactly what he was trying to provoke. I refused to give him the satisfaction.

Shanna looked like she was the one who'd been slapped. "Will? What are you doing?"

"Nothing, babe." The Kid spoke to her as he might to a small child. "Just warming up to a source."

"You kissed her!"

"Making friends, that's all."

"Why would you want to be friends with her?" She glared at me as she clutched his arm, claiming him. With her other hand she waved the scissors.

"She's a friend of Amy's family, babe, close to the case—she has to know lots of good stuff."

Get me away from these two, I thought.

"You know, Will, someone who hangs around kidnapping cases, who shows an undue interest—it can make people suspicious."

A dark expression crossed his face. "What do you mean?"

I didn't say more.

He took a step away, pulling Shanna with him. "Hey, if you're accusing me of something, you're way off base."

I stayed silent. I was freezing. My toes were going numb in their city boots.

"You know as well as I do, they're looking at Shanna's father for it."

"Will!" Shanna cried. "You said you didn't believe that."

"Of course I don't, babe. I'm making a point, is all." He didn't tell us what his point was.

"You're writing a story for real, aren't you? A lead feature, you said."

"Totally." Then, less assuredly, "That's the idea, anyway."

Shanna picked up on his backpedaling. "What do you mean, the *idea*? You said they promised you."

"Sure, if the story's good enough."

"Good enough? You're their top freelancer."

"Yeah, well." This time his sheepishness looked genuine. "After this article, I will be. Especially if sweet Cleo here plays nice and helps me out."

"I thought I was the one helping you out."

"Shanna, get real," I said. "This clown has never published a line in his life."

"That's not true!" She released his arm. "Is it?"

"I told you—I've published lots of stuff."

"Ask him to show you some clips," I said.

"Can you do that, Will?" A frown etched a crooked furrow between her brows; it reminded me of a question mark. "Do you have clippings?"

"Well, it's not like I carry a scrapbook around."

"Have you been lying to me? What else have you lied about? Her?" Shanna pointed the scissors at me. "'Sweet Cleo!' What kind of 'friends' are you and her really? The same kind you've been to me this weekend? Anything to get the story, that's what you said. I'm beginning to see what you mean."

"Jesus, babe—"

"Tell me, damn it. I want the truth."

I pushed between them, ripped the black tape off the taillight and stuck it on the Kid's parka. "Get out of here, both of you. If I catch you near me again, I'm pressing charges."

Shanna stomped off, marching as determinedly as her low-heeled pumps would permit on the rutted ice. After shooting me a vicious glance, the Kid followed, calling, "Shanna! Don't listen to her."

They got into a dirty white Chevy Cruze. The engine roared to life but the car didn't move. I saw the two people inside making wild gestures, as if they were arguing. After a moment their heat steamed up the window glass and I couldn't make them out anymore.

When the Cruze finally pulled out of its parking space, my anger dissipated, to be replaced by vague guilt. Poor, lonely Shanna—when she finally finds someone, the romance goes sour and it's my fault. William Paveleck was no prize, but it wasn't up to me to decide where someone else should place her heart. My own heart was more than enough to manage.

What appealed to Shanna, I decided as I crossed the parking lot, might be less the Pizza Kid himself than the story he was pursuing. A major crime, a devastated family—in some ways Amy's case paralleled the horror that Shanna was flung into when her sister Robin was murdered.

I felt guilty, too, about letting Paveleck get away so easily. What if my impulsive accusation was on target? Hard to believe the Kid was more than he appeared to be—an aspiring reporter whose ambition exceeded his skill or good sense. But just suppose ...

If what I learned here didn't lead us to Amy, I'd take a long, hard look at William Paveleck.

Opening the door to Mountain Guy's, I was hit by a rush of warmth and strong, appetizing odors—coffee, chili, frying onions. A radio played a country ballad accompanied by an undertone of static. The interior looked as rustic as the outside: dark and low-ceilinged, with unpainted wooden walls. The worn planks of the floor were damp with tracked-in mud and slush. Half general store, half cafe, Mountain Guy's was set up to purvey almost anything the weekend Sierra traveler might need: beer, soda, sandwiches, cans of soup, boxes of cereal, Sterno, motor oil, trail maps, woolen gloves. Hmm, gloves—good idea.

I selected a pair, forest green to match my jacket, and got in the line at the single checkout counter. A large man sporting a bushy red-orange beard was working the register with cheerful efficiency.

Racks of snack items were conveniently positioned within easy reach of the clientele. Here in the mountains, beef jerky was the favored treat, judging from the huge amount on display. Maybe the protein helped people acclimate to the cold and the altitude. I debated between the teriyaki and barbecue flavors, then grabbed a package of peanut M&Ms. The peanuts would take care of the protein and I'd have all the nutritional advantages of the chocolate as well.

I'd eaten a third of them by the time I reached the register. I placed the gloves and the candy bag on the counter.

"Hi," I said as the man rang up my sale. "I'm looking for the owner of this place."

"You found him," he said with a smile. He was wearing a yellow-and-black checked lumberjack shirt that reeked of pipe tobacco. "Guy Fletcher. What can I do you for?"

"You called a police hotline about a girl who's missing?"

His expression instantly grew serious. "Yeah, that was me. You a cop?"

"A private investigator working with the police." I told him my name.

"Let's go over there and talk. Hang on a moment." He cupped his hand to his mouth and called, "Mandy!"

A teenage girl appeared in a doorway at the back of the restaurant section. A kitchen, I guessed; she was wearing an apron.

"Yeah, Dad?"

"Come take over the register for a few minutes."

When his daughter was installed in his place, Fletcher led me to an oilcloth-covered cafe table next to a wood-fired stove. I sat and stretched my grateful feet toward the warmth. He filled two large mugs with coffee and took the other seat.

He said, "I hardly slept all night, wondering if the kid I saw was really her."

"I hope she was," I said. "We'll be that much closer to finding her."

"I didn't make the connection when they were here. Then last night on TV they showed the girl's picture. It looked like it might be the same kid. At first I brushed it off—I mean, there's lots of little girls with dark hair, right? But then I got to thinking, what if something like that had ever happened to Mandy."

"Tell me about the girl you saw."

"She was maybe seven or eight years old. She and her mother—at least, I thought it was her mother—got here yesterday around dusk. The lady came in and bought a few groceries, a six-pack of root beer, some coffee to go."

Root beer. My heart jumped. Amy's favorite.

"And you saw the girl then?"

"Not then. She must've been waiting in the car. But ten minutes later they came back. Needed to buy some tire chains and get them put on. I went out and did it myself. Usually there's some fellows here that do it, they pick up extra money, but late Saturday's a slow time. People coming up to the mountains for the weekend are already here, and the ones going home wait till Sunday."

"What happened when you put on the chains?"

He shrugged. "Nothing really. I did the job, she paid the money. The girl showed up while I was working on the car. I think she'd been around back in the restroom."

"Was the woman nervous? Was she trying to hide the girl?"

"Nervous, yeah, but I thought it was because she wasn't used to driving in the snow. She seemed okay about the girl."

"Was the girl all right? Did she seem hurt? Was she frightened of the woman?"

"Actually, she seemed more scared of me. It was like she didn't want to be seen. When she saw me at the car, she acted real shy. Skittish, you might say. She pulled up her jacket collar like she was trying to hide her face. Turned away so I couldn't get a clear look at her."

"But you did get a clear look?"

He nodded. "Pretty much."

I handed him one of the flyers. "This is Amy, the missing girl."

"Yeah, same picture they showed on TV. I can't swear absolutely it's the same kid, but it's sure possible."

"The woman—what did she look like?"

He set down the flyer and picked up his mug. "A redhead. Brighter hair than yours, more like these whiskers of mine." Fletcher stroked his flame-colored beard.

Red hair. Like the driver of the car that Hannah Holcomb saw zooming down the street around the time Amy disappeared. "What else did you notice about her?"

"Not much, I'm afraid. She had on a tan raincoat with a belt tied around the waist. I remember thinking neither one of them was dressed right for the kind of weather we're having."

"What kind of car was it?"

"Buick Regal."

"What color?"

"Gray. Maybe silver. Wish I'd written down the license plate. A California tag, I'm sure of that."

Excitement zinged through me. Yes! A gray Buick Regal. Same car, same woman. I was on the right track—please, let me be on the right track.

But why would Amy not want to be seen? She wasn't shy. I could understand the kidnapper trying to hide her, but surely Amy would be eager to be recognized. She was a resourceful, resilient kid—why hadn't she seized a chance to be rescued?

"Is there anything else you can tell me? Did either of them call the other by name? Did they say where they were going?"

He shook his head. "No, no names, no destination. Once the chains were on, the woman thanked me and they left. Must have headed east, since they needed the chains."

I finished my last sip of coffee and stood up to leave. To call Nick, then head east and hope to spot a gray Buick Regal.

"Thanks," I said to Fletcher. "You've been a big help."

"Wish I could tell you more. Do you think you'll find her?"

"No question." I put more confidence into my voice than I felt. "We'll find her."

I went back out into the cold. The clouds had darkened and sunk lower to the earth. The wind was sharp against my face.

As I walked across the frozen parking lot, a voice called me from the cafe door. I turned to see Guy Fletcher.

He smacked his forehead dramatically. "I can't believe I forgot this. It's because she asked earlier, while she was paying for groceries, and just now my mind was focused on the little girl and the car."

I returned to the porch where he stood. "The woman with Amy? What did she ask?"

"Pineland Road. She asked for directions to Pineland Road."

Pineland Road. The name rang a faint bell deep in my memory, but I couldn't place it.

I intended to find out soon, though. I got Guy Fletcher to give me the same directions he'd given Ms. Redhead.

"What are you driving?" he asked.

"That Cherokee over there." I pointed to Kit's car.

"Hmm. You'd be okay with the four-wheel drive if you were staying on Fifty. But those back roads, most of them haven't been cleared real well. Might be wise to invest in some chains."

"I've got some," I said. "Come on, Guy, help me get them on."

I skimmed over the ice and slush to the Cherokee.

CHAPTER 34

T HE CHEROKEE VIBRATED and rattled as I pulled onto the pavement. Less than a mile down the highway, I reached the chain-control point. Cars were parked on both shoulders, their drivers struggling in the slush with their chains. On the eastbound side, hawkers were selling the precious items for double the price at Mountain Guy's. The sedan ahead of me was forced to turn back, but when the officer saw my vehicle was properly equipped, he waved me on.

A few yards later, my chains bit into hardpacked snow.

East on 50 toward the summit, right on Muir Ridge Road—Guy Fletcher's directions had been simple and clear. Pineland Road would be a left turn a few miles along Muir Ridge.

While Guy Fletcher installed my chains, I'd left messages for Nick, Mac Doyle and the local sheriff, telling them about the lead to Pineland Road. So far no one had called back.

I drove slowly and cautiously. The Cherokee handled differently than my comfortable old Toyota. The chains and the snow beneath them made the steering tricky, and my goal was to return Kit's car unscathed. Behind me a pickup driver flashed his lights and leaned on his horn. I ignored him. There was no place to pull over and let him pass, and I didn't dare go faster.

More important, I didn't want to miss my turn.

Fat snowflakes swirled in the air. At first I convinced myself they were blowing off the trees, but as they fell thicker and faster, that hope was dashed.

Pineland Road, Pineland Road. The name chafed the edge of my consciousness. Where had I heard it before?

Daylight was waning. Already the world had been reduced to muted shades of gray. Trees, road, falling snow, snow on the ground, the air itself—all without form, all nearly indistinguishable.

I'm coming, Amy. I'm on my way.

Then the doubts hit, as dark and shapeless as the trees looming in the grayness. What if I found not Amy but some other girl at the end of this trek? What if Amy was there but I arrived too late? What if I slid off the road into a ditch and was buried by the falling snow, never to reach her at all?

There it was—Muir Ridge Road. The sign was obscured by a low-hanging branch, so I nearly missed the turn. I cut the wheel hard to the right. The Cherokee skidded. Heart hammering, I jerked the wheel the other way and fishtailed into the road. At least the snow that covered the narrow lanes felt smooth and solid.

Behind me, I heard a gasp.

I glanced over my shoulder, nearly losing control of the car again.

A trick of the wind. Or a swish or a squeal as I hit a patch of slush. I knew no one was there.

No one but Amy, in spirit. I could almost feel her presence settling into the passenger seat.

I thought of the last day I'd seen her, the day we chose each other for sisters. We held a ceremony to make our new family status official. I poured root beer into two of my best wineglasses, Irish crystal that had belonged to my mom, and we clinked the glasses as we offered a toast.

"To my favorite sister," I said.

"To the best sister in the world," Amy responded. "We'll be sisters forever and ever. Can we drink the root beer now?"

Then we exchanged works of art—works of heart really. I gave Amy a watercolor I'd done of Scruff as a puppy. She presented me with a portrait she'd painted as a warmup for her mother's birthday gift. A quick sketch of me, with stars in my emerald green eyes and my scarlet hair flying. I hung it on the front of my refrigerator, above a painting she'd done on New Year's Day. That one was a mountain scene, purple triangles for the mountains, green triangles for—

Amy's voice suddenly echoed in my memory: "It's the pine land. See all the trees?"

Of course! Not a descriptive term. Not a landscape out of her imagination. A place Amy knew, a place where she'd been.

Pineland Road.

Muir Ridge Road twisted higher into the mountains. Keeping my eyes straight ahead, I groped to reach the cell phone in my purse, without success. I wanted to call Nick again, tell him I'd figured out where Amy was, and with whom.

The car swerved, and I tightened my grip on the steering wheel. Snowflakes pelted the windshield faster than the wipers could clear them. I felt like I was driving blind.

Someone sneezed. And it was not Amy's spirit.

My whole body froze.

"H-hey!" Make yourself sound brave, Jess. Pretend you're in control. "Show yourself, whoever you are."

Nothing moved.

I listened to the engine's hum, the chatter of the chains, the swish of the wipers. Above all those sounds, I was sure I heard breathing.

Spotting a break in the endless snowbank that lined the road, I pulled over. Someone's driveway, apparently. The rutted track disappeared into darkness. No sign of a house or cabin.

I left the engine running.

"Right now!" I demanded. I fingered the door handle, ready to open it and flee—as if there were somewhere I could go. "I know you're there."

Slowly a head and shoulders emerged from under the tarp.

Shanna Moritz.

I was flooded with relief, and I couldn't help it expressing as anger.

"Shanna, damn it! What the hell are you doing in my car?"

"Don't be mad," she said in a small voice. "Can I come up there?"

Without waiting for a reply, she slipped out the back door and opened the passenger door in front. Shoving my purse to the floor, she wriggled into the seat where a moment ago the imaginary Amy had been.

Shanna's eyes were bloodshot and her face blotchy; tears had left dirty streaks. Her limp hair drooped against the collar of her windbreaker. She hunched her shoulders as if she were trying to draw her head, turtle-like, into the jacket. She clutched a nylon backpack to her chest like a mother cradling a baby. She no longer looked like a woman in love; once again she was the lost child.

I looked into the back. The tarp now sagged over the shapes of the toolkit and the earthquake box. "Your turn, Mr. Pepperoni. Show yourself."

"No. I'm alone. Will is ..." Shanna flapped her hand to indicate what Will was, leaving it for me to interpret—gone, dismissed, a hopeless case?

"What happened?" I asked. "Are you all right?"

"God, I need a smoke." She fumbled a package of cigarettes from her backpack.

"Please don't. Not in this car."

But she had a cigarette lit almost before I finished the sentence.

"It's all your fault, you know," she said.

"My fault? What is?"

I thought she wasn't going to answer. Then she said, "That thing with Will."

"Did you two have a fight? I thought you were driving back

home. Did he kick you out of his car? Did you jump out and run away, or what?"

She blew out a plume of smoke. It stung my eyes.

"I was so happy with Will. I loved him so much. I thought, at last I've found someone who will love me back."

"Shanna," I said gently, "you've only known him for two days. Isn't it a little soon to be talking about love?"

Her voice trembled. "It's been the best two days of my life. We were together every single minute, and he loved me. You can't imagine how good we made each other feel. Till you came along back there."

A car rumbled by, the only one I'd seen since turning onto Muir Ridge Road; its rear wheels kicked up a shower of ice.

"I'm sorry if I disillusioned you about William Paveleck, but—"

"'The lovely Cleopatra!' You think I'm deaf? Or blind? I saw how you two were looking at each other."

"Whoa! I don't know what you think you saw, but you totally misread it."

"Well, you can't have him. I made damn sure of that."

Those words filled me with alarm. "Shanna, what are you saying? What happened to Will?"

"Everyone I've ever loved has been taken away from me." She burst into tears.

I slid the dangling cigarette from between her fingers and stubbed it out in the ashtray.

She was right, I realized. No wonder she felt angry and lost. That long-ago car accident robbed her of her mother. Then grief stole her father, making him incapable of giving his daughters the love they needed. Instead he abused them, an evil and twisted perversion of the love they craved, if the prosecutors were right about Carl Moritz's motive for killing Robin. And with that horrific act of violence he took away Shanna's sister, and her infant nephew and …

"Eric Nielsen," I said aloud as the light dawned.

Shanna's head snapped up. She stopped crying mid-sob. "What did you say?"

"Nolan Aldridge told me you introduced Robin to Eric. He thought you were playing matchmaker. But that wasn't it, was it? Really, you wanted her to meet your boyfriend."

"You're crazy!" Sliding forward to the edge of the seat, she turned to glare at me.

It was starting to fall into place. "Only things went wrong. Robin and Eric fell in love with each other." Love at first sight, so romantic. And poor Shanna again was left out in the cold.

"So what! So what if that bitch did steal him from me! What does that prove?"

You can't have him. I made damn sure of that.

"It proves nothing, Shanna. Calm down."

I touched her shoulder, intending to settle her back into the seat, but she resisted, made herself rigid. Snow had piled up on the windshield, hiding us from the world, robbing us of what little light the late afternoon still held. My body was covered in cold sweat.

"Look where it got them," Shanna said. "They're dead, both of them."

"And their baby too. Your father—was it your idea that he kill them?"

She shook her head and mumbled something I couldn't make out.

"What did you say?"

"I ... I'm so sorry about the baby."

"Wait—that's who you meant, isn't it? In the restroom at the Hall of Justice, that first time we met. I asked about Amy, and you said you were sorry about the child. You were talking about Michael, not Amy." Keep Shanna talking, Jess, while you figure out what to do.

"I meant her too. I don't want any child to ever get hurt."

277

"But you did want to hurt Robin and Eric?"

She sat back finally, giving a tiny nod. I couldn't believe I'd ever felt sorry for this woman.

"I was driving down Haight Street that day. Going home. I saw them walk into the bookstore. I knew they were there to show off the baby. *My* baby, that's what he should have been—mine and Eric's. I couldn't stand for them to ... to be so happy."

Her tears welled up again. She pulled a woolen bundle from her backpack, a folded blue muffler. A fringed tail was hanging loose, and she dabbed at her eyes with it.

"The g-gun was in my car. In the glove compartment. My f-father gave it to me. He wanted ... he wanted me to be safe. I drove around and around the block until I saw them come out of the store. And then I ... I c-can't even remember what happened. I never meant to hit Michael. I was going to raise him. Let him be *my* little boy."

And at last she would have had someone to love. But at such a cost.

"How did your father find out you killed them?"

"I told him. I didn't mean to ... but I was so upset."

"And he decided to protect you."

"It's the only nice thing he's ever done for me."

A hell of a way to make up for past hurts. "And he's kept on protecting you, even though he's on trial for their murder."

She stroked the scrunched-up muffler in her lap. "It's so weird they arrested him. I never dreamed that would happen."

"Don't you care that he's going to be sent to prison, maybe executed, for something you did?"

"But he won't—he's innocent! He'll never get convicted. They wouldn't dare."

Damn! Oh, damn. How was I going to handle this? I should drive Shanna back to civilization. Turn her in to the cops, get them to find Will Paveleck. And Amy, find Amy on Pineland Road. But Shanna would never come willingly. Call the county sheriff? No, my phone was in my purse, trapped under her feet. Probably wouldn't even work here in the middle of nowhere. Flag down a passing car for assistance? Great idea, but there weren't any. The only vehicle I'd seen since I turned onto Muir Ridge Road was long gone.

I ventured, "Shanna, I want to help you—"

"Oh," she said with sudden calmness, "you've done more than enough already. To ruin my life, that is."

She held up the folded muffler, and I felt a chill deeper than any that winter could cause. Protruding from the woolly blue nest was the barrel of a gun.

"First Robin and Eric," she said. "Now Will and you. None of them got away with hurting me, and you won't either."

CHAPTER 35

If she kills me I'll never find Amy.

In my torrent of thoughts and emotions, that one stood out crystal clear.

"The reason I'm telling you all this," Shanna said, "is because Robin never got to find out why she died. When you meet up with her in hell, I want you to explain it to her."

"What about Amy?" I said. "Do you know where she is?"

Shanna frowned. "Amy? Why do you keep bringing her up? I've told you and told you, I have nothing to do with what's happened to her. Not me, not my father, not anyone we know."

Why? Because someone took to suggest the connection, sending notes to the police implying that Moritz or some cohort of his had engineered Amy's kidnapping. But I no longer believed that was true. If Amy had been taken to Pineland Road, the notes must have been false tips, deliberately misleading. Unless—suppose Shanna knew somehow about Amy's holiday trip to the mountains. What if she and Will Paveleck hadn't really followed me from Creekhaven, but drove up here yesterday with their small captive? Shanna didn't fit Guy Fletcher's description of the woman in the Buick Regal, and he hadn't mentioned a man in the car. But it had been dusk, hard to see, and eyewitness reports, though they might be sincere, were notoriously unreliable.

"I've been trying to help find her," Shanna rattled on. "I volunteered at that concert, I was assisting Will with his story ..."

280

The gun in her hand wavered as she blinked back tears. "I want to rescue her."

I had caught my breath. As I exhaled, it hung in the air, a cloud of frost. "Then join forces with me, Shanna. We'll find her together. You'll be a hero."

"Right. Like you know where she is."

"I think I do. That's where I was heading when—"

She snorted. "When you were so rudely interrupted."

"If you'd rather, I'll drive you back to Mountain Guy's. You can call someone to come pick you up and—"

"Take me to jail? No, thanks. This car right here will take me anywhere I want to go. And I don't need you to be the chauffeur."

She lifted the gun again. All she had to do was lean forward slightly and set the barrel squarely between my eyes. I could almost feel the pressure of the cold metal against my skin.

"Shanna, please. You don't want to kill me."

"Why not?"

Because if you did, you'd have pulled the trigger by now. I didn't speak the words out loud; she might consider them a challenge. If I said the wrong thing, provoked her anger, she could blow me away. I was freezing, yet sweating. My stomach was twisted into a hard knot.

She shifted position, grinding her heel into my purse. No way could I reach it. My pockets held only my gloves. There might be potential weapons under the tarp, but Shanna would hardly give me permission to search for one.

Wait—there was something I could use, directly behind my seat—if only I could reach it.

Heart in my throat, I leaned back, slumping against the driver's door.

"Amy's depending on us, Shanna. Please put the gun away. You know how awful it is for a kid when everyone lets you down."

I slid my arm between the door and the seatback. Felt around. Felt nothing. Damn, where was it?

"Think how great you'd feel if you saved her life. Think how people would love you."

"How do you know she's alive?"

"I don't. But I'm praying she is."

There it was—thank God. My hand closed around the tripod.

Shanna shook her head. "I can't. They'll find me and send me to prison."

"They'll find you anyway. It doesn't matter how far you run. But if you rescue Amy, that would be a mitigating circumstance. It would count in your favor. You'd get a lighter sentence, maybe probation."

"They wouldn't do that," she said.

No, they probably wouldn't. I hefted the tripod, lifted it over the top the headrest.

"Hey!" Shanna yelled.

The gun fired. A huge *boom* rocked the car. Behind me, the window shattered.

I smashed the tripod down onto her head.

Shanna's body folded over, trapping the gun between her thighs and her ribcage. She fell heavily against the dashboard.

I was shaking; I couldn't move. My ears rang from the gunblast. Cold and snow rushed through the broken window. I leaned back, hanging my head outside, gulping the freezing air as if I would never again have a chance to fill my lungs.

Finally, I made myself reach out to Shanna's immobile form. Her hair was sticky with blood. Her skull at the point of the wound gave slightly under my touch. But when I moved my fingers to her temple, I felt a ragged pulse, and thin puffs of breath brushed my hand when I held it beneath her nostrils.

She was alive. For now anyway.

Oh, God, what had I done?

First priority, retrieve the gun. Trying not to jar her too much, I pried it free from her crumpled body and put it in my jacket pocket.

Second, find some supplies. I opened the door and slid off the seat and planted my boots in the new snow. As soon as I took a step, my knees buckled. Bracing myself against the car, I staggered to the rear and opened the hatch.

A length of rope. A heavy-duty flashlight. A first-aid kit. I found everything I was looking for in Kit's earthquake box. Another item inside was a bottle of brandy. I unscrewed the cap and took a swig. It burned all the way down.

I wrapped the items in the plaid blanket and shuffled to the front of the car again. Setting my bundle in the snow on the car roof, I opened the passenger door.

Third, disentangle my purse from Shanna's feet and take out my pocketknife so I could cut the rope into suitable lengths.

By the time I had tied Shanna's hands and feet, ministered to her broken head and covered her with the blanket, I was exhausted.

Sitting in the driver's seat once more, I took out my cell phone. I'd try Nick again, call 911.

No signal.

I shook the phone. Hit the power button and hit it again.

Nothing. Just as I feared. The damn phone didn't work.

Now what? What was the right thing to do? Shanna needed quick medical attention. I could take her back to the chain-control post, get the officer to summon the sheriff and an ambulance.

But what about Amy? I couldn't be more than a mile from Pineland Road.

Twenty-four hours had passed since Guy Fletcher had seen the redheaded woman and the girl with dark hair.

One hundred twenty hours since Amy had vanished.

Every second counted.

Shanna moaned. Her skin was clammy, her breathing shallow and sporadic. She was right here beside me, possibly dying. If I went back, I had a good chance to save the life of a murderer.

But if I went forward, trying to help Amy—a child, a fellow

artist, my chosen sister—I'd be gambling against nearly impossible odds.

You're not the judge or jury, an inner voice whispered.

If Shanna dies, it's your fault, another one said.

I started the engine. The wipers strained to push the accumulated snow from the windshield. Snowflakes danced in the yellow beam of the headlights, flurried in through the broken window to sting my face.

I would turn around. Deliver Shanna into safe hands, recruit reinforcements from the sheriff's office and then resume my search for Amy. That was the right decision.

But the Cherokee, as if it had a will of its own, moved straight ahead.

CHAPTER 36

A MILE FARTHER ON, I found Pineland Road.
At the signpost I turned and aimed the Cherokee through a narrow opening in the trees. The road carried me across a creek on a small stone bridge, then twisted up a steep hillside. The surface was rough—earlier cars had carved icy ruts that were rapidly filling with new snow. I crept around the curves, praying I wouldn't encounter a vehicle coming downhill.

I had the heater running full blast to fight the frigid wind blowing in through the broken window. Snowflakes stung my face.

I passed a cabin nestled among the evergreens, then another. Both were dark and still, no vehicles parked nearby, the snow around them untrammeled. Probably vacation homes. No sign that anyone had visited them for weeks.

The Cherokee kept climbing. Nothing to see but trees and rocks, blurred by the snowflakes in the air. I could still make out remnants of tire tracks, so there must be more houses farther along.

Coming around a sharp bend, the car skidded. As I struggled to bring it under control, Shanna's body shifted and she groaned. I stopped in the middle of the road—no place to pull over—to check her bandage and straighten the blanket.

"You're doing fine, Shanna," I told her. "Don't die on me."

I placed my hands on top of the steering wheel and lowered my forehead onto them. This was a quixotic venture, a hopeless quest. I'd been wrong to push on after Shanna got injured. After I injured her. I didn't want to be responsible for her death. I should go back, get help, let the authorities take charge. As soon as I could find a place to turn around, that's what I'd do.

I put my foot on the gas. The Cherokee stalled.

Damn! I cut off the heater and the headlights, then turned the ignition key again. The engine made a grinding sound and died. I tried once more. Same result.

Now what was I going to do?

I punched buttons on my cell phone. Still no signal. I fought an urge to fling it through the open window.

The snow was so thick on the windshield that I couldn't see through it. Night would be here soon.

Okay, Jess, think this through. Screaming will not help. Crying will not improve the situation. Sending smoke signals won't work in this weather. You have two choices: sit and wait for someone to come along, or get out and try to scare up some assistance.

My entire being voted to sit and wait. Yet I heard myself say, "Hang in there, Shanna. I'll be back as quick as I can."

Kneeling on the seat, I reached back, grabbed the tarp and wrestled it forward. I wrapped it around Shanna over the plaid blanket. The best I could do to protect her against the cold.

I got out of the car, flinching as my feet disappeared into the snow. I put the flashlight in one of my jacket pockets. Took Shanna's gun out of the other and checked it. Fully loaded, except for the one shot she'd fired.

There was no telling what might lie up the road, how far it was to the next house. Plan A, I would walk back downhill to the nearest cabin, break in and see if there was a working phone. Illegal, yes, but surely justified under the circumstances.

I'd worry about the consequences later.

I pulled on my new gloves and fervently wished I'd brought my knit hat.

Placing my feet with care, I pushed away from the car. Whiteness whirled around me. For a moment I felt dizzy. Nerves, that's all. Breathe deep, Jess, get steady.

Woodsmoke. I caught a whiff of woodsmoke.

Then it was gone. I wasn't sure I'd smelled it at all.

I inhaled deeply again. A sharp cold breath. Then another. Yes—woodsmoke, definitely.

No one could be out here camping. There must be a house close by.

The road ahead climbed for a short distance and disappeared into the pines. The source of the smoke couldn't be far beyond that point.

I began trudging up, and up, and up. My boots plowed through the snow. I tried to keep to the ruts dug by some earlier car. The road narrowed; trees closed in. Branches overhead gave me some protection from the falling snow, but they cut out what little was left of the daylight.

Then I reached a break in the trees. The wind whooshed, and the air turned solid with snow. The world was white, gray, blank ...

Panic slammed me hard, doubling me over like a punch in the stomach.

I couldn't move; I couldn't breathe; I didn't dare take another step.

Flipping on the flashlight, I scanned the edges of the road, looking for ... what? I was puzzled at first, then realized I was hoping to glimpse a purple mitten on a stick. I was searching out places where a seven-year-old girl might take shelter among the rocks and the pines.

A seven-year-old who wasn't Amy but me.

I looked up toward where the sky would be if the trees and snow weren't blocking it, wishing a ranger would magically appear, just as my rescuer had back then.

No such luck. This time it was up to me to set things right.

I pushed on.

A few hundred yards farther along, I reached the crest of the hill. On the other side, the road descended briefly, then leveled off. The trees parted to open up a meadow. At the far end of the clearing, a house stood against a backdrop of pines. Through the scrim of the snowfall, it looked larger and newer than the cabins I'd passed down the road.

And it appeared as if someone were home. Smoke rose from the chimney. Big windows glowed yellow with lamplight. The place looked warm, inviting: *Welcome, stranded traveler. You will find help and comfort here.*

Was this where Amy was being held? If so, I wouldn't be greeted with smiles and a cup of tea. Gunfire more likely, the way Philip Vandergriff had been met at the blood-soaked apartment on Cole Street.

Think positive, Jess. I visualized myself running in, grabbing Amy from under the nose of the kidnapper and fleeing. I pictured Amy home again, in her parents' embrace. What I couldn't see was how we would get away, with the Cherokee dead, my cell phone not working, and the storm growing more fierce by the minute.

I felt its rising power the instant I moved beyond the trees. In the clearing the snow fell harder, the flakes blown nearly sideways by the gusting wind.

I tried to keep to the road, placing my feet carefully in the tire tracks, feeling through the snow to find their icy edges. My wimpy boots were soaked through, and I could no longer feel my toes. As I brushed my hair out of my face, I realized the wet strands were beginning to freeze.

The rutted tracks veered sharply to the right, leading up a driveway to a car parked close to the house. Pineland Road continued straight, but beyond this point the snow on the road was unbroken. No one had gone up or down since long before this storm began.

The car was draped with a fresh mantle of white. Keeping an eye on the house, I crept up behind it, trying to keep out of sight until I had a better idea of what I was dealing with. I brushed some snow off the fender.

Yes! A gray Buick Regal. My heart would have leapt if it weren't frozen in place.

I memorized the license plate, then crouched behind the car, watching the house. It was a handsome, contemporary structure built of stone, wood and glass. A deck with a railing stretched across the front. Draperies covered the floor-to-ceiling windows, letting light through but concealing the interior from view. I thought I detected a shadowy movement inside but couldn't be sure.

I heard a sudden sound: a call, a scream, an animal's howl. Or perhaps just the rush of wind.

I crept out from behind the car. In front of the house, someone had built a snowman, using pinecones to create eyes, nose and mouth. A thick row of pine needles had been poked into the snow beneath the nose to suggest a mustache.

As I moved forward I became aware of patterns pressed into the snow—shapes with heads, long skirts and sweeping wings.

Snow angels.

Half a dozen of them. Each with a crinkly halo made of aluminum foil.

Illumine foil. Haloes made of light. Like the one Amy and I made in my studio.

Tears formed. I blinked them back so they wouldn't fall and freeze on my face.

Please be here, Amy, I whispered. *Don't let this be like Cole Street. No dead body this time. No signs you were here but now you've vanished again.*

Hand on the gun in my pocket, I stepped up to the deck. Someone had cleared away most of the snow, leaving the surface glazed with ice. My feet slipped and I fell heavily.

Wincing with pain, I picked myself up and touched the tender spots. I'd landed on my hip, banged a knee and whacked my shoulder against a railing post. I would have major bruises, but no bones were broken so far as I could tell. My bigger worry was whether anyone had heard the thud.

At least the gun hadn't fired.

I stood totally still, listening. No sound from inside. Moving with extra care, I crossed the deck.

When I touched the latch, the door inched open. The last person to go in or out had failed to close it tightly.

I kept the gun ready as I let myself inside.

CHAPTER 37

I stood stock still inside the doorway. Snow dripped off my boots and jacket. I didn't dare enjoy the relief that my body felt at being out of the storm.

I could see and hear no one. The silence had weight and shape, the way it does when it fills an empty space. Yet all the signs indicated there were people in this house.

I was in a large room—living space, dining area and kitchen combined. Every lamp was lit, imparting an amber glow to the pine-paneled walls.

A blaze burned in the massive stone fireplace. Half a dozen logs were stacked and ready on the hearth. I moved to it quickly and thawed myself in front of the flames.

A muted TV flickered in the corner. The remote control and a mug half filled with coffee sat on a low table in front a leather sofa. I tested the liquid with my finger; still warm. The sofa cushions bore the indentation made by a person sitting there not long ago.

On an end table I found the cradle for a portable phone, but to my dismay the handset was nowhere in sight. So much for calling for help.

A newspaper lay beside the phone. Yesterday's *Chronicle*. Philip Vandergriff's photo smiled at me from the front page. Above the picture were the words: "Tech Company President Murdered."

How ironic to see that horrific headline in Philip's own house. Because that's what this had to be. The place Amy had visited for her Christmas trip to the pine land.

Where were they?

I opened the sliding glass door at the rear of the room. Cold air rushed in; tumbling flakes brushed my face.

Back here was another deck, partially cleared of snow, though a picnic table in one corner was covered with more than a foot of white stuff. I saw no outbuildings, no shelter where Amy and her kidnapper could be hiding.

I shut the door and leaned against it, rubbing my painful shoulder. They must be here in the house. But where?

A short hallway led to three closed doors.

Nerves on high alert, I crept to door number one and opened it, revealing a small room furnished with a bureau and a double bed. The mattress was bare, the drawers and closet empty.

But the bathroom behind door two had been recently used. Pink toothbrush on the sink, half-used bar of soap on the tub rim, damp washcloth hanging on the rack. Not daring to breathe, I pulled the shower curtain aside. No one there.

The third room was another bedroom. This bed had been made, but carelessly, pillow askew and covers wrinkled. I looked underneath it. Nothing but dust. The closet held only some twisted wire hangers. I opened the bureau drawers. Empty, empty, empty, then paydirt—socks and underpants, a couple of T-shirts, a red sweater.

All child-sized. Amy-sized. My hand trembled as I touched them.

But what really made me catch my breath was a crayoned drawing that had been taped to the wall. It showed two artists dressed in knee-length smocks, standing at an easel. The bigger one had orange corkscrews of hair; the smaller one had brown hair and a red crescent smile. Their arms were upraised, a paintbrush in each hand. Next to them was a dog with tail and ears like Scruff's.

At the bottom, printed in green crayon, was the name *Amy* and today's date.

No tears, Jess. Not now. Just find her.

Near the kitchen, a flight of steps rose to a balcony that overlooked the living area. Ignoring the protests of my bruised hip and knee, I ran upstairs. Amy had to be up there; I'd looked everywhere else. Grim pictures formed in my mind, ones I couldn't shake—Amy being brave and resolute as the kidnapper held a gun to her head, a knife to her throat, a thin sharp wire around her neck.

At the top I slid my hand into my pocket and closed it over the grip of Shanna's gun.

Halfway along the balcony, there was a double-doorway. One door was open. I tiptoed to it and peeked in, exposing as little of myself as possible.

The master suite. Empty. Damn it, where were they?

I went inside.

The kingsize bed had been slept in and left unmade. A pillow had slid to the floor, and a patchwork quilt was snarled with a sheet and a couple of blankets.

The adjacent bathroom was more sumptuous than the one downstairs. Acres of mirrors and an oversized Jacuzzi tub. Not long ago someone had used lotion or soap in here, scenting the room with lavender.

And she'd left behind her hair.

On the marble counter sat a pink plastic head topped with a red wig. I fingered the fuzzy strands. If I wasn't mistaken, Guy Fletcher had seen this hair and so had Hannah Holcomb.

Where was the wig wearer now?

She and Amy had to be hiding in the walk-in closet.

Heart in my throat, I eased open the door, listening for the softest whisper of breathing, the slightest rustle of movement. All was silent.

No one there.

I wanted to scream with anger, frustration, disappointment.

The closet was empty of people but full of clothes—jeans, flannel shirts on hangers, heavy sweaters folded on a shelf. Based on their size, I guessed they were Philip's, kept here to avoid the need for packing when he came up for weekends. I was surprised to see nothing that looked like Terri's.

A tan tote bag hung from a brass hook. It looked familiar. I took it down and peeked inside, much as Scruff had tried to do when he encountered it on Thursday afternoon outside of Philip's house—just hours, it turned out, before Philip died.

Two more wigs—one black, one curly and gray—and beneath them, a theatrical makeup kit.

Of course. Why hadn't we thought of wigs? The brunette Atom saw on Cole Street and the redhead who drove past Hannah Holcomb's house and bought tire chains at Mountain Guy's—they were the same woman.

The gray wig baffled me. Maybe it was a spare, never used.

As I replaced the tote bag and turned to leave the closet, I spied something wedged into a corner.

Another bag. This on was made of white plastic, emblazoned with Japanese calligraphy and a circular red sun.

For half a second I worried about getting fingerprints on it. But of course my prints were already there. I'd taken this bag to the Japanese Tea Garden and left it there.

Careful to avoid smudging any prints the kidnapper had left, I looked inside.

Cash. Lots of cash, rubber-banded into neat bundles.

The ransom money.

I shoved the bag back into place, so the cops could find it where the kidnapper had left it.

Crossing the bedroom to the door, I again noticed the tangle of bedclothes. Suddenly I was filled with dread. The bundle was too small to have anything hidden inside. But I had to make sure.

Holding my breath, I unknotted the covers, and almost cried with relief when I didn't find Amy's body wrapped up inside.

Downstairs again, I paced the floor.

I was too late.

The thought scraped my brain like sharp claws. Amy had been here and now was gone, just like on Cole Street. I'd almost found her but I'd failed.

I was too damn late.

I needed help but had no way to summon it. Shanna was in my car with potentially mortal injuries. I had no idea where Amy was.

Too late. If they died, it would be all my fault.

Stop it, Jess. For God's sake—shake yourself to your senses.

I drew to a halt in front of the fridge. The door was adorned with snapshots of what looked like a festive Christmas celebration. Amy with a big red stocking. Amy in front of a tinseled tree. Philip and Terri together, Terri raising her left hand to show off her spectacular diamond ring. All of them smiling, enjoying a merry holiday, looking forward to a bright future.

Scarcely a month ago. How quickly the world could turn upside down.

A glass on the counter contained melting ice cubes and a couple of inches of brown liquid. I took a sniff. Root beer. I found the crushed can in the trash, along with a crumpled package that had held chocolate chip cookies. The smell of the remaining crumbs flashed me back to the Cole Street apartment. I had stood in that kitchen, weak in the knees, examining crumbs in a cookie tin while the police dealt with Philip's body in the next room. *Do you think she likes chocolate chip?* said a voice in my memory. The cookies in the tin came from Terri's house. I'd smelled them baking.

Earlier I'd noticed a litter of papers on the dining table. Now, feeling sore and disheartened, I sat down to give them a closer look. It was hard to concentrate. Part of me wanted to curl up on the sofa, go to sleep, let a blessed stupor overtake me. A kind of mental hypothermia.

A folder from AmeriCar contained the rental agreement for the Buick; like the lease for the Cole Street apartment, it was signed by Theresa Shaw.

A batch of documents pertained to SalesCom Technologies— financial statements, payroll reports, marketing memos. SalesCom was Lacey's now, most likely. Unless Philip had already changed his will in Terri's favor, anticipating their wedding, his sister was the obvious heir.

Lacey, the tech genius who designed the revolutionary software that was the linchpin of SalesCom's success. Lacey, the actress who gave up her share of the company to chase a dream of stardom that never came true.

McCabe and Rovinsky thought Terri had kidnapped her own daughter in order to extort one hundred thousand dollars in ransom money from Philip. But wasn't Lacey the more likely suspect? Perhaps Philip had forced out of SalesCom. Maybe she felt cheated of the wealth the company generated after she left it. So she found a way to kill her brother, grab his wealth and frame Terri as the guilty party.

Lacey in the red wig was the one who snatched Amy on her way to Evelyn's house.

Lacey in the dark wig tended to Amy in the Cole Street apartment. When Philip discovered them there, Lacey shot him and fled.

Lacey in the gray wig and elderly makeup—yes, I could guess what the gray wig was for. She wore it when she collected the ransom money in the Japanese Tea Garden. She'd counted on blending with a cluster of tourists and lucked out—the unsuspecting seniors church group from Arkansas provided a perfect cover.

But where the hell was she now? Where was Amy? I started to stand up—I had to figure out how to find them.

My foot skidded as I put weight on it, and I landed hard on the chair seat again. Looking down in frustration, I saw the culprit that had made me slip—a manila file folder lying on the rug.

I picked it up and flipped it open.

A sheaf of articles about the Moritz murder trial, clipped from newspapers and printed out from Internet sites. Drafts of letters, typed on a computer but annotated and corrected by hand. On one sheet, Nick's name and Hall of Justice address was written in black ink above the words:

> *Inspector Gardino, If you want to see your daughter again, forget everything you ever knew about Carl Moritz.*

I recognized that handwriting. I had a sample in my purse. Philip Vandergriff had used the same thick, angular script when he wrote his cell phone number on the back of his business card.

So Philip was not the victim of extortion after all—at least not at first. Instead it looked like he was the mastermind of Amy's kidnapping.

But why? How could he do such a terrible thing?

My thoughts were shattered by someone yelling outside, then a series of loud, sharp cracks.

Gunfire!

CHAPTER 38

A BLAST OF COLD AIR hit me as the sliding door opened and Lacey Vandergriff, sodden and disheveled, burst into the room. Eyes crazed, movements twitchy, she looked like a savage animal in a trap. A gun dangled in one hand.

A tight fist squeezed my heart. *Oh God, she's just done something terrible to Amy.*

I pulled Shanna's weapon from my pocket.

Lacey halted abruptly.

"What are you doing!" she cried. "Get out of here!"

She aimed a backward glance at the sliding door. The doubled glass panes reflected the room with its amber light; the open half was curtained by falling snow.

My mind turned to stone yet raced at triple speed. "Sit down, Lacey. Give me your gun and sit."

She snapped around to face me, lifted her gun.

I tightened my grip on Shanna's gun, pointed it at Lacey. The trigger felt hot under my finger.

I heard a shout from outside.

"Who's out there?" I demanded. "What's going on?"

Lacey used both hands to hold her gun level.

Shoot first, an inner voice urged. I couldn't make myself do it.

More shouting.

"Oh God," Lacey said.

Count to three, Jess. Then shoot.

Suddenly Lacey let go.

Her gun clattered onto the table. My hand shaking, I scooped it up, dropped it into my pocket.

"You've got to help me," Lacey moaned.

"Where's Amy?" I tried to keep my voice steady.

"I don't know. Oh God, it wasn't supposed to turn out like this."

"Damn it, Lacey! Where is she?"

She ran a hand over her tawny hair. Her natural hair. It was soaking wet, plastered to her scalp.

"No one was supposed to get hurt. Honest."

"Is Amy hurt? Lacey, you have to tell me—"

"Philip wanted to be a hero, that's all. To rescue Amy so Terri would love him."

I couldn't believe what I'd heard. "You mean this whole mess happened so he could impress his fiancée?"

Lacey nodded. "Terri wanted to break their engagement. He couldn't stand the idea of losing her."

"Amy's the one we've lost!" I nearly screamed it. Calm down, I told myself. You'll get more answers if you let Lacey tell this her own way. I said, more softly, "And you went along with this insane idea."

"He paid me. I needed the money. We set it up to look like Amy was kidnapped because of the Moritz trial."

"But you tried to frame Terri. Signing Theresa Shaw on documents. Using Terri's gun."

Lacey shrugged, or maybe shivered. Her thin jacket appeared to be drenched through. "I figured the Moritz people would use a made-up name. Phil gave me Terri's gun. That one"—she gestured toward my pocket—"that's Phil's. I found it here in the house."

"After you killed him, you mean."

"No! I never—"

"The ransom was your idea, wasn't it. Philip was shocked when he heard about the demand letter. That wasn't in the plan."

Lacey's hazel eyes flashed with anger. "He owed me big time.

The bastard got rich off my software design. A hundred thousand dollars was nothing."

"So he went to Cole Street, argued with you about it, and you shot him."

"No, I swear I—"

Her anger was no match for mine. "And you grabbed Amy and ran. Took the money and ... God, Lacey, you got what you wanted—why didn't you let Amy go?"

"I was going to. I tried. I drove her to the playground, but she wouldn't get out of the car, she was crying ..."

"Where is she now? Damn it, Lacey, you've got to tell me."

I heard the scuffling of footsteps on the decks, front and back.

"Oh shit, they're here." Lacey looked around frantically, as if trying to decide which way to run.

"Who? Who's out there?"

A pounding on the front door. "Police! Open up!"

Lacey yelled, "I've got a hostage! Go away or I'll kill her!"

"No!" I called. "She's unarmed. She's under control."

The front door slammed open and two men burst in, guns drawn. Another entered through the sliding glass door, stamping snow off his boots.

Nick, Mac Doyle and a uniformed sheriff's deputy.

I felt a tremendous weight lift from my shoulders.

"Nick! Am I glad to see you."

"Amy!" he yelled. "Amy, it's Daddy! You're safe now."

Lacey didn't resist as the deputy cuffed her hands behind her back.

I tried to approach Nick but Doyle cut me off. "Figures that you'd be here."

"Yeah, I ... well ..." I was too fatigued, too rattled to explain anything coherently or defend myself from accusations.

Nick prowled the big room, taking in the embers dying in the fireplace, the clippings on the table, the photos on the fridge. Then he disappeared down the hallway in search of Amy.

Doyle said, "Thanks for the message about Pineland Road. We'd have been here sooner but Route Fifty's closed. Homicide investigation, someone shot a guy driving a Chevy Cruze. Had to get a sheriff's escort to get us around it."

I said, "His name's William Paveleck."

Doyle lifted an eyebrow. "You know him?"

"Shanna Moritz shot him. She's in my car, a Cherokee down the road, she's injured, she—"

"We found her," Doyle said. "Couple of officers are taking her to get medical attention. Care to tell me what happened?"

Nick came back just in time to see the deputy maneuver Lacey to the open front door.

"Wait!" He rushed to her, grabbed her shoulder. "Amy's here, right? Where is she, upstairs?"

Lacey stared at the floor.

"She's not in the house, Nick." My heart ached as I said it. "I searched the whole place."

"Then where—what the hell have you done to her, Lacey?" Nick's hands went to her throat. "For Christ's sake, if you've hurt her, I'll—"

Doyle pulled Nick back. "Don't do it."

"She ran away," Lacey whispered.

"She what!" Nick's face was flushed; he looked ready to explode.

Tears glistened in Lacey's eyes. "Amy saw someone—it must have been Jess—coming toward the house. She got scared. She ran out the back, into the woods."

"You let her go?"

"I tried to stop her, I really did. I went out and looked, but I couldn't find her. It's so dark out there. So cold. I thought for sure she'd come back by now."

Nick pivoted toward the sliding glass door. "Mac, you guys can handle Lacey, right? I've got to find Amy."

"We'll send help," Doyle said. "A search team."

301

"Can't wait." He was already running.

I dashed out into the snow right behind him.

CHAPTER 39

"A MY! *AY-MEE!*"
Shouting her name, Nick and I crossed the deck, half-slid down the icy steps, and waded out into snow that came nearly to my knees. Beyond the house, the forest loomed. The tumbling flakes, whipped by the wind, made pale, shifting patterns against the black backdrop of trees.

"*Ay-mee!*"

Nick turned on a flashlight. I retrieved mine from my pocket. Switching it on, I was startled by the sudden brilliance of the snowflakes in the air.

We swept the beams over the white ground. My light caught a line of what looked like freshly broken snow—Lacey's tracks, I guessed, returning to the house. They led out from a gap in the trees. Beside and beneath them were other footprints, less distinct, their depths and edges blurred by the snow that had fallen since they were made.

"Nick! Over here." I beckoned with the flashlight.

We followed the tracks into the woods. Under the trees the going was easier; the drifts were less deep, the snowfall less heavy.

A few yards in, our path intersected with a wider one, probably a fire road. To my dismay, footprints led off in both directions.

"I'll go this way," I told Nick. "You go that way."

"Better stick together," he said.

"What if we choose the wrong way? If we separate, we double our chances of finding her."

He nodded. "Keep to the trail. Don't you get lost too." He touched my shoulder, then set out to the left, following his flashlight beam.

"Amy!" he yelled, his voice muffled by snow and wind.

He rounded a bend and disappeared.

I stood there alone, surprised at the hollow feeling in the pit of my stomach. As the snowflakes hit my face, I felt abandoned and bereft. I took a deep breath. Stamped my feet, going numb in my soaked boots. Brushed snow off my shoulders. I wished again I had a hat or a hood. My hair was getting soaked, and my ears tingled.

As an experiment, I turned off the flashlight, and was overwhelmed by the near-total darkness. I couldn't see the house at all, but occasionally I caught glimpses of Nick's distant beam floating like a ghost among the trees.

Shivering, I turned my light back on. What was I doing out in a fierce storm? The warmth and safety of the house pulled on my nerve fibers the way a magnet pulls on steel.

Be adventurous! Take risks!

The whisper of falling snow, but it sounded like Amy's voice.

I picked my way along the narrow road, shining the flashlight into the tangled undergrowth and echoing Nick's shout:

"Amy!"

Why did she dash away into this awful night? Because she saw me approaching the house, Lacey said. The idea that I'd made her run wrenched my soul. Even if she didn't recognize me, wouldn't she welcome having someone come to her rescue?

The road grew steeper, switchbacking up a hill. I could still make out footprints, a single set now, shallow indentations in the snow. Child-size? Hard to tell.

"Ay-mee!" I yelled. The wind whisked the sound away.

Amy must have fled because she was scared. Perhaps when she saw me outside the house, she thought I was someone else. Someone who meant danger. Who could that be?

The trees and brush closed in. A thorny branch scratched my face.

"*Ay-mee!*"

My foot snagged on a buried rock or root, and I pitched headlong. I sprawled in the snow, unable to move or breathe.

Give up, go back, my inner voice said.

After a moment, I mustered strength from somewhere and dragged myself to my feet.

As I shook off the snow, I heard my hair crackle. Ice coated the soggy strands. I rubbed it away with the wool of my glove.

Never in my life had I felt so cold.

How long could a child last out here? Amy had run outside when I arrived at Philip's house—what, an hour ago? Far too long to brave a storm like this.

Rounding a stand of trees, I panicked. I'd lost the road.

I flashed my light here, there, over that way. The trees pushed tightly together; no gaps to suggest a trail among them.

No more footprints.

My stomach twisted into a tight knot.

Wait, there were the tracks, circling behind a bent pine.

I went that way, plunging through a thicket of brambles, and heaved a sigh of relief when the road widened again. But the snow here was deeper, the footing less solid.

At the right-hand edge of the road, the ground dropped away into a canyon. I aimed the beam down the slope. The light hit large rocks far below, marking the course of an ice-clogged creek.

No sign of a child down there.

Keeping far to the left, I pushed onward.

Lacey said she'd taken Amy to the merry-go-round in Golden Gate Park, intending to deliver her as promised after grabbing the ransom cash. But Amy refused to get out of the car. She didn't want to go home.

Why not? Was someone at home hurting her? Abusing or molesting her? By kidnapping Amy, Philip had done her great harm—but she must know Philip was dead. Surely she wasn't afraid of her mother? Or Nick? I began to feel sick to my stomach. Oh God, don't let it be Terri or Nick.

Then who?

"Amy! *Ay-mee!* It's Jess! Where are you?"

No answer but the wind sighing and the trees cracking and groaning under the weight of snow.

I wracked my brain, trying to think of any hint of trouble I might have missed, any signal that Amy needed my help, my protection. I came up with nothing.

"Amy!"

But she'd given a sign to Guy Fletcher, I realized—even if she hadn't intended to. At Mountain Guy's, she'd tried to hide from him, to avoid being noticed. So maybe it wasn't a person she feared. Maybe she was frightened by the very idea of being rescued.

Why? Because she'd have to go home. Was she anxious about something at school? Or afraid she faced punishment for some misbehavior? If so, it must be something she'd done after I'd seen her last but before she disappeared. Or—I was struck by the thought—something she'd done during these recent terrible days. What if—

With a sudden whoosh, a large bough released its burden, pummeling me with snow. As I dodged the onslaught, my feet skidded out from under me and I slid over the edge of the trail.

I plunged downhill, trying to curl into a protective ball. I wanted to pray to whatever gods might be listening. I wanted to shout "I love you!" and hope the wind would carry the words to all the right ears.

All I managed was a wordless shriek that bounced off the canyon walls.

I braced myself for the sensation of smashing against rocks and ice.

Then abruptly I stopped falling.

To my astonishment I was still alive. I sucked in a deep breath to make sure. The air was so cold it seared my lungs.

I didn't have the nerve to open my eyes. When I finally peeked, everything was black except for a smudge of light in the snow above me.

My flashlight. I must have dropped it on the road.

I became aware of pain. Of numbness in my fingers and feet. Of snowflakes prickling my face.

When I tried to move, whatever was beneath me shifted. I heard twigs snapping.

I'd landed in some bushes on a narrow ledge.

Carefully, slowly, I gathered myself into a crouch, balancing on the rocky shelf. If I moved any more, I would tumble to the bottom of the canyon and break myself to bits. If I didn't move, I would die of exposure; my blood would freeze solid, just like my tears were freezing to my cheeks.

I couldn't go on.

I couldn't give up.

Be adventurous! Take risks!

Bracing myself against the canyon wall, I inched up until I was more or less standing. I leaned there, breathing hard. Every muscle ached. Every bone felt like jelly. An intense pain burned through my left shoulder.

Okay, Jess, now what?

Aim for the light, I told myself. It's not far, just a few feet. You can make it. Pretend the light is the park ranger, come like an angel to rescue you.

I stayed still, giving my eyes time to assess whatever they could in the blackness. Gradually I made out shapes: boulders, shrubs, vines, all shrouded in snow. I closed my fingers around a rock that protruded overhead and tugged. It held. I kicked at the snow until I carved out a foothold. I hoped it was solid; my toes were so numb I couldn't tell.

I pulled myself up. Didn't fall. Hung there a moment to catch my breath. Groped for another handhold, praying my frozen fingers wouldn't refuse to work.

My hand brushed something thin and round. A slender tree trunk, angling upward toward the trail. Below me, I could barely discern the tangle of dead leaves and branches that had once been the treetop. Up above, the flashlight beam revealed broken, twisted roots poking into the air.

If I was lucky, maybe some of the roots still held the tree fast.

I crept sideways until I could grasp the trunk with both hands. I yanked it gently, holding my breath, afraid I'd dislodge it and shoot the tree and myself straight into the ice-choked creek.

It didn't budge.

I worked my way upward, hand over hand, inch by painful inch. In summer, in daylight, I could have scrambled up the slope in no time. This climb took weeks.

At last I crawled onto the fire road and collapsed. My shoulder was throbbing. I didn't have the energy to pick myself up.

I had never felt so exhausted. The snow felt almost comfortable. The thing to do was to lie here, get some sleep. Yes, that was the best plan. I'd pillow my head in a snowdrift and let the falling flakes cover me like a warm blanket. I pulled off one of my gloves. I could put it on a stick—forest green this time, not a purple mitten—and wait for the angel to …

Except—what about Amy?

Come to your senses, Jess. Don't be an idiot.

Rubbing my shoulder, I struggled to sit up.

"Amy!" My voice sounded feeble.

I picked up the flashlight, distressed to see that its beam was growing dim. Before long, the batteries would give out.

I forced myself to stand. Tried yelling again.

"Ay-mee!" A little stronger this time.

I could still make out faint footprints on the road, though they were rapidly filling with snow. They led me on, into the darkness.

The road climbed uphill.

At least I thought I was still on a road. Maybe I was just moving through a series of gaps between trees. Perhaps the dents in the snow weren't human footprints but the tracks of some beast. A grizzly bear. A ravening wolf. Sasquatch.

Stop it, Jess. Concentrate. Don't let fear run away with you.

I swept the flashlight beam in slow arcs, left to right and back again. Trees to rocks to footprints to undergrowth. No colors at all in the landscape, just blacks and grays.

No sounds either, or only the tiniest ones. A branch creaking. The whoosh of the wind. My boots crunching into the snow, one step and then another. My shoulder ached. My whole body felt like one enormous bruise.

I couldn't tell how long I'd been walking. Time operated under different rules out here. Instead of minutes marching forward in a line, it was as if eternity was shaking them out of the sky, so that they fell to earth in the form of snowflakes.

"Amy!" I yelled.

I rounded a bend and the footprints stopped.

No! I wanted to scream. To weep. To lie down and let the snow bury me.

I closed my eyes, then opened them again, hoping I'd see something different.

Beyond this point, the snow on the trail was smooth and unbroken.

The footprints probably weren't Amy's anyway. More likely someone had come out this afternoon for a hike through a winter wonderland.

Or I could have been chasing Lacey's steps, and reached the point where she'd given up searching for Amy and turned around.

But I'd been following only one set of prints. Coming and going, Lacey would have left two distinct tracks.

I flashed the light around. Where had the person who made the prints gone? The faltering beam picked out trees, an outcropping of rocks, a fallen log …

A flash of red.

There, next to the log. Something red.

I could see now how the snow near the trail was scuffed and churned. It looked as if someone had fallen, then crawled into the woods.

I wanted to run. Impossible. I slogged and stumbled through the snow to the place where I saw the red.

The log, some boulders and a cluster of trees had created a sheltered nook where hardly any snow had accumulated. In the center, curled into fetal position on a layer of pine needles, was a girl in a red ski jacket.

"Amy!"

I knelt beside her. I could hardly see. Tears clouded my vision.

She didn't stir. Oh God, don't let it be too late.

"Amy? It's Jess." I kissed her cheek. Cold, but not icy. I felt shallow breathing.

I lay down next to her, tight against her body, hoping to warm her.

A wiggle, a moan. The most welcome sound I'd ever heard.

"Come on, Amy. Let's get to someplace warm." I wracked my brain trying to come up with the first-aid steps for treating hypothermia, but I couldn't think clearly. My brain just repeated over and over: *Warm, warm, warm.*

"Can't," she mumbled.

"Sure you can," I said, far more heartily than I felt. "We'll make it. We'll have you home in no time."

I stood up, then stooped and lifted her into my arms. Pain shot through my shoulder. That and the sheer weight of her made me stagger, but I managed to gain my balance.

"Okay, Amy, here we go." One step at a time, Jess. Take it one step at a time.

Holding her made it awkward to handle the flashlight. I got it fixed in one hand, pointing ahead and slightly down. That would have to be good enough to guide us. Now if only the batteries would hold out.

Amy murmured something against my chest.

"What's that, sweetheart?"

"Don' 'ake me home."

"We have to find shelter. Get you warm."

"I di' a bad thing."

I placed my feet carefully, first one, then the other. "Don't think about it now."

She clutched me tighter. "Oh Jez. Wha' we gonna do?"

"Don't worry, sweetheart. I promise you, everything will be fine."

We were back on the fire road. Now if I could just get Amy down the steep stretches without sliding.

One slow, painful step at a time. With each step Amy grew heavier and my body hurt worse. I couldn't make out any landmarks. Couldn't be sure we were heading in the right direction. Had no idea how far we'd come, or how much longer I could last.

Way down the trail I saw bobbing lights.

"Hey!" I called. "Hello!" I waggled the flashlight, hoping the erratic darting of the beam would be a signal.

Someone yelled, "Jess!"

"Nick? Nick! Up here!"

Amy tensed in my arms. She whispered, "Don' let him find me."

Before I could answer, Nick came into view. There were people behind him—Carmen Aguilar and two more, probably the searchers from the sheriff's office.

"Jess! I heard a scream," Nick said. "So we came this way and ... Amy! Oh my God—Amy!"

Amy's body went rigid as he lifted her from my arms. Then I saw her sag against his shoulder.

"Oh Daddy!" she cried. "I'm so sorry I shot Philip. Please don' put me in jail."

CHAPTER 40

N EVER IN MY LIFE had I been so glad to see a cup of tea—even a paper cup from McDonald's.

"Thanks," I said to Carmen Aguilar, who brought it to my bedside in the Placerville hospital the next morning. "I really appreciate this. Room service in this hotel is terrible."

She rewarded my quip with a bigger chuckle than it deserved. "The FBI is always glad to help. How are you doing?"

"I'm okay." I pried the lid from the cup, bent my face over it and inhaled the steam. Heat, glorious heat. "I've been thoroughly poked, prodded and probed. All that's wrong is a wrenched shoulder, a whole lot of bruises and some superficial frostbite in my toes. I don't know why they wouldn't let me out of here last night."

In truth, I'd been happy to spend the night tucked between white sheets in the hospital bed. I was exhausted and achy; my shoulder throbbed, my toes throbbed and tingled, and every muscle I had was sore. I'd slept poorly, if at all. Amy's words kept echoing in my brain: *I'm so sorry I shot Philip.*

What a terrible burden for a seven-year-old child to bear.

"How's Amy?" I asked, then sipped the tea.

"I'm told her prognosis is good," Aguilar said. She moved toward the door. "I have to leave. We're taking Lacey back to the Bay Area so she can be turned over to the local authorities."

"Wait. Before you go, tell me—what does Lacey say happened that night when Philip was killed? Does she back up Amy's story?"

"Not exactly. Apparently it was a chaotic moment. Lacey thought she'd pulled the trigger herself."

"What!"

"We didn't tell her about Amy's confession, just asked her to tell her story. She'd have been smart to ask for a lawyer when she was read her rights, but we're lucky she didn't. The ransom letter was all her doing. She told us Philip was so furious when he heard about it that he went to Cole Street and started beating her up. They were yelling and screaming. Amy was terrified—who wouldn't be? So she grabbed the gun."

"I don't understand. How did Amy get hold of it?"

"Lacey had in her tote bag under all of those wigs. Amy discovered it earlier in the day. So when Philip got violent she knew where to find it."

"So Amy *was* the one with the gun."

Aguilar nodded. "At first she was. I'm not sure if she wanted to scare Philip into stopping his assault or give it to Lacey so she could protect herself. But Lacey thinks she took the gun from Amy and was holding it when it went off. By chance, she claims. Philip tried to seize the gun and it fired during the struggle."

"So Amy didn't kill Philip?" My heart lifted, just a little.

"It was a few seconds of confusion and craziness. Hard to be certain what happened. What we do know is that Lacey panicked. She grabbed Amy and bolted." She took gloves from her pocket. "I've got to run."

"Thank you. For the information and the tea."

When she was gone, I eased myself out of the bed and, mindful of my damaged toes, took cautious steps to the cupboard where the nurse had stashed my personal belongings. Most of my body parts seemed to be more or less in working order. I got out my phone and carried it back to the bed. I wanted to send a text. After some thought about what to say I decided to keep it simple: *Kit, please call me. I have a lot to tell you.*

When I looked up, Nick was standing at the door. He looked

gray with fatigue.

"How're you doing, Jess?"

"I'll be fine. And Amy ...?"

Nick said, "Thank God we found her when we did. If she'd been out there any longer ..."

I shuddered. "Let's not think about it. We did find her, that's all that counts."

"Physically, the docs say she'll be all right. Emotionally, though ... I don't know. After what she's been through ..."

"It's a lot of trauma to deal with. But at least she doesn't have to feel guilty about killing Philip. Carmen Aguilar told me Lacey is the one who pulled the trigger."

Nick rubbed the spot between his eyebrows; strain and tension had carved a deep furrow. "What's ironic is, that was the night when Philip planned to stage his rescue of Amy. Think of the agony we'd have been spared if Lacey hadn't been so damn vengeful and greedy."

"Think of the grief we'd have been spared if Philip hadn't been such a total bastard."

"Like I told you yesterday morning, Jess, at the coffee shop—too many assholes in this world, and they're winning."

"The good guys won this one, Nick. And Amy's safe."

"Yeah. She's safe. Right now, nothing else matters."

"Are you still thinking of quitting the SFPD?"

"Nothing that's happened in the last couple of days makes me feel different." His expression softened. "Amy was asking about you, Jess. Are you up for seeing her?"

I swung my legs out of the bed. "Absolutely."

Just then a nurse poked her head in the door. When she found out what I intended to do, she insisted that I make the trip through the corridors in a wheelchair, accompanied by an orderly.

As we came up to the ICU, I saw a deputy sheriff sitting outside a closed door. Nick nodded to her and said to me, "Shanna Moritz is in there."

"Will she be okay?"

"She's hanging in." He shook his head. "You know, she killed four people, let her father take the rap on three of them—I'm finding it hard to care if she lives or dies."

"I care." I did not want Shanna's blood on my hands. Let a jury decide if she would pay for her crimes with her life.

Amy's face on the pillow was pale against her dark hair. It was unnerving to see her amidst a welter of tubes and monitors. I said hello, and she answered my greeting with a weak smile.

Nick's phone rang and he stepped into the hallway to take the call.

"Jess," Amy said, "what are you doing in that thing?" She reached out and touched the rubber tire of the wheelchair.

"I thought I'd ride in style to visit you," I told her.

She nodded as if what I'd said made sense. "As soon as I get home, can come to your house? So I can finish my portrait of Mom. And see Scruff."

"Of course."

"Good. That's settled then." She smiled and closed her eyes. When Nick came back in, she was asleep.

He slid his phone into his pocket. "That was a friend of mine who works in the crime lab in San Francisco," he said. "The trigger of Terri's gun showed a single fingerprint, very clear. It belongs to Philip. And there was gunshot residue on his hand."

"Wait—you mean the struggle for the gun ended with Philip accidentally shooting himself?"

"We may never know for sure. But yeah, that's what the evidence suggests." Nick laid his hand gently on his daughter's cheek. "And that's what I'll be telling her."

The doctor who'd been treating me insisted that I stay in the hospital for another night. As morning light touched the room, the nightmare phantoms that had haunted my dreams retreated into shadowy corners of my brain. I was aware of their lingering presence, but their power was diminished. I got up and readied myself to go home.

Looking out the window, I saw the storm had passed. Here and there in the cloud-cluttered sky were scraps of blue. Snow lay thick on everything—the cars in the parking lot, the lawns, the distant hills. For an instant the sun peeked out, and the world glittered with a diamond brilliance that hurt my eyes.

Before leaving, I peeked in on Amy. She was asleep again. Her cheeks looked rosier than yesterday and her countenance was peaceful. I kissed her cheek and whispered a promise we'd get together soon.

I went to a garage and arranged to have the Cherokee towed there and repaired. Then I rented a car and drove home. As I headed west the clouds in front of me grew thicker and darker—the next storm getting ready to roll in.

When I stepped up on my front porch I saw a curtain flap in Mrs. Fiorelli's bay window. Her door popped open and Scruff bounded out, nearly bowling me over with his enthusiasm. Davy and Mrs. F were at his heels. I hugged all three of them at once, then took Scruff upstairs.

My phone had rung while I was driving, so I checked my messages. I heard my brother Teddy's voice.

"Hey, Jess, I'm home from my ski trip. Totally awesome! I even skied one of the black-diamond slopes; you know, for experts. If you'd just try skiing you'll love it. I dunno why you've got this weird thing against snow."

Amy placed nine candles on top of the lopsided chocolate-frosted cake. Three red ones stood for a decade each. The six yellow ones signified single years.

"You think Mommy will like it?" she asked.

"I know she will."

"It will be a good party, won't it?" She sounded as if she wasn't sure.

"Definitely. The best," I promised her.

She carried the cake out to my studio and set it on the worktable. I followed with napkins, plates and forks. Instead of painting, Amy and I had devoted our lesson time on this mid-February afternoon to the art of baking. I didn't have much more experience than she did, and Scruff's only contribution was to clean up spills. Our creation wasn't exactly Escoffier quality but it would do just fine.

The doorbell rang. The guest of honor was here. Amy flew down the stairs to welcome her mom.

She showed Terri around my flat as proudly as if it were her own home. Their final stop was the studio, where two easels were set up in the middle of the room. Amy pointed out the canvas on the taller one.

"This is Jess's latest painting," she explained. "It's about being in the snow."

It was a brand-new work. My earlier painting of winter had proved a false start. For two weeks after that terrible, wonderful day when I'd found Amy, I couldn't bear even to look at it. Then one dark morning at three a.m., awakened by nightmares yet again, I came into the studio and covered what I'd done before with a solid coat of midnight blue. I began again, working in such a frenzy that the new painting was complete by the time daylight showed at the edges of the window blinds. Tall looming shapes in black and deep grays; occasional elusive dabs of white; and in one corner a splash of purple, a radiant flash of red.

Amy wouldn't tell me if she had nightmares too. She insisted on maintaining her silence about her ordeal. I knew she was seeing a therapist, and I hoped those sessions were helping. So far she'd painted no pictures of snow.

The shorter easel was covered with one of my bedsheets. "What's under there?" Terri asked. Amy giggled but didn't answer.

The doorbell rang again, and Amy went to greet our other guest. When she escorted Nick into the studio, she looked anxiously from her mother to her father.

"Nick, hello." Terri politely extended her hand.

"Happy birthday, Terri," Nick said. Ignoring the offered handshake, he kissed his ex on the cheek.

She looked startled, then smiled. Amy's face was flooded with relief.

As we gathered around the cake, a gust of wind rattled the windows and pelted them with rain. This winter was breaking century-old records. We had six long weeks to go before the storm season would end.

Amy clapped her hands. "Make a wish, Mommy. Blow the candles out."

Terri kissed her fingertips and touched them to her daughter's forehead. "I already have what I wished for," she said. "We got you back again."

Nick said, "You'll never know how glad I am that that wish was granted."

"Me too. So make a different wish," Amy instructed. "But you can't tell what it is or it won't come true."

Terri closed her eyes tightly, then opened them and blew. Eight candles were extinguished immediately. The ninth resisted, its flame flickering sideways. Then it too winked out.

Amy, Nick and I applauded. Scruff barked his appreciation.

"Shall I cut the cake now?" Terri asked.

Amy eyed the chocolate frosting but decided, "Not yet. First let's do the—what do you call it, Jess?"

"The unveiling," I said.

"That's it. Daddy, come help."

She grabbed one corner of the sheet covering the small easel. Nick took the other.

"Jess, you count. Mommy, watch now."

"One ... two ... three!"

They flipped off the sheet, revealing the portrait Amy had painted. Terri gasped. "Oh, sweetheart!"

"Happy birthday, Mommy!"

The painting was obviously the work of a child, but its likeness to its subject was unmistakable. Terri's SalesCom Technologies employee ID photo was still clipped to the top. Amy had carefully rendered the waves of the dark hair that framed the face, the high cheekbones and the narrow chin. With remarkable skill, she had captured the hint of sadness in the wideset brown eyes, and the way the mouth curved, almost but not quite a smile.

"Amy! It's beautiful." Terri grabbed her daughter into a hug.

"It sure is, sunshine," Nick said. He'd known the portrait was in the works, but Amy hadn't let him have an advance peek. "You are one very talented young lady."

"I'm an artist," she said.

"You definitely are," Terri agreed. "No question."

"We'd better cut that cake now," Nick said. "Jess has a date tonight, so we've only got a short while."

"Plenty of time," I assured them. "Kit won't be here for a couple of hours." I was nervous about seeing him. It would be the first time we'd been together since New Year's Day. The Cherokee had been repaired and returned, and explanations provided, but we'd connected only by phone, text and email. Kit had stayed in Hawaii after his photo assignment was over to explore the idea of moving there. He came home two weeks ago, and we'd been planning and postponing this reunion ever since.

Terri cut the cake and passed around plates. Nick poured drinks into stemmed glasses—champagne for the grownups, root beer for Amy.

"Wait," said Amy. "I almost forgot. There's another picture."

She ran into the hall and reappeared with a rolled paper. "I had something up my sleeve when I got here today, Jess. My jacket sleeve, I mean. You didn't even see it."

She pushed the cake aside and spread out the paper on the

worktable. A tempera painting showing six figures—a man, two women, a girl and a pair of dogs.

"I did this in school," she said. "We all made family portraits. There's Mommy and Daddy and me, and I put in Jess because we decided to be sisters. My teacher said there's all kinds of families, it doesn't just have to be people you live with."

"Your teacher is wise," said Terri. "But what about the dogs?"

"Well, that's Scruff." Amy pointed to the yellow-brown figure with the long tail. "He's part of the family too. And this one"—she put her finger on the small black dog—"that's the puppy you're going to get me for my birthday." She looked up with a grin.

"We'll have to think about that," Terri said.

"Real artists all have dogs," Amy said with complete assurance. "Right, Jess?"

"Absolutely." What else could I say?

Nick raised his glass. "Time to make a toast."

"Let me do it," Amy said, picking up her root beer. "To us."

"Hear, hear," we all said, and we clinked our glasses.

ACKNOWLEDGEMENTS

THIS BOOK was a long time in the making, and it never would have come to fruition without the generous help, intelligent suggestions, and kind support of numerous people. Among those I would like to particularly thank are Ken Gwin, Gwen Kauffman, Jonnie Jacobs, Rita Lakin, Bette Golden Lamb, J.J. Lamb, Camille Minichino, Shelley Singer, Nicola Trwst, Sharri Wolfgang, and Judith Yamamoto. And, of course, Charlie.

ABOUT THE AUTHOR

MARGARET LUCKE flings words around as a writer and editorial consultant in the San Francisco Bay Area. She is fascinated by the power of stories and the magic of creativity.

Her novel *A Relative Stranger,* featuring artist and private eye Jess Randolph, was nominated for an Anthony Award for Best First Mystery. She is also the author of *House of Whispers,* a tale of love, ghosts and murder on the Marin County coast, and two how-to books on writing, *Schaum's Quick Guide to Writing Great Short Stories* and *Writing Mysteries.*

A former president of the Northern California chapter of Mystery Writers of America, Margaret teaches fiction writing classes for UC Berkeley Extension and other venues. She welcomes visitors at www.margaretlucke.com.